DEBBIE MACOMBER

Changing Habits

mira

ISBN-13: 978-0-7783-0794-5

Changing Habits

Recycling programs
for this product may
not exist in your area.

For questions and comments about the quality of this book, please contact us at
CustomerService@Harlequin.com.

Harlequin.com

Printed in U.S.A.

Also available from Debbie Macomber and MIRA Books

Blossom Street

The Shop on Blossom Street
A Good Yarn
Susannah's Garden
Back on Blossom Street
Twenty Wishes
Summer on Blossom Street
Hannah's List
The Twenty-First Wish
   (in *The Knitting Diaries*)
A Turn in the Road

Cedar Cove

16 Lighthouse Road
204 Rosewood Lane
311 Pelican Court
44 Cranberry Point
50 Harbor Street
6 Rainier Drive
74 Seaside Avenue
8 Sandpiper Way
92 Pacific Boulevard
1022 Evergreen Place
Christmas in Cedar Cove
   (*5-B Poppy Lane* and
   A Cedar Cove Christmas)
1105 Yakima Street
1225 Christmas Tree Lane

The Dakota Series

Dakota Born
Dakota Home
Always Dakota
Buffalo Valley

The Manning Family

The Manning Sisters
   (*The Cowboy's Lady* and
   The Sheriff Takes a Wife)

The Manning Brides
   (*Marriage of Inconvenience* and
   Stand-In Wife)
The Manning Grooms
   (*Bride on the Loose* and
   Same Time, Next Year)

Christmas Books

A Gift to Last
On a Snowy Night
Home for the Holidays
Glad Tidings
Christmas Wishes
Small Town Christmas
When Christmas Comes
   (now retitled *Trading
   Christmas*)
There's Something About Christmas
Christmas Letters
The Perfect Christmas
Choir of Angels
   (*Shirley, Goodness and Mercy,
   Those Christmas Angels* and
   Where Angels Go)
Call Me Mrs. Miracle

Heart of Texas

Texas Skies
   (*Lonesome Cowboy* and
   Texas Two-Step)
Texas Nights
   (*Caroline's Child* and
   Dr. Texas)
Texas Home
   (*Nell's Cowboy* and
   Lone Star Baby)
Promise, Texas
Return to Promise

Midnight Sons

Alaska Skies
   (*Brides for Brothers* and
   The Marriage Risk)
Alaska Nights
   (*Daddy's Little Helper* and
   Because of the Baby)
Alaska Home
   (*Falling for Him*,
   Ending in Marriage and
   Midnight Sons and Daughters)

This Matter of Marriage
Montana
Thursdays at Eight
Between Friends
Changing Habits
Married in Seattle
   (*First Comes Marriage* and
   Wanted: Perfect Partner)
Right Next Door
   (*Father's Day* and
   The Courtship of Carol Sommars)
Wyoming Brides
   (*Denim and Diamonds* and
   The Wyoming Kid)
Fairy Tale Weddings
   (*Cindy and the Prince* and
   Some Kind of Wonderful)
The Man You'll Marry
   (*The First Man You Meet* and
   The Man You'll Marry)
Orchard Valley Grooms
   (*Valerie* and *Stephanie*)
Orchard Valley Brides
   (*Norah* and *Lone Star Lovin'*)
The Sooner the Better
An Engagement in Seattle
   (*Groom Wanted* and
   Bride Wanted)
Out of the Rain
   (*Marriage Wanted* and
   Laughter in the Rain)
Learning to Love
   (*Sugar and Spice* and *Love by Degree*)

You…Again
   (*Baby Blessed* and
   Yesterday Once More)
The Unexpected Husband
   (*Jury of His Peers* and
   Any Sunday)
Three Brides, No Groom
Love in Plain Sight
   (*Love 'n' Marriage* and
   Almost an Angel)
I Left My Heart
   (*A Friend or Two* and
   No Competition)
Marriage Between Friends
   (*White Lace and Promises* and
   Friends—And Then Some)
A Man's Heart
   (*The Way to a Man's Heart*
   and *Hasty Wedding*)
North to Alaska
   (*That Wintry Feeling* and
   Borrowed Dreams)
On a Clear Day
   (*Starlight* and
   Promise Me Forever)
To Love and Protect
   (*Shadow Chasing* and
   For All My Tomorrows)
Home in Seattle
   (*The Playboy and the Widow*
   and *Fallen Angel*)
Together Again
   (*The Trouble with Caasi* and
   Reflections of Yesterday)
The Reluctant Groom
   (*All Things Considered*
   and *Almost Paradise*)
A Real Prince
   (*The Bachelor Prince*
   and *Yesterday's Hero*)
Private Paradise
   (in *That Summer Place*)

Debbie Macomber's
   Cedar Cove Cookbook
Debbie Macomber's
   Christmas Cookbook

CHANGING HABITS

To my cousin Shirley Adler,
who lived the life

{Prologue}

1973

Kathleen waited in the cold rain of a Seattle winter as her brother placed her suitcase in the trunk of his car. She felt as awkward and disoriented as she probably looked, standing there in her unfashionable wool coat and clumsy black shoes. For the last ten years she'd been Sister Kathleen, high school teacher and part-time bookkeeper for St. Peter's parish in Minneapolis. Her identity had been defined by her vocation.

Now she was simply Kathleen. And all she'd managed to accumulate in her years of service was one flimsy suitcase and a wounded heart. She had no savings, no prospects and no home. For the first time in her life, she was completely on her own.

"I'll do whatever I can to help you," Sean said, opening the car door for her.

"You already have." Tears stung her eyes as her brother backed out of his driveway. She'd spent the last two months living at his house, a small brick bungalow in this quiet neighborhood. "I can't thank you enough," she whispered, not wanting him to hear the emotion in her voice.

"Mom and Dad want you to come home."

"I can't." How did a woman who was nearly thirty years old go home? She wasn't a teenager who'd been away at school, a girl who could easily slip back into her childhood life.

"They'd never think of you as a burden, if that's what you're worried about," her brother said.

Perhaps not, but Kathleen was a disappointment to her family and she knew it. She didn't have the emotional strength to answer her parents' questions. Dealing with her new life was complicated enough.

"You're going to be all right," Sean assured her.

"I know." But Kathleen didn't entirely believe it. The world outside the convent was a frightening place. She didn't know what to expect or how to cope with all the changes that were hurtling toward her.

"You can call Loren or me anytime."

"Thank you." She swallowed hard.

Ten minutes later, Sean pulled up in front of the House of Peace, a home run by former nuns who helped others make the often-difficult transition from religious to secular life.

Kathleen stared at the large two-story white house. There was a trimmed laurel hedge on either side of the narrow walkway that led to the porch. She saw the welcoming glow of lamplight in the windows, dispersing a little of the day's gloom.

Still, she missed the order and ritual of her life. There was a certain comfort she hadn't appreciated: rising, praying and eating, all in perfect synchronization with the day before. Freedom, unfamiliar as it was, felt frightening. Confusing.

With her brother at her side, Kathleen walked up the steps, held her breath and then, after a long moment, pressed the doorbell. Someone must have been on the other side waiting, because it opened immediately.

"You must be Kathleen." A woman of about sixty with short white hair and a pleasantly round figure greeted her. "I'm Kay Dickson. We spoke on the phone."

Kathleen felt warmed by Kay's smile.

"Come in, come in." The other woman held open the door for them.

Sean hesitated as he set down Kathleen's suitcase. "I should be getting back home." His eyes questioned her, as if he was unsure about leaving his sister at this stranger's house.

"I'll be fine," she told him, and in that instant she knew it was true.

{ Part One }

THE CALL

The harvest is plentiful, but the workers are few.
—Matthew 9:37

{ 1 }

Angelina Marcello
1948 ~ 1958

"Angie, come here," her father called in heavily accented English. "Taste this." He held out a wooden spoon dripping with rich marinara sauce.

Obediently Angelina put her mouth over the spoon and closed her eyes, distinguishing the different spices and flavors as they met her tongue. "Not enough basil. You should add fresh chopped parsley, too."

Her father roared with approval. "You're right!" He tossed the spoon into the restaurant's large stainless steel sink. Then he reached for eight-year-old Angie and lifted her high in the air before hugging her tightly. It was 1948, and Angie's world revolved around her father and, of course, the family-owned business, the restaurant named after her. It was a well-known fact that Angelina's served the finest Italian food in all of Buffalo, New York.

Unlike other children her age, Angie's first memories weren't of being plopped on Santa's knee in some department store for a candy cane and a photograph. Instead, she recalled the pungent scent of garlic simmering in extra-virgin olive oil and the soft hum as her mother bustled about the kitchen. Those were the warm years, the good years, during the big war, before her mother died in 1945.

Sometimes, late at night, she'd heard giggles coming from her parents' bedroom. She liked the sound and cuddled up in her thick blankets, her world secure despite all the talk of what was taking place an ocean away.

Then her beautiful mother who sang her songs and loved her so much was suddenly gone; she'd died giving birth to Angie's stillborn brother. For a while, any hint of joy and laughter disappeared from the house. A large black wreath hung on the front door, and people stopped, stared and shook their heads as they walked past.

Only five years old, Angie didn't understand where her mother had vanished, nor did it make sense when strangers crowded into her home. She was even more confused by the way they put their heads together and whispered as if she wasn't supposed to hear. A few wept openly, stopping abruptly when she entered the room.

All Angie understood was that her mother was gone and her father, her fun-loving, gregarious father, had grown quiet and serious and sad.

"You're going to be a good Catholic girl," he told her soon after her mother's death. "I promised your mother I'd raise you in the Church."

"Sì, Papa."

"Use English," he insisted. "We live in America."

"Yes, Daddy."

"I'll take you to Mass every Sunday, just like your mother wanted."

Angie listened intently.

"And when you start first grade you'll attend St. Gabriel, so the nuns can teach you."

She nodded; her father made this sound like a promise.

"It's just you and me now, Angelina," he whispered.

"Yes, Daddy."

"You're going to be a good Catholic girl," he said again. "You'll make your mother proud."

At that Angie smiled, even though she dreamed of being a cowgirl when she grew up so she could ride the range with Hopalong Cassidy. Her hero didn't look Italian but she made him so in her dreams and he ate at her father's restaurant and said it was the best food he'd ever tasted.

In 1948, by the time Angelina entered the third grade, she wore her thick black hair in two long braids that her father dutifully plaited each morning at the breakfast table. He put down the newspaper, giving his full attention to her hair, and when he'd finished, he carefully inspected his daughter. It was the same ritual every morning. Awaiting his approval, Angie would stand tall and straight, arms held stiffly at her sides. She wore her blue-and-gray-plaid school uniform with the pleated skirt and bib front and anxiously awaited her father's nod, telling her she'd passed muster.

"Smile," he instructed on this particular day.

Angie obediently did as he said.

"You're as beautiful as your mother. Now eat your breakfast."

Angie slipped into the chair, bowed her head and made the sign of the cross before and after grace, which she said aloud. Then she reached for her spoon. She hesitated when she noticed her father's frown. Studying him closely, she wondered what she'd done wrong. The worst thing she could imagine would be to disappoint her father. He was her world and she was his—other than the restaurant, of course.

"It's nothing, *bambina*," he reassured her in gentle tones. "I just hope your mother forgives me for feeding you cold cereal."

"I like cold cereal."

Her father nodded, distracted by the newspaper, which he folded back and propped against the sugar canister while Angie ate her breakfast.

"I want to leave early this morning," she told him, struggling to hold back her excitement. "Sister Trinita said I could sing with the fifth- and sixth-graders at Mass." This was a privilege beyond anything Angie had ever been granted. Only the older children were permitted to enter the choir loft at St. Gabriel's, but Sister Trinita, the fifth-grade teacher, was her special friend. She chaperoned the children who attended Mass at St. Gabriel's every morning before school—children who rustled and fidgeted and talked.

Angie knew it was important to show respect in church. Her father had taught her that and never allowed her to whisper or fuss during Mass. She might not understand the Latin words, but she'd learned what they meant, and she loved the atmosphere of the church itself—the lighted tapers, the stained glass windows and shining wood, the Stations of the Cross telling their sacred story. Sister Trinita had commented one morning, as the children streamed out of the church and hurried toward the school, that she was impressed with Angie's respectful behavior.

That first time Sister had spoken to her, Angie knew she'd found a friend. After school the same day, she'd visited Sister Trinita's classroom and volunteered to wash the blackboards. Sister let her, even though Angie was only in third grade.

After that, Angie used every excuse she could invent to visit Sister Trinita. Soon she was lingering in the school yard after classes until she saw Sister leave. Then Angie would race to the nun's side so she could walk Sister back to the convent house, which was situated across the street. Sister Trinita looked for Angie, too. She knew, because the nun would smile in welcome whenever Angie hurried toward her. It became her habit to walk Sister Trinita home.

"You're going to sing with the choir?" her father asked, raising his eyes from the newspaper.

Angie nodded, so excited she could barely contain her glee. "I like Sister Trinita."

"Good."

His curt nod told Angie that he approved.

Scooping up the last of her Cheerios, she set aside her spoon and wondered if she should tell him that she'd started waiting for Sister Trinita outside the convent door each morning. She walked Sister to the church and then slipped into the pew where the third-graders sat.

"Sister Trinita says I'm her favorite." She hesitated, waiting for her father's reaction.

"Who is Sister Trinita?" her father asked unexpectedly. "Tell me again."

"The fifth-grade teacher. I hope I'm in her class when *I'm* in fifth grade."

He nodded slowly, obviously pleased with her acceptance by this nun. Pleased, too, with her daily attendance at Mass—even though he himself didn't like

going. He went to Mass on Sundays because he'd promised her mother he would. Angie knew that. He'd made a
deathbed promise to the wife he'd so desperately loved.
A man of his word, Tony Marcello faithfully escorted
Angie to church each and every Sunday and on holy
days.

At night when he returned from the restaurant and
sent the housekeeper home, he drilled Angie on her
catechism questions. And on the anniversary of her
mother's death, they knelt before the crucifix in the
living room and said the rosary together. At the name
of Jesus, they would bow their heads.

This morning, her father smiled as he drank the rest
of his coffee. "Ready?" he asked. "If my little girl's
going to sing in the choir, then I'll have to get you to
church early."

"Ready." With her braids flapping against her navy
blue uniform sweater, Angie grabbed her books, her
Hopalong Cassidy lunch bucket, and reached for her
father's hand.

For two years, Angelina Marcello walked Sister
Trinita to and from the convent each weekday. It broke
her heart when Sister was transferred to another school
in 1950, the year she entered fifth grade. Angie had
turned ten.

After a while Angie stopped thinking about Sister
Trinita, but she never forgot the nun from the order of
St. Bridget's Sisters of the Assumption—the woman
who had lavished her with attention when she'd most
needed it.

In the summer of 1953, her father enrolled her in St.
Mary's School for Girls. She would always remember
that he sang "That's Amore" as he drove her home following her interview with Sister St. George.

"Your mother would be proud of what a fine young lady you are," he told her, stopping at the restaurant on the way home.

At age fourteen, Angie was waiting tables during the summer and cooking with her father, along with Mario Deccio, the chef. She knew the recipes as well as she did her own name. The restaurant was her life—until her senior year in high school.

Everything changed then.

"You *want* to do this?" her father asked, reading the senior class permission slip for the annual retreat. He looked at her carefully. "You want to travel to Boston for this retreat?"

"It's just for the weekend," Angie explained. "Every graduating class goes away for retreat."

"At a convent?"

"Yes. Sister St. George said it was a contemplative time before we graduate and take our place in the world."

Her father read over the permission slip again. "You know your place, and that's right here next to me at Angelina's."

"Everyone's going," Angie protested.

"All the girls in your class?" He sounded skeptical.

"Yes." She wasn't entirely sure that was true, but Angie wanted to be part of this retreat. After attending twelve years of parochial school, she was curious. Convent life was so secretive, and she didn't want to lose this one opportunity to see it from the inside.

"All right, you can go," her father reluctantly agreed.

He was right, of course; her future was set. She would join him at the restaurant and cook or wait tables, whatever was needed. The restaurant was the only life she knew, and its familiarity a continuing comfort.

Early that June, St. Mary's School for Girls' senior class left by charter bus for Boston and the mother-house of St. Bridget's Sisters of the Assumption. It was three weeks before graduation. The first thing Angie felt when the bus pulled up to the convent was a sense of serenity. The three-story brick structure was surrounded by a tall fence and well-maintained grounds. While traffic sped by on the busy streets surrounding the convent, inside the wrought-iron gates there was tranquility. Angie didn't know if her friends felt it, but she did.

Friday evening the sisters served dinner.

"They aren't going to eat with us?" Sheila Jones leaned close and asked Angie. Sheila and Dorothy French were Angie's two best friends.

"Haven't you ever noticed?" Dorothy whispered. "Nuns never eat with laypeople."

Angie hadn't noticed, hadn't thought about it until then.

"I wonder if they've ever tasted pizza," Dorothy said.

"Of course they have," Angie insisted. "They eat the same food as everyone else."

"I wouldn't be so sure of that," Sheila murmured.

Angie wondered. She couldn't imagine life without pizza and fettuccine Alfredo and a dozen other dishes. These were the special recipes her father had entrusted to her care.

Later that evening, Angie was intrigued by the Spartan cell she'd been assigned for the weekend. The floors were bare, as were the walls, except for a crucifix that hung above the bed. One small window took up a portion of the outside wall, but it was too high to see out of and only allowed in a glimmer of sunlight. The single bed had a thin mattress and the bed stand could hold a lamp and a prayer book, but little else.

That first night when Angie climbed into bed, the sheets felt rough and grainy against her skin. She'd expected to fall asleep almost instantly, but her mind spun in ten different directions. This was holy ground, where she slept—holy ground on which she walked. Women who had dedicated their lives to the service of God had once slept in this room. This wasn't something to be taken lightly, she realized. She finally fell into a deep sleep sometime after midnight.

The second day of the retreat included an hour of solitary prayer. Each girl was to spend time alone to assess her calling in life. No talking was permitted, but they could speak to one of the sisters if they desired. Angie took pains to avoid her friends because it would be too easy to break silence.

"Angie!" Dorothy French's loud whisper echoed through the chapel as she loped down the center aisle.

Angie cringed and ignored her.

Undaunted, Dorothy slipped into the pew next to her. She rattled her rosary as she lowered her head and pretended to pray. "I'm going to bust if I have to go another minute without talking."

Angie glared at her friend.

"What about you?" Dorothy pressed. She stared at Angie. "Don't tell me this silence doesn't bother you, too?"

In response, Angie shook her head, slid past her and left the chapel. She'd been deeply involved in saying the rosary and resented the intrusion. Fearing someone else would distract her, she walked out of the building and decided to do the Stations of the Cross. The fourteen stations, which illustrated the stages in Christ's journey to crucifixion, followed a path that meandered through the lush grounds. The air was warm and perfumed with the scent of spring, and Angie felt an unmistakable surge of well-being.

It was at the fourth station, where Jesus met His mother on the road to Calvary, that Angie came upon an older nun sitting on a bench, her head bowed and her hands clasped in prayer. Not wanting to disturb the other woman, Angie decided to leave.

Just as she was about to turn away, the nun glanced up and as she saw Angie, a flash of recognition came into her eyes.

Angie took a second look. No, it couldn't be. "Sister Trinita?" she whispered.

The nun smiled. "Is it really you, Angie?"

"Yes...oh, Sister Trinita, I've thought of you so often over the years."

"I've thought of you, too. Are you a high school senior already?"

Angie nodded. "St. Mary's School for Girls."

"The years go past so quickly." Sister smiled gently. "I can hardly believe you're almost grown-up." She moved farther down on the bench, silently inviting Angie to join her.

"I was so disappointed when you were transferred," Angie told her. "I looked forward to fifth grade for two years." After her mother's death, Sister Trinita's departure had been the second big loss of her life.

"It was difficult for me to accept that I wouldn't be your teacher, but it was for the best. The decisions of the motherhouse always are."

Angie didn't agree. Sister Trinita's transfer, her disappearance from Angie's life, had seemed so unfair. "You had no choice?"

"No, but that's not the point. When I became a bride of Christ, I promised obedience in all things."

"I could never do that," Angie told her. She didn't like admitting to such a weakness, but it was true.

Sister Trinita laughed softly. "Of course you could. When God asks something of us, there's no thought of refusing."

Sister sounded so calm and certain, as though there was never any question when it came to obeying God, never any doubt. Angie was sure she'd turned God down any number of times.

"You've grown into a fine young woman," Sister Trinita said, her eyes soft with affection. "I imagine your father is very proud."

Angie shrugged. "I suppose so."

After another moment she asked, "You're assigned to the motherhouse?"

Sister Trinita smiled, but she hesitated before she answered. "For now."

"Oh."

There was a long silence, or maybe it only seemed long to Angie. Just as she started to speak, Sister Trinita rose slowly to her feet, tucking both hands in the capacious sleeves of her habit.

"It's been good to talk to you," Sister said.

"You, too." Angie wasn't ready to leave, and it seemed she was being dismissed. "Sister," she said, "could I ask you about being a nun?" It was the only question she could think of that would prolong the conversation.

Sister Trinita sank back onto the bench. "What would you like to know?"

Angie clasped her hands and gazed into the distance. It was so peaceful here in these gardens. The sound of traffic was muted by the many trees throughout the property. "When did you first realize you had a vocation?" she asked.

"Not until after I graduated from high school."

That surprised Angie. "So late?"

Sister smiled. "I was nineteen."

"But how did you *know?*"

Sister Trinita glanced down at her hands, which she'd removed from her sleeves. "That's not easy to explain. I felt it in my heart." She brought one hand to the stiff white bib of her habit. "I longed to serve God, to follow Him wherever He led me."

"Even if that meant not marrying or ever having children?" This was the most difficult aspect of a vocation for Angie to understand.

"It was what God asked of me."

"I couldn't imagine living without a husband," Angie confessed. "I'm sure I'd feel incomplete."

"I'm married to Christ, Angie. He is the one who makes me whole."

Angie didn't think she could ever feel the same. It wasn't as if Christ was here on earth. She wanted the same things in life that her friends did—a husband, a real flesh-and-blood husband. One who would hold her close and talk with her and…and kiss her. She wanted children of her own, too.

"Has your father remarried?" Sister asked next.

She shook her head. Her father never would. There was no room in his heart for another woman. No room for anyone other than Angie.

"Do you think your father is incomplete?" Sister asked. "He's lived all these years without a wife."

"Not at all," Angie said quickly, aghast at the suggestion. Her father was content. He owned a thriving business, had his friends—he bowled one night a week with his cronies—and focused his hopes and dreams on her.

"Neither am I," Sister said. "You see, with obedience comes joy, and there is no greater joy than serving our Lord."

No greater joy, Angie repeated in her mind. It was at that moment that the idea sprang to life.

"Sister," she whispered, her voice trembling with excitement. "I think God might be speaking to me." It frightened her to admit it, to actually say the words aloud.

"Do you, Angie?"

"Yes, Sister." She exhaled sharply. "Oh, no!"

"No?" Sister asked with a gentle smile.

"My father—he won't like this." God was calling her. Angie felt the desire to serve Him gaining strength in her heart, becoming more real with every minute. When she'd first sat down with Sister Trinita, she'd had no idea where the conversation would take her. God had brought this special nun back into her life at exactly the right moment. It was His way of speaking to Angie and revealing her vocation. As always, God's timing was perfect.

"I have a boyfriend, too," Angie murmured, thinking of the obstacles she had yet to face. "He works part-time at the restaurant and he's cute, but..."

"Are you and this young man serious?"

"No...we're not going steady or anything." The truth was, Ken was more of a friend than a *boy*friend. They'd gone to her school prom together and they talked on the phone once or twice a week, but it wasn't anything serious. Ken would probably understand if Angie announced that she wanted to become a nun. But her father never would.

"Might I suggest you keep this matter to yourself for now?" Sister said.

Angie blinked back tears of joy. "I don't know if I can. I feel like my heart's about to burst wide open." She hurriedly wiped her eyes. "I really think God's calling me to be His bride. What should I do now?"

"Pray," Sister said. "He will lead you. And if your father objects, God will show you the way."

Shortly after she returned from Boston, Angie realized how right Sister Trinita was. She should've kept the call to herself. Instead, she'd made the mistake of telling her father she wanted to enter the convent.

"No! Absolutely not," Tony Marcello bellowed at his only child. "I won't hear of it."

"God is calling me."

Her father slapped the kitchen table with such force, the napkin holder, along with the salt and pepper shakers, toppled to the floor. His unprecedented violence shocked them both, and they stared at each other, open-mouthed. Her father recovered first. "What did those nuns say to you while you were in Boston?"

"They didn't say anything."

"You're not entering the convent!" he shouted. "I won't allow it." His face had gone as red as his famous sauce and he stormed out of the house, slamming the door behind him.

Tears pricked Angie's eyes, but she refused to let them fall. Sister Agnes, Mother Superior of St. Bridget's Sisters of the Assumption, had warned the girls that if any of them had vocations, they might encounter resistance from their families. She'd said it was common for parents to have questions and doubts.

Angie had known her father wouldn't be pleased, but she hadn't expected him to explode. In all her life, her father had never even shouted at her. Not until the day she announced her vocation.

Two weeks after graduation, Angie broached the subject a second time.

Her father was in his restaurant office doing paperwork when Angie walked tentatively into the room. She closed the door, sat in the chair beside his desk and waited.

Her father glanced up and seemed to know intuitively what she'd come to discuss. "The answer is no, so don't even think about asking."

"I want you to talk to Mother Superior."

"Why? So I can get even angrier?"

"God is calling me to serve Him," she said simply.

Her father glared at her. "Your mother, God rest her soul, asked me to raise you as a good Catholic. I promised her I would—but I never agreed to this."

Angie's voice trembled. "Please, just talk to Mother Superior."

"No. Your place is here with me. This restaurant will be yours one day. Why do you think I've worked like a slave all these years? It was for *you*."

Although her heart was breaking, Angie held her ground. "I don't want the restaurant," she said, her voice a mere whisper now. "I want God."

Slowly her father stood, his face contorted with rage. "You don't mean that. If I thought you could truly believe such a thing, I—I don't know what I'd do. Now get out of my sight before I say something I'll regret."

Angie's sobs came in earnest as she rushed from the office. Nearly blinded by her tears, she stumbled past Mario Deccio, her father's friend and chef. Despite his concern, she couldn't explain what was wrong, couldn't choke out the words.

For two days Tony Marcello didn't speak to his daughter. For two days he pretended she wasn't in the house.

"Daddy, don't be like this," Angie pleaded on Sunday night. The restaurant was always closed on the traditional day of worship.

Her father ignored her and stared at the television screen while Ed Sullivan announced his lineup of guests.

Disheartened, Angie sat in the chair beside her father's. She started to weep. He'd never been angry with her before and she couldn't bear it, couldn't bear not having him speak to her. "Tell me what you want me to do," she pleaded between hiccupping sobs.

"Do?" he asked, looking at her for the first time in two long days. "What we've always planned for you. That's all I want."

"What *you* always planned for me," she corrected.

Her father's gaze returned to the television. "God took your mother and my son away from me. I'll be damned if I'll give Him my daughter, too."

"Oh, Daddy." Her heart ached to hear him utter such terrible words.

"Enough, Angelina. There's nothing more to talk about."

Defeat settled over her. "All right."

Frowning, he glanced at her. "All right?"

"I won't go."

His eyes narrowed, as though he wasn't sure he should trust her. Then he nodded abruptly and said, "Good." That settled, he returned his attention to the small black-and-white television screen.

She did try to forget God's call. Angie wrote Mother Superior a letter and said it was with deep regret that she had to withdraw her application. Her father would never accept her vocation and she couldn't, *wouldn't,* disappoint him. She was all he had left in the world.

Sister responded with a letter of encouragement and hope, and stated that if God truly wanted her to serve Him, then He would make it possible.

Angie wanted to believe Sister Agnes, but God had His work cut out for Him if He was going to change her father's heart.

To all outward appearances, he was dead set against her joining a religious order.

In July and August, Angie worked at the restaurant every day. At night, mentally and physically exhausted, she hid in her room and wept bitter tears. She feared that if she was unable to follow her vocation, her life would be a waste. She prayed continually and begged God to make it possible for her, as Mother Superior had said. Every night, on her knees, she said the rosary until her mind was too numb to continue.

The first week of September, just three days before the convent opened its doors to postulants, her father burst into her bedroom.

"Go!" he roared at her like a demon. He loomed in the doorway, his shoulders heaving with anger. "You think God wants you? Then go!"

Angie was too stunned to speak. She looked up from where she knelt, the rosary in her hands.

"I can't stand to hear you crying anymore."

Slowly Angie came to her feet. Her knees ached, her back hurt, but she stood there shocked, unmoving.

"Go," he said again, his voice lower. "It won't take you long to realize I was right. You're no nun, Angelina. It isn't God's voice you're hearing… I don't know who put this idea in your head, but they're wrong."

"Daddy."

"You won't listen to me. I can see that. If I make you stay, in the end you'll only hate me. This is a lesson you need to learn on your own."

"I wouldn't do this if I didn't sincerely believe I have a vocation."

He muttered something in Italian that Angie didn't understand. From his tone, she suspected it was just as well.

She wanted to explain that God had taken hold of her soul and she couldn't refuse Him. But she was afraid that if she gave him the slightest argument, he might reverse his decision.

"Thank you," she said, lowering her eyes, humbled that he had given in to her.

He didn't say anything for the longest while, and when he spoke, his voice shook with emotion. "I said you can go, but God help me, I refuse to drive you there."

"I can take the bus."

"You'll have to."

Saying goodbye to her father that September morning in 1958 was the most difficult thing Angie had ever done. He dropped her off at the Greyhound bus depot and hugged her tight. Then, with tears glistening in his eyes, he loudly kissed her on both cheeks.

"You'll be back," he muttered, backing away from her.

Angie didn't argue with him, but she knew otherwise. She'd been born to serve God as a St. Bridget's Sister of the Assumption.

{2}

Kathleen O'Shaughnessy
1951 ~ 1963

Kathleen always knew she'd become a nun. She knew it from the day she received her First Communion. She heard her mother say it.

Kathleen stood with three of her cousins for a group photograph. She wore a white dress with a satin sash, a short veil and white gloves. It was the same Communion dress her three older sisters had worn. The same dress her cousin Molly had borrowed a year earlier. Kathleen held the white prayer book, clasped her hands and bowed her head devoutly for the camera.

"Kathleen looks like an angel," her aunt Rebecca said to Kathleen's mother.

Annie O'Shaughnessy nodded. "She does, doesn't she? I have the feeling Kathleen's going to be our nun."

"You think so?"

"Ned and I are sure of it."

Kathleen was sure, too. It was 1951 and she was all

of six years old. By the time she entered high school on Boston's east side, there were ten mouths to feed in the O'Shaughnessy household. Kathleen ranked number five of the eight children sired by Ned and Annie O'Shaughnessy, only two of them boys. Everyone old enough to work was employed in the pub owned by her uncle Patrick O'Shaughnessy.

Kathleen and her sisters attended St. Mark's High School and were taught by St. Bridget's Sisters of the Assumption. After school each day, Kathleen and her year-older sister, Maureen, walked to the pub, where they worked as janitors in order to pay for their tuition at the parochial school.

They could have been twins, she and Maureen, they looked so much alike. Both had long thick auburn hair and eyes so blue they sometimes appeared violet. Kathleen's hair fell to the middle of her back and had the sheen of a new car, or so her mother claimed. It was her greatest delight, her hair, and she religiously brushed it a hundred strokes a night.

"Do you think nuns cut their hair?" Maureen asked her as they walked to the pub one cloudy spring day in March of 1962. Her siblings enjoyed riling her about convent life. They were jealous of the special attention their parents gave her because of her vocation.

"They probably do," Kathleen returned, refusing to allow Maureen to upset her. If chopping off her hair was what God asked of her, then so be it, she told herself. Nothing would dissuade Kathleen from her vocation.

"How can you stand it?" Maureen asked curiously.

"Having my hair cut? Don't be silly." Although the remark was flippant, it wouldn't be easy for her to lose her precious locks.

"No," Maureen countered. "How can you give your

life to God? Don't you even wonder what sex is like and what you'll be missing?"

"Maureen!"

"Well, don't you?"

In fact, Kathleen thought about sex a great deal. She didn't want to admit it for fear her sister would tease her. Try as she might, she couldn't keep her unruly mind from wandering down that forbidden path. Obviously, anyone who wanted to be a nun shouldn't allow herself to dwell on such profane matters. It worried Kathleen immensely. She was about to renounce sex forever, and she had no idea what she was giving up.

"Don't you?" Maureen pressed, unwilling to drop the subject.

Kathleen increased her pace, but Maureen kept up with her. "I think about it some," she finally muttered.

Maureen slowed her steps and then in a low voice, said, "Robbie and I did it."

Kathleen came to a complete standstill and stared at her in shock. Maureen had lost her virginity? "When?" she gasped. Jesus, Mary and Joseph, her sister was *crazy* to risk getting pregnant.

"Last week… We weren't planning to do it, but his parents were out and we got to kissing, and the next thing I knew we—well, it just happened." Flustered, her sister tucked her schoolbooks tightly against her and looked straight ahead.

Kathleen's mind buzzed with a hundred questions, but she asked the most important one first. "Have you been to confession?"

"Not yet."

"Maureen, you're putting your immortal soul in jeopardy." Without absolution from a priest, her sister was headed for eternal damnation.

"I'll go to confession on Saturday, same as always," Maureen said, casting Kathleen an exasperated look. "Don't you want to know what it was like?"

God help her, Kathleen longed to hear every sordid detail. "Did it hurt?"

Maureen shrugged. "Some, at first. I thought we must be doing it wrong because Robbie couldn't make his…you know…go inside me."

Kathleen could no longer breathe and closed her eyes, mentally fighting off the image of Robbie squirming on top of her sister, pushing into her.

"When he did, I thought he'd ripped me wide open."

"Was there blood?"

"Judas Priest, I hope not! We were in the middle of the living room carpet… Anyway, if there was, Robbie took care of it. He's the one who'd have to explain it to his parents."

Kathleen's head started to pound. She was horrified that her sister had been so careless. "What happened after he put it in?"

Maureen looked away, but not before Kathleen caught a glimpse of her disappointment. "Nothing. Robbie kept saying how sorry he was and how he never meant to hurt me. Then he grunted a little and started to pant and before I knew it, he was finished."

It all sounded rather disgusting to Kathleen. "You'd better not wait until Saturday to go to confession. What if you get run over by a bus before then?"

Maureen rolled her eyes. "I can't go any earlier," she said.

"Why not?" She couldn't understand why her sister would take risks with her salvation, especially when Father Murphy heard confessions every morning before eight o'clock Mass. Maureen could slip into church on her way to school.

Kathleen was about to remind her of that when Maureen announced, "Robbie wants to do it again tonight."

"You can't!" Kathleen was aghast that her sister would even consider such a thing.

"His parents are going out of town and he said he'd pick me up at the pub once I'm finished cleaning." Maureen defiantly flipped her thick red hair over her shoulder. "I already said I would. There's just *got* to be more to it than what we did."

"Are you nuts? You can't take this kind of chance," Kathleen cried. "What if you get pregnant?"

"I know, I know… But Robbie said he'd use something so I wouldn't end up with a baby. And even if I did get pregnant, Robbie said he'd marry me."

"You're not even eighteen. What about college?" Her sister received top grades. She could get a scholarship; Kathleen was positive of that. No one in their family had gone to college yet. Sean had joined the Army when he graduated and Mary Rose was married and the mother of a two-year-old. Joyce and Louise shared an apartment and worked at the pub. Joyce was a waitress and Louise made sandwiches back in the kitchen. They split the tips. After they'd moved out, Kathleen had a bed of her own for the first time in her life.

"You're only seventeen," Kathleen wailed. "How do you know you want to marry Robbie?"

"How do you know you want to be a nun?" Maureen flared back.

That shut her up. "Just be careful," Kathleen cautioned.

"You won't tell Mom, will you?"

Kathleen promised she wouldn't.

Late that same night, Maureen woke her out of a deep sleep. Moonlight shimmered in through the sheer drapes, and the sound of the television traveled up the stairs like distant whispers.

"Are you awake?" her sister asked, putting her hand on Kathleen's shoulder and lightly shaking her.

Kathleen propped herself up on one elbow. It sounded like *Ben Casey* playing downstairs, which would keep her mother distracted. Maureen's eyes sought hers.

"Did you do it?" Kathleen whispered.

Maureen nodded. "Twice."

"In one night?"

Again her sister nodded.

Kathleen shouldn't be this anxious for details, but she had to know, despite the fact that she'd never experience physical love herself. She sat up and wrapped her arms around her bent knees. "Tell me what it was like."

A soft smile lifted the edges of her sister's full mouth. "I know why Mom and Dad had eight of us. It feels so good, Kathleen. It's like…oh, I don't know. It's like nothing else in the whole world."

Kathleen leaned against the headboard and bit her lower lip, taking in her sister's words. "Did Robbie use…protection?"

Maureen lowered her eyes.

"Maureen!" Sure as anything, her sister was going to end up pregnant before graduation and the whole family would be disgraced.

"He put it on, but he said it wasn't as good and—"

"You should've made him do it." Kathleen covered her mouth with both hands, equally dismayed at her sister's foolishness and her own willingness to abandon the Church's stand on birth control. "If you get pregnant, Mom and Dad will kill you."

Indignant, Maureen leapt off the bed. "Robbie said it was a big mistake to tell you. I should've listened to him. Miss Goody Two-shoes. No wonder entering the convent is all you talk about."

"That's not true," Kathleen snapped.

"If you tell Mom or Dad, I'll never forgive you."

"I'm not going to tell."

Maureen hurriedly undressed in the dark. "I could never enter the convent," she whispered, calmer now.

"Because you've lost your virginity?"

"No," she returned with a snicker, "because I could never live without sex. You're better off not knowing, Kathleen. If you did, you wouldn't be so keen to listen to that call from God you're always saying you hear."

Thankfully Maureen wasn't pregnant, although once she and Robbie had started having sex they couldn't seem to stop. Three months after graduation, Maureen had an engagement ring, and all thoughts of attending college were discarded like yesterday's newspaper.

In the last month of her junior year, Kathleen was elected prefect of the Sodality, the society dedicated to the devotion to Mary, the mother of Christ. She felt elated that her classmates had entrusted her with this honor—until her uncle Patrick unexpectedly pulled her aside at the pub one afternoon.

Kathleen was sure he intended to offer her a weekend job as a waitress. She was a good worker and the extra money would mean she could afford a few extras without having to ask her mother.

"Sit down, Kathleen," her uncle said, showing her to a table at the back of the pub. She wondered why he'd chosen to sit in the shadows.

He pulled out a chair for her, and as she sat, she glanced down at the floor; even in this dark corner it shone. She took whatever task she was given seriously. There wasn't a spot or a speck of dust on the polished oak floor.

"I've never hidden the fact that you're my favorite niece," her uncle said, folding his arms across his big chest.

He wiped the back of his hand across his mouth, and Kathleen wondered if he was already into the beer. Her uncle had a weakness for his own product.

"Since you *are* my favorite, it pains me to tell you this. Damn, it doesn't seem right, but your mother and father said…" He let his words fade, then took a deep breath. "I'm afraid I'm going to have to let you go."

Kathleen thought she must have heard wrong. Let her go? It sounded as though her own uncle was firing her. She couldn't imagine what she'd done to deserve this. Furthermore, without the job, she had no way of paying her tuition. When the shock wore off and Kathleen managed to find her tongue, she said, "You don't want me working at the pub any longer?"

Her uncle stood abruptly. "Back in a minute." With that, he trotted toward the bar and drew himself a mug of Harp. He took a healthy swig before he sat down at the table again. "Let me tell you a story."

Her uncle was the best storyteller she'd ever met. It was one reason the pub was so popular. Boston didn't lack for Irish pubs, but every night her uncle's tavern was filled with music and laughter. And every night, the affable Patrick O'Shaughnessy entertained the crowd with a story or two. He had the gift, and what a gift it was. But if not for her father's handling of the accounts, she feared her uncle would have lost the pub ten times over. Although he was a wonderful host and told a grand story, her uncle Patrick had no sense when it came to money or beer.

"Did I do something wrong?" she asked before he could get caught up in one of the Irish legends or folk-tales he loved.

"Wrong? My Kathleen? Never!"

"Then why are you telling me I can't work in the pub anymore?" Apparently her mother and father already knew because her uncle had discussed it with them. Come to think of it, her father generally did the hiring and firing for the pub. Not this time, though.

Uncle Patrick leaned over and clasped her hand in his. "Your parents and I talked it over, and we decided it just isn't right for you to be here."

"But why?"

"Kathleen, you've a calling from God!"

"Yes, but…"

"Next year you'll be in a convent. And now that you're head of the Sodality, well…it isn't seemly to have you working in a tavern."

"But Father O'Hara is here two and three nights a week."

"Father O'Hara isn't a nun. It's different with priests. I don't know why, but it is. Now, I realize this comes as a shock—and that you need the money for tuition."

A sick feeling settled in the pit of her stomach. It wasn't her father or even her uncle who'd come up with this outlandish notion. That…that sodden priest must have planted the idea in their minds. "Is this Father O'Hara's doing?" she demanded.

"None of that matters, Kathleen. Just accept that we all want the best for you. This is hard on me, too, you know. Your beautiful face won't be gracing my after-noons any longer, now will it?"

In less than a year she'd be a postulant. When Kathleen entered the religious life, she'd be required to relinquish the things of the world, but that was months away yet. She hadn't thought she'd have to give up her job quite so soon.

"I feel bad about this," her uncle continued.

Kathleen tried not to show her distress. She'd need to make certain sacrifices in order to serve God. She was willing to cut her hair if God asked it of her, although she prayed He wouldn't. Sex was out of the question for her, too, even though Maureen insisted on filling her in on all the details of what she and Robbie were doing. She hadn't even walked through the convent doors and already she was expected to behave like a nun. It hurt that her only source of income was to be taken away from her, and all because of Father O'Hara.

"Will I have to leave St. Mark's?" It would be a bitter disappointment not to graduate with her friends.

"Now, that would be a sin," her uncle told her, sipping his lager. "Your tuition's been paid up for the remainder of the school year."

Kathleen gasped. "You did that?"

"I can't have my sweet Kathleen worrying about paying her school fees, now can I?" He winked boyishly at her above his mug. "Father O'Hara and I worked out a deal."

He didn't need to tell her what the deal was. Beer in exchange for tuition. Still, she had no complaints as long as she graduated from St. Mark's.

To her surprise, Uncle Patrick's eyes misted. "You're the pride and joy of this family," he whispered. "We all hoped one of the O'Shaughnessy brood would heed God's call. You make us proud."

She murmured her thanks, a little uncomfortable at his emotion.

"You have always been a sweet girl. No wonder God wants you."

The summer of 1963 was the most carefree of Kathleen's life. Knowing that she'd be entering the order of St. Bridget's Sisters of the Assumption in September, she spent lazy afternoons listening to the Beach Boys and Martha and the Vandellas. She even took up the guitar and managed to pick her way through a whole repertoire of songs. The Singing Nun had made "Dominique" popular and for a time Kathleen entertained the notion of forming a band of singing postulants. She wondered what Reverend Mother would feel about that. Maybe nuns could be actresses, too. *Lilies of the Field* had been one of the most popular movies of the year. It would've been far more authentic if they'd used real nuns to act with Sidney Poitier, Kathleen mused.

The highlight of the summer, however, came in August, when her oldest brother Sean was home on leave from the Army. He was so handsome that Kathleen nearly burst with pride when she saw him.

"What's it like being a Green Beret?" she asked, sipping a tall glass of iced tea on the front porch swing. She wore cutoff jeans and a sleeveless blouse and no shoes. This was her last fling before the convent.

"Good." Sean sat down on the porch step and dangled his arms over his knees. "I'd forgotten about summers in Boston," he said, wiping the sweat from his brow.

"Are you enjoying Seattle?"

"Yeah." He leaned against the porch column and stared up at her. "You're absolutely certain about this,

Kathleen?" he asked, frowning. "You don't look like someone who wants to be a nun."

She smiled and wondered if he knew what a wonderful compliment he'd given her. "I leave for the convent in two weeks."

"What if you don't like it?"

"I will," she said with utter confidence. She hadn't made a contingency plan because she was sure she wouldn't need one.

Sean reached for his iced tea. "I was thinking back the other day, and I can't remember a time when we didn't know you were going to be a nun."

Kathleen stretched out her bare legs. "First grade I knew."

"At six years old?"

She nodded solemnly. "It was during my First Communion that I heard God calling me."

"Was that God or was it Mom and Dad?" Sean asked with more than a little sarcasm.

"What do you mean?"

"Everyone just kind of assumed this was right for you. Is it something you truly want or did you just accept what the family decided?"

"Oh, Sean, don't be ridiculous."

"Have you ever been kissed?"

"Why do you want to know that?" Answering with a question saved her the embarrassment of admitting the truth.

"You haven't experienced life yet. All you know is home and school and working at Uncle Patrick's place. There's a whole world out there. Don't get me wrong, I love Mom and Dad, but we've lived a sheltered life. Take a few years, travel, go off to college and meet a boy or two before you make your final decision about this nun business."

"This is what I want, Sean. Be happy for me, all right?"

Sean didn't comment for several moments. Then he said, "Promise me one thing."

"What?"

"If you ever decide the convent isn't for you, you won't hesitate to leave."

"Break my vows?" Kathleen had never heard of anyone doing something so dreadful.

"Yes, if that's what it takes."

She was positive he didn't mean that. "Would you ever leave the Army?"

"It's different, Kathleen."

"Is it?"

"Just promise me. I'll rest easier giving my sister to God, knowing that if you change your mind you'll have the courage to walk away."

What an unusual request. She tried to laugh it off, but he wouldn't let her.

"I'm serious," Sean insisted. "I need to hear you say it."

Kathleen weighed her words. This was the strangest discussion she'd ever had with her oldest brother. "I promise." But her decision had been made years earlier. She belonged to God.

{3}

Joanna Baird
1965 ~ 1967

"Greg, we can't," Joanna managed to say between increasingly deep, urgent kisses. "Not again. We promised." Her boyfriend dragged her mouth back to his. Already his hands were inside her blouse, fumbling with the snap of her bra.

"I can't help it," Greg Markham groaned. "I've missed you so much. I need you, baby."

In the backseat of his 1956 Chevy Bel-Air, Joanna made one last desperate attempt to clear her head. It was too late to reason with Greg, though, and she knew it. She'd missed him, too. Just back from basic training, her high school boyfriend was about to leave for Vietnam, and their time together was limited. Without further protest, she rolled up her skirt and worked off her underwear. Soon he was positioned over her in the cramped car.

Joanna wound her arms around his neck as he slowly

sank his body into hers. Closing her eyes, she sighed audibly as she arched up to receive him. She gave herself over to the familiar sensations. Frenzied now, she and Greg churned against each other until his release came in a deep, guttural moan.

Breathing hard, he buried his face in the curve of her neck. "I'm sorry, baby, so sorry."

She didn't know why he felt the need to apologize. She'd wanted him as much as he'd wanted her. Perhaps even more. She might have made a token protest, but she'd been the one who'd purposely set out to arouse him. Using her body to tempt him gave her a sense of power, a sense of control, and she loved it. Loved *him*. Catching his earlobe between her teeth, she relished his body's shiver of renewed arousal. Moving provocatively against him, she whispered, "I haven't even finished my penance from the last time."

"Me neither," Greg said and laughed softly.

When Greg had gone to confession, his penance had been harsh and unreasonable, Joanna thought. Father Kramer had instructed her to say the Rosary six times, but he'd ordered Greg to give up cigarettes for seven whole days. Greg hadn't managed to go without his smokes for five hours, let alone a week. It was unfair of Father Kramer to be so hard on Greg while letting her off so lightly.

Raising himself, Greg awkwardly yanked up his jeans. She heard his zipper close as she struggled to sit upright with her skirt around her waist. He climbed out of the car for a smoke while Joanna tried to rearrange her clothes. She searched for her nylons and sighed with relief when she found them both. The last time they'd made love in the car, one of her nylons had been tucked under the seat. They'd spent an anxious ten minutes looking for it. If she were to walk into the house without it, her parents would know she'd been up to no good.

"Are you dressed?" Greg asked as he opened the car door.

Joanna glanced out. "Is anyone coming?"

Greg chuckled. "Just me."

She groaned. "You know what I mean."

His gaze held hers and the amusement left his eyes. "Oh baby, what am I going to do?"

In a week Greg would be shipping out to Vietnam. In May, shortly after they graduated, he'd enlisted in the Army. His timing was perfect; just a month later, in July, President Johnson had announced the escalation of the war in Vietnam and said that draft calls would be doubled.

"You'll wait for me, won't you?" Greg pleaded.

Joanna didn't understand why he kept asking her that. "You know I will." She'd be starting nursing school at Holy Name Hospital in Providence a few weeks from now. Between her studies, hospital work and writing Greg, she wouldn't have time to meet anyone else. She didn't want to, loving Greg as much as she did.

Stepping out of the car, she wrapped her arms around his middle and wriggled sensually.

"Baby," he moaned and twisted around, backing her against the passenger door. "You know what that does to me."

Joanna sighed and slid her arms around his neck. "I love you, Greg."

"I love you." He leaned away slightly and his eyes held hers. "How am I going to survive an entire year without making love to you?"

"I'll wait for you."

He frowned as though he wasn't sure he believed her, no matter how many times she repeated it.

Then, two days before Greg was scheduled to depart for Vietnam, Joanna arrived home to find him sitting in the living room, talking intently with both her parents.

"Hi," she said, entering the house. She hadn't expected him, but it wasn't unusual for Greg to stop by unannounced. What *was* unusual was to find her parents with him.

"Joanna." He automatically stood when she walked into the room.

Her mother wiped a tear from the corner of her eye and smiled warmly at Joanna.

"What's the matter?" Joanna asked. Clearly *something* was from the way everyone was staring at her. She seemed to be the only one who didn't get whatever was going on.

"Nothing's wrong," her father assured her, steering his wife from the room. "Not a thing."

"Greg?" Joanna asked.

The next moment, he actually got down on one knee. "Joanna," he said, gazing up at her, "will you marry me?"

Joanna gasped as he pulled a small velvet box from his pocket. Greg opened the ring box to display a solitaire diamond in an antique gold setting. They'd talked about the future and decided they wanted to get married, but their plans were for an unspecified date sometime in the future. Marriage would come after she'd received her nursing degree and Greg was settled in with his father's business. Vietnam, however, was about to change all that.

"Greg, yes! Yes, yes, oh yes."

He slipped the ring onto her finger and kissed her. Her parents, smiling broadly, wandered back into the room. Her father wrapped his arm around her mother, who was struggling to hide her tears of joy.

"I came to ask your family for their permission," Greg explained. "I want to do everything right, just the way my father did."

Joanna wiped the tears from her own cheeks. "Mom, look." She held out her left hand so her mother could inspect the small diamond.

"Your father asked me to marry him just before he left to fight in World War Two," she said, hugging Joanna and then Greg.

"What's happening?" Rick, her sixteen-year-old brother, asked as he sauntered into the room, munching a crisp apple.

"Joanna and Greg are engaged."

"Joanna's getting married?" Rick noisily bit into his apple. "I thought you were going to be a nun."

"Rick!" She couldn't believe her brother would bring up that long-ago ambition now.

"A nun?" One corner of Greg's mouth turned up in the start of a smile. Knowing the things he did about her, he had reason to be amused. Joanna elbowed him in the ribs before he could let out their secret.

"You're stealing my little girl away from God," her father said.

"Daddy," Joanna protested, furious that her family would take such delight in teasing her.

"Cut it out, you two." Her mother stepped in to rescue her. "Joanna considered the convent when she was a high school freshman. That's all there is to it."

"Well, God can't have her," Greg said, throwing his arm around her. He kissed the top of her head. "I've got her now."

Rick took another loud bite of his apple. "When's the wedding?"

Greg and Joanna exchanged glances, and then burst out laughing because they didn't know. Soon, they decided. Greg would serve his year in Vietnam and when he returned, they'd get married. While he was off at war, Joanna would make all the wedding arrangements.

Eventually the date was set for September of the following year. That gave Joanna and her mother a little more than fourteen months to plan.

Two days later, Greg left for Vietnam. Joanna rode with him to the airport, where—along with his mother and father—she tearfully saw him off. As the jet zoomed into the sky, she felt a sensation of dread and wondered if this would be the last time she saw Greg.

A week following his departure for Asia, Joanna entered the hospital nursing program. Within a matter of days, her world revolved around her studies, writing Greg and all the planning that went into a big wedding.

"I don't know what I'd do if I didn't have the wedding to distract me," she wrote Greg early in December as her hi-fi belted out "I Can't Get No Satisfaction" by the Rolling Stones. "If I wasn't busy thinking about the wedding, I'd be worrying about you. Now, honey, please take care of yourself. I love you so much."

Greg's letters were full of details about his assignment and his life in Saigon, where he was stationed. He spoke of the squalor and the effects of the war on the people of the Southeast Asian country. He mailed her small things he found in the local shops—a bracelet, silk pajamas, an ivory-handled mirror. He was fortunate not to be in a combat situation; instead, he'd been assigned to desk duty with the Military Police and typed up volumes of paperwork whenever a soldier was sent to the stockade. One bonus to this assignment was that he had plenty of time to write. In the beginning, he mailed a long letter nearly every day.

January 3, 1966

Sweetheart,
Thanks for sending me the fabric swatches for the bridesmaids' dresses. You sure you want *five* bridesmaids? Never mind, you can have ten if it makes you happy. I like the green one best, but you decide. I'll come up with five ushers, but I'll probably need to ask a cousin or two.

It was hard not being home for Christmas. I hope you like your gift. A set of bone china isn't as romantic as I would've liked, but that was what you said you wanted. I hope you like the pattern I picked out. Just think—one day you'll be my wife and you'll cook me dinner and serve it to me on those very plates.

Write soon. I live for your letters.
Greg

Joanna lived for his letters, too. Each day she hurried home from school and sorted through the mail, suffering keen disappointment if there wasn't one.

"I don't think there's a letter from Greg," her mother said. It was a cold February afternoon, and Joanna, still wearing her coat, flipped through a stack of envelopes on the kitchen table.

"I haven't heard from him in three days."

"I'm sure he's fine."

"I'm sure he is, too," Joanna said, but she wondered and worried all the same.

That evening her best friend phoned. "We're going to see *My Fair Lady.* Why don't you come along?"

Joanna was tempted, really tempted. She enjoyed musicals and it would be a welcome break, but she hesitated.

"Everyone's going to be there," Jane urged her. "Bob and Gary and Sharon and just about everyone."

"I can't," Joanna said reluctantly.

"Why not?" her friend asked. "You haven't gone anywhere in months, not since Greg left."

"That's not true. You and I went shopping last week."

"You spend more time with that girl at the hospital than you do with any of us."

"You mean Penny?"

"Whatever her name is. You're always there. Who is she, anyway? It isn't like she went to school with us. You barely know her."

Jane was right. Penny had leukemia and after her classes Joanna often stopped in to visit the teenager. Sister Theresa had introduced Joanna to Penny. These days Joanna had more in common with the hospital patient than her high school friends. Penny's boyfriend was also in Vietnam; they compared notes and discussed news about the war. Sister Theresa had mentioned how beneficial these visits were for Penny, but she didn't understand how much Joanna got out of them, too.

"You're right, we did go shopping," Jane went on, "but that was just the two of us. You haven't gone out with the crowd. We used to all hang out, remember?"

As if Joanna could forget.

"I'm engaged." She didn't feel comfortable meeting

her friends in situations that often involved couples pairing up. Not when she wore Greg's engagement ring.

"That doesn't mean you're dead," Jane muttered.

"I know, but it bothers me...." Greg didn't like it either. When she happened to mention running into their old gang, he'd plied her with questions. He hadn't asked her *not* to hang around with their high school friends, but she could tell from his letters that he worried when she was out with the guys. She couldn't find it in her heart to write him long, chatty letters in which she conveniently forgot to mention that she'd sat beside Paul or Ron at the movies.

Greg was the possessive type, but she didn't mind. She saw it as proof that he loved her. Besides, it wasn't his fault that he was in the middle of the war while several of their friends had gotten college exemptions.

Penny understood Joanna's dilemma on an entirely different level. She didn't want to write Scott, her boyfriend, about her experiences in the hospital or the progression of her disease, so Joanna helped her think up cheerful news to convey to her sweetheart half a world away.

"Do me a favor," Jane said. "Ask Greg. Do you honestly think he wants you to stay home, pining away for him?"

To Joanna's astonishment, when she did bring it up, casually—with the assurance that she'd stayed home—Greg protested. "Jane's right. You should be going out with our friends," he wrote. "I know you love me and I love you. I might be cut off from everyone while I do this stint in the Army, but that doesn't mean you have to be, too."

Joanna read his letter a second time, just to be sure there wasn't any hint of resentment. She detected none and wondered if she would have acted as magnanimous had their roles been reversed. Still, she wrote him every day, rain or shine, whether her moods were up or down.

His letters came intermittently now, always with a good excuse about why he hadn't been able to write. "I'm sorry, Joanna. Has it really been a week? Forgive me, sweetheart, but it's crazy over here. I promise to look at the wedding invitation samples and get back to you soon." Then he'd remind her of his love and everything would seem perfect again.

Joanna's studies at the hospital continued. Despite her fears that Greg's absence would make the time drag, this first year was flying by.

"Was it hard for you to wait for Daddy?" Joanna asked her mother as they sat out on the patio in the bright June sunshine.

"The war seemed interminable," her mother said, relaxing on a chaise longue. "Like you and Greg, we were engaged, I kissed him goodbye when he left for the South Pacific and then we didn't see each other for twenty-two months."

"I could never wait that long," Joanna said. She sipped her soda and tried to calm her anxieties. There hadn't been a letter from Greg in four days. Lately he hadn't been writing real letters, either. They were more like notes he dashed off early in the morning before he went on duty. But Joanna didn't care; it didn't matter how long his letters were. All she needed was the knowledge that she was in his thoughts.

"You do whatever is necessary," her mother told her. "That's what women have always done."

"Twenty-two months." Joanna couldn't bear to be apart from Greg for almost two years. Already it

seemed far longer than that since she'd last seen him—
and since they'd last made love.

"I didn't know from one day to the next if your father was alive or not," her mother added.

"I think I'd know if anything happened to Greg." She
hadn't meant to say it out loud, but Joanna felt certain
her heart would tell her if he was injured...or worse.
They were so closely linked, so deeply in love.

"How's Penny?" her mother asked.

Joanna sighed. "Back in the hospital. Sister Theresa
called earlier to let me know. I'll go up to see her first
thing tomorrow."

The phone rang and Joanna raced into the kitchen.
Twice now Greg had managed to reach her stateside and
they'd talked, however briefly. Her emotional high had
lasted for days afterward.

"Hello," she answered cheerfully. The kitchen radio
played the Beatles song "I Want to Hold Your Hand"
and she made a mental note to take Penny her transis-
tor radio.

Ten minutes later, Joanna put down the receiver.
"Mom, Mom," she cried, so excited she could barely
stand still. "That was the fabric store in Boston. The
material's in." At fifty dollars a yard, the stuff was hor-
rendously expensive, but her mother had ordered Belgian
lace anyway. It was for Joanna's wedding dress, after all,
which the best seamstress in town was sewing.

"Did you ask her to mail it?"

"No... I didn't think of it."

"Good." Her mother sat up and removed her sun-
glasses. "Because you and I will be personally picking it up."

"We're going to Boston?" Joanna shrieked.

"We are," her mother said, sounding delighted, "and we're going to shop. Every bride needs a trousseau."

"Oh, Mom, really?" Joanna felt like crying with gratitude and excitement. The wedding had seemed so far away, but now that the lace had arrived it had suddenly become real.

"I want everything to be perfect for you," her mother said.

"What will Dad say?"

"Leave him to me."

They left the next morning and were away for three glorious days. This trip was exactly the restorative Joanna needed. Sure enough, a long letter from Greg awaited her when she returned. She immediately sat down and wrote him back, describing the shopping spree and the hotel and what a fabulous time she'd had.

Because Joanna and her mother had left on the spur of the moment, she hadn't been to the hospital to visit Penny yet.

Packing up the lacy silk gown she intended to wear on her wedding night, plus her going-away suit and shoes, Joanna arrived at the hospital late on Tuesday afternoon. Penny would enjoy seeing everything, and Joanna was eager to show off her purchases.

Sister Theresa was at the nurses' station when Joanna walked off the elevator.

"Joanna," Sister said abruptly.

"Hello, Sister. I'm here to see Penny."

Sister's face fell and she sighed softly. "I'm so sorry to tell you, we lost her yesterday afternoon."

"Lost her?" The hospital didn't *lose* people. Then it dawned on Joanna. "Penny…died?"

"I'm sorry, Joanna. I know what good friends the two of you became."

A sob broke free from the constricted muscles of her throat. The shock of Penny's death sent the room spinning. Joanna hadn't seen her in two weeks, but they'd talked on the phone and Penny had always seemed so optimistic. Never once had she mentioned her leukemia. Whenever Joanna asked, Penny had brushed aside the question. It was clear she didn't want to talk about her illness and Joanna hadn't pressured her.

"Come and sit down," Sister said, gently sliding her arm around Joanna. "Penny often told me how much she loved your visits. Her other friends had drifted away, but you were there for her."

Only she hadn't been, Joanna realized, sick to her stomach. While Penny had been lying alone and friendless in the hospital, Joanna was off shopping as though she hadn't a care in the world. The guilt tarnished her happiness, made it seem trite.

In Greg's next letter a few weeks later he tried to console her. "You couldn't have known, Joanna. Stop blaming yourself. You *were* there for her. You visited when she needed you."

But even his words didn't help and Joanna didn't know if she could ever forgive herself. She walked around in a daze. She'd never lost a friend before and felt that she'd failed Penny. Sister Theresa talked to her several times, offering both compassion and common sense. The nun's kindness made a real difference.

"I heard from Scott," Sister told Joanna the following week.

"Penny's Scott?" Joanna asked.

Sister nodded. "He knew from the first that Penny wasn't going to recover, but like her he pretended she would. He's taking it hard, but he's a strong Catholic and has accepted the will of God."

Joanna wished she had the faith to be more accepting. Her own relationship with God had suffered since that first time in the backseat of Greg's Chevy. Oh, she faithfully attended Mass every week, sitting in the pew with Rick and her parents. Her brother was bored by church, but he went because he didn't have a choice. Joanna's attitude wasn't much better. Religion had become irrelevant to her. It wasn't only Penny she'd let down; it was God, too.

"If you ever need to talk," Sister Theresa invited, "you know you can tell me anything."

It was as though the nun had read her thoughts. Penny's death had shaken Joanna, and no one else understood that. Not her parents. Not Greg either, although he tried. He seemed to be more and more preoccupied lately. Judging by one or two comments he'd made, he appeared to be involved in some trouble of his own—something to do with his commanding officer. Joanna knew she should ask, but she didn't. School and the wedding demanded all her energy. Then, in July, as Greg's year of duty drew to an end, he wrote to say that it was important for them to talk.

Talk? About what? She wrote and asked, but Greg said he'd explain everything once he got home. And that was fine with her. She needed him, wanted him close. The wedding was less than a month away; she should be excited—in a few weeks, she would be Greg's bride. His *wife*. Instead of making love in the backseat of a car, she would enjoy the luxury of waking in a real bed, wrapped in her husband's embrace.

Just as Joanna finished preparing the wedding invitations, she received word that Greg was flying home. It was early, but she had no complaints. This was the best news she'd gotten in weeks. No, months. She wondered if this unexpected reprieve was linked to his troubles with the military, but Joanna didn't care. Whatever the reason, she was grateful.

"We'll have a long heart-to-heart when I'm home," he wrote again.

"I need you," she wrote back. She craved his arms around her and the release his body would give her. It wasn't only physical satisfaction she sought but emotional, too. With Greg she could be herself. She could let him see her grief over Penny. What had seemed impossible to convey through letters would be easier to explain in person.

Joanna didn't sleep the night before Greg was scheduled to arrive. His mother had called to say—testily, Joanna thought—that Greg's family would meet him at the airport alone. Joanna could see him later. It was as though Mrs. Markham was purposely excluding her from this reunion and Joanna resented it.

"Mrs. Markham doesn't want me there," she complained to her mother.

Her mother didn't bother to hide her irritation. "Greg is your fiancé, for heaven's sake."

"I'm sure he'll be expecting me." Joanna didn't know why his mother was being so unreasonable, but she had no intention of waiting silently at home. "I'm going to the airport on my own."

Her mother nodded. "I think you should. You don't need to ride with Greg's parents."

At the airport, Joanna felt a little silly sneaking behind his parents' backs. She couldn't stay away, though, and considered it cruel of his mother to have suggested it.

When Greg's plane touched down, she saw his parents standing apart from everyone else. They seemed to be arguing. Joanna would have said something, revealed her presence, but she didn't want to embarrass them. His mother took a handkerchief from her purse and dabbed her eyes.

Soon the passengers disembarked, and Joanna strained for a glimpse of Greg. The instant she saw him, her heart leapt with joy. She had to force herself not to run straight into his arms.

It was a good thing she didn't.

Seconds later she realized Greg hadn't traveled from Vietnam alone. There was a woman with him—a petite Vietnamese woman who was obviously pregnant.

Confused, Joanna stared at them. Greg was bringing a foreign woman to the States? A pregnant woman? It didn't make sense.

As if watching a movie unfold before her eyes, Joanna stayed out of view as Greg put his arm around the woman and steered her toward his parents. Mr. and Mrs. Markham stepped forward, and the Asian woman bowed her head at the introduction.

"Greg?" Unable to remain silent any longer, Joanna moved away from the pillar where she'd been standing. "Who is this woman?"

"Joanna." Greg looked at her, and then his mother. The blood seemed to drain from his face.

"Oh, Joanna," his mother groaned. "You should never have come."

Joanna ignored her. "Who is this woman?" she demanded a second time.

Greg exhaled and refused to meet her eyes. "This is Xuan. My wife."

"Your…wife?"

Her question was met with an embarrassed silence. If the news that he was married wasn't shock enough,

Joanna's gaze fell to the small round belly. "She's pregnant?"

Greg swallowed visibly and nodded.

Still Joanna couldn't take it in. "The baby is yours?" That wasn't possible. Greg was engaged to marry *her*. Their wedding was only weeks away. She'd just had the final fitting for her wedding gown, and the bridesmaids had their dresses with shoes dyed to match, and her aunt Betty was flying in from San Francisco to attend the wedding, and… *Of course* there was going to be a wedding.

Joanna read the regret and sorrow in Greg's eyes. "I'm sorry," he whispered.

"You couldn't tell me? You left me to learn this on my own?" Doing something so underhanded was horrible enough, but to humiliate her just four weeks before the wedding was cruel beyond words.

"I *couldn't* tell you," he cried. His eyes pleaded with her for understanding.

"My father important man," the Asian woman said boldly. "He—" she pointed at Greg "—marry me. Take me to America. Big trouble for him if not." Xuan faced Joanna and stared at her. "He love me." She planted her hands on her stomach as if to say she bore the evidence of Greg's love.

"Yes, I can see that he does," Joanna said quietly.

"Joanna, please—this is awkward enough." Greg's mother moved toward them. "Do you think it would be possible to have this discussion elsewhere?" Mrs. Markham glanced self-consciously around her.

His mother was right. This was neither the time nor the place to deal with such—what had she called it?—awkwardness.

"I should never have come," Joanna said in a voice she barely recognized as her own.

"Now you know why I asked you to stay home." Mrs. Markham sounded angry.

"We couldn't say anything," his father said, obviously taking pity on Joanna. "It wasn't our place." He was kind enough to escort her to the parking lot. Joanna followed obediently but it felt as though she was walking in a fog.

"Greg should have explained the situation," he said when they'd reached her vehicle. "He said he couldn't do that to you in a letter. You'd already had one shock this summer."

Joanna stared up at him blankly.

"Your friend died."

"Oh, you mean Penny."

"Perhaps I should drive you home," he suggested, and held out his hand for her car keys.

Joanna stared at his palm. "Did I tell you Mom and Dad got the country club for the wedding reception?"

"Joanna, there isn't going to be a wedding."

She blinked rapidly. He was right. No wedding because there was no groom. Her fiancé was married to someone else. A Vietnamese woman, who'd told them that her father was a powerful government official. So this was the trouble Greg had been alluding to in his letters, the trouble that had involved his commanding officer. His Vietnamese wife was the reason Greg had been sent stateside early.

"I'll be fine," she said and opened the car door herself. Once inside, she pressed her forehead against the steering wheel and waited for the waves of shock and disbelief to dissipate before attempting to drive. When she noticed that Greg's father was still outside, she hurriedly started the engine and drove away.

As soon as the news of the cancelled wedding was out, Joanna's family and friends rallied around her. By the end of the first week of August, there was no evidence that she'd ever been engaged.

The wedding dress disappeared from her closet. The invitations, all stamped and ready to be mailed, vanished. Her family and friends tiptoed around her, and Greg's name was no longer part of anyone's vocabulary.

His wife, Joanna learned, was living with his parents. Their baby was due in three months. That meant Greg had been unfaithful to her soon after he'd landed in Southeast Asia.

No wonder he'd graciously urged her to get out with their friends. He was "getting out" himself. Oh yes, her fiancé sure had the world by the tail, she thought bitterly. He had a fiancée stateside who loved and missed him, plus a mistress in Vietnam.

The only place Joanna experienced peace was inside church. In the afternoons when she'd finished her classes, she sat in the hospital chapel and absorbed the serenity and peace of the empty room.

After the first couple of weeks, she felt a long-forgotten desire begin to reemerge. As a high school freshman, she'd considered joining the convent. Every good Catholic girl entertained the idea at some point; Joanna was no different. Perhaps, she reasoned, her broken engagement was just God's way of leading her back to the religious life. She'd give it time, but not discuss it with anyone until she'd made a tentative decision.

A month later, Joanna sought out Sister Theresa. "You said I could talk to you anytime I needed."

"Of course." Sister led Joanna into her office and closed the door.

"You heard?" Joanna asked, not wanting to explain her humiliation.

Sister Theresa nodded. "I realize this must be a very painful time for you, Joanna, but God allows these burdens to come into our lives for a reason."

"I believe that, too."

Sister smiled approvingly. "You're wise beyond your years."

Joanna didn't feel wise; she felt wounded and weak. "I've been doing a lot of praying since Penny died and I learned about Greg. I wonder if God is using this situation to point me in a completely different direction."

"How do you mean?"

Joanna figured she might as well be direct. "These days the only place I feel any comfort is in church."

"God is eager to listen to our prayers," Sister said.

"I sense His presence. I pray and afterward I feel better. I've started thinking that maybe God is calling me to a life of prayer."

Sister didn't reveal any emotion. "Are you saying you're considering the convent?"

"Yes…"

"Do you feel you have a vocation, Joanna?"

"Yes."

Sister sighed. "I don't want to discourage you, especially if God *is* calling you to the religious life. But it's important that you enter the convent for the right reasons. Not because you have a broken heart."

Joanna understood Sister Theresa's concern. "I feel God purposely took Greg out of my life. It was His way of asking me to work for Him."

Sister regarded her steadily. "God doesn't want to

be your second choice, Joanna. He wants to be first in your heart."

"He is, Sister. He was until…until Greg and I became involved. I want to serve as a St. Bridget's Sister of the Assumption."

Sister Theresa paused. "Nothing would please me more, but I want you to wait."

"Wait?" Joanna was ready to enter that very moment. Greg wasn't right for her. They'd led each other into sin and she so desperately wanted to be at peace with God again.

"Give it six months," Sister Theresa added.

Reluctantly, Joanna nodded.

"Have you mentioned this to your parents?"

"Yes." It hadn't gone well. Her mother insisted that Joanna was just reacting to the broken engagement. Her father, on the other hand, had encouraged her, which only infuriated her mother.

"Give it six months," Sister repeated, "and if you're still convinced this is what you want, then I'll recommend that you be admitted in February as an incoming postulant."

{ Part Two }

BRIDES OF CHRIST

As a bridegroom rejoices over his bride, so will God rejoice over you.

—Isaiah 62:5

{4}

Angelina Marcello
1958 ～ 1972

As Angie disembarked from the Greyhound bus that September morning in 1958, she was impatient to start her new life. The farewell scene with her father lingered in her mind. Still, she couldn't allow his disparaging remarks to spoil her first day at the convent. He seemed so sure that entering the order was wrong for her, but if that was true, why did her heart burn with zeal for God?

Her father found it hard to let her go, Angie realized with a swell of compassion. She loved him all the more for his willingness to step aside and allow her to follow her own path, despite the fact that he was convinced she'd made the biggest mistake of her eighteen years.

He'd wept openly as she boarded the bus, the tears streaming down his cheeks. She would always remember her last sight of him: as the bus pulled out of the station, he'd taken the handkerchief from his pocket and dabbed at his eyes. Then with slumped shoulders, he'd turned and walked away. She'd watched sadly, wishing she could have spared him this grief and knowing she couldn't.

Despite Angie's eagerness to enter the religious life, she was nervous. She arrived in Boston midafternoon and caught a cab that deposited her in front of the motherhouse. She was cheered to see that the wrought-iron gates were open wide as though to welcome her. Carrying her small battered suitcase—originally her mother's—Angie walked resolutely up the brick walkway to the convent's entrance and rang the bell.

"Angelina. I see you made it on your own." A tall nun, so thin and sleek that she resembled a crane, stepped forward to greet her.

Angie didn't recall meeting her before.

"I'm Sister Mary Louise. We met briefly when you made your application. Don't worry if you don't remember me. You met a lot of us that day."

Angie smiled in relief. There'd been so many, and their faces and names were a blur in her mind.

"I'm the Postulant Mistress. We'll be having tea shortly. Now, come inside and make yourself comfortable. Several other girls are already here."

She was ushered to a formal room furnished with a dining table and chairs. Angelina recognized Mother Superior there; she also saw three young women, obviously the other postulants. What surprised her was the immediate sense of connection she experienced. These girls, who sat self-consciously at the table, sipping tea and munching cookies, would become her new community. Her family.

"Mother Superior, I'm sure you remember Angelina Marcello," Sister Mary Louise said, escorting Angelina to the older nun.

Angelina hesitated, uncertain if anything was required of her, such as bowing or genuflecting. She knew priests kissed the bishop's ring, but she wasn't up on etiquette for meeting such an important woman.

Sister Agnes's smile was warm and encompassing. "Of course I remember Angelina. You come to us from Buffalo, New York. I'm right, aren't I?"

Angie nodded, holding herself stiff for fear of saying or doing something wrong.

"I thought so. Is there a chair for Angelina, Sister?" Mother asked and Angie was offered an empty place at the table. As soon as she sat, Mother Superior introduced her to the others. "Meet Karen. She's from Boston and Marie is from Columbus, Ohio. Josephine comes to us all the way from California. We're so pleased you're here to be part of us."

By the end of the day, Angelina had been introduced to twenty women ranging in age from seventeen to twenty-two. The postulants were served an early dinner, with only Mother Superior joining them. Because they sat across from each other, Angie and Karen had a chance to talk.

"Did your family bring you?" Angie asked, aware that most girls had been accompanied by their parents and sometimes siblings.

Karen gazed down at the polished tile floor and shook her head. "They were unhappy with my decision." Her hair was dark and straight and fell to the middle of her back. She had a pretty face, Angie thought.

"My father was too," she confessed. This trip to Boston was the first time Angie had traveled anywhere outside of New York State. She'd worried about making the trip by herself but in the end, she'd managed quite nicely. That reassured her, in some small way, that she'd made the right choice.

"I think this is such a beautiful life," Karen told her. Her eyes held a dreamy look. "The habits are lovely, aren't they?"

Angie's smile was vague. She'd never stopped to think about the habits or that she'd soon be wearing one herself.

A few moments later Sister Mary Louise appeared in the refectory doorway and signaled them to follow her. They paraded through the convent, through a series of corridors and passageways, arriving at a heavy wooden door.

"This is the entrance to your dormitory," Sister explained. Angelina had been a visitor earlier in the year during her high school retreat, but it had all felt so different then.

With the others, Angie slowly entered her new living quarters. The soon-to-be postulants clustered together, their shoes clattering against the stone floor. No one seemed willing to walk all the way inside.

"Come in, come in," Sister Mary Louise encouraged. Then one by one, she led them down the hallway and assigned them rooms.

"This will be your cell," the Postulant Mistress told Angie. "I put you next to Karen."

Angie's eyes linked with the other girl's and they shared a smile. It would be good to have a friend, especially one who understood how difficult it had been to go against her father's wishes. As soon as Sister Mary Louise pointed out her room, Angie moved inside, curious about the place where she'd be spending so many hours. It was stark, with only a bed, table and lamp, similar to the one she'd slept in just a few months earlier.

She couldn't help wondering how many other young women had prayed and slept and struggled with doubt and fear in this very room. How many other women had come to St. Bridget's Sisters as she had, with a heart longing to serve? How many had stayed and how many had left? These were things she might never know.

Sister Mary Louise hurried into Angie's cell. "Here are your new clothes." She set a stack of folded garments on the end of the bed.

Angie waited until the nun had left before examining the unfamiliar garb. She could hear nervous giggles coming from the other cells. She discovered black woolen stockings, which she put on after the plain cotton underwear. Next was a dark tunic with long sleeves; they fell past her fingertips and she had to fold them back over her wrists. Then came the black vestlike shirt and pleated ankle-length black skirt, followed by a short cape. Last were the shoes—what she'd always thought of as "nun shoes"—one-inch-thick heels that laced up.

When Angie had finished changing out of her street clothes and into her new ones, she stood in the cell doorway. Sister Mary Louise nodded approvingly when she saw her. "Does everything fit?"

Everything hung loosely on her, but Angie suspected that was exactly how it was supposed to be. "I believe so, Sister."

"Very good. Now we'll give you a veil." She set Angie down on a stool in the hallway and retrieved a hairbrush from her pocket. With swift strokes, she pulled Angie's hair severely from her face and fastened it in the back with hair clips, then secured a veil to her head. Only a few wisps from her bangs were visible.

Soon all twenty of them were dressed and veiled. "This is your introduction to St. Bridget's Sisters of the Assumption," Sister Mary Louise explained. "During the induction ceremony a few minutes from now, Mother Superior will read a special prayer. I want you to bow your heads and listen carefully. Absorb as many of the words as you can and hold on to their meaning. This prayer is asking God to grant you whatever you need to be a good nun." Sister Mary Louise paused briefly, glancing around at the assembled postulants.

"Let me add," she said, her expression serious, "that this time as a postulant is a period of testing. You are asking for the privilege and honor of becoming a novice. You are studying us and we'll be studying you to ensure that you genuinely belong with us."

The Mistress of Postulants paused for a moment, meeting several girls' eyes. "There will be many questions you will answer in the next year. Important questions. But first and foremost, you must decide if you are ready to set aside your own selfish desires and replace them with a close relationship with God.

"You will learn the lessons of obedience and poverty. From this moment forward, you own nothing. Everything you have, right down to your toothbrush, belongs to the Order. You must be absolutely ruthless in your rejection of the world."

Angie gave a deep sigh. She *was* ready to relinquish the world, ready to cast aside all that she owned and would inherit, including the family restaurant. She wanted this life and was determined to pursue it wholeheartedly.

"For many of you, silence will be your greatest struggle. It is just one of the ways we use to empty out all the clutter in our minds. Silence allows God to fill our heads with His thoughts. Grand Silence begins shortly after dinner at seven-thirty. You are not to speak until the next morning. All of this will be further explained in due course. Now follow me."

Sister Mary Louise led them into the chapel for the short ceremony in which they were officially welcomed as postulants into the motherhouse. After that, they were taken back to the dormitory.

Sister Mary Louise stood in front of them. "I know that most of you are feeling confused and a little numb. It's been a busy day, one that signifies the beginning of an important stage of your lives. You will pray together, eat together and study together. However, you'll be separated from the professed sisters at all times, except in chapel and during meals and Sunday evening recreation."

Angie's head was swimming. There seemed to be so much to remember.

"In the morning the alarm rings at four-forty-five. As soon as you hear the bell, you will rise and immediately kneel beside your bed and recite the Our Father. You are to remain silent from the time you hear the bell until after Mass. The bell indicates silence and offers each of us the opportunity for a short daily retreat as we lovingly prepare for Mass."

All Angie heard was the ungodly hour at which the alarm rang. Everything after that was a blur. Four-forty-five in the morning. But, Angie reminded herself, this time set aside for prayer was the very reason she'd entered the convent. She'd come searching for the way to serve God to the fullest.

"Following chapel and breakfast, you will start your first classes." Angie nodded eagerly; she'd always enjoyed school and these would be the most vital lessons of her entire life.

That night, Angie slipped into the long flannel gown

the convent provided and crawled between the coarse sheets of her bed.

The classes that first day were full of valuable information, some of it familiar, some brand-new. Angie took careful notes.

"The history of our Order gives us a rich legacy," Sister Mary Louise said, "thanks to the woman who founded St. Bridget's Sisters of the Assumption. I know many of you have already heard the story of Fionnuala Wheaton."

Angie had read about the life of this wonderful Irishwoman before she was accepted into the convent.

"What can you tell me about her?" Sister asked.

The room was silent, and then Karen tentatively raised her hand. "I know she was married to an English landowner."

"She was widowed at an early age," Angie added.

"That's correct," Sister said, smiling appreciatively in Karen and Angie's direction. "Fionnuala and William had a good marriage. They were devoted to each other."

"She was disappointed that they'd never had children," another postulant said.

"Yes, but we know this was all part of God's plan. God had other things in mind for our founder."

Angie was beginning to understand that God's ways were not those of the world.

"After her husband's death, Fionnuala was devastated by grief and turned to the Church for comfort. The priests of St. Bridget's Parish encouraged her in acts of charity. Soon her generosity was widely known throughout the region. It wasn't long before other widows asked to join her. The small group decided to live and work together. It was Fionnuala's intent to heal the sick and educate the poor."

Angie sat up straighter. This was her heart's desire, too—to help the poor, to teach, and endlessly offer herself to whatever work the Church asked of her.

"In 1840, with the approval of Pope Gregory XVI, St. Bridget's Sisters of the Assumption formally received the blessing of Rome and was established as a religious order."

"This was in Ireland?" one of the girls asked.

"Yes." Sister smiled at Bonnie, the girl whose cell was across from Angie's. "These were the days of the terrible potato famine and as you know, many Irish immigrated to the United States. Conditions were deplorable in Ireland and in the United States, too, as the immigrants struggled to make new lives. In an effort to help, St. Bridget's Sisters of the Assumption sent many young nuns to America. They arrived in Boston and established the convent here. Soon the demand for nuns was high, and by the turn of the century more and more women were offering their lives to the service of the Church."

"When was the motherhouse transferred here?" Karen asked. "From Ireland, I mean."

Sister Mary Louise walked toward the blackboard. "Just before the first of the two World Wars. We're proud of our order, which has grown and expanded through the years. As of today, we have ten convents situated across the United States. I'm pleased to tell you that we are one of the most prominent religious orders in the country. God has continued to bless our efforts.

"While the motherhouse here in Boston is our oldest convent, it isn't our largest. That honor goes to our convent in Minneapolis, Minnesota."

Angie had read about the Minneapolis convent in the brochure she'd received at the time of her high school retreat. The Sisters worked as nurses at St. Elizabeth's Hospital and teachers for the thriving Catholic schools within St. Peter's diocese.

Besides attending her classes, Angelina was required to fulfill housekeeping duties around the convent. Her first assignment was in the laundry room, situated next to the kitchen. After several weeks of bland meals, Angie could remain silent no longer, especially when she realized the cook planned to make spaghetti.

"Let me help," she suggested. She'd already finished sorting and folding that day's clean laundry.

"Help?" The cook, an older woman hired from the community, looked up at her in surprise.

"I'm Italian. I know about herbs and spices." She dipped a spoon into the bubbling red sauce on the stove and tasted it, then slowly shook her head. Her father would throw himself in front of oncoming traffic rather than serve anything this bland. "Bring me the basil," she said with such authority that the lay cook hurried to comply.

Searching through the spice rack, Angie added a pinch of this and a handful of that, tasted, tested and wasn't satisfied until she had something that at least resembled the sauce she knew and loved.

That evening the sisters raved about the meal. The two nuns who'd drawn kitchen duty tried to explain that it had been Angie's work, but it was risky to give her credit. Angie had been assigned to the laundry, not the kitchen. Not once was she ever asked to cook, although the other postulants helped prepare meals on a regular basis.

Whenever the mail arrived, Angie searched for a letter from her father, but she never found one. Karen didn't hear from her family, either. Angie's father could come up with no more effective way to discourage her. It was with a heavy heart that she offered up her disappointment to God.

At the end of her first year, in which she'd received only one terse letter from her father, Angie entered the novitiate. This was known as the contemplative year of silence. Speaking was allowed for only half an hour each evening, and all contact with family was prohibited. She never knew if her father wrote during that year but suspected he hadn't. He was still angry with her.

Nor did he write during her second year as a novice. She spent her days in prayer, studying Scripture and Church history and performing household tasks. The slow, peaceful days in this year of silence helped to shape her thoughts. They taught her patience and a willingness to yield her life to the dictates of God and Mother Superior. By the end of her time in the novitiate, Angie was approached by the Mistress of Novices regarding her new name as a professed sister. She was asked to submit three, but final approval rested with Mother Superior.

The Mistress of Novices stopped her one afternoon as Angie swept the dining room floor. Her eyes brimmed with sadness. "I understand you knew Sister Trinita?"

"Yes," Angie said, keeping her gaze lowered out of respect for the nun's position. The term the convent used was "custody of the eyes." "Sister Trinita was a favorite teacher of mine in grade school," she explained.

"I thought you should know Sister passed on to our heavenly Father last week."

"No," Angie gasped and her hand flew to her throat.

"She'd been seriously ill for some time."

"I... I had no idea."

"Sister didn't wish to burden others. She was suffering from cancer." She paused. "You were a special friend and I thought you'd want to know."

Tears welled in Angie's eyes but she refused to let them fall. The woman who had so greatly influenced her life was gone to be with God. Angie felt the loss as keenly as she had when she'd lost her mother.

"I believe one of the names you chose was Sister Frances?"

Angie nodded. Sister Trinita had long ago told Angie it was her given name before she'd entered the convent.

"I'll talk to Reverend Mother and do what I can to see that you receive the name Sister Frances."

"Oh, thank you," Angie whispered. "That would mean the world to me."

"I can't make any promises, Sister."

When she saw Karen during the recreation period after dinner, her friend knew immediately that something was wrong. "What happened?" she asked, squinting at the needle she was threading. All the second-year novices worked diligently on sewing their own habits, using three battered old machines and doing the finer work by hand. Until they spoke their final vows of chastity, poverty and obedience, their clothing was known as dresses or gowns. Only professed Sisters wore habits.

"Sister Trinita died…she had cancer." Thinking back to their chance meeting on the convent grounds three years earlier, Angie recalled the hesitation in her manner. When Angie had asked about her latest assignment, Sister Trinita had passed over the question. She'd said "For now," and Angie was convinced the nun knew about the cancer then.

"I'm sorry," Karen whispered.

"I am, too… She was so wonderful to me."

That same evening, Angie wrote her father. She expressed her love for him as she inquired about his health and the restaurant. She didn't give him an account of her life inside the convent. It would only rub salt in his wounds. Neither did she tell him the news about Sister Trinita. He wouldn't understand why it affected her so intensely. Just as he didn't understand that the convent's rules and routines now filled her world, and everything she'd once known had faded away. Everything outside these gates represented the world she'd renounced.

In the spring of 1962, Angelina Marcello took the name of Sister Frances as she spoke her first vows. For three long years, Angie had waited for this, and it was a source of deep pain that her father had refused to share such a momentous day with her. The vows were said during Mass, followed by Holy Communion. Forming a procession, the novices came forward, each in a pure white gown and a veil like a bride. Indeed, Angie *was* a bride; she'd agreed to become the bride of Christ. This was a solemn betrothal.

"I am the bride of Him whom the angels serve," Angie said in unison with the other novices.

At this point, the priest ceremonially removed each bridal veil and replaced it with the black veil of St. Bridget's Sisters of the Assumption. When he'd finished, the novices chanted, "As a bride, Christ has adorned me with a crown."

When they turned to face the congregation, all wearing their black veils, Angie felt a surge of triumph. As of that moment, Angelina Marcello became known as Sister Frances.

Her first assignment was teaching in San Antonio, Texas. For ten years, Angie taught high school there, mostly classes in religion and home economics. She heard from her father only once a year on her birthday.

In 1969, after Vatican II, St. Bridget's Sisters of the Assumption were given the option of retaining their chosen names or reverting to their original names. Angie asked to be called Sister Angelina. Her father seemed pleased with her decision when she phoned to let him know.

At the end of the school year in 1972, Sister Angelina learned that she would be sent to St. Peter's High School in Minneapolis. After nearly fifteen years, she'd been assigned to the order's largest convent.

Her time in Texas felt like an apprenticeship, a preparation for this new and special task. And it *would* be special; she was sure of it.

{5}

Kathleen O'Shaughnessy
1963 ~ 1972

Kathleen's send-off was a giant family affair with her sisters, aunts, uncles and a multitude of nieces, nephews and cousins all present for the farewell party. Her uncle Patrick closed the pub for a day and unashamedly wept as he hugged her.

"Your smiling face is going to be sadly missed," he said, stepping back to get one last look at the girl he'd always known and loved. Shortly afterward she would no longer be his Kathleen but a nun. Tears glistened in his eyes as he gently clasped her shoulders. "You're making us all proud, Kathleen. God be with you."

Her parents drove her to the convent. Her mother's eyes shone with happiness as Sister Mary Louise, the Mistress of Postulants, led Kathleen and the other young women into the motherhouse to begin their new lives. That first evening Kathleen was given her new garments and taken to the chapel for the welcoming ceremony.

She took easily to the change in lifestyle and enjoyed being a postulant. The concept of owning nothing wasn't new to her; after all, she and her sisters had always shared clothing, makeup, magazines, records—all the paraphernalia of a 1960s teenager. She wasn't allowed to keep anything of her former life, not even the clothes she'd worn the day she entered the convent. Her dress was taken from her, washed and given to the poor.

"Everything we do and ask of you," Sister Mary Louise explained early in Kathleen's instruction, "is for a reason. At times you will understand and agree, and at other times it will remain a mystery. It isn't necessary to understand everything. What *is* necessary is obedience."

Owning nothing was liberating, Kathleen decided. She felt privileged to share everything with her fellow sisters, and her life became much simpler. She no longer wore makeup, had no radio, no books. Nothing. The temptations tied to having such possessions disappeared. It was as though she'd been born into another world.

Kathleen tried to be ruthless in her rejection of the world. She looked forward to emptying herself of all that kept her from loving God. Her sense of righteousness hit its first snag, however, when it came time to cut her hair—her beautiful, waist-length, auburn hair. For easier grooming, she and the others were told, their hair must be cut short.

This was hard. Much harder than any sacrifice Kathleen had made so far. She cringed as she saw several girls with their hair clumsily hacked off. Surely there was some way to forgo this. But when her turn came, she knew it was senseless to ask.

"Sister Kathleen." Sister Mary Louise motioned to the chair.

Kathleen bit her lower lip as she sat on the hard-backed chair.

The Mistress of Postulants hesitated, scissors raised. She, too, seemed to regret shearing away such beautiful hair. "It's necessary," she murmured.

"Yes, Sister," Kathleen agreed as she felt the scissors along the side of her neck.

"Otherwise the bulk of our hair becomes too cumbersome under our veils," Sister Mary Louise continued.

The first fat locks fell unceremoniously to the floor. Kathleen closed her eyes rather than watch and swallowed the lump growing in her throat. She felt the second strands drop onto her lap, and despite her best efforts, tears slid down her cheeks.

Her weakness and vanity embarrassed her. It was just hair. It would grow back and later, as a fully professed nun, she could keep it any length she desired. Besides, with her hair hidden under the veil, no one would know or care what it looked like. For all the world knew, she could be bald.

God would find a way to compensate her for this sacrifice, Kathleen reasoned, and He did. With music. Seven times a day, the sisters gathered in the convent chapel to chant the Divine Office. These times of prayer, known as "Hours," were such a spiritually uplifting experience that Kathleen felt transformed. She loved the simplicity and beauty of the music and reveled in the glory of worshiping with her fellow sisters. Losing her lovely hair—her one vanity—was a small price to pay.

That November, President John F. Kennedy was assassinated, and to Kathleen, it seemed like a personal blow. The entire convent reeled with the shock of his death. The president had been the nuns' ideal; not only was he a good Catholic, but he'd once lived in Boston.

Nineteen sixty-four was an eventful year. In February she received a letter—already opened—from her oldest brother, Sean. Although no one ever said as much, Kathleen knew all mail addressed to postulants and novices was censored. Sean wrote to tell her he was engaged to a girl named Loren Kruse. The wedding would take place early that summer, and Kathleen's parents, plus the three youngest O'Shaughnessys, were traveling to Seattle for the event. It went without saying that Kathleen would be unable to make the trip.

She held the letter so tightly that she crumpled it. Family had always been important to Kathleen, and Sean was her favorite. Although he was almost ten years older, there'd always been a close bond between them. He was the only member of her family to question her vocation, and although she'd dismissed his concern, she'd also appreciated it.

Sister Mary Louise knew right away that something was troubling Kathleen. "Distressing news, Sister?" she asked.

"Oh no, this is happy news," Kathleen said and forced a smile. "My oldest brother will be married in June. The family's attending the wedding."

"And you'd like to be there, as well?"

Hope flared inside Kathleen. "If I could… It would mean so much to me, Sister."

Sister Mary Louise frowned, as though Kathleen's response had disappointed her. "Sister Kathleen, you have a new family now."

"But…" She knew instantly that it was both wrong

to interrupt and pointless to argue. "I'm sorry, Sister," she said and her voice trailed off.

Sister nodded, accepting her apology. "I realize this is still new to you. You've only been with us for six or so months, and our way of life is still somewhat foreign. But by now you should be willing to make any and all sacrifices to serve God. You must release your family. You belong completely to God now."

"Yes, Sister," she said obediently. But she wanted to protest. She *had* made sacrifices, lots of them, and made them gladly. Her family, though…

"You must die to self before you can be born again."

Kathleen swallowed painfully. She couldn't be with Sean and Loren on their wedding day, at least not in person, but she would be with them in her heart.

That night as she said her evening prayers, Kathleen's conscience bothered her. Her attitude was all wrong. She couldn't allow herself to think she was being cheated because she'd been forbidden to attend Sean's wedding. She'd entered the convent in the hope of living a godly life. If she kept all the rules and obeyed and did whatever was asked of her, eventually she'd find the path that would lead her to God. If she struggled with something as unimportant as a family wedding, it could be years before she broke through the bondage of self. Before she became the kind of nun she truly wanted to be.

Summer passed and with it Sean's wedding. On the day he claimed his bride, Kathleen fasted and prayed and offered this sacrifice up to God. When she went to bed that night, her empty stomach growled and tears dripped from her eyes. As hard as she tried, as hard as she prayed, she couldn't suppress the feeling of loss. Of disappointment. This was a day for celebration, and she'd desperately wanted to share it with her beloved brother.

In August of 1964, Kathleen entered the novitiate and began her year of silence. In addition to the seven times of prayer each day, which constituted the Divine Office, Kathleen spent a half hour in prayerful meditation, plus two examinations of conscience. Each morning she was required to recite the Rosary; each evening she spent a half hour on private prayer and spiritual reading. All told, her prayers outside chapel took up as much as five hours a day.

In addition to her prayers and her examinations of conscience, Kathleen was assigned kitchen duty. As if Sister Clare Marie, the Mistress of Novices, was aware of her distaste for cooking and meal preparation, Kathleen drew her least favorite task three weeks in a row. Because she was observing the year of silence, she wasn't allowed to speak to Mrs. O'Halloran, whom the convent employed as a cook, unless it was absolutely necessary. It seemed unnatural to Kathleen to work with this woman and not be able to speak to her. The two of them bustled around in the kitchen, where they were sometimes joined by other sisters.

Unfortunately Mrs. O'Halloran was a talker. Even knowing that Kathleen couldn't respond, the cook chatted away.

"I saw my son off to school today," she said as Kathleen entered the kitchen for her chores one September afternoon. "Off to junior college my Kevin went. He's the first of my brood to take college classes. His father, God rest his soul, would've burst his buttons with pride." She paused in her chatter and dumped a ten-pound bag of potatoes into the sink, then handed Kathleen a paring knife.

Kathleen nearly groaned. Of all kitchen tasks, she hated peeling potatoes the most. Another sacrifice, she mused, her forehead creasing in a frown.

"We're going to have to come up with the money for tuition," Mrs. O'Halloran prattled on. "But from what I make here cooking for the sisters, plus what I collect from the government for Social Security—God bless Franklin Delano Roosevelt—and Kevin's janitorial job, we should be fine."

Kathleen smiled and reluctantly reached for a potato.

"Being a widow all these years, I've learned how to pinch a penny, I can tell you that."

After peeling the first potato, Kathleen dutifully picked up the next.

"You tell me when you've finished with those, Sister, and I'll set you to work cutting up lettuce for the salad."

Keeping the silence with Mrs. O'Halloran was definitely a struggle, but Kathleen managed. Barely. She found the work mundane and unchallenging. She hadn't entered the convent to peel potatoes, she thought rebelliously. She possessed an active and inquisitive mind.

In the middle of her first year in the novitiate, Sister Clare Marie asked to speak to her.

"I noticed that the mashed potatoes with last night's dinner were lumpy, Sister. I understand you were the one responsible."

"Yes," Kathleen admitted. If she peeled one more potato she'd scream. Mrs. O'Halloran's favorite side dish was potatoes in one form or another. Kathleen had peeled potatoes every day that week and she was sick of it.

"Do you consider working in the kitchen beneath you, Sister Kathleen?"

"No, Sister... I just don't seem to have the knack for

it." Her sewing skills were much better and she was fortunate in this regard because several of the other novices had difficulty constructing their clothes.

"You've always done well in school, haven't you?"

Kathleen lowered her gaze, following the tradition known as custody of the eyes. She was pleased that Sister Clare Marie was aware of her high grades. She'd worked hard to achieve her academic standing and it seemed like a waste not to be partaking in some kind of study, other than simply learning the requirements of the religious life.

"Do you know why you aren't in the classroom this year, Sister?"

Kathleen nodded. "Because of the year of silence." One glance told her that she'd only partially answered the question. "And because mundane tasks help free one's mind for God," she added, knowing this was the answer the Mistress of Novices sought.

Sister Clare Marie seemed to carefully measure her words. "You're answering with your head and not your heart," she finally said. "You seem to think that is what I want you to say, but I want much more from you, Sister Kathleen, and so does God."

Kathleen hung her head. How right Sister was.

"Performing these mundane tasks *is* important work. It is while you are peeling potatoes that you learn to set aside your own will and your own selfish desires. It is while you're holding a peeler in your hand that the demand for self is broken. Remember, only when you are broken can God truly use you."

"But Sister Janice loves to work in the kitchen." Kathleen didn't know why she was arguing. She knew it was wrong to raise objections or to contradict the

Mistress of Novices. Kathleen's reaction revealed to her how far she had yet to go.

"You think it would be easier for Sister Janice to work in the kitchen and for you to serve elsewhere. Is that what you're suggesting, Sister?"

Timidly Kathleen nodded. If she could've erased her earlier remark, she would have done so.

Sister Clare Marie sighed heavily. "That's where you're wrong. It's far better for Sister Janice to face her own struggles with a task that challenges her will. I have assigned all of you to work in areas I know you actively dislike. You think this is punishment, don't you?"

That was exactly what Kathleen assumed.

The Mistress of Novices shook her head. "Let me assure you, Sister Kathleen, it isn't. I'm working hard to help you be a good nun."

"But Sister, I'm failing. It's a losing battle. The potatoes are winning."

Sister Clare Marie smiled. "Those potatoes have brought you to the point of frustration and boredom, haven't they?"

"Yes."

"Then you're exactly where you need to be before you can die to self."

Kathleen let the words sink in. Her confusion started to clear and Sister Clare Marie's statement found a home within her heart.

"I feel you've made significant progress this afternoon," the older nun said warmly.

Kathleen felt she had, too. What had seemed a burden and a pointless task earlier now made sense. The convent was using those mounds of unpeeled potatoes to shape her into a malleable, useable instrument of God.

That conversation stayed with Kathleen a long time.

It showed her that despite her resolve to the contrary—
and despite her own wrongful pride in her sacrifices—
the world still held on to her heart. When Sister Clare
Marie had first mentioned the lumpy mashed potatoes,
Kathleen had felt a small surge of hope that she might
be reassigned. Instead, she'd come away determined
to perfect the peeling and mashing of potatoes. Because now she knew that each potato would bring her
closer to God.

As the weeks progressed, the silence that had
seemed unnatural in the beginning became the norm.
Kathleen didn't know what was happening in the world.
Little outside the convent gates made its way to her
ears. Lyndon Baines Johnson had stepped in as president after the assassination of John Kennedy; she knew
that much but was completely unaware of his policies.
Whatever laws Congress had passed was unimportant
to her. Secular music—oh, how she'd once loved the
Beatles—movies and their stars meant nothing. Silence
was her only reality. Everything outside the convent
was alien. Never again did she want to become influenced and corrupted by the world's values.

That summer, just before Kathleen entered her second year in the novitiate, she was allowed a visit from
her family. As the long-awaited weekend approached,
Kathleen grew apprehensive. It had been more than
twelve months since she'd last seen her parents. Family
was considered a distraction in the year of silence. Kathleen wondered if they'd recognize her. She'd changed
from the immature teenager who had stepped through
the convent doors two years earlier and even from the
postulant of last summer.

Her mother and father arrived early and Kathleen
nervously met them for a walk around the grounds.

She kissed her mother's cheek, but took care to maintain the proper decorum.

"Kathleen," her mother said, searching her face. She blinked back tears. "I always knew you'd make a beautiful nun."

Kathleen lowered her gaze, uncomfortable with the comment about her outward appearance. "Hello, Dad," she said, hugging him lightly. He looked older. His hair was almost completely gray and the wrinkles at his eyes were deeper and more pronounced.

"You seem well," her father said.

"I am well." She buried her hands deep in the sleeves of her gown. "How's Uncle Patrick these days?"

"Good," her father assured her. "He sends his love."

"He was in Ireland this spring," her mother told her.

Her father chuckled. "He kissed the Blarney stone while he was there—not that he needed to."

Her parents laughed at the small joke.

"How's Maureen?"

"Pregnant again. She and Robbie are good Catholics." Pride gleamed in her mother's eyes as she said it. "So many young people are using birth control, but not Maureen and Robbie."

"But Wendy's still a baby." Kathleen didn't know much about family planning, but it didn't seem good for her sister to be giving birth to a second child within a year's time.

"Irish twins, that's what they'll be," her father boasted.

Rather than belabor the conversation, Kathleen changed the subject. "And Sean? How are he and Loren?"

Her parents' eyes met.

Something was wrong, and Kathleen could tell they were hoping to keep it from her.

"Mom? Is everything all right with Sean and his wife?"

"Of course," her father leapt in. "They're very much in love."

Her relief was instantaneous.

"Sean enlisted for another hitch in the Army," her mother said brightly. Her enthusiasm didn't ring true.

"Yes," her father added. "Sean reenlisted just in time to get shipped off to Vietnam."

"Vietnam?" she repeated as a sense of dread settled over her.

Again her parents exchanged looks. "America's involvement in Southeast Asia is escalating," her father explained.

"Sean's going to Vietnam?" Kathleen was shocked that more news of the war hadn't filtered into the convent. Vietnam had been a minor and faraway conflict when she became a postulant; President Kennedy had merely committed a few troops and military advisors. Surely Mrs. O'Halloran would have mentioned such a significant change in the military's role. The cook chatted endlessly, and Kathleen had learned to tune out much of her trivial conversation, finding the other woman's voice discordant and disruptive. Silence had its own beauty and listening to Mrs. O'Halloran distracted her. Still, she would've noticed and remembered news of this magnitude.

"It's not a declared war," her father said.

"But the president's sending over American men to fight?" Kathleen glanced at her mother and then her father. She was most concerned about one enlisted man, however, and that was her brother Sean.

"Sean sends his love," her mother said, and her voice trembled just enough for Kathleen to detect her worry.

"You're afraid for him, aren't you?"

Her mother nodded. "Loren is, too. She wrote to tell us that Sean's already been in one battle. The fighting was fierce… We don't know what'll happen. Pray for him, Kathleen. Promise me you'll pray."

"Of course! Of course."

Her parents left shortly after, and while Kathleen had enjoyed their visit, she discovered that she was more than ready to return to the growing familiarity of silence. Sister Clare Marie was right. With time, she'd learned to prefer silence to talking.

Her second year in the novitiate was everything Kathleen had hoped it would be. She excelled in her classes and enjoyed her studies on church history and theology. These were exciting times for the Catholic Church. In 1959, several years before Kathleen entered the convent, Pope John the XXIII had called for an ecumenical council, the first since 1869.

It took place in 1962. Twenty-six hundred cardinals and bishops from around the world had rallied to the Pope's call. So now, in 1965, Vatican II had already been in session for three years and the changes within the Church were gradually making their way down to the people.

Many outmoded customs and rituals were being set aside in favor of a more contemporary worship. For instance, the priest no longer faced the altar with his back to the congregation; instead, the altar was turned toward the people. But the most dramatic change for Kathleen was the translation of the Mass from Latin to the vernacular. It delighted her to hear Mass said in English. Others, including many of the older nuns, felt it was sacrilegious. They were certain these changes would create problems; perhaps they were right.

Only last Sunday, Mrs. O'Halloran told Kathleen that there'd been guitars and tambourines played at Mass in her local parish. A "folk Mass" she'd called it. At first Kathleen found it scandalous to think of such secular instruments in a church—but then again, perhaps it wasn't. After all, Christians were exhorted to "make a joyful noise unto the Lord." What was more joyful than the sound of guitars and banjos and flutes? The more she thought about it, the more she liked the idea. Perhaps in time, this kind of worship could be introduced into the convent's celebration.

Within a few weeks of saying her final vows, Kathleen learned that some religious orders had decided to discard the tradition of wearing habits, substituting secular attire.

To Kathleen, it seemed unbelievable that any woman who'd struggled to separate herself from the world would willingly wish to become part of it again.

"I know you've heard rumors of changes in our traditional habit," Sister Clare Marie announced one afternoon. "After a recent discussion with Mother Superior, I can tell you that St. Bridget's Sisters of the Assumption will not be making any such changes for the time being."

Kathleen was glad to hear it. She'd worked very hard for the privilege of wearing a habit and she didn't want to see it eliminated.

"Mother Superior feels that Pope John's intention was to open the windows of the Church and let in a breath of fresh air. He anticipated a soft breeze, not a tornado."

Again Kathleen was in full agreement.

"We are a large order, one of the most populous in the United States. We welcome small changes, but anything this substantial will develop slowly for us. We have dressed in this same habit since 1840 and we are unwilling to let go of what is most familiar."

Several heads nodded.

"However," Sister said, "one change that might enhance our order has come to the attention of Mother Superior." She smiled as though this was a matter close to her own heart. "Instead of taking a saint's name at the time you say your vows, you may retain your own name if you wish."

That meant Kathleen could be referred to as Sister Kathleen instead of Sister Lydia, the name she had chosen as the first of her three alternatives.

"Think it over carefully and decide within the next week."

As Kathleen deliberated on all the changes, she began to feel a sense of excitement. For three years she had struggled in vain to let go of her earthly family in order to be part of God's. Now she was given the chance to be part of both.

The first person she would tell was Sean. Of all her family, she knew her oldest brother would definitely approve. She wrote him a lengthy letter and, as she'd expected, his response was gratifying.

On August 14, 1966, a Sunday afternoon, Kathleen O'Shaughnessy said her vows. Her parents, four of her five sisters and her youngest brother were in attendance. They watched as the bridal veil was replaced with the full veil of a professed sister.

"Do you know where you're going to be assigned?" her mother asked anxiously. Kathleen knew her family prayed it would be nearby so they could visit on a regular basis.

"I won't find that out until later." Kathleen was as

curious as her family. She'd waited three long years for this moment. She'd entered the convent as one of thirty postulants, but over time eleven had chosen to leave. Their vocations hadn't been strong enough to hold them.

A week later, Kathleen learned that she was being sent to attend education classes at the University of Minneapolis. The following September she'd be teaching first grade at St. Peter's School.

Of the nineteen new sisters, she was the only one assigned to the convent in Minneapolis.

{6}

Joanna Baird
1967 ~ 1972

"**J**oanna," her mother said, twisting around from the front seat of the 1965 Ford Fairlane to look her full in the face. "Are you *positive* that life in a convent is what you want?"

"Mom, please! I've already said it is. I feel God is calling me." She stared out the window, at the softly falling snow.

"Sandra, for the love of heaven, will you leave the girl alone?"

"Mark, don't you see what's happening?" her mother cried. "How can you simply drive our daughter to a convent like this? She's overreacting to what Greg did. Can't you *see* what a terrible mistake she's making?"

Joanna wanted to clap her hands over her ears to block out the angry exchange between her parents. Her mother had been dead set against Joanna's entering the convent from the moment she'd mentioned it six months earlier. Her father, on the other hand, was all for it. His own cousin was a Dominican nun and he'd felt strongly that this was the right decision for Joanna. As her parents, he'd argued, it was their duty to stand by her and support her in whatever she wanted for her own future.

"She's doing this on the rebound," Sandra Baird insisted.

"I'm over Greg," Joanna said from the backseat. She rarely thought about Greg or the broken engagement anymore. He was part of her past. God was her future. Greg's wife had given birth to a robust and healthy daughter they'd named Lily. To prove there were no hard feelings, Joanna had mailed Greg and Xuan a congratulatory letter, in which she told them of her decision to enter the convent.

"Joanna is old enough to know what she wants," her father continued. "You didn't question her decision to enter nursing school, did you? Now she wants to dedicate her life to God. Why are you against that?"

Her mother crossed her arms. "Why?" she cried sarcastically. "Because in my heart I know the convent isn't the place for our daughter, despite what you think."

"If you're right," Joanna said, struggling to remain calm, "I won't stay. Please, Mom," she begged, "try to be happy for me."

"I am, honey," her father said, taking his eyes off the Boston traffic just long enough to send her an encouraging smile. "Your mother and I approve of whatever endeavor in life you choose."

Her mother glanced over her shoulder and pleaded with Joanna one final time. "I'd be happy if I truly believed you belonged in the convent. Just promise me that if you ever decide you want out, you won't be too proud to leave."

"I promise." Joanna hated to be the cause of this struggle between her mother and father. Even today, when they were delivering her to the motherhouse, her parents continued to argue as if it were *their* decision instead of Joanna's.

Once they arrived at the convent, Joanna felt reassured. The quiet, serene atmosphere brought her a sense of peace and renewed her purpose. When it was time to leave, Sandra hugged Joanna tightly. Tears shimmered in her eyes as she released her, then hurriedly turned away.

"I couldn't be more proud of you," her father said, as he handed her over to Sister Mary Louise, the Postulant Mistress.

Joanna didn't see her parents leave. Without another word, Sister Mary Louise directed her to the dormitory and assigned her a cell. The room was stark compared to Joanna's bedroom at home. There she had a canopy bed and a hi-fi set with stacks of albums. But she'd walked away from that life and was eager to embrace another.

"You'll need to change out of your clothes and into these," Sister instructed, giving her the simple garb of a postulant.

"Are there any others entering this month?" Joanna asked. It was mid-January, and the majority of women seeking the religious life came in September.

"Just three. You're the last to arrive. Now I'll let you change into your new clothes," Sister Mary Louise said.

Unexpected emotion swept through Joanna as she stripped off her sweater and skirt. A moment later she realized why. It was as though the sins she'd carried with her since losing her virginity were being stripped away as well. She didn't blame Greg; they'd both been

virgins that first time. They'd led each other into sin.
But now she was beginning anew.

When Joanna was interviewed by Sister Agnes in
November, the head of the convent hadn't asked if she
was a virgin. Grateful, Joanna hadn't volunteered the
information, either. It was too embarrassing to confess
to Mother Superior.

The sin of impurity had already been confessed to
her parish priest. She'd received absolution and com-
pleted her penance. What she'd done with Greg was in
the past and no one need ever know.

As Joanna donned the skirt, blouse, cape and veil,
she experienced a feeling of release, a spiritual cleansing. She paused to close her eyes and thank God for
His forgiveness and for this opportunity to serve Him.

Sister Mary Louise returned shortly and nodded with
approval. "Everything seems to fit nicely."

It was a nice fit in more ways than the obvious, Joanna mused, smiling.

That evening at dinner with the other postulants—
both those who'd been there since September and the
four who'd come today—Joanna was warmly welcomed. Three of the postulants performed a skit in
which a confused new recruit arrives at the convent
door. The humor made her laugh so hard, Joanna's sides
ached. She hadn't known what to expect from the other
postulants, and she was grateful for the laughter and
camaraderie. Later, at Compline, the evening prayers,
the four women entering as postulants stood before the
priest. Joanna willingly surrendered everything to God,
her first step toward becoming a bride of Christ.

The glow of welcome lasted all week. But because
she was unfamiliar with the rules, adjustment was a
bit difficult those first few days. The Grand Silence,

which lasted from after evening prayers until breakfast the following morning, proved to be the most challenging. Joanna didn't realize how hard it would be to stay quiet. Each day there seemed to be so much she wanted to share with the others, questions she longed to ask, but there simply wasn't time.

In her first letter home, she wrote confidently about her new life.

February 11, 1967

Dearest Mom and Dad,
I love it here. I really do. You wouldn't believe the welcome the other postulants gave me. There's such laughter and joy at St. Bridget's.

Mom, I know you're worried that this isn't the place for me. Although I made it sound like I knew exactly what I wanted, I confess now that I had my doubts. How could I not? Less than a year ago I was engaged to be married. If everything had gone the way we assumed, I'd be a wife by now.

Sister Theresa suggested I wait six months before entering the convent and that was good advice. Those months helped me deal with my disappointment and recognize my growing desire to serve God. It was important for me to be sure that my vocation wasn't simply a reaction to what happened with Greg. Today I can tell you from the bottom of my heart that it isn't.

In a manner of speaking, I'm engaged again. This time the groom won't disappoint me. This time I don't need to worry about my fiancé breaking my heart. This time, I made a better choice.

I'm happy, sincerely happy, and more confident than ever that I'm making the right decision.

Much, much love,
Sister Joanna

A week later her mother wrote back.

February 18, 1967

My dearest Joanna,
Your letter was just the reassurance I needed. You do sound happy—almost like your old self once again. These have been such heart-wrenching months for you. You can't blame me for doubting this sudden decision of yours to become a nun.

I want what every mother wants for her daughter, and that's your happiness. It's been a struggle to put my own desires for your future aside and accept your wishes. If you're convinced God is calling you to serve Him, then I have no right to question your vocation. But, Joanna, let me ask you for the last time: Have you fully considered everything you're giving up? Are you sure you'll never want a child of your own? You and Rick have brought me incredible joy. I hate the idea that you'll never experience motherhood. Just be aware of what you're going to miss out on if you go through with this.

FYI, I ran into Greg's mother in the grocery store yesterday. She tried to pretend she didn't see me, but I wasn't letting her off that easily. I stopped her to say hello. When I mentioned that you'd joined the convent she was shocked. Apparently Greg didn't say anything to her about it. (I still don't think it was a good idea to write him, but that was up to you.)

I understand you're only allowed to receive one letter a month. I'll write a little bit every day so you'll receive an extra-long letter from your family.

Your father and I love you deeply, and although Rick would never openly admit it, I know he loves you, too. He misses you, just as your father and I do.

Please think about what I said.

Love,
Mom

The next six months passed in a blur of activity for Joanna. Although she'd entered the convent later than most of the other candidates, she was able to become a novice at the same time as her fellow postulants.

She mentally prepared herself for the year of silence. No letters from home, no contact with the outside world, nothing that would distract from her commitment to Christ. This was her year of contemplation.

Joanna recognized that for her, this would be a true challenge. She enjoyed talking with the others, especially when the postulants gathered around Sister Mary Louise during nightly recreation. That was one of the best times of the day.

Silence for a year. It wouldn't be so bad, Joanna told herself repeatedly. At least it wouldn't be a complete and total silence. Five to seven times a day there'd be singing and prayers. Then, for a half hour each evening at recreation, she'd be permitted to speak to her fellow novices.

One morning as she swept the chapel, Joanna started humming Bob Dylan's "Mr. Tambourine Man." It wasn't a conscious decision. The music that morning had been melodic and lovely, but somehow the Dylan song had entered her mind and refused to leave. She didn't know why a tune she hadn't heard in ages was stuck there, but it was.

As soon as Joanna realized what she was humming, she stopped, shocked at herself. Although it hadn't been intentional, she felt guilty. Humming Bob Dylan in the chapel was sure to be considered sacrilegious. Still, within minutes she was back at it, keeping her voice low so as not to be heard.

Her own rebelliousness upset her. Humming was bad enough, but breaking silence inside the chapel was that much worse.

Nights were the most difficult for her. After a full day of work, study and prayer, she often fell into a deep sleep without even trying. It was in her dreams that Greg came to her.

The first time she dreamed of him, she woke abruptly, terrified that she might have called out his name. That would've mortified her. Her mind waged battle with her soul as Greg continued to make frequent visitations while she slept.

The dreams disturbed her. During her waking hours she managed to suppress her anger with Greg but these dreams, in which he begged her forgiveness, told Joanna the truth about her emotions. She was furious with him and she *couldn't* forgive him. It got to be so that she was afraid to fall asleep for fear Greg would show up. The memory of his betrayal would linger for hours every morning and she'd have to make an active effort to force it from her mind.

A month or so later, Joanna was summoned to Sister Clare Marie's office. A shiver of apprehension shot through her. Perhaps one of the other sisters had heard her humming while she cleaned the chapel floors. Joanna wondered if her foolish rebellion was about to get her into trouble.

With pounding heart, she knocked politely at the door and waited for a response before entering.

"Sister Joanna," Sister Clare Marie said from behind her desk. "Sit down."

Joanna settled quietly in the chair. She folded her hands in her lap and lowered her gaze as required, although she longed to read the other nun's expression.

"I imagine you're wondering why I asked to speak to you."

"Yes, Sister."

The older nun waited a moment. "Sister, are you happy with your life here?"

"Very much so," Joanna said in a rush. Her panic was immediate. Perhaps the convent was going to dismiss her, send her away.

"I'm pleased to hear that."

Joanna closed her eyes and made herself relax.

"I've noticed a certain…restlessness about you in the last few weeks. Are you sleeping well?"

It would be so easy to blurt out her dreams and beg the older, wiser nun to tell her how to vanquish them. But fear held her back. Fear of rejection if she revealed this unforgiving part of her nature. Fear of what the dreams said about her.

Because the ugly truth was that Joanna wanted Greg to suffer. She wanted him to have a miserable marriage and an equally unhappy life. She wanted him to pay for what he'd done to her.

"Sister?"

Joanna looked up in surprise.

"Are you sleeping well?" the other nun repeated. "I'm afraid the answer is obvious. Perhaps you'd better tell me what's troubling you."

"It's nothing," Joanna answered, hoping to make light of her telltale hesitation.

Sister Clare Marie leaned forward. "The eyes cannot hide what is in the heart, my child," she said gently. "Is this about the young man you'd once planned to marry?"

Keeping her head lowered, Joanna nodded reluctantly.

The Mistress of Novices released a soft breath. "I thought it might be that."

"I've had...dreams about him."

Sister sat back in the hard chair. "Dreams?"

She nodded again. "Dreams in which he wants me to forgive him for what he did—and Sister, I can't make myself do it."

"From your reaction, it appears that your inability to forgive him distresses you."

Joanna wanted to weep. The anger was back and so close to the surface it demanded all the restraint she could muster to remain seated. This nun couldn't know the pain and embarrassment Greg had brought her. Sheltered as she was, Sister Clare Marie couldn't know what betrayal did to a woman's soul.

"How often do you recite the Our Father every day?"

Joanna gave a quick shrug. "Ten times?"

"Ten times," Sister Clare Marie repeated, then added in the same serene manner, "and forgive us our trespasses as we forgive those who trespass against us."

In other words, Joanna realized, her inability to forgive Greg was hindering her own spiritual life. "You don't know what he did to me," she cried, pleading for understanding.

"But I do," the nun continued undaunted. "I also know that you love him."

"Loved," she corrected. Joanna felt nothing but disdain for Greg now. Some days she thought she hated him, and that frightened her more than anything.

"No, my child, you're still in love with him. Otherwise you would be able to release him from your mind."

The lump in Joanna's throat hardened. "Are you going to…send me away?"

Sister Clare Marie smiled faintly. "Not unless you wish to return to the world."

"No, Sister, I want to stay right here." She'd discovered what she'd been seeking behind these walls.

The comfort and love of her parents, the loyalty of her friends and her own righteous indignation had offered little compensation for her loss. Only when she'd accepted God's call to become a nun had she found the peace and serenity she desperately sought.

"The convent isn't a hiding place."

"I know that, Sister." Joanna took a deep breath. "I'll forgive Greg if that's what you want." She choked out the words with a sob.

Sister Clare Marie's eyes filled with compassion. "You've read me correctly, Sister. I do want you to forgive this young man, but not for his sake. You need to forgive him for your own."

Joanna recognized the truth of those words, but she was emotionally incapable of acting on them.

"Unless you can find it within yourself to forgive this young man…"

Forgive. The word reverberated in her mind.

"…and release your anger and bitterness…"

Anger and bitterness clashed with *forgive*.

"…I fear you'll be caught in a vicious trap. A trap that will make it impossible for you to progress in the religious life." She paused. "Do you understand what I'm saying, Sister Joanna?"

"I think so. If I can't forgive Greg, then the bitterness will eat away at me until I've lost the very thing I've come to seek."

The Mistress of Novices nodded. "Exactly."

"But how can I do it?" Joanna pleaded. Sister made it sound easy. "I pray for Greg, but I don't *mean* the prayers. I can't stop feeling that he deserves to be miserable after the way he humiliated me."

"We all deserve misery for the sins we've committed," Sister returned.

Of course that was true, but knowing it didn't help Joanna deal with the sense of betrayal. She'd had the wedding invitations all but mailed. Her bridesmaids' dresses had been ordered and paid for, and her own wedding gown with its overlay of Belgian lace had cost her father far too much money. Now it was tucked away in the back of the closet like a forgotten prom dress.

"Pray for him," Sister Clare Marie urged. "Ask God to bless him, his wife and his family."

Joanna swallowed hard. She *couldn't* do this. She couldn't.

"You must." Then bowing her head, Sister closed her eyes and her lips began to move in silent petition.

Joanna couldn't hear her prayer but she felt the effect of it immediately. The resistance, the uncontrollable anger, suddenly seemed to leave her heart. Her eyes flooded with tears as she bowed her own head and asked God to make her willing to forgive Greg. That was the first step and a necessary one if she was to remain part of this life she loved.

When they'd finished praying, Sister Clare Marie looked up. "You may return to your duties now."

Joanna wiped the moisture from her cheeks. "Thank you," she whispered brokenly and started to turn away.

"One last thing."

Joanna turned to face her again. "Yes, Sister?"

"I was just wondering if a Bob Dylan song is appropriate music to be humming in chapel."

Joanna's jaw sagged. Sister knew. Had she heard or had someone told her? "No," she managed to say.

"I didn't think so myself." Sister Clare Marie raised her eyebrows and dismissed Joanna with a nod.

Joanna left the office and leaned against the outside wall. After the shock of the question had dissipated, she began to smile. A nun who had a reputation for being strict and unyielding had treated her with genuine kindness.

Joanna was determined never to forget this conversation. It would be the turning point for her, she decided. The path to God had come to a crossroads and she'd chosen to follow Him. She'd chosen to discard the baggage that impeded her travels and move forward.

That night the dreams stopped. Greg had disappeared into some hidden corner of her mind—and she had Sister Clare Marie to thank for that. She hadn't forgiven him, but she was now willing to believe it might be possible.

In her last year as a novice, the world seemed to be in a state of chaos. It was 1968 and on April 4, Martin Luther King, Jr., was assassinated in Memphis. Riots broke out across the country. Sister Agnes, the Mother Superior, asked for a day of fasting and prayer.

Then in June, Robert Kennedy was fatally shot in Los Angeles after winning the California primary. His death hit Joanna hard, and she wept openly. After the assassination of his brother less than five years earlier, it felt as though the world had turned into an ugly place. No one was safe, not the president, not the men fighting in Vietnam, not the country. More than ever, Joanna was grateful for the protection of the brick wall around the convent; it gave at least the illusion of keeping the world at bay.

The war in Vietnam was worse than ever and her mother wrote about her fear of Rick being drafted. He'd made it through his first year of college, but if the war continued, his draft number was sure to come up. Joanna worried about him incessantly.

With so many concerns, Joanna found herself on her knees more and more often, praying for the president and the country. After two and a half years in the convent, she felt separate and apart from world events, and yet aware of them. It was as though she was looking on from a distance. She knew from some of the older nuns that compared to even a few years ago, the world was encroaching on the convent and its serenity.

In August of that year, when she took her vows, her brother and parents arrived for the ceremony. Joanna waited with the other novices and prayed fervently that God would use her to touch lives. It had already been decided that she would continue with her nursing program over the summer, but not where.

The ceremony was as beautiful as it was simple. She knelt before Bishop Lawton and vowed to live a life of poverty, chastity and obedience. In her heart, she gave everything to God. She offered up all her romantic dreams and all her hopes for the future.

After the ceremony, her father had tears in his eyes. Her mother looked tired and worried. Rick seemed uneasy.

"Hey, it's me under all these clothes," she teased her brother.

"You don't look the same," he returned.

"I am."

"Are you?" her mother whispered.

"Now, Sandra." Her father placed his arm around her mother's shoulders.

To her credit, her mother attempted a smile. "You look radiant."

"Thank you, Mom." Joanna gave her a hug. Even now—almost three years after Joanna had entered the convent—her mother held out hope that she'd change her mind.

"Do you know where you're going to be assigned?" Rick asked. "Dad said you might come back to Providence."

"I might." But Joanna felt that was unlikely. "I don't know where Mother Superior will send me." It went without saying that she would go without question and serve wholeheartedly wherever Sister Agnes saw fit to assign her.

"When will you know?" her mother pressed.

"Soon," Joanna assured her family.

The next week she received her orders. "Minneapolis," she wrote her family. First to finish nursing school. Later, after she'd obtained the necessary credentials, she'd work at St. Elizabeth's Hospital.

{ Part Three }

LIVING THE VOWS

I have come that you might have life and have it abundantly.

—John 10:10

Sister Angelina
1972

Angie was thrilled to be assigned to St. Peter's. A progressive high school with co-ed classes, it was the pride of the Minneapolis diocese.

On the first day of classes, Angie entered her homeroom for her last period of the afternoon. She immediately noticed a teenage girl who sat on her desktop, uniform skirt rolled up at the waist and her blue eye shadow screaming at the world to pay attention.

The class hushed as Angie moved silently toward the front of the class, her habit swishing softly against her legs.

"Good afternoon," she said, tucking her hands inside the wide sleeves. "I'm Sister Angelina, and this is tenth-grade Health. If your class schedule does not show Health in sixth period, then I suggest you find the classroom where you belong now."

She watched as the girl with the long thin legs and

the vibrant eye shadow read over two schedules and dejectedly shrugged her shoulders. She handed the young man she'd been speaking to one of the schedules. The boy reached for his books and slid them off the desk before sauntering out of the room.

"Very well," Angie said in her best teacher's voice. After ten years in the classroom, she'd become proficient at recognizing the troublemakers. Already she could tell that this girl was going to be one of them. At roll call she learned that her name was Corinne Sullivan.

Angie had just started to pass out textbooks when Corinne's hand shot into the air.

"Yes, Corinne?"

"Are we going to learn about sex this term?"

Angie certainly hoped not. "Do you mean sex education?"

Corinne nodded eagerly and smacked her wad of gum.

Chewing gum was an abomination as far as Angie was concerned. Without so much as a pause, she picked up the wastebasket and walked down the aisle to Corinne's desk.

"Regarding sex education, I believe there is a short introduction to the basic facts." Angie held the wastebasket up for the girl, who stared at her blankly.

"Your gum, please."

"Oh." She spat the wad into the basket and Angie returned to the front of the room. "Does anyone else have questions about our curriculum for this term?" When no one responded, she murmured, "Good."

Health class was Angie's least favorite teaching assignment. She preferred the Home Economics classes where she taught food preparation and cooking skills. Her talent in the kitchen made her a favorite with the other nuns and often the parish priests. It wasn't uncommon for Angie to deliver a bowl of her fettuccine Alfredo to the rectory on a Sunday afternoon.

For the remainder of the period, Angie reviewed the curriculum.

Just before the bell rang ending the class period and the day, Corinne waved her arm again. "Is there going to be a lot of reading for this class?"

"There will be some, but no more than your other classes."

Scowling, Corinne sank lower in her seat, as though the thought of cracking open a textbook would be asking too much of her.

The bell rang and Angie walked over to Corinne's desk as the classroom emptied quickly. "Could you stay a few minutes after class?" she asked.

"Sure." Corinne exchanged looks with another girl, Morgan Gentry, if Angie remembered correctly.

"Am I in trouble, Sister?" The words tumbled out. "Because it's only the first day, and I forgot the rule about gum. If I am, I hope you'll give me a break. I don't usually get a demerit until the second week."

Angie struggled to hold back a smile. "Do you deserve a demerit?" she asked.

Corinne appeared to give that some thought. "Just for the gum, and that's a minor offense, don't you think?"

"Your uniform skirt's rolled up at the waist."

Corinne groaned. "Come on, Sister. I have to do that or this thing would drag on the ground." She ran her hands down the hips of the plaid pleated skirt and then flipped back one roll of the waistband. "Better?"

"Much," Angie said.

The girl grinned, her dark eyes sparkling. "Anything else?"

Angie hesitated to mention the eye makeup.

"Most of the nuns object to my blue eye shadow," the girl cheerfully informed her. "You can complain, too, if you want."

"You think I should?"

"Nah." Corinne shrugged. "Why be like everyone else?"

Exactly. "You can wear as much eye shadow as you want in my class."

"Really?" Corinne smiled sheepishly. "I think you're going to be a lot of fun to have as a teacher."

Angie smiled despite her effort not to. She could see that Corinne wasn't a belligerent girl, just inquisitive and social.

"Can I go now?" Corinne asked.

"Yes, but, Corinne…"

"Yes?"

"No more passing notes to Morgan or I'll have to confiscate and read them."

Corinne's heavy sigh could be heard as she walked out the door. "Yes, Sister."

Angie's amusement lasted as she walked home to the convent later that afternoon. She was going to enjoy Minneapolis. The community here was strong and the school staff seemed supportive and dedicated.

To her delight, Angie discovered a letter from her father tucked inside her mail cubicle. She hesitated before opening it. Tony Marcello had never fully accepted her decision to be a nun. Even now, twelve years after she'd professed her vows, he refused to call her anything other than simply Angelina. Not Sister Frances. Not Sister Angelina.

The day she'd entered the convent, he'd stopped attending Mass. It was his private rebellion against the

Catholic Church for stealing away his only child. Angie had been praying for years that her father would return to the Church; the thought that he might die without last rites sent a chill through her blood.

Still, a letter from her father was a rare treat and she greedily read the handwritten pages. She hadn't visited him more than four or five times over the last fifteen years. He hated seeing her in a habit; that was obvious whenever she stayed with him. Many of the other orders had modified theirs to a more modern skirt and blouse with only a short black veil to signify their religious status. St. Bridget's Sisters of the Assumption were currently—and reluctantly—considering such a change. It was coming, and soon. Angie wondered if her father would be more comfortable with her if she wore a less restrictive style; somehow, she doubted it.

"News from home?" Sister Kathleen asked, checking her own cubicle for mail.

"Yes," she said, flipping from one page to the next. "It's from my father." Angie smiled and closed her eyes. She could almost smell the marinara sauce. Her grin widened when she noticed that the last sheet of his letter was a handwritten recipe, a new one he was planning to serve at Angelina's. An unexpected wave of homesickness practically knocked her off her feet.

Worst of all was the knowledge that she'd found God, but as a result her father had lost his faith.

{ 8 }

Sister Joanna

Joanna loved Minneapolis and the entire state of Minnesota. The first time she heard someone say, "Sure, ya betcha," she laughed outright. Overall, the people were hardworking and dedicated. The Catholics were a tight-knit group. Plenty of good, solid Swedes and Germans had immigrated to the area, and their descendants retained a deep faith and strong family values.

Joanna's assignment as a floor nurse at St. Elizabeth's Hospital was demanding, but rewarding, too. She worked on the surgery floor and cared for patients once they were released from the Recovery Room. Apart from her initial training in Providence, her entire nursing career had been spent at St. Elizabeth's, first as a senior nursing student and then as a registered nurse.

"Sister?" an elderly woman whispered from her bed as Joanna entered the room. She was a recent arrival and gazed up at Joanna. "I thought for a moment you might be an angel."

Joanna smiled and lifted the woman's fragile wrist to

take her pulse. Patients sometimes confused the nursing sisters with angelic beings. She supposed it was because of the white habits they wore at the hospital. Older patients often needed their glasses and were disoriented following surgery. More than once she'd been asked if this was heaven.

"You're doing just fine, Mrs. Stewart," Joanna assured the woman.

"I am?" Mrs. Stewart didn't sound as if she believed her.

"Are you in any pain?" Joanna asked.

"Some. If you must know, it feels like someone took a hatchet to my stomach."

"Are you complaining about my sewing technique?" Dr. Murray asked as he entered the room. He stood on the opposite side of the bed, across from Joanna, and gently lifted the blankets. "This is some of my finest stitching, if I do say so myself."

Mrs. Stewart snorted. "I feel like someone ran over me driving a two-ton truck." Her eyes were still dull from the anesthesia.

"It sometimes feels like that. I told you before we went into this that having your gallbladder removed is major surgery."

"So you did, Doc, so you did." Mrs. Stewart's eyes fluttered closed as she drifted back into a drug-induced sleep.

Dr. Murray replaced the blankets and then reached for the chart at the foot of the bed to read Joanna's latest entry. He glanced up and caught her eye. "Could I have a moment of your time, Sister?" he asked.

"Of course." She followed him out of the room. She hadn't known Dr. Murray long, but she liked him better every time she saw him. Certainly better than Dr.

Nelson, with whom she'd clashed earlier in the week. Dr. Murray had recently finished a stint in the Army, she'd heard via the hospital grapevine. Word was, he'd served in Vietnam, although he'd never mentioned it himself. His dealings with her had always been strictly professional; however, Joanna knew that several of the younger nurses were vying for his attention. It must have flattered his ego, but, as far as she knew, Dr. Murray had done nothing to encourage them one way or the other.

He stopped at the nurses' station. Mrs. Larson, the day-shift lead nurse, glanced up from the large wraparound desk as Joanna and Dr. Murray approached.

"Mrs. Larson," he said, leaning against the counter, looking relaxed and at ease. He grinned boyishly. "Would it be possible to assign Sister Joanna to care for my surgery patients? She's got half of them convinced she's an angel and it doesn't do any harm to let them think they've reached the pearly gates. Keeps down the complaints."

Joanna was amused by his remarks—and surprised by his request. She knew half a dozen nurses who would envy her the position.

The shift lead looked equally amused. "I'll see what I can do, but I don't think that'll be a problem."

"I'd appreciate it," the surgeon said. "Do you have any objections, Sister?"

"None," she murmured.

"Good." With that, the conversation was over and he turned to leave.

Mrs. Larson's gaze followed Dr. Murray down the polished corridor. "Now, that's one mighty talented surgeon."

Joanna nodded; she certainly couldn't disagree.

"He's a master of tact, too," the other nurse added with more than a hint of admiration.

"How do you mean?"

"Dr. Murray's young and single. Frankly, he's not hard on the eyes, either."

Of course, Joanna had noticed that Dr. Tim Murray was tall and dark-haired and that he possessed classic features with enough ruggedness to give his face unmistakable masculinity and character. But she'd noticed all this objectively, without personal interest. Dr. Murray's social life, or lack of it, wasn't any concern of hers. They had a professional relationship; he was a physician and she was a nun. He apparently approved of her nursing skills and that pleased Joanna. And it hadn't hurt her ego any that he'd asked for her to attend to his patients. Although ego should be sublimated, she reminded herself. It remained one of her greatest challenges.

"But why do you say he's a master of tact?" Joanna asked curiously. What did his looks have to do with it?

"He asked to work with you, didn't he?" Mrs. Larson said. "By having you assigned to his patients, he isn't offending any of the nurses who've requested the privilege."

"Oh." So much for the boost to her ego. Dr. Murray was using her as a shield against unwanted female attention. In requesting Joanna, he hadn't been acknowledging her skills, but protecting his own interests.

"It's more than the fact that you're a nun," the lead nurse added thoughtfully, almost as if she'd read Joanna's mind. "I'm sure he genuinely admires your work. He asked me earlier who'd been assigned to the care of Mrs. Masterson and Mr. Stierwalt. When I said it was you, he commented on what a good job you'd done."

Joanna instantly felt better. She didn't recall those two people, but surgery patients usually stayed on her ward only three or four days. With so many, it was easy to lose track of their names.

"Is it true that Dr. Murray was recently discharged from the Army?" Joanna asked.

Mrs. Larson nodded. "I hear he's been through quite a bit. He doesn't talk about it, but there've been rumors." Then, as if she realized she'd overstepped her bounds, the other nurse shook her head. "Such carnage…so many lives lost."

Joanna tried not to think about the war, even though the headlines had screamed of little else for nearly seven years. She could only imagine the butchery Dr. Murray had seen in his years of duty. His skills were exceptional, and she suspected that was the result of working on the mangled bodies of America's young men.

Following her shift, Joanna returned to the convent. After dinner the nuns partook in a half-hour period of recreation. Then later, before bedtime, there were the nightly prayers.

That evening several of the nuns watched the Summer Olympics taking place in Munich, West Germany. While the convent had a television set, it was hardly ever turned on. Evenings were usually spent in meditation, prayer and quiet pursuits. There wasn't much interest in what television had to offer, but the Summer Games were an exception. Why, only the day before, an American swimmer by the name of Mark Spitz had won an incredible seven gold medals.

Joanna recalled carefree days as a teenager spent at the local swimming pool. Greg was part of those memories, but she could think of him without bitterness now.

As she said her Rosary that evening, Joanna's mind drifted from the Hail Marys to Dr. Murray. It was vain of her to be this pleased—an impulse she should try to curb—but she couldn't help it.

Joanna closed her eyes and forced herself to concentrate on the words of the prayer. *Hail Mary, full of grace, the Lord is with thee. Blessed are thou amongst women and blessed is the fruit of thy womb, Jesus...*

She paused and bowed her head at the name of Jesus.

Briefly she found herself wondering if Tim Murray had returned from Vietnam with wounds of his own. Outwardly it didn't seem so, but men often concealed their emotions. She had the feeling that there was more to Dr. Murray than met the eye.

{9}

Sister Kathleen

Kathleen was one sister who'd have no objection when St. Bridget's order finally got around to making changes to the habits. Every day it became more of a trial to hide her thick auburn hair beneath her veil. Her hair was long again, almost the same length as when she'd entered the convent.

The habit was due to be altered soon. In a few months—perhaps as little as a few weeks—the modified habit would allow the professed nuns to stop dressing like nineteenth-century Irish widows.

With the last of her afternoon bookkeeping classes at the high school dismissed, Kathleen was technically finished for the day. She sat at her desk and graded her students' papers, becoming absorbed in her task. Amazing how easily these kids could forget basic concepts like—

"Sister Kathleen."

At the sound of her name, Kathleen jerked her head up. Father Sanders, the parish priest, came into her classroom, looking a bit disgruntled. The pastor was medium height and middle-aged, with thinning hair and a bit of a paunch. A jovial sort, he was known to liven up his sermons with a joke or two, just to keep the congregation alert and in good spirits. He reminded Kathleen of Father O'Hara, who'd been a friend of the family while she was growing up.

For years Father Sanders had been the only full-time priest serving St. Peter's, but the demands on his time were too much for one man. Only recently had a second full-time priest been added to assist him. Father Brian Doyle, barely two years out of the seminary, was young and idealistic and had a genuine heart for God. Kathleen viewed him as the perfect priest. Never had she met any man more comfortable in a collar. His sermons touched her, although delivered in the self-conscious, faltering manner of an inexperienced speaker. Still, it was obvious that he'd spent hours working on each one. Father Sanders's chatty style was more popular, but in her opinion there was far less substance to his words. Few parishioners, however, appeared to notice.

"What can I do for you, Father?" Kathleen asked.

The older priest crammed himself into one of the student desks with their attached chairs and stretched his legs out in front of him. He leaned back, wearing one of the most forlorn looks she'd ever seen. "Bookkeeping is a job fitting for the saints," he mumbled.

Like her father, she'd always had an affinity for practical mathematics. Over the last few summers she'd taken college-level courses in business math and as a result was now teaching ninth- and tenth-grade bookkeeping. It was a challenge she welcomed, although her actual experience was limited.

Kathleen grinned. "You think so, Father?"

His brows rose toward his receding hairline. "I know so." He straightened, sitting upright in his cramped seat. "Sister Kathleen, I'm here to throw myself upon your mercy."

It was hard not to laugh when Father Sanders had such a flair for drama. "I *desperately* need your help," he said, widening his dark eyes.

Kathleen held her red pencil between her open palms. "What can I do for you, Father?" she asked again.

The priest's shoulders fell. "Mrs. Stafford, who's been doing the books for the parish for the last twenty-five years, is on an extended vacation. She suggested a couple of replacements to keep the books during her absence, but fool that I am, I didn't think getting someone in for such a short time was necessary. I figured I could assume the task myself." He glanced pleadingly in Kathleen's direction. "Just how difficult can it be to enter the weekly collection amounts and write a check whenever necessary?" he asked.

"Not difficult at all, if you know what you're doing," Kathleen assured him with a grin.

"My point exactly." With a hopelessly lost expression, he turned up his palms. "Frankly, Sister, I *don't* know what I'm doing. There, I've admitted it." He continued to stare at Kathleen as though he expected her to comment.

Kathleen wasn't sure what he was asking, although she was beginning to suspect. "What would you like me to do?"

"Could you...would it be possible for you to lend me a hand for the next few weeks?" He gave a helpless shrug. "Just until Mrs. Stafford returns. She's only been gone two weeks, and will be back—" he hesitated "—about a month from now. Could you do that, Sister?"

His request presented something of a problem. While she was willing to assist where she could, nuns and priests generally didn't work together. The priests had little or no say over the nuns' duties and assignments. "I'd be happy to help, but I'll need to check with Sister Superior." Sister Eloise would need to approve before Kathleen could take on any assignment other than her teaching duties, which had to be her first priority.

"Leave Sister Eloise to me," the priest said, brightening considerably as he slid out of the desk. "I can't thank you enough."

He was gone so fast, it almost seemed that he was afraid she might change her mind.

That very night, after the evening meal, Sister Eloise asked to speak to Kathleen.

"I understand Father Sanders visited your classroom this afternoon."

"He did," Kathleen admitted.

"Father says he needs help keeping the church books until Mrs. Stafford is back from her vacation. Apparently he's already spoken to you?" Her frown suggested disapproval. "Is this a task you feel comfortable undertaking?"

"I think it would be good for me," she said honestly. Her own experience was limited to occasionally counting out cash from the till at her uncle's pub. All other bookkeeping knowledge had come from a textbook.

"Do you have time for this?"

"I'll make time," Kathleen told her, eager to accept the assignment. It was an opportunity to accumulate some real experience, and she couldn't imagine that the parish books would present any significant problems.

She knew there must be an office at the rectory, although she hadn't seen it; presumably that was where she'd work. She'd been as far as the front hallway a couple of Sunday evenings, when she'd gone with Sister Angelina to deliver dinner to Father Sanders and Father Doyle. That was all she'd ever seen of the place.

Sister Superior's frown deepened.

"I wouldn't do it at the expense of my prayer life," Kathleen said quickly.

Sister's brow relaxed, and she eventually nodded. "Father asked if you could walk over to the rectory after school three afternoons a week. I agreed, with the stipulation that you be back in time for dinner."

That meant Kathleen would need to bring her students' papers to the convent and grade them at night. "That's fine," she said. The experience she'd gain from working on the books, Kathleen reasoned, would be worth any lost personal time.

"I hope Father Sanders appreciates your sacrifice."

"I'm sure he does," Kathleen murmured.

"Somehow I doubt it, but let's hope so."

The following day, Kathleen arrived at the rectory shortly after her last class. Her briefcase was filled to overflowing with papers she'd have to grade that evening.

Mrs. O'Malley, the housekeeper, greeted her. The scent of simmering beef wafted into the church office.

"Irish stew?" Kathleen asked as she sat down at the big desk the housekeeper had shown her.

"It is. Me own mother's recipe."

Kathleen hadn't tasted authentic Irish stew since she'd entered the convent. The aroma reminded her of home and family, of childhood, and her mouth all but watered as she closed her eyes. For a moment, it was as if she'd slipped back in time and sat at the large kitchen table, between Joyce and Maureen....

Her mother wrote regularly, filling her in on the details of family life in Boston. Over the years Kathleen had visited a number of times, but nothing was the same. How could it be? She was a different person from the young girl who'd walked through the convent door nine years earlier. The changes weren't only with her, either. Her three younger siblings were like strangers to her, and the four older ones had all married and made their own lives. Their letters were few and far between. Only Sean made the effort to keep in touch with her.

"I see my salvation has arrived," Father Sanders said, bursting into the room. He carried a large cardboard box and set it on a corner of the cluttered desk.

"Hello, Father." She stood courteously. "What's that?" Kathleen was almost afraid to ask. She'd assumed that Mrs. Stafford had left the books in good order and she'd merely be stepping in for a brief period.

The priest didn't answer. "I can't tell you how much I appreciate your help in this matter, Sister Kathleen."

She peered inside the box and found a large green ledger, numerous wadded-up receipts and a stack of checks. Kathleen had the uncomfortable sensation that she was about to plunge into water well over her head. Eager as she was to help, this favor suddenly felt overwhelming.

"I don't think this should take long, do you?" Father Sanders said hopefully. "You're a bright one and seeing that you teach bookkeeping, you should have this mess cleared up in a couple of hours."

"It might take me a little longer than that," she muttered, sinking into the padded leather chair.

Father nodded solemnly. "You take all the time you need."

"Would you care for a cup of tea, Sister?" Mrs. O'Malley asked.

Kathleen shook her head. As she started to empty the box, both the priest and the housekeeper disappeared.

Kathleen worked steadily, identifying and sorting collection receipts, hardly looking up from the desk. When she lifted her head, she was shocked to notice that it was past six.

Her heart nearly exploded with urgency as she placed the receipts, now tidied and tallied, in envelopes and set them aside. Then she flew out of the room and almost collided with Father Doyle, who was walking in the front door.

"Oh, Father! I beg your pardon."

"Sister Kathleen?" He was clearly shocked to find her at the rectory.

"I'm sorry, Father, but I have to get back to the convent right away," she said breathlessly. "I'm helping Father Sanders with the book work while Mrs. Stafford's on vacation." She edged away from him, walking backward and gripping her briefcase.

"I'll walk you."

"No, no, that isn't necessary, but thank you." She didn't have time to walk at a normal pace; she had to hurry. In her rush it might appear that she was being rude and Kathleen didn't want to risk that.

"You're sure?"

"Oh, yes."

"Have a good evening, Sister."

"You, too, Father." Without prolonging her departure, she grabbed her long skirts and raced down the short flight of wooden steps outside the rectory.

A nun was standing by the convent entrance. Kathleen dashed past her, rosary beads clattering at her side.

She stopped abruptly when she realized it was Sister Eloise.

"You're late, Sister."

"I'm sorry, Sister," she said, shoulders heaving. "The...the time got away from me."

Sister Superior wasn't pleased and it showed. "I was afraid something like this would happen. I should never have agreed to Father Sanders's request."

"I won't be late again," Kathleen promised her, and she sincerely hoped that was true.

The other nun walked ahead of her. Kathleen paused a moment to catch her breath and placed a hand over her pounding heart.

{ 10 }

Sister Angelina

Corinne Sullivan hurried past Angie on the way to her desk just as the bell rang for class. The heavy stench of cigarettes clung to the teenager like cheap cologne. Corinne had obviously been smoking, which was strictly prohibited while in school uniform.

Angie liked Corinne, even if the girl was something of a challenge. She enjoyed pushing the limits, testing Angie's authority and asking outrageous questions. It was all for the sake of attention. A brief look at Corinne's school records confirmed that she was the second child of three and the only girl. Experience in the classroom had taught Angie to recognize the characteristics of a middle child.

"Corinne," Angie said as she stepped to the front of the room. "Could I speak to you after class?"

"Again?" Corinne said with a low moan.

"Again," Angie echoed.

"Is it about the smell of cigarette smoke?" The teenager slid gracefully into her desk. "I wasn't smoking, Sister, I *swear*."

"We'll discuss that later, but it's interesting you should mention cigarettes because that's the very subject we'll be discussing in class this afternoon."

A couple of the students opened their textbooks and stared up at Angie, confused. There hadn't been anything about smoking in the chapter she'd assigned them as homework.

"Aw, Sister," Corinne groaned, "are you going to tell us smoking's bad for us?"

"As a matter of fact I am." Recent studies had proven that smoking was detrimental to one's health. Despite that, cigarettes were more popular than ever, especially among teenagers. Angie considered it a disgusting habit, even though her father had smoked for years and as far as she knew, still did.

A low protesting moan rumbled through the class.

"Why do people smoke?" Angie asked, genuinely curious as to what her students would tell her.

Loretta Bond raised her hand. "It helps relax you." Then, as though she realized what she'd said, she added, "That's what my mother told me. She's been smoking since I can remember."

"Cigarettes taste good," one of the boys offered.

"How many of you have ever smoked a cigarette? Just once, just to try it out." Nearly every hand in the room went up.

Corinne Sullivan's hand was one of the first to shoot into the air. She glanced around and looked absolutely amazed. "Wow."

That was Angie's reaction, as well. The class was made up of sophomores, fifteen- and sixteen-year-old students. They seemed too young to be smoking.

"Okay," Angie said, as her students lowered their arms. "Loretta, tell me why you lit up the first time."

Loretta appeared to be unsure about answering. "My mom threw away a pack and there was one cigarette left in it, so I decided to see what smoking was like. I thought it might be cool."

"How old were you?"

Loretta cast down her eyes. "Ten."

Angie swallowed a gasp. When she recovered, she asked, "And how was it?"

Loretta laughed. "I nearly choked to death."

"They're nasty-tasting," Morgan added. "At first, anyway."

"Tell me about *your* first cigarette," Angie said to the girl who'd been exchanging notes with Corinne at the beginning of the year.

"I lit up for my boyfriend," she said, glaring at Mike Carson. "He was busy driving and asked me to get out a cigarette for him. I did and it tasted awful, but after a while—I don't know, they kind of grow on you."

"One lady saw me smoking and thought I was twenty," Cathy Bailey inserted proudly.

Angie wasn't surprised. "In other words, you assume that if you smoke you'll look more mature?"

Several heads nodded.

"Everyone smokes, Sister," Corinne said.

"But not you?"

Corinne sighed and reluctantly admitted, "Okay, okay, I smoke, but not every day, just sometimes."

"But not today?"

"No, it was Jimmy's smoke, I swear." She snapped her mouth shut as if she'd said more than she should have.

"Jimmy," Morgan echoed, her eyes round and horrified.

Angie didn't know what that was all about, but she couldn't ask right then. "Next question," she said, resting against the edge of the desk. "Who in this class has never smoked?"

Three timid hands went up. Only three out of a class of thirty students, and all girls.

Angie nodded, acknowledging their response. "That was very interesting," she said. "I appreciate your honesty."

"Sister." Corinne's hand snaked up over her head. "We were honest with you, but will you be honest with us?"

"What do you mean?"

The teenager beamed a smile. "Have *you* ever smoked?"

The question stunned Angie. In all her years of teaching, not a single student had ever inquired about her life outside the convent. But it was plain that every one of these kids was eager to hear her answer. They leaned forward in their desks.

"Once," Angie said. "I was about sixteen and my father smoked. I tried it, thought it tasted vile and that was the end of it."

The class stared at her with astonished expressions, apparently finding it impossible to imagine her as a teenager. "It might surprise you to know that I was once very much like you."

"I want to know what you were like before..." Corinne insisted.

"Before what?" Angie said. "Do you think that because I wear a nun's habit I've never had a life?" She laughed at the teenager's stricken look.

"What about boys?" Morgan asked.

Angie shook her head. "This is Health class, not Ancient History."

A few of her students laughed.

"It's hard for me to think of you as someone my age," Corinne said, propping her chin in her hands.

"Let's return to our discussion," Angie suggested.

"Did you always want to be a nun?" Morgan asked.

Angie could see that the class wasn't going to be satisfied until she gave them a small detail of her life before the convent. "All right, if you must know, I did have a boyfriend once, a hundred years ago. He worked part-time in my father's restaurant."

"Your father has a restaurant?"

"What kind?"

"With a name like Angelina, you need to ask?" Corinne twisted around to mock her classmates.

"You're Italian?" Cathy Bailey cried, as though Angie had told them she walked on water.

"Enough," Angie said and picked up the textbook. "Open your books to page fifty-six. Cathy, would you please read the opening paragraph?"

Her class reluctantly complied. Books could be heard opening and pages flipping. Cathy read the text and Angie reverted to her original plan for the class.

Holding the book in both hands, Angie paced the classroom and directed the discussion, which concerned early childhood development. Angie gave them their homework assignment and then the bell rang, signaling the end of the school day.

"I want you to answer all the even-numbered questions at the end of the second chapter. Anything else before we finish?"

Charlotte Chesterfield, who was also in Angie's Home Economics class, raised her hand. "Sister Angelina, I'd love to learn how to cook a few Italian dishes. Are you going to share any family recipes with us?"

"We'll discuss that in Home Economics, Charlotte."

"But…"

"My mom says that the way to a man's heart is through his stomach," Corinne inserted, as though this were an insider's secret.

"You have plenty of time to think about finding a husband later on," Angie told her as the rest of the class gathered their books.

"No, I don't," Corinne muttered. "I'm looking for one right now."

Angie's shock must have shown, because Corinne said, "I plan to get married the year I graduate."

"But why?"

"Oh, Sister, don't you know? Can't you guess? I don't care if I ever go to school again. I'm not much good at it. All I want is a man."

Angie wanted to argue with her, to explain that there were so many options and possibilities other than tying herself down in a relationship at such a young age.

"Do you still want to talk to me?" Corinne asked, walking backward toward the open door.

Angie shook her head. Everything she'd planned to say had already been discussed in class. "You can go."

Corinne's face brightened with a smile. "Thanks."

Just before she left for the day, Angie walked past the principal's office. "Sister Angelina," the lay secretary called out, stopping her. "What happened in Health class today?"

"What makes you ask?"

"Corinne Sullivan, Loretta Bond and about five other girls came in and requested transfers from study hall to Home Economics."

Sister Kathleen, who taught bookkeeping, chuckled as she moved past Angie in the wide hallway. "Word must've gotten out about your marinara sauce."

Angie answered with a groan, and the other nun broke into an outright laugh.

Soon Angie was smiling, too. She was dismayed about her Home Economics class filling up with young women trying to lure men into early marriage. She didn't understand it, especially with women's rights issues prominent in the headlines. Nevertheless, she had to admit she was pleased to be so popular with her students.

{ 11 }

Sister Joanna

Joanna was sitting at the nurses' station going over the medication records when Dr. Murray strolled up to the desk. He folded his arms along the top. "Good afternoon, Sister Joanna."

"Dr. Murray." She looked up and was struck anew at what an attractive man he was. That wasn't something she consciously wanted to notice, but it would be impossible not to. Despite his smile and the friendly expression in his intensely blue eyes, she felt a lingering sadness in him. For some inexplicable reason, she wanted to console him.... "Uh, is there anything I can do for you?"

He shook his head and straightened, almost as if he'd read her thoughts and was embarrassed by her sympathy. "I notice Mrs. Stewart is doing better this afternoon. She'd like to go home, but I'm inclined to keep her an extra day."

Joanna approved. The widow didn't have anyone to help her at home and wouldn't until the weekend. It was often like that with older people. Joanna was grateful that the physicians took home care into consideration before releasing a patient.

"She said you sat with her late yesterday afternoon when your shift was over and read to her."

Now it was Joanna's turn to be embarrassed. Like many patients, Mrs. Stewart was bored, eager to get back home to what was familiar, but still weak and slightly disoriented. Joanna had sat with her for a couple of hours.

"She said she'd been wanting to read *The Godfather,* seeing how popular it is," Joanna said, feeling somehow that she should justify her time, even though it had been after her shift. "She said she didn't know if she'd live long enough to see the movie."

Dr. Murray continued to study her. "You should know she sang your praises for a good ten minutes. It was very thoughtful, what you did."

Joanna dismissed his praise. "It was nothing." The older woman craved companionship. She was alone and away from family and had recently lost her husband of fifty years.

Dr. Murray started to turn away and then seemed to change his mind. "Would you mind if I asked you a personal question?"

"I…no, I guess not." Joanna stood so she could meet his eyes. Unaccountably, she could feel her pulse quicken.

A slight frown came over his face. "What happened? I mean, what makes someone like you decide to become a nun?"

Joanna hid her embarrassment behind a laugh. "Someone like me?"

"*Something* must have happened."

Joanna didn't know whether to be insulted or flattered. "What do you mean?"

Dr. Murray seemed to regret having said anything. "Trust me, when I was in school I never had any nun who looked like you. They were all old and crotchety."

Joanna felt heat invade her cheeks.

"That probably isn't something one's supposed to say around a nun. Sorry." He shook his head. "Listen, do me a favor and forget I said anything. I just figured you must've had a reason for entering the convent."

"I did," Joanna confirmed. "God asked it of me."

Her answer appeared to confuse him even more. "You mean there was never a boyfriend?"

"I didn't say that."

He brightened and raised his index finger. "Aha, so the truth comes out. You did have a boyfriend."

"Once, a long time ago."

"And he dumped you."

"In a manner of speaking." She reached for another chart and sat down, indicating that the conversation was over. This subject was far too uncomfortable—far too personal.

"He dumped you, broke your heart and you decided to join the convent," he said, as though this was what he'd suspected all along.

"Wrong," she said. "Yes, I was hurt, but it was for the best that we split up. It would never have worked. It was while I was working through my pain that I felt God pulling me toward Him. I answered His call and I've never regretted my decision."

He stared at her as though absorbing her words.

"My turn to question you," she said.

He held up both hands. "Okay, I'll admit it—I'm a lapsed Catholic. But don't try to bring me back, Sister, because I have no intention of resuming any kind of relationship with God."

That hadn't been her question, but now that he'd raised the subject, she was curious. "Why not?"

He glanced at his watch. "We don't have two or three days to debate this. Suffice it to say, the Church and I had a parting of the ways about three years ago."

"When you were in Vietnam?" she asked, standing once more.

All the teasing laughter left his eyes. "Yes," he said curtly, "but—"

"But?"

"There are plenty of subjects we can discuss, Sister. Vietnam isn't one of them."

"Can you tell me why?"

His gaze narrowed and for a long moment it was as if he'd been transported to a time and place he no longer wanted to remember. "I think it was the closest I'll ever get to hell on earth. Yet even with death and devastation at every turn, there was honor and decency and bravery above anything I'm likely to witness again." He looked away and seemed chagrined by the power of his feelings. "Is that enough?" he said in a mocking manner.

"That's enough," she said gently and then to her amazement she did something completely out of character. Joanna felt compelled to touch him. Almost against her will, she leaned toward him and placed her hand on his shoulder. With someone else it might have made her feel self-conscious, but not with Dr. Murray. She didn't quite know why that was.

Now, more than ever, she was determined to pray for the young surgeon. To lift him before God and plead for the salvation of his eternal soul. After a few seconds, she dropped her hand and said quietly, "Several of the boys in my high school class went to Vietnam."

"Anyone special?"

She must be easy to read, Joanna decided. "I had a boyfriend who went over there."

"Did he come back?"

Her laugh was tinged with a note of bitterness. "He did, only he returned with a pregnant Vietnamese wife."

"I see."

"Like I said, it was for the best. Greg and I were never meant to be." She'd already said more than she wanted and hoping to end their conversation on a subject other than herself, she asked, "What about you? Did you leave anyone behind when you went overseas?"

"I had a whole slew of lovers waiting for me," he returned flippantly.

Joanna snickered softly.

"What? You don't believe me?"

"All nurses, no doubt."

He shook his head and seemed grateful that the conversation had taken a lighter tone. "No, not a one."

"I suppose you left a string of broken hearts in Vietnam, too."

"Sorry to disappoint you. Actually I wasn't nearly as good-looking then as I am now."

Joanna rolled her eyes.

"It's true. I was the class brain and what prom queen wants to date a guy who's more interested in science than in her bra size?"

Joanna knew exactly the kind of girl he was talking about. There'd been some in her high school class, too.

"Later, while I was in med school, I met someone special. We might've gotten married if things had turned out differently."

"What do you mean?"

Dr. Murray pointedly checked his watch again, implying it was time to go.

"You'd better confess now."

He sighed and she could tell he didn't want to discuss it, but she wasn't letting him off that lightly. "Come on, you dug around until you got the information *you* wanted."

"All right, all right. Don't ever try to escape a nun." He smiled as he said it, taking the edge off his words. "If you *must* know, I'll tell you."

"I must."

"After I shipped out to Nam, she met someone else."

It was the reverse of her story. Greg had married a girl from Vietnam, and Dr. Murray's sweetheart had left him for someone stateside.

"Do these sorts of things happen often?" he asked, sounding disgruntled. "Do people come up to you and immediately start confessing their deep, dark pasts?"

"On occasion." A couple of months ago, on a rainy Sunday after the last Mass of the day, a young soldier had stopped her outside the church and asked her to pray for him. That was all he'd said, but there had been tears in his eyes and emotion throbbed in his voice. She could only speculate about why he'd asked, but she'd remembered him in her daily prayers for weeks after that chance meeting.

"If it's any comfort, I've never mentioned Greg to anyone else."

Dr. Murray nodded solemnly.

Despite his casual attitude, he'd been hurt by this woman in med school, just as she'd been devastated by Greg's actions. That pain had shaped them both into the people they were, Joanna mused. The people they'd always be.

{ 12 }

Sister Kathleen

Kathleen was exhausted from teaching all day and then rushing over to the church office, but she gave Sister Eloise no cause for concern after that first night. She made sure she was always on time for dinner. Knowing Sister Angelina would be cooking on Friday, Kathleen eagerly anticipated the evening meal.

Sister Angelina had arrived that summer and quickly become a favorite of Kathleen's. The newest convent member had bonded easily with the other sisters, as well. She was a talented cook, and anyone fortunate enough to sample any of her dinners wasn't likely to forget it. She had a gift for adding whatever a dish needed to make it special. The instant one of the sisters sought her advice regarding a new recipe, Sister Angelina tore into the spice cabinet with enthusiasm and a dash of adventure.

Sister Angelina did the same thing to their lives, Kathleen reflected. She added spark and wit and joy. And she'd quickly become one of the most popular teachers in the school. They were only a few weeks into the school year and already there'd been a number of requests for transfers to her classes. The students loved her.

Kathleen didn't know Sister Joanna well, but she appreciated her sense of fun. Because the other nun worked on the postoperative floor at St. Elizabeth's Hospital, they'd had only a few opportunities to get to know each other. Five nuns worked at the hospital, two fewer than the previous year. Sister Penelope and Sister Barbara had both taken sabbaticals. It was rumored that they were thinking about leaving the convent. That seemed to be happening more often in the years since Vatican II, to the point that Kathleen had become alarmed.

The bell rang signaling dinner, and the nuns formed a silent line, walking with their heads bowed and hands folded into the dining room. They took their places at the long tables and waited to be served. As with all domestic tasks at the convent, they cooked and served meals on a rotational basis. The following week it would be Kathleen's turn to carry the plates from the kitchen out to the waiting sisters. Exhausted as she was, she didn't relish the additional duty. It was difficult enough to manage her high school bookkeeping class and the parish finances.

Once the food was arrayed on the table, Sister Superior stood, and with one voice they said grace. Whatever Sister Angelina had cooked smelled heavenly. Kathleen closed her eyes and drew in a deep breath, appreciating the scent of fresh garlic and a blend of herbs she could never hope to name.

Even after six years of convent life, Kathleen wondered if she'd ever grow accustomed to silence at meals.

In the beginning it had so unnerved her that she'd been half-tempted to stand up and shout that this was unnatural.

Meals at home had been boisterous affairs with her mother leaping up from the table, rushing over to the stove and back. Her brothers and sisters chatted incessantly, usually all at once. Kathleen had never thought she'd miss the "infernal racket," as her mother used to call it, but she did.

After the main course—a delectable lasagne—Sister Joanna and Sister Angelina brought the dessert plates to the tables. They set down big round platters piled high with fresh-baked brownies, three per table. Kathleen eyed the brownies, which oozed with melting chocolate chips. She reached into the middle of the table and grabbed one. It was everything she'd hoped it would be. However, Sister Martha seemed to be having trouble biting down on hers. After one bite, she yanked the brownie out of her mouth and examined it, then spat out the offending bit. A piece of half-chewed rubber fell on her plate. Kathleen immediately realized that the two nuns had played a joke on them, mixing fake brownies in with the real ones.

She couldn't help it; she burst out laughing. Knowing she'd contravened the rules of conduct, she covered her mouth. A moment later, someone else started to laugh, and then another, almost hysterically.

In the meantime Sister Angelina and Sister Joanna sat with straight faces.

"Sisters, Sisters." Sister Eloise bolted to her feet and looked around the table, but Kathleen could see that she was struggling to hold back a smile herself.

The laughter faded. Kathleen reached for a second brownie and realized it was made of rubber. Maintaining silence was nearly impossible and small bursts of giggles continued to erupt here and there. Kathleen could see that the other nuns were having as much trouble keeping silent as she was.

Friday evenings, after dinner, were set aside for what was known as the Chapter of Faults. Once a week, the Sisters were to come before their Superior, in front of their fellow nuns, and confess their weaknesses and faults. It was a time for humility, for self-examination— a time to openly acknowledge one's failings that week.

One at a time each nun would kneel before Sister Eloise. Head bowed and hands piously folded, she would state, "Before God Almighty and you, Sister Superior, I confess the following list of faults."

When it was Kathleen's turn, she knelt before Sister Eloise and lowered her head. As hard as she strived for perfection, Kathleen knew she continually failed. She was never at a loss for failings and weaknesses.

All the convent rules, including custody of the eyes and silence at mealtime, served the function of shaping her into God's faithful servant. To an outsider, they might appear harsh or, as she'd once thought, unnatural, but every rule had a purpose.

"Sister Superior," Kathleen began, "I have been weakened by pride in assuming that I could help Father Sanders. Pride was what led me to believe I might be of service to the parish."

Sister Eloise nodded. "I was afraid you were stretching yourself too thin. Be careful, and remember that pride goeth before a fall."

"Yes, Sister." Kathleen quickly rose and returned to her place.

Sister Jacqueline stepped forward and knelt. She bowed her head.

"Sister?" Sister Eloise said when the nun hesitated.

As though to offer assistance, Sister Ruth, one of the older nuns, spoke up. "Sister Jacqueline displayed a lack of charity toward Sister Mary Catherine. Sister Catherine had asked for the scissors and Sister Jacqueline used them herself before passing them on to the one who had asked."

Sister Jacqueline reddened.

"Is this true?" Sister Eloise asked.

The nun in the center of the circle nodded. "It is."

"Very well. I would urge you to be more charitable and patient in the future." Sister Eloise glanced toward Sister Ruth and frowned as if to say that when it came to charity, the other nun had a few lessons to learn herself.

"I will," Sister Jacqueline murmured.

She was one of the youngest nuns in the convent. Kathleen had noticed that fewer and fewer young women had stepped forward to seek the religious life— just as more and more were seeking to return to secular life. There had been much discussion as to why.

Kathleen had her own conjectures. The Church was torn by controversy over the issues of birth control and women's rights. The religious life, she feared, was losing its appeal and that saddened her.

Then there was the way women left the convent. It was always done in such secrecy. One day a chair at breakfast would be empty, but nothing was ever said or explained. They all knew, however, that another sister had decided to leave them.

With so many nuns reverting to their given names and some orders altering their habits, Kathleen felt that those who'd chosen the religious life had lost part of their identity. At the same time, she herself often craved a less restrictive life. Many of the older nuns, steeped in tradition, were adamantly opposed to any and all changes, while the younger ones welcomed them.

Aware that her feelings—a reverence for tradition on the one hand, and a desire for more freedom on the other—were contradictory, Kathleen didn't know what conclusions to draw.

She'd entered the convent with high ideals. Those ideals had felt poignantly beautiful when she was eighteen, and in fact, they continued to be. Still, there were times, like that very evening, when she would've given anything to laugh freely and joke with the other nuns. She suspected her fellow sisters felt the same way, but the rules were not to be broken.

"Sister Joanna, meals are a time of silence, and with your childish prank, you disobeyed that precept."

Caught up in her thoughts, Kathleen had missed Joanna's confession and part of Sister Superior's rebuke. The rubber brownie incident had been funny, but their order frowned upon such frivolity.

In spite of Sister Eloise's sharp words, Kathleen was sure she detected a note of humor in her voice. Could it be that Sister Superior longed for the free exchange of conversation at meals, like Kathleen did?

Some answers didn't come easy.

{ 13 }

Sister Joanna

Joanna didn't know why she'd done something as silly as set out those rubber brownies. Sometimes she couldn't help herself. It had been childish, just as Sister Superior had said during the Chapter of Faults.

Saturday was a rare day off from the hospital, and Joanna devoted herself to prayer. She needed to focus on her calling and her ongoing struggles with pride and vanity. After Mass on Sunday, during which she sang with the other nuns in the choir at St. Peter's, she returned to the convent and spent time in the chapel.

Of all the nurses he could have chosen, Dr. Murray had asked *her* to be assigned to his surgery patients. Joanna had allowed his request to go to her head. He had other reasons for requesting her; she knew that. Because of her status as a nun, she was a safe choice. Still, she'd been unable to prevent a feeling of pride. Then there had been that brief discussion later in the week. She was astonished now that she'd told him about Greg and that she'd actually touched him. She sighed. It was wrong to feel this way about a man.

In retrospect, her feelings for Dr. Murray could have been the very reason she'd pulled that ridiculous stunt with the brownies. She'd taken the attention away from her real weakness and cast it on yet another fault.

As soon as she realized that she'd concealed one weakness by exposing another, Joanna sat in the chapel and spilled out her heart to God, asking His forgiveness and pleading for insight into her sinful nature. Even in the convent, devoting her life to God, she struggled with obedience. Joanna sometimes wondered if she would ever become the woman God wanted her to be. Would she ever gain the maturity to win the constant battle she waged against self? At times such as these, the answers to her questions were in doubt. It wouldn't get better, she acknowledged, especially when the order implemented the coming changes.

Rumors had whispered through the convent about the imminent redesign of their habits. The modification itself would upset some of the sisters; what concerned Joanna was the fact that it symbolized shifting attitudes about the religious life and its role in the world.

That Sunday evening, Sister Superior stood before them. "I heard from Boston this afternoon. The modernization of our habits is now complete. Sister Angelina has agreed to model it for us." She turned and waited while Joanna's friend walked slowly into the room, wearing the new shortened habit of their order.

Several of the nuns shifted in their seats for a better look. Joanna was impressed. The skirt was definitely shorter, hitting just below the knee. The veil, which had fallen over their shoulders, was now the approximate length of a scarf. It fit the back of the head with what seemed to be a simple clip. For the first time in their 133-year history, St. Bridget's Sisters of the Assumption would display their hair, part of their arms and their legs.

Murmurs rippled across the room, but they were immediately silenced by a look from Sister Eloise.

"Are there any questions?"

Sister Josephina raised her hand. She was in her seventies and had joined the convent in the 1920s. She stood on shaking legs and glared at Sister Angelina, as if seeing the other nun for the first time. For a moment, she had trouble speaking. "These…these new habits have received the approval of the motherhouse?"

"Yes, Sister." Sister Eloise didn't seem eager for the changes, either, but she had stepped forward in obedience and submitted to the decisions made by her superiors.

Joanna understood Sister Josephina's unspoken concern. For the last fifty years, the other nun's hair had been cropped and hidden beneath yards of heavy fabric. Now she was being asked to display what had once been considered intensely private. It wasn't only her hair that would be revealed to the world, but her legs too. For someone who had worn the same dress for fifty-odd years, this was a drastic change.

"I… I don't know how to style my hair, Sister," another of the older nuns said, her voice trembling.

"Which of us does?" Sister Eloise returned, gesturing in a forsaken manner.

The nuns looked at each other with despair.

"Will we be required to wear nylons?" Sister Margaret asked. "Or can we continue to wear our cotton stockings?"

Sister Superior seemed at a loss as to how she should answer. "I believe the choice will be an individual one."

There were so few individual choices in convent life that this was a revolutionary thought to many of the sisters.

"Our arms will show," Joanna heard Sister Charlene whisper to Sister Josephina. She tucked her hands deep into the bulky sleeves that marked their habit, as though to hide them from view.

The discontented murmurs continued well into the evening. Joanna recognized that many of the older nuns were shaken by the changes. She would adjust easily enough, but then she was young and had worn the current habit only six years; some of the others had worn it for fifty and sixty. Some orders had made the changes optional, but for whatever reason, Sister Agnes, their Mother Superior in Boston, had decided against that.

At the hospital the following afternoon, Joanna ran into Dr. Murray.

"Good afternoon, Sister," he said when he swiftly passed her in the corridor.

She acknowledged him with a polite nod, but her heart raced at the sight of him. Either he was late for his rounds or he was covering for another surgeon because he rushed past her.

Joanna struggled with disappointment. Despite all her prayers and promises, she wanted to see him. She'd hoped for another chance to chat, to know him better; apparently he wasn't interested. This was wrong, this desire of hers. It had to stop. Her awareness of him was too personal, too intense. She had to bring it under control.

At lunch, Joanna joined the other nuns in their private dining room. She'd never understood why they weren't allowed to eat with the seculars. At one time she'd asked about the practice and been told simply that it was tradition. Questioning further would have shown a lack of faith and a rebellious attitude.

Dr. Murray drifted into her mind again. She couldn't help wondering what he'd think when he saw her in the new habit. Her legs were long, and at one time she'd considered them her best feature. After entering the convent, she'd given up all thoughts of her physical appearance. As a postulant, she'd been homesick and turned to food and quickly gained ten pounds. It hadn't bothered her. Anything to do with personal appearance was forgotten. Eventually she'd lost the weight, but not because of any diet. She wasn't even sure how the extra pounds had disappeared.

Now she'd need to shave her legs again. The idea of wearing her cotton stockings was ludicrous. After going through the washing machine two or three times, those stockings were faded and pilled. No, she would wear white nylons the same as the other nurses.

Mirrors! My goodness, the sisters would require mirrors if they were going to style their hair. Joanna wondered if Sister Eloise had thought of that. Knowing how concerned Sister Josephina and several of the other nuns were, Joanna had offered to help with their hair. However, it had been so long since she'd fiddled with rollers and hair spray, she was afraid her fellow sisters might end up resembling the Supremes. That image made her laugh.

After lunch, Joanna returned to the floor to find Dr. Murray out of surgery. He still wore his greens.

"I have another patient for you," he said as she approached the nurses' station. His manner was professional and none of his earlier banter was in evidence now. "His name is Fredrick Marrow. He just had his appendix out. Unfortunately his appendix ruined a perfectly good afternoon—his *and* mine."

"A date, Dr. Murray?" she asked, then wished she could withdraw the words. It had been unethical of her to ask.

"A hot one," he said. The sudden smile he flashed her could have melted concrete. "I'm in a rush to get back to my golf game. Take care of Freddy for me, will you?"

"Of course." Joanna instantly felt better. His date had been on the golf course with a set of clubs. But he should be dating, should have an active social life. That was what she wanted for him, she told herself, but the small voice in the back of her mind claimed otherwise.

{ 14 }

Sister Angelina

"How are you going to style your hair, Sister?" Corinne Sullivan asked, cocking her head as she studied Angie.

Like the rest of the Health class, she'd been assigned to read her textbook in silence. "I'll give you a few hints, if you want," she offered excitedly. "I'm good with hair. I styled Megan's." Turning around in her desk, she looked at her handiwork while Megan pretended to be reviewing the chapter.

"Read," Angie whispered in warning, not wanting to disturb the others. While most had their heads obediently bowed over their reading assignment, Corinne continued to assess Angie as she walked down the aisles between the rows of desks.

"I'm just interested," Corinne said in a low voice when Angie glared at her.

Corinne might be interested, but for Angie the whole subject of hair was a source of anxiety rather than pleasure. In the past fourteen years Angie had done nothing more than run a brush through her hair. She'd noticed the other day that there were several gray hairs in her brush. It didn't surprise her. For most of her life her father had been completely gray; in fact, the last time she'd seen him, his hair had gone white. Premature graying ran in the family. Which brought up another question: would...should Angie color her hair? Would that be allowed? Somehow she doubted it. Vain and contradictory though it was, she didn't want to appear old— or, at least, any older than thirty-two. She sighed at the prospect of all these decisions she didn't feel equipped to make, all these changes she wasn't ready for.

Redesigning the habit was a sign of the upheaval taking place within the Catholic Church, an upheaval that would profoundly affect the religious life—was already affecting it. Angie felt more and more uncomfortable with the loss of traditions that had defined the order for more than a century.

"Didn't you ever think about marriage?" Corinne pressed, still watching Angie, who paced up and down. "I'm sorry, Sister, it's just that I've never really thought of you as a *woman* before, you know?"

That was understandable enough, Angie mused. For that matter, she didn't consider herself one, either. Her menstrual cycle was a nuisance and her breasts were useless appendages she struggled to contain and minimize.

"We heard you're going to be wearing dresses just like everyone else!"

Before Angie could hush the girl a second time, the class bell rang and the students, including Corinne, surged out the door. Weary after the last class of the day, Angie sat down at her desk and flipped absently through the homework papers she'd collected earlier.

"You busy?" Sister Kathleen asked as she stepped

into the classroom. Tiredly she leaned against the door-jamb. "Were you drilled about the new habits all day? I don't understand it. You'd think we were about to break a 130-year-old tradition or something," she teased.

Angie chuckled. "I got my share of questions."

"If it's this bad now, can you imagine what it'll be like once we actually start *wearing* the habits?"

The students were merely curious, whereas Angie was worried. In all the years she'd spent in the convent, every bit of individuality had been methodically stripped from her. And now...

"I'd better get over to the rectory," Sister Kathleen said with a noticeable lack of enthusiasm.

Angie encouraged her with a smile. The church books must be a disaster if Father Sanders had requested Sister Kathleen's help. Angie liked both parish priests. Father Sanders, who often celebrated Mass at the convent, was congenial in that bluff, hearty way, and from personal experience, she knew it was hard to refuse him. Father Doyle was younger, obviously idealistic and more serious in his manner. Angie suspected he never would have made such a request.

"I'll see you later," Sister Kathleen said as she left.

As Angie gathered up her papers and placed them inside her briefcase for the short walk back to the convent, she glanced out the window overlooking the parking lot below.

She immediately found Corinne, who was talking to a young man sitting in a car. Angie didn't have a clue what kind it was, but it appeared to be new. The driver's window was rolled down and his elbow rested on the edge. He took a puff on a cigarette and offered it to Corinne. Angie was relieved that the girl shook her head and declined. That relief was short-lived, however. A moment later, Corinne shrugged and reached for the smoke. Looking carefully around, the girl leaned close to the car and took a deep drag on the cigarette before handing it back to the young man.

Angie picked up her briefcase, and feeling mildly depressed, headed out of the classroom. Generally she walked directly to the convent, which was down the street from the school. However, at the last minute, she decided to take a more circuitous route and went around the back of the building, toward the parking lot. Corinne had probably left with her boyfriend already, but if not, maybe Angie's presence would remind her of their earlier discussion about smoking—and the fact that it was forbidden on school premises.

She was in luck, she saw. Corinne was half in and half out the car when Angie sauntered past.

"Good afternoon, Corinne," Angie said casually, as though she often took this out-of-the-way route.

"Sister Angelina?" Corinne's eyes went wide with shock—and then guilt.

Without waiting for an introduction, Angie nodded in the direction of the driver. The young man was quick to avert his gaze.

"This is Sister Angelina. She's my Health teacher... I tried to get into her Home Ec class, too, but I haven't heard if there's room yet. Everyone wants Sister to teach them how to cook a real Italian dinner."

"I got the paperwork this afternoon. I guess you'll be joining us, after all," Angie told her.

"I'm in?" Corinne nearly exploded with excitement.

"I don't believe I caught your name," Angie said to the boy. He was attractive enough, with dark hair and eyes, and he didn't seem particularly tough-looking. That reassured Angie.

"Oh, Sister," Corinne said eagerly, "this is Jimmy Durango, my steady."

"Do you attend school here?"

"No." Jimmy shrugged. "I'm not a Catholic." He said this as though he expected her to disapprove. He was studying her, though, and trying not to be obvious about it. Angie understood his curiosity; this was possibly the first time he'd ever seen a nun up close.

"Where do you go to school, Jimmy?" she asked.

"Garfield High in Osseo."

"Isn't that quite a ways from here?"

"He comes to town to see me," Corinne put in.

"And your parents have met Jimmy?"

"Oh, yes." She gave her boyfriend her hand and they entwined their fingers, expressions fervent. "Mom wants me to date a Catholic boy," Corinne said, "but I don't like any of the guys around here." She made it sound as though any boy at St. Peter's couldn't possibly meet her exacting requirements, although Angie distinctly remembered a young man who'd followed Corinne into class that first day.

Jimmy's eyes narrowed; he seemed to assume that Angie would agree with Corinne's parents and discourage the relationship. She wouldn't. That wasn't her job. Angie was a teacher, not a counselor. She liked Corinne a great deal; the girl had spunk and a sense of humor, and she didn't hesitate to question what she didn't understand. Those were traits Angie admired. She'd just have to hope that Corinne had enough common sense and self-respect not to do anything foolish.

"Nice to meet you, Jimmy."

"You, too...." He hesitated, apparently uncertain about how to address her.

"Oh, just call her Sister Angelina."

"Even if I'm not Catholic?" Jimmy asked.

Angie nodded. "Of course."

"You aren't going to change your name when you get your new habit, are you, Sister?" Corinne asked.

"No, I'll still be Sister Angelina Marcello."

"You have a last name, too?"

"Yes, Corinne, most of us do." Try as she might, Angie couldn't keep the amusement out of her voice.

"I know that," Corinne said with a sheepish grin. "It's just that I've never heard yours before. Wow, that is so cool! Sister Angelina Marcello," she repeated reverently.

Angie was about to turn away, but Corinne stopped her. "Jimmy sometimes has questions I can't answer about the Church. Would it be all right if I asked you, Sister?"

"Corinne." Jimmy's voice was low and full of warning.

"Jimmy?" Angie smiled at the young man, thinking he might be more comfortable asking her himself.

"It's nothing important," Jimmy insisted, looking pointedly at Corinne. His face had gone red, as though his girlfriend had betrayed a confidence. When he realized that Angie was studying him, he grew even more flustered. He turned abruptly and started the engine.

"You coming?" he asked Corinne.

She looked torn. "I don't know yet," she said, holding her books tightly.

The nuances of what was happening were beyond Angie. It was time for her to leave. "Once again, it was a pleasure to meet you, Jimmy."

"Thanks, Sister. You, too."

"Bye, Sister," Corinne said. She suddenly raced around the front of the vehicle and slid into the passenger side next to Jimmy.

Remembering years ago when she'd been a teenager herself, Angie stood back and watched as the two of them roared off. She liked Corinne's boyfriend, she decided.

{ 15 }

Sister Kathleen

"Sister, I was wondering when you'd arrive," Mrs. O'Malley said when Kathleen stepped into the rectory. A blast of chilly air followed her inside. "I have tea brewing if you'd care for a cup."

Kathleen didn't have time to spare. The housekeeper was an inveterate talker—like Mrs. O'Halloran back at the motherhouse—and if Kathleen took the time for tea, the woman might easily waste an hour with her chatter.

"Thanks for the offer, but I can't today. I'd better get to work," she said grimly. Kathleen had come to realize that her being at the rectory, accepting this task, was a sign of weakness—not the kindness and generosity she'd first thought. Well, it was in part, but she knew that generosity wasn't her primary motivation. She was eager for recognition, eager to leap in and save the day for the parish priest, eager for praise.

"I'll just go into the office," Kathleen said.

With a disappointed nod, the housekeeper returned to the kitchen.

The church office was quiet. After Father Sanders had given her the books and his receipts that first afternoon, Kathleen hadn't seen him again. Father Doyle wasn't around much, either. Even when she did happen upon them, they exchanged only the briefest of pleasantries.

In the back of her mind—and Kathleen was embarrassed to admit this—she'd assumed that once she was in the rectory she'd have the opportunity for interesting discussions about theology and various church matters with one or other of the priests. Friendly discussions, because no nun would dare question a priest or challenge him in any way. She reminded herself that even entertaining the notion that any priest would care to hear her philosophy was to assume a higher opinion of her own intelligence and position than warranted.

Taking her chair, Kathleen opened the ledger and penciled in the deposit from Sunday's collection. That was easy enough. The monthly bank statement had arrived, so Kathleen sorted the checks by number and marked them off as having cleared. This was the first statement she'd seen. Previous ones must have been destroyed or stored elsewhere; they hadn't been in the box with the other material.

The first problem she encountered was a discrepancy in the deposits. It wasn't much—twenty dollars in the first deposit and fifteen in the second. The ledger showed one thing, while the bank statement noted a lesser amount.

Kathleen set the statement aside until she had a moment to ask Father Sanders who, she assumed, had deposited the Sunday collections. Normally Mrs. Stafford would have seen to the task first thing Monday morning, but she'd been on vacation since mid-August, when Father Sanders had assumed her duties.

Kathleen worked diligently for the next hour, reconciling the accounts, but she found one small discrepancy after another. It was as though whoever was making the deposits had skimmed a bill or two off the top each time. She couldn't imagine Father Sanders doing such a thing, but he was the one who made the deposits. It didn't make sense. She also discovered that receipts for rectory expenses didn't tally with amounts deducted in the ledger.

The bell above the rectory door chimed and she glanced up just as Father Doyle strolled down the hallway toward the kitchen. He paused when he noticed Kathleen.

"Good afternoon, Sister. Beautiful day, isn't it?"

Kathleen smiled in agreement. She did enjoy these lovely autumn afternoons, when the air was crisp with intimations of winter. They reminded her of Boston and the big leaves falling from oak trees on the street outside her family home.

"Father," she said, stopping him before he disappeared. "Do you happen to know where Father Sanders is?" If she could have ten minutes of his time, she might be able to clear up these discrepancies. She was certain he'd have a logical explanation.

"Father is out for the rest of the day. Can I help?" he asked, moving into the office.

"No, no... I have a few questions I need answered, but they can wait for another day."

"You're sure I can't be of assistance?"

She appreciated his willingness but she needed the older priest. "No, unfortunately, I have to discuss this with Father Sanders."

Father Doyle shrugged, then said slowly, "I'll ask him to be available for you the next time you're here."

"Thank you." Kathleen glanced up and saw that Father Doyle was frowning. She'd never really looked at him before. Or rather, had never looked beyond his collar. Although he bore a solid Irish name, his facial features betrayed none of the typical signs of being from Ireland. He might be one of the so-called Black Irish, she decided. It was said that Spaniards had settled in Ireland at the time of the Armada, which accounted for the blue-eyed, dark-haired men.

Loud jovial singing could be heard coming from the kitchen. "That must be Father Sanders now," Kathleen said. She wanted her questions answered as quickly as possible. Otherwise she might be held up for several days.

"I'll check and see." Father Doyle hurried toward the kitchen and left the door between the rectory and the private dining room open in his rush. The singing became louder and more boisterous.

Father Sanders joined her a moment later, obviously in an expansive mood. "Good day to you, Sister Kathleen."

"Good afternoon, Father."

"I understand you have a question for me?"

"I do." As simply as possible, she explained the differences between what the bank statement had noted for the deposit and the amount he'd entered in the ledger.

"I must've written the deposit amount incorrectly," the priest said. "Like I explained earlier, this accounting business is beyond me. Just change what you need to so it comes out right."

His advice shocked her. "Father! I can't do that."

"You can if I say so."

"But…but what will Mrs. Stafford think when she returns?"

Father sighed sharply, and she caught a whiff of mint on his breath. "She won't think a thing of it, seeing I was the one who made the mistake. Mrs. Stafford makes allowances for my many flaws and you should, too."

"Yes, Father." He was growing impatient with her, but Kathleen hesitated to alter the books simply because Father told her to. While it wasn't a lot of money, she had no moral or legal right to do that.

"Anything else?"

Kathleen hesitated.

"I don't have all day, Sister," Father said.

Kathleen felt properly chastised. "Just one more thing," she said, drawing in a deep breath. She could feel the embarrassment redden her face. "I'm afraid the receipts you gave me for expenses don't reconcile with—"

"Reconcile?" Father's voice was too loud. "Speak English. How am I supposed to know what that means?"

"I… I—"

"Father." The younger priest appeared, almost as though he'd been waiting in the wings. "Perhaps it would be better if you discussed this later."

"Yes, yes, it would," Father Sanders mumbled, suddenly deflated. He stared down at the floor in apparent confusion.

"I believe Mrs. O'Malley has coffee for you, Father."

"Coffee?" Father Sanders repeated with a scowl. Father Doyle artfully steered the older priest back toward the kitchen. He glanced over his shoulder at Kathleen. Feeling his gaze, she looked up and read the apology in his eyes.

It was then that she knew. At that moment she recognized what should have been obvious from the first. Father Sanders was drunk. It'd been years since she'd seen anyone in that condition. And yet, now that she was aware of it, she wondered how she could have missed all the signs, from the mouthwash or peppermints masking his breath to the too-careful enunciation and mood swings.

Just as she was clearing off the desk, Father Doyle returned. He hesitated, evidently unsure of what to say.

When he finally did speak, his voice was regretful. "In the future it might be better if you came to me with your questions, Sister."

"Perhaps you're right." Father Doyle preferred to handle the situation on his own—preferred not to involve her—which was understandable, she supposed. Understandable and very kind. What he probably didn't realize was that she was already embroiled in Father Sanders's troubles.

Father Doyle was the most honest and ethical man she'd ever known and if he wanted to protect Father Sanders, then she could only agree.

"As Father said, he doesn't have a head for numbers."

Kathleen offered him a weak smile. "So it seems," she murmured.

Father Doyle was studying her, as if to gauge how much she'd discerned from the other priest's behavior. She considered explaining that she'd been around a tavern most of her growing-up years, but Father Sanders's drinking was a subject that needed to be handled with discretion.

Singing exploded from the kitchen again, loud and badly off-key.

Father Doyle's gaze sought hers.

Kathleen recognized the song from her uncle's pub. "My uncle used to sing that," she said in a whisper.

"Your uncle?"

They were tiptoeing around each other, neither wanting to say what was obvious. "He's…a favorite uncle of mine. My father works at the pub my uncle owns. Uncle Patrick doesn't have a head for business, either, and so my dad helps tend the bar and he does the books."

Father Doyle's relief was unmistakable. "Father Sanders is a good priest," he said seriously. "He has his struggles, as we all do, and I'm sure he'll…improve."

Kathleen was relieved, too. Father Doyle was taking care of the situation. She needn't worry. "I'm sure he will."

The younger priest grinned. "So it appears your uncle Patrick and Father Sanders share a certain weakness for…numbers."

Kathleen grinned back. She could keep a secret and she wanted Father Doyle to know that. As far as she was concerned, the fact that Father Sanders liked to drink would stay between the two of them.

{ 16 }

Sister Angelina

"What did you think of Jimmy?" Corinne excitedly asked Angie the following Monday when she arrived for her first Home Economics class. It was the twenty-fifth, and the last week of September.

"He seems very nice," Angie said, busy setting out all the ingredients for the recipe her class would be working on.

"Are we cooking today?" Corinne asked, glancing at the kitchen countertop, laden with plum tomatoes, olive oil, onions, garlic, parsley and fresh basil.

"We are. I'm going to teach you how to make a proper red sauce."

"Red sauce?" Corinne wrinkled her face as though she'd never heard of it before.

"Better known as spaghetti sauce here in the States," Angie qualified.

"Oh, good," Corinne said as the other class members slowly filed into the room. "When I told him about the class, Jimmy said he couldn't wait to have me cook for him. Mom and I are going to Italy this summer. I want to learn as much about Italian food as I can." She looked over her shoulder to see who'd entered the room before lowering her voice. "Jimmy says Italian women are hot-blooded."

"Hot-blooded," Angie repeated, making sure Corinne heard the displeasure in her voice.

"Not you, Sister," Corinne said quickly with a horrified look.

"I should hope not," Angie said with a small irrepressible laugh. Hot-blooded, indeed!

"Sorry, Sister. It's just that…well, Jimmy's special and I want to be the perfect wife for him."

Angie struggled to keep her voice calm. "You two don't need to think about marriage for a long time."

"Uh-uh." She shook her head. "I'm going to marry Jimmy."

"And how does Jimmy plan to support you?"

Corinne's face hardened. "He has a part-time job at the lumberyard and he thinks pretty soon they'll take him on full-time."

"But what about school?" Angie certainly hoped Corinne's young man hadn't dropped out of school. That was a sure way to mess up his future and possibly Corinne's.

"He didn't drop out, Sister, if that's what you're worried about."

"No," Morgan Gentry said, joining Corinne and Angie, "he got expelled. A week ago."

Corinne glared at her best friend. "That wasn't Jimmy's fault and you know it."

"I don't know any such thing and if your mother finds out you saw Jimmy again, you'll be grounded until graduation."

Furious now, Corinne whirled around to confront her.

Just then, thankfully, the class bell rang and cut off their disagreement before it could develop into a full-blown fight.

Home Economics went faster than any of Angie's other classes. It was a subject she held dear, especially the food and cooking sections. Her father had taught her well, and she'd become an inventive and confident cook.

The one drawback of teaching these classes was the memories they stirred of her youth. She'd spent so many hours with her father at his restaurant. *Her* restaurant, she mused sadly. It would've been hers if she hadn't entered the convent. In some ways Angie wished she could be two women. She wanted to serve God; she also wanted to earn her earthly father's love and praise by giving Angelina's the same passion and dedication he had all these years.

"Sister?" Morgan looked at her, face slightly tilted. "I was asking about the red pepper flakes. Aren't they hot?"

"Very, so they should be used sparingly."

"Simmered in the olive oil?"

"Yes."

Another hand shot into the air. "Does it have to be extra-virgin olive oil?"

The girls giggled as if this were a smutty joke.

"The term extra-virgin signifies the first run of the press. And no, it isn't necessary." It would be a sin to use anything else, but only in her father's kitchen. In a high school class, where every penny was carefully considered, less costly oil would do. "You can use any good oil." She nearly choked on the words. "But olive oil *is* preferable."

"Fresh parsley?" One of the other girls threw out the question, taking notes as she did.

"Fresh," Angie repeated. "Always fresh whenever possible. Use dried only if you have no choice."

Her students leaned over their notebooks and scribbled furiously. This recipe was the most popular of all the ones she'd taught over the years.

"Why do you call it red sauce instead of spaghetti sauce?"

"Because it's used on more than pasta."

Her students glanced quizzically at one another. "Like what?" Corinne asked.

"Like pork roast or spread over top of a meat loaf. My family had at least a dozen dishes that required red sauce. A good Italian cook will make up a large batch on Saturday."

"Every week?"

"Without fail," Angie said. "And the sauce is used for the next few days." She tried to think of a comparison. "It's a little like hot sauce. Some people put Tabasco on their fried eggs, right?"

"Maybe some people, but not me," Morgan said, shaking her head.

"Well, ketchup then." Angie shuddered.

"Red sauce isn't a condiment, is it, Sister?"

"Not exactly…" The bell rang and her class moaned with disappointment.

Lunch period was next and the girls hurried out. All except Corinne. She walked over to Angie's desk. "I don't want you thinking the wrong things about Jimmy," she said.

"It isn't my place to judge another." Angie gathered up her books.

"I know, but Morgan made him sound bad."

Angie hesitated. "Is it true that Jimmy was expelled?"

Corinne frowned and nodded reluctantly. "But it's not like it sounds. He wasn't the one at fault, but Garfield's principal has it in for him and…" She let her voice fade. "I love him, Sister. I really, really love him."

Angie gave the girl her full attention. "What do your parents think of him?"

Again Corinne looked uncomfortable. "My dad doesn't like him, and my mom thought he was all right until he got expelled. Now they don't want me to see him anymore."

That explained a great deal.

"But you're continuing to see him?"

"Only sometimes. We tried to stay away from each other, but it's no good. We were meant to be together." Her face held that dreamy look of young love. "When you saw us the other day, it'd been more than a week since we talked and it just wasn't any good, Sister. Not for Jimmy and not for me."

"Is it good to meet behind your parents' backs?"

"No," Corinne agreed quickly enough. "We hate it. Jimmy's going to talk to my dad, face-to-face. He said it's the way a man does things."

Angie's estimation of Jimmy went up a notch. "Good. And he's asking you questions about the Church?"

Corinne looked at the floor. "Some." She looked back at Angie, smiling widely. "We went to Mass together last Sunday."

No doubt without her parents' knowledge. If they *had* known, they would've disapproved.

"I wish Morgan hadn't said anything," Corinne said as she walked out of the room. "I hate it when people hear something about another person and then judge that person without even knowing the details. It's so unfair."

"Yes, it is," Angie agreed. "But unfortunately that's the way it is in life." If Jimmy didn't return to school for his diploma, he'd carry that stigma wherever he went.

"He was talking about going into the Marines, but they said they wouldn't take him until he graduated." She continued to hug her books.

Morgan was waiting for Corinne at the end of the hall. "Gotta run. See you later, Sister."

Angie smiled as the girl ran down the hall. Parenting must be an extremely difficult task—much more so than teaching, she decided. She prayed God would grant Corinne's parents wisdom in dealing with their daughter.

{17}

Sister Joanna

Joanna was all aquiver. That was how she'd describe her feelings, although "quiver" was certainly an old-fashioned word. She'd come across it in an ancient novel she'd found in the convent library, the kind written by an "authoress" a century ago. Nevertheless, *aquiver* summed up her emotions perfectly. Because this was the first day of her modified habit with its short veil. Her naturally blond hair was artfully styled around it.

The nuns were required to make the modifications to their own habits. The sewing machines at the convent had been humming all weekend. Joanna had never seen such chaos. It was crazy and funny and exciting in ways that baffled her.

Her hair. She'd spent an inordinate amount of time fussing with it, positive that any style she wore would be ridiculously outdated. Joanna wasn't alone in that; many of the nuns had complained about having to find time for personal grooming in their rigid schedules.

The shorter skirts and veils were only the beginning of what was going to be a difficult adjustment for them all.

As she stepped on to the city bus that would drop her outside the hospital, Joanna felt breathless, full of mixed emotions. She couldn't help wondering if Dr. Murray would comment on the change in her dress. Perhaps he wouldn't notice.

She shouldn't be thinking about him. It was a matter of discipline. A matter of obedience. She had no right, no possible excuse, to allow a man to linger in her thoughts. It was flirting with danger, and Joanna knew that as well as she knew her own name.

She hurried into St. Elizabeth's, and as she'd feared, her appearance on the third floor attracted immediate attention. It seemed that everyone, right down to the maintenance man, turned to stare at her. This was decidedly unnerving.

"Sister?" Lois Jensen, a lay nurse, blurted out when Joanna awkwardly approached the station. All of a sudden she didn't know what to do with her arms and tucked them behind her.

"You look…" Lois was obviously at a loss for words.

"Different?" Joanna supplied, hoping to ease the other woman's discomfort—and her own.

"Yes! Different."

"Let me have a look," Julie Jones, a hospital volunteer, said eagerly. She came around the front of the nurses' station to get a better view.

Julie took Joanna by the shoulders and turned her slowly around, studying her from head to toe.

"You two are embarrassing me," Joanna said, feeling herself blush.

"So this is the new habit we've heard so much about," Julie said. "It's quite a change, isn't it?"

Flustered, Joanna nodded. Thinking it would help if she immediately got to her work, she moved toward the tray of prescriptions to be dispensed to her patients.

"Come and look, Dr. Murray," Julie called.

Joanna wanted to grind her teeth in frustration. The last person she wanted to see right now—or be seen by—was Dr. Murray. She'd hoped to avoid encountering him until the unfamiliarity of this new habit had worn off. Clearly, that was not to be.

"Well, well," the physician said, joining the small group of onlookers. He crossed his arms and gave her a thorough inspection. "What have we here?"

"Sister has legs," Lois said.

"Good ones, too," the doctor added appreciatively.

"Would you kindly stop," Joanna pleaded.

"And hair," Julie felt obliged to point out. "I didn't know you were a blonde, Sister."

Joanna's hand involuntarily went to the side of her head. "You three might have time to waste, but I don't." Eager to escape, she reached for the tray and headed down the corridor.

Dr. Murray caught up with her ten minutes later, when she entered the room of one of his patients. Mr. Rolfson had undergone extensive cancer surgery. No one needed to explain to Joanna that his time on earth was limited. He was receiving massive doses of medication and was in a lot of pain. He was asleep when she walked in.

Dr. Murray glanced up. "Let him sleep," he instructed.

She nodded and was about to turn away when he stopped her. "I didn't mean to embarrass you earlier."

"You didn't," she said wryly. "Lois and Julie already took care of that."

"You look very nice." His gaze held hers a moment longer than necessary.

Joanna immediately dropped her eyes. The silence that followed was rife with a tension she didn't understand, but she resisted looking up. It wasn't hard to guess what he was thinking.

"Why do you do that?" he asked, sounding irritated with her.

"Do what?"

"Refuse to look at me."

"It isn't anything personal," she said quickly. "Actually it's part of our religious training."

"Why?"

With the woman's movement in full swing, the concept of "custody of the eyes" must sound hopelessly outdated. Nonetheless, she explained as simply as she could.

He listened and then in a lower voice said, "I don't like it."

She didn't respond.

"It isn't you," he added.

She couldn't keep from smiling. "Unfortunately, Fionnuala Wheaton didn't clear the practice with you when she founded St. Bridget's Sisters of the Assumption."

"You aren't the meek and mild kind of woman."

"You don't know me," she countered, impatient with him now. She wasn't sure why they were both angry, but it was difficult not to raise her voice. Dr. Murray apparently had no such qualms.

Joanna looked over at the sleeping patient. He seemed oblivious to their conversation, but it distressed her that their words might be invading his rest. "I don't think this is the place for a…a personal discussion."

"You're right. We'll continue in the hall." He reattached the clipboard to the foot of Mr. Rolfson's bed and moved out of the room, then waited for Joanna to follow.

With dread, she joined him. "This conversation is unnecessary."

"I disagree." He raised his eyebrows. "You're a fraud, Sister."

"I beg your pardon?" How dared he say such a thing to her! She glared up at him, unable to hide her outrage.

Delighted, he laughed and clapped his hands. "There," he said, nodding with satisfaction. "What about this 'custody of the eyes' business now?"

"I am allowed feelings." For the most part, however, displays of emotion must be controlled. Dr. Murray seemed to enjoy exposing her failings and weaknesses.

"I am not a fraud," she said, struggling to hide the hurt his words had inflicted.

"Do you know why I asked that you be assigned to my patients?" he asked abruptly.

She did know. "I was a compromise so you could avoid encouraging any of the single nurses."

"Wrong. I asked for you because I saw you argue with Dr. Nelson. You stood up to that pompous jackass and wouldn't let him discharge a patient. You were right. The woman wasn't anywhere close to ready for discharge. You were fearless and unwavering, and eventually he backed down. All it took was someone with enough courage to confront a man who ranks himself right up there with God Almighty."

Joanna recalled her impassioned plea for Mrs. Brock in vivid detail. Dr. Nelson was indeed a jackass, but unfortunately he had no idea how others viewed him. She'd risked his anger that day, but considered it a risk worth taking. Perhaps it was her religious status that

had made him listen and eventually concede. Whatever the reason, Joanna was grateful on behalf of the
older woman.

"And where was 'custody of the eyes' *that* day?" Dr.
Murray asked.

"I…" Joanna bit down on her lower lip, afraid of what
he might read in her if she allowed him to meet her eyes.

"My point exactly," he added, his voice softer now. "I
knew then that you were the one who should be caring
for my patients. Someone who's both fearless and gentle. It didn't have anything to do with diplomacy toward
the other nurses. I simply wanted you on my team."

"And I want you on mine," she murmured.

He frowned. "What do you mean?"

"Dr. Murray, it's time you started attending Mass
again." As a lapsed Catholic, he'd turned his back on
God and Joanna couldn't remain silent any longer.

His short, derisive laugh didn't really surprise her.
"Are you trying to save me, Sister?"

"I'm looking out for the care of your eternal soul."
She was serious and she hoped he saw her determina-
tion.

Dr. Murray shook his head. "Like I told you, I gave
up on the Church a long time ago. I appreciate your
concern, but this ploy of yours isn't going to work."

"What ploy?"

A slow and far-too-sexy smile slid into place. "I
know what you're doing."

It was her turn to ask, "What do you mean? I'm doing
exactly what I told you."

"You're diverting attention away from yourself by
focusing on me and my relationship with the Church. It
isn't going to work. We were discussing *you.*"

Joanna was bored with that subject. She had her own

rounds to perform and a long list of tasks that would consume the next eight hours. She couldn't allow herself to be distracted from what was important—her work.

"I can't," she insisted. "I have duties, the same as you do."

He raised his hands as though in surrender. "All right, all right. Go, but we aren't finished."

She retreated two steps, walking backward. "Yes, Doctor, we are. And don't think I've given up on getting you back to church. I'll be praying for you."

He chuckled and rolled his eyes. "You go right ahead. Oh, and Sister—" that sexy grin was back "—I like the changes in your habit."

Joanna self-consciously glanced down at her shorter skirt and absently smoothed her hand along her side.

"It's long overdue."

She nodded, agreeing with him, but the order hadn't asked her opinion and she hadn't been foolish enough to offer it.

"What a sin," Dr. Murray muttered.

"A sin?"

"Keeping those legs of yours hidden all these years." Then he whirled around without another word and walked resolutely away.

Despite her best efforts, Joanna experienced a warm glow from his compliment. Just as she was getting ready to leave for the day, Gina Novak approached the nurses' station. Gina was young and pretty and possessed a quick wit and easy laugh. Joanna liked her.

"Good afternoon, Sister," Gina said, pulling out a chair and sitting down next to Joanna. She gave her the once-over just as everyone else had that day. "So, how do you like the new habit?"

"Oh, I'm getting used to it," Joanna said, hoping to bring the conversation to a quick close.

Gina seemed to accept her remark. She nodded, then asked, "Did you hear about my date last night?"

Joanna finished making a notation. "No. Who's the lucky guy?"

"Dr. Murray." She sighed as she said it.

"Our Dr. Murray?" Joanna's stomach twisted and a chill raced down her arms.

"The one and only. I think he's *wonderful*." Gina gave a dreamy smile. "I've wanted to go out with him for ages and ages. I dropped subtle hints, but he didn't seem to notice, and then out of the blue he asked me out."

"Apparently he got your message." Joanna didn't imagine it had been a subtle one, either, and immediately chastised herself for unkind thoughts.

"I'd just about given up," Gina continued.

"I hope you had a good time." God would forgive her for the lie.

"We did."

"Where did he take you?" Joanna hoped she didn't sound inappropriately curious.

Gina rolled her chair back from the desk. "To dinner and a movie. He's very interesting, you know?"

"Will you be seeing him again?" she asked.

Gina shrugged. "I hope so. He hasn't asked me yet, which is fine. Since we sometimes work together, it'd probably be best if we played down our relationship."

"I think that might be a good idea," Joanna said, trying hard to sound unaffected by the news.

"I will tell you this, Sister," Gina said, lowering her voice. "He's a great kisser."

The thought of Gina and Tim Murray kissing fixed

itself in her mind. Dear heaven, she was *jealous*. She longed to be the one he was holding, the one he was kissing. This was all wrong, but that knowledge did little to settle her stomach and even less to settle her heart.

{ 18 }

Sister Kathleen

On her way to the rectory the following week, Kathleen walked through the elementary school playground during the last recess of the day. Laughter and shouts filled the air as the first-through-sixth-graders scrambled about. The children, dressed in their school uniforms, took eager advantage of their fifteen minutes of freedom. There was a lively dodgeball game going on, some of the girls were jumping rope, while others played hopscotch on the pavement. It reminded her of her own early years at St. Boniface, the grade school where she'd first been introduced to teaching nuns.

Just then a stray ball rolled in Kathleen's direction. "Sister, Sister, throw me the ball."

"No, me! Sister, throw it to me!"

Kathleen lifted the ball over her head and lobbed it toward the group. The children loved to see her join in, and she was much freer to do so in the shortened skirt. She suspected the kids purposely sent the ball in her direction for the pleasure of seeing her react. The ball landed halfway between the two boys, and both raced after it.

"Not a bad shot for a nun," Father Doyle commented as he walked down the hill from the church rectory. The wind ruffled his dark hair.

The instant the children saw Father Doyle, they abandoned their game and dashed toward him. He laughed into the October sunshine and good-naturedly caught a ball one of the boys threw him. He feinted, pretending to throw it back, then spun around and tossed it at another boy behind him.

Kathleen smiled, watching him. The children were thrilled by his attention and begged him to play for "just one more minute."

It'd been a week since their talk. A week since she'd learned the carefully hidden truth about Father Sanders. Both priests had been absent from the rectory when she'd arrived Monday afternoon; Kathleen had done what work she could and left feeling thwarted. She could only do so much when a number of serious questions remained unanswered. Handling the church's accounts was difficult enough without this additional complication. She'd considered mentioning Father Sanders's weakness to Sister Eloise but feared that might only make things worse. Sister had been against her working on the church books as it was. No—much better to leave the matter in the capable hands of Father Doyle.

Suddenly in no rush to get to the rectory, Kathleen held one end of a jump rope and turned while the eight- and nine-year-old girls leapt in and chanted the same playground songs that had been part of her own childhood.

On the mountain stands a lady
– Who she is I do not know
Not last night, but the night before
Twenty-four robbers came knocking at my door

The rope slapped against the pavement as the girls jumped in and out. Kathleen recalled how she and her sister had loved to jump rope at this age. Now Maureen was a divorced mother of three and working two jobs to make ends meet. She rarely wrote and when Kathleen had visited Boston the previous summer it seemed that the sister who'd once been her closest friend was a stranger.

All too soon the bell rang, and the children were gone. Kathleen found herself on the playground alone with Father Doyle. Seeing the hopscotch squares, she couldn't resist and tossed her marker into the center, then hopped through the numbered squares.

"Way to go, Sister," the priest called out. "Not only are you a whiz with numbers, but you're a master at childhood games."

Kathleen laughed. "I can see you're easily impressed."

"Oh, not really. But I do think kids can show you how to enjoy the moment."

"I do, too." Kathleen tucked her hands inside her sweater pockets. Speaking of moments, she should be at the rectory by now, but she dreaded another afternoon of trying to understand a situation she couldn't explain.

"Are you working today?" He nodded toward the rectory.

"Yes." Kathleen realized her reluctance must be obvious.

"More problems?" His question was tentative, as

though he was afraid of the answer or perhaps already knew it.

The bank deposit was off again. Father Sanders had made the deposit and then forgotten to enter it in the ledger, or so he claimed. He'd left her a note apologizing and promising to do better.

Kathleen had thought it would be a simple matter of phoning the bank and getting the information she needed. She'd done that and the bank had been completely accommodating. How she wished it had ended there, but once again the deposit was short.

The head ushers had tallied the collection, taking the weekly donations from the envelopes. Part of her duty was to record donation and envelope numbers for income tax purposes. The ushers had given the weekly donations to Father Sanders to deposit—only the amount deposited was a hundred dollars short of what had been counted. This was the largest discrepancy yet, and she didn't know how to handle it. She explained the situation to Father Doyle. "What should I do?" she asked, hoping he could provide a solution.

Father Doyle's expression was sad. "I'll speak to Father Sanders and suggest I make the deposits from here on out."

That might solve one problem, but it didn't help Kathleen with the discrepancy in the account books.

But even knowing what she did about Father Sanders, she couldn't help liking him. It was the same with her uncle Patrick. Both were generous, happy-go-lucky men who were often a pleasure to be around. Especially when they were sober…

"Is he worse?" she whispered, although no one could possibly overhear.

Father shook his head. "No." But he sounded unsure.

"Have you spoken to Mrs. O'Malley?" Surely the housekeeper knew, although she, like Father Doyle, seemed bent on silence. Kathleen understood it, but she wasn't convinced secrecy was the best approach. However, she couldn't think of any other.

"Mrs. O'Malley and I have talked," Father Doyle admitted. "Her husband, God rest his soul, was an alcoholic and I'm afraid she's grown accustomed to handling Father Sanders's...moods."

Kathleen swallowed hard and wondered if the older woman had been buying alcohol for the priest. She was a gentle soul who strived to please, and if she'd been caught in that same trap in her marriage—well, there was no telling what she'd do. It wasn't inconceivable that she was supplying Father Sanders; Kathleen couldn't imagine where else he was getting the booze.

As far as she knew, Father Sanders didn't drink outside his room in the rectory. If he went to liquor stores or bars, people in the community would recognize him. She was beginning to feel that this situation couldn't remain hidden much longer.

"The bishop knows," Father Doyle said, walking with his hands clasped behind his back.

"Bishop Schmidt?" Kathleen had been sure the parish was destined for trouble if word of Father Sanders's weakness leaked out, and to the bishop of all people. But if he knew...

"I believe that's the reason the bishop assigned me to St. Peter's." Their steps slowed as the rectory came into view. "I shouldn't be talking to you about this, Sister."

But there obviously wasn't anyone else he could talk to.

"I feel I've failed Bishop Schmidt."

"Failed him?" This made no sense to Kathleen.

"Father Sanders is in spiritual trouble. I was assigned to St. Peter's to steer him away from alcohol and back to God, and I've fallen short of accomplishing my task."

Father Doyle was a good priest, devout and dedicated to God. Kathleen understood why the bishop had given him this assignment. He was a man of prayer, and if anyone could influence Father Sanders, it would be Father Doyle. But that was a lot of responsibility to place on one priest's shoulders, Kathleen mused. Was it really fair?

"I don't think you can blame yourself," she said, looking down at her feet, wishing she knew what to say.

"I can't—"

Father Doyle's words were cut off in midsentence as a car careened around the corner with such speed that for a few seconds it balanced precariously on two wheels. Kathleen gasped, horrified, as the vehicle narrowly missed two parked cars before it fell back onto four tires again. The car landed with such force that it actually seemed to bounce.

Kathleen released a shaky breath, thinking the worst was over, but she was wrong. As though momentarily stunned, the blue Dodge sat in the middle of the street, then turned and aimed for the driveway leading to the garage behind the rectory.

"It's Father Sanders."

Kathleen couldn't believe her eyes as the priest steered the car into the rectory driveway. Unfortunately he missed the driveway and drove across the lawn, leaving deep tire tracks. The car quickly disappeared behind the priests' residence.

Father Doyle raced toward the rectory. He outdistanced Kathleen, but she caught up with him at the car. Father Doyle had opened the driver's side door and had apparently gotten the keys out of the ignition and away from the older priest.

It terrified her to think of Father Sanders driving drunk—to think of what could have happened, what *might* have happened.

While Father Doyle assisted the other man from the vehicle, she hurriedly inspected the car for signs of an accident or a hit-and-run. She thought her heart was going to roar straight out of her chest, it was beating so fast. Fortunately, there was no sign of any impact.

"I need help," Father Doyle shouted, struggling to keep the other priest upright with one arm around his waist. Father Sanders, who outweighed Father Doyle by a good fifty pounds, was leaning heavily against him. Drunk, he seemed incapable of walking.

Kathleen hurriedly wrapped her arm around him from the other side, and using her shoulder for leverage, offered him as much support as she could.

"Mrs. O'Malley, put on coffee," Father Doyle shouted as they carefully made their way up the back steps. At the top, Father Sanders turned to get a look at his rescuers. Kathleen gasped as he nearly sent all three of them crashing backward. She was convinced the angels must have prevented the fall, because there was no other explanation.

"Mrs. O'Malley's…gone for the day." Father Sanders badly slurred his words.

"Gone?"

He laughed as though this had been a brilliant idea. "I gave her the day off."

Kathleen could guess why. "I'll make the coffee," she said, once they were safely inside and away from prying eyes.

The younger priest pulled out a chair at the kitchen

table and with Kathleen's help managed to lower Father Sanders onto it.

Once he was settled, Kathleen started opening and closing cupboards until she located the coffee grounds. In a few minutes she had a pot brewing. No one spoke and the silence seemed to expand in the large kitchen.

When the coffee was ready, Kathleen poured Father Sanders his first mug. She set it in front of him. He stared at it as if he didn't know what to do with it. His eyes were rheumy, with deep pockets beneath. He looked lost and sad and frightened.

"I'm so sorry," he whispered brokenly after he'd finished the coffee. He couldn't look at Kathleen as she refilled the mug.

"I know, Father." And she did. When her uncle Patrick gave in to his weakness for drink, he was regretful and melancholy for long days afterward.

"Did you hurt anyone?" Father Doyle asked.

Silence returned as Kathleen and Father Doyle awaited his reply.

Father Sanders buried his face in his hands. "Just me." He wept openly into his palms. "Forgive me, forgive me," he pleaded.

Father Doyle was suspiciously silent.

"It won't happen again," Father Sanders vowed. Lowering his hands, the older priest lifted his head and large tears rolled unrestrained down his cheeks. "Never again. I swear it, never again. I've hit rock bottom, and God as my witness, I don't want to go back there."

"You've said this before," Father Doyle told him.

"I know," the older priest sobbed piteously. "I do. I'll never touch another drop. This time I'm serious. I swear by everything holy that I'll never drink again."

Father Doyle's eyes met Kathleen's and she could

tell that he badly wanted to believe the priest. "This is the end," he said finally.

"The end. Yes. I'm sorry. I'm sorry." Then Father Sanders started to weep in earnest.

Standing with her back against the counter, Kathleen found herself fighting tears. This was hard, so hard. Father Doyle had a terrible decision to make. He should probably bring the matter to Bishop Schmidt; Father Sanders's drinking today—and his subsequent behavior—was out of control. But the older priest sounded sincere and repentant. And they both liked him, *wanted* him to succeed.

She was glad she wasn't the one making the decision.

{ 19 }

Sister Angelina

Thursday night after school, Angie wrote her father a long newsy letter, telling him about the new habits. Ever since her Health class had learned she was Italian, Angie's head had been full of childhood memories. In the convent you weren't Italian or French or American; nationality was ignored. All nuns were considered children of God who'd come to dedicate their lives to His service.

As she wrote, Angie brooded on what had happened this afternoon. Her Health class had gone poorly. The discussion had gotten out of hand and Angie blamed herself for the resulting chaos as she'd lost control of the class.

She sat at the table and stared down at the letter, realizing that she'd always turned to her father when she was bothered by something. It was a childhood habit. He rarely answered her letters, though. He had a good command of the English language, but his writing skills were poor and it embarrassed him that he had such trouble spelling.

Even though he didn't write, she felt his love. He'd never recovered from the disappointment of losing her to God. He discounted her happiness and still insisted that she'd made a mistake in entering the convent. She wondered if he worked as many hours at the restaurant as he had while she was growing up and what he thought of all this election fuss. It seemed to her Nixon would surely beat McGovern, but she was no judge of that. The nuns always voted Democrat.

"You're looking thoughtful, Sister," Joanna said, sitting in the chair across from her. She pulled out her cross-stitch—of a stylized sailboat—and carefully worked on one of the sails. It was a Christmas gift for her brother and his wife, she'd told Angie.

Angie set her fountain pen aside. She wasn't aware that she was so transparent. "We discussed birth control in class this afternoon. I did a poor job of explaining the Church's position." In retrospect, she wished she'd invited Sister Joanna to come as a guest speaker. As a nurse, Joanna would have presented the information in a manner that was far more enlightening than her own awkward approach.

Sister Joanna's gaze briefly left the fabric. "That's not a subject I'd want to discuss with teenagers, especially these days."

So much for that idea! The more she thought about this afternoon, the worse Angie felt. If she had more knowledge of male-female relationships, more experience, it would help, but she'd dated so little and when it came to sex she knew even less.

"When I was a teenager, sex was something that

simply wasn't discussed," Sister Joanna said, concentrating on her cross-stitch.

"I feel so inadequate talking to my students about anything having to do with it," Angie murmured. "But it isn't like I can avoid talking about birth control when we're ordered to discuss it." Sister Superior was adamant that all Health classes hear what the Church had to say on the controversial subject. Corinne's insistence on answers complicated everything; she wanted to know what other forms of birth control worked if the pill was forbidden. Angie didn't feel she should even mention the rhythm method, the form of birth control acceptable to the Church, to teenagers who shouldn't be engaging in sex in the first place.

"The girls giving birth seem to be getting younger and younger, too." Sister Joanna put down her cross-stitch project and leaned back in her chair. "Dr. Murray assisted Dr. Nelson with a cesarean on a fifteen-year-old who was having twins. At fifteen! It's hard to believe a fourteen-year-old girl would be sexually active."

At that age, Angie was listening to records and the radio and laughing on the phone with her girlfriends. The thought of having sex so young—and dealing with diapers and bottles—was beyond the scope of her imagination.

"What did you tell your class?" Sister Joanna asked.

"Well…" Angie mulled over the question. "I said the same things Sister told us."

"That the pill is against God and nature?"

Angie nodded. "I thought it was important my students understand that the medical community doesn't know what effect the pill will have on a woman twenty years down the road."

"Personally I think what the Church is most worried about is that the pill will promote promiscuity."

Angie looked around to make sure no one was listening. "I think a few of the girls might already be... active with their boyfriends." She had her suspicions, especially concerning Corinne.

"That wouldn't surprise me."

"It does me," Angie cried. "They're so young, and they have their whole lives ahead of them."

"Don't you remember this age?" Sister Joanna asked. "Everything was so urgent. So crucial. I was constantly afraid that life was going to pass me by. My biggest fear was that I wasn't going to experience any of it."

Angie shook her head. "I didn't feel that way. My father and I were close. I knew that no matter what happened, he'd be there for me." A childhood friend who lived on the same street came to mind. Maria Croce. Angie hadn't thought about Maria in years. Her friend was constantly afraid her house would catch fire. There'd been a fire down the block and although the family escaped, the dog had died. From that point forward, Maria lived in constant fear of a house fire. Angie never gave the possibility a second thought because she knew nothing would prevent her father from rescuing her. He would walk through flames to save her, and she knew it. With that kind of love and security, Angie hadn't felt the same sense of urgency about life that Joanna had.

"Frankly, my class didn't *want* to hear the Church's opinion on birth control," Angie continued, thinking back.

Corinne was the worst offender; in fact, she had openly scoffed. "One girl," Angie murmured, "said she didn't think it was any of the Church's business whether or not a woman practiced birth control."

"More and more women feel that way," Joanna said as she resumed her cross-stitch.

Angie couldn't get the class out of her mind. Especially Corinne. The girl was quick to state her opinion and often critical of others when they disagreed. Rarely, though, did anyone take offense.

Corinne seemed to revel in being outrageous, but beneath all the show was a good heart. Angie usually enjoyed their talks and looked forward to the days Corinne hung around after class so they could visit.

Today hadn't been one of those days. Corinne couldn't get out of the room fast enough. Sure enough, when Angie looked out the window to the school parking lot, she recognized Jimmy's car.

Corinne ran across the lot and threw herself inside as if she'd been waiting for this moment all day. Angie couldn't tell exactly what was happening in the car, which didn't leave for several minutes. She guessed Corinne hadn't been sharing the quadratic formula with her boyfriend.

"You said you thought a few of your students are sexually active," Sister Joanna said. "Is this something you feel comfortable talking to them about? Privately, of course."

Angie's eyes widened with dismay. *Her* talk about sex? She didn't even know how to approach the subject. And what could she possibly have to say about it?

Sister Joanna glanced up, looked at Angie and then started to laugh. "God *is* the one who created sex, you know."

"Not to talk about." Angie was sure of that.

"Just discuss it with them the same way your mother talked to you," she advised.

"My mother died when I was five. My father's the one who explained the birds and the bees."

"Your dad?" Sister Joanna lowered the cross-stitch to her lap.

"Dad told me everything. He got books from the library, drew me a picture and explained the way a woman's body works."

"He wasn't embarrassed?"

At the time Angie had been so caught up in what he was telling her that she couldn't remember. "I don't think so."

"But you are?"

She nodded. After years of living in a convent, in which every aspect of her femininity had been ignored, Angie could no more discuss the matter of physical intimacy than she could perform brain surgery.

"It might be a good idea if you did talk to these girls, Sister."

Angie marveled at Sister Joanna. She seemed to believe such a discussion should come naturally—and for her, it probably would.

"I...couldn't."

"I didn't think I could put a needle into someone's arm, but I learned," Joanna said briskly. "We do what we have to. Your students respect you, and I'm sure they'd welcome the opportunity to speak freely with you."

Angie rested her spine against the back of the chair as she considered talking to Corinne about such a deeply personal subject.

"They'd feel safe with you, I think," Sister Joanna went on. "For one thing, you aren't their mother."

"Wouldn't they worry about me judging them?"

"You're not like that and they know it."

Maybe she *could* talk to some of the girls, Angie mused. Maybe she could have a frank and honest discussion with Corinne, just like her father had with her when she was a teenager.

{20}

Sister Joanna

Singing with the choir at Sunday morning Masses had never been Joanna's favorite task. Music wasn't her gift and she struggled to stay on key, but Sister Martha insisted Joanna's talent or lack of it didn't concern her. All the choir director needed that Sunday was another voice. It didn't matter that Joanna's undisciplined singing drifted between alto and second soprano, sometimes within the same musical bar.

Her attention drifted, too, as she sat through the eight, nine and now the ten o'clock Mass. Father Sanders had said the eight and nine o'clock Masses but he'd been replaced by Father Doyle for the ten o'clock.

Sitting at the organ, Sister Martha played the multi-tiered keyboard, and the church echoed with the crescendoing tones. Joanna raised the hymnal and joined her fellow nuns in song as Father Doyle entered from the back of the church with a small procession of altar boys. The first carried the six-foot-tall crucifix, with two of the younger boys behind him, followed by Father Doyle, who held a large Bible.

Joanna was more impressed with the younger priest than ever. His sermons focused on the importance of God in the contemporary world, and he wasn't afraid of difficult concepts, which he tried to explain in clear and relevant ways. Granted, his delivery was a bit dry and sometimes faltering, but he was improving every week. Not long ago he'd quoted the lyrics to a popular song Joanna remembered from her own teenage years. *To know Him is to love Him.*

The priest's words had stayed with her, and she knew they had with others, too. To take something as simple as the lyrics of a familiar song and to use that as the basis for a sermon on God's unconditional love struck her as divinely inspired. The tune ran through her mind for days and she knew she'd never think of it the same way again.

Sister Kathleen had casually mentioned how helpful the younger priest had been to her, too. Joanna worried about her friend, who was burdened with the task of sorting out the church books. It seemed to be weighing heavily on her, although she never complained.

As Father Doyle approached the altar for the beginning of the ten o'clock Mass, Joanna noted that the church was far more crowded than it had been for the previous two. Father Doyle was becoming popular with the parishioners; she hoped that wouldn't cause problems for him with Father Sanders. Joanna quickly rejected that thought. Father Sanders was such a friendly, likeable priest, she doubted he'd care one way or the other.

As the organ music faded, Joanna saw a lone male figure move up the side aisle, searching for space at the end of a pew. If she didn't know better, she would've thought it was Dr. Murray, although of course it couldn't be.

She peered closer, or tried to without being obvious. The man, whoever he was, certainly resembled the doctor, she decided absently. Their gait was similar and—

It *was* Dr. Murray.

Once he'd found a seat, he turned around and glanced over his shoulder. She gazed down at his face. Dr. Murray, the lapsed Catholic who'd emphatically stated that he had no intention of attending Mass again, was in church.

At first Joanna was dumbstruck, and then so excited she nearly dropped her hymnal. Dr. Murray had actually come to Mass! This was what she'd been praying for since their first conversation, what she'd wanted more than anything. He *had* been listening to her, had felt her concern for him. He'd come back to church!

The rest of the hour passed in a blur. She couldn't remember what she sang, or even if she did. Nor did she recall more than two words of the sermon, or climbing down the stairs with the other nuns when it came time to receive Communion.

The minute Mass was over, Joanna set aside the hymnal and hurried down the stairs, hoping to catch Dr. Murray before he left. Unfortunately, she was caught in the crowd of parishioners as they exited. For one frantic moment, it was impossible for Joanna to move.

People stopped to greet her and Joanna couldn't be rude. She smiled and remarked how good it was to see them, then quickly excused herself in an effort to find Dr. Murray.

Once outside, she paused at the top of the church steps, certain she'd missed him. Disappointment flooded her as she scanned the crowd and didn't see him.

"Looking for someone?" the familiar deep-throated voice asked from behind her.

"Dr. Murray!" Joanna whirled around and breathlessly placed a hand over her pounding heart. She stared up and smiled at him, so pleased that for a moment she couldn't speak. "I'm *so* glad you're here."

He looked different without his hospital whites. Good. Better than any man had a right to look. So handsome it was a sin for her to even notice—yet she couldn't help herself.

"I figured you'd be at this Mass," he said.

"I was at the eight and nine o'clock Masses, too."

"I thought we Catholics were only required to attend one a week."

"You are, unless you're singing in the choir. Sister Martha needed an extra voice and—" She stopped, wanting to kick herself for rambling. "What made you decide to come to Mass?" She blurted out the question without even a hint of finesse.

His expression mildly uncomfortable, Dr. Murray shrugged. "I don't know. I woke up, there weren't any emergencies and I decided what the hell, why not? I kept thinking about you praying for me and it seemed the least I could do." He grinned. "By way of thanks, I mean."

Apparently he hadn't been on any Saturday-night dates, which pleased her even more.

Then, because she wasn't sure what to say next, she asked, "Have you met Father Doyle?"

He shook his head and didn't seem especially interested.

"You must," she insisted. "He's wonderful." On impulse she reached for his hand, clasping it in her own as she led him toward the priest. It felt…odd, being linked with him like this. It meant nothing, and yet Joanna felt his touch ripple though her in a way that was all too sexual. Almost at once, the need to be held and touched and loved felt overwhelming. It'd been so long since she'd had any physical contact with a man, so long since she'd been wrapped in a man's arms. Her breath caught in her throat and she suddenly jerked her hand free. Trying to cover for her uncharacteristic actions, she gave him a weak smile and said, "Father's right over here."

Father Doyle stood at the main doors, exchanging greetings with his parishioners. Since he was busy talking, they had to wait a few minutes. Joanna felt awkward standing there, afraid to say anything for fear Dr. Murray would comment on the fact that she'd pulled her hand away from his.

"Are you all right?" he asked, his voice lowered.

Her face was flushed and she could feel the heat in her cheeks. "I'm fine," she said, forcing a light note into her voice. "What about you?"

When he didn't answer she was compelled to look at him. His eyes met hers. "I don't know."

In other circumstances, she might have delved into the question, but right now she was afraid of where the conversation would take them.

As if Tim realized he'd said more than he should, he changed the subject completely. "I liked Father Doyle's sermon."

"I did, too," Joanna said automatically, grateful to escape the tension between them. The truth was, she didn't remember the sermon. She'd tried to listen, honestly tried, but her mind refused to concentrate while Dr. Murray was in the church.

"I didn't know they ordained men that young," he added.

"He's older than he looks."

"Really. And how old are you?"

"Me?" Joanna glanced up at him, wide-eyed with shock. Age wasn't something she thought about, especially her own.

"You don't look much older than a teenager yourself."

"And you're so ancient?" Joanna teased.

"I'm thirty-two and I feel forty."

"Ooh, that's old," she said with a laugh.

"You're not kidding. Now answer my question. How old are you?"

Joanna had to stop and calculate her age. "Twenty-six. I think."

His eyes narrowed. "Good grief, you're just a kid."

"I don't feel like one." Especially just then. What she felt like was a woman, with a woman's heart and a woman's desires, and frankly it terrified her. Since entering the convent, she'd ignored the fact that she was a woman. But unlike a virgin, she'd experienced the delights of the flesh, and the memories refused to leave her.

At just that moment, Father Doyle turned his attention to Joanna. His smile revealed his pleasure at seeing her. "Good morning, Sister Joanna." His gaze slid from Joanna to Dr. Murray and he nodded.

Joanna stepped closer. "Father Doyle, this is Dr. Tim Murray, who's a surgeon at St. Elizabeth's Hospital."

Father Doyle extended his hand, which Dr. Murray gripped firmly. "I don't believe I've seen you in church before."

"Good eye, Father," Dr. Murray said. "I told Sister

Joanna that I was a lapsed Catholic and she took it upon herself to pray for me."

Father nodded approvingly toward Joanna. "The effective prayer of a righteous nun availeth much," he said, grinning boyishly.

"You're telling me," Dr. Murray muttered. "Now every Sunday morning I wake up and the first thing I think about is Sister Joanna praying for me. Then I start thinking about all those years I attended Mass as a kid." He shook his head. "To tell you the truth, Father, I gave up on religion a long time ago."

"You were in Vietnam?"

Dr. Murray reluctantly nodded.

"Perhaps we could talk about it one afternoon. Are you free anytime this week?"

Dr. Murray shrugged. "Wednesday. Although I'm not sure you're going to want to hear what I have to say."

"Maybe, but I've got a good ear—as well as a good eye. I'll put you down on my calendar for two o'clock, if that works for you."

"All right. Do you want to meet here?" He gestured in the direction of the church.

"No, come on over to the rectory," Father Doyle said, "and I'll have the perfect excuse to ask Mrs. O'Malley to bake up a batch of her gingersnaps."

"I'll look forward to it, Father."

"So will I." There was no doubting the sincerity in his voice.

Sister Martha and Sister Kathleen, followed by three other nuns, came out the side doors of the church. It was Joanna's signal to leave and return to the convent.

"I have to go." She couldn't quite hide her disappointment.

"So soon?" Dr. Murray sounded equally dejected. "I thought I'd take you to lunch."

Sadly Joanna shook her head. Other, less conservative religious orders had relaxed their rules with regard to these situations. But eating with laypeople other than family remained strictly prohibited for the nuns of St. Bridget's Sisters of the Assumption.

"I can't," she said.

"Perhaps another time then," he suggested, almost flippantly.

Again she shook her head. "That isn't possible. I'm sorry."

"Right," he said, his own voice impatient.

He was drawing away from her. Physically and emotionally.

"I keep forgetting you're Sister Joanna, not Nurse Joanna," he muttered.

He wasn't the only one with the memory problem, Joanna thought. She kept forgetting it herself.

{ 21 }

Sister Angelina

Late Wednesday afternoon, as she left the school, Angie saw Sister Kathleen walking from the rectory to the convent house. She sped up to join her friend. Angie was worried about Sister Kathleen and had been for some weeks. Apparently her work at the church wouldn't last much longer, which was a blessing in Angie's opinion.

The normally good-natured, fun-loving Kathleen had become introspective and subdued in the last little while. Twice now, Angie had seen her in conversation with Father Doyle. Angie hadn't been close enough to hear what was being said, and even if she had been, she would've moved away. Whatever the topic, it appeared to be of deep concern to them both. Their body language said as much—their heads were lowered and their voices had dropped to a whisper. Father Doyle stood with his hands behind his back and Sister Kathleen was leaning toward him, hands clasped in front of her.

Father Doyle hadn't been himself lately, either. It

seemed that he, too, was preoccupied by some serious matter. Angie's thoughts came to an abrupt halt. No, it couldn't be—but stranger things had happened. Could Father Doyle and Sister Kathleen have fallen in love? That would make sense, since Sister Kathleen was at the rectory three afternoons a week and it would only be natural for the two of them to talk and get to know each other. They shared a love of God, and well…oh dear, this could be trouble. Angie swallowed hard and considered all the difficulties such a relationship would bring to both the diocese and the convent.

These were trying times for the Church. Nuns, and priests, too, were leaving the religious life in record numbers. Already five nuns had left the Minneapolis convent that year. Five! Unfortunately, there weren't any replacements, and the school had been forced to hire lay teachers, which automatically raised tuition. Many families were already burdened by the expense of private school. Angie feared that these added costs might threaten the very existence of the parochial school system.

Angie worried about the nuns who'd chosen to reject their vows. They were walking into an uncertain future without savings and without jobs. She prayed that God would direct their lives.

"You look a little troubled," Sister Kathleen said as they walked side by side toward the convent.

"Me?" Angie asked with a short laugh. "I was just thinking the same thing about you. Is everything all right?" She hoped Kathleen would be honest with her— not that there was anything Angie could do to help.

Sister Kathleen took so long to reply that Angie wanted to stop and grab her by the shoulders and look her full in the face. Finally the other nun said, "Everything will work itself out soon."

Soon, Angie repeated mentally. Then, risking Sister Kathleen's rebuke, she said, "These things sometimes happen when a man and a woman work together." She took a deep breath, hoping she wasn't embarrassing them both as she broached the uncomfortable subject. "Through no fault of their own, of course."

Sister Kathleen gave her an odd, puzzled look. Her face was blank. "Sister, what are you talking about?"

Angie instantly regretted opening her mouth. "It was nothing. Forgive me."

Sister Kathleen grew quiet, frowning as they quickened their pace. "You think Father Doyle and I are… attracted to each other?" At that, she burst into delighted laughter. "Father Doyle and I are *friends,* nothing more. Nothing else, either, I promise you."

Angie's relief was intense. She hated the thought of Sister Kathleen leaving the order because she'd fallen in love with a priest. But her amusement was quickly cut short.

As they neared the convent, Angie recognized Corinne Sullivan sitting on the low brick wall outside the door. When Angie approached, Corinne, agile and athletic, leapt down to the sidewalk, landing solidly on both feet.

"Hello, Sister. Have you got a minute?" The girl's eyes were ablaze and Angie could only speculate about what was on her mind.

"Go ahead, Sister," Kathleen told her, stepping a few feet away to give them privacy.

"What's the problem?" Angie asked, focusing on Corinne.

"It's not you, Sister. I think you're great. It's the Church. You're going to lose us and all the girls in the high school if they continue with this nonsense about birth control and—"

Angie held up her hand. "I can assure you, Corinne, that the Church's stand isn't nonsense."

"But it *is*, Sister," Corinne insisted. "What right does a bunch of old men have to tell a woman what she can and can't do with her own body?" she blurted out. "A married couple should be able to decide how many children they want—not some pope who's never been married and doesn't know a thing about raising a family. It's just *wrong*."

Angie was still marshaling her thoughts when Corinne asked, "Sister, do you know who Gloria Steinem is?"

Angie shook her head. "Sorry, no."

"Then you've never heard of *Ms. Magazine,* either, have you?"

Again Angie shook her head. She wasn't sure what this other woman had to do with the conversation, but Corinne apparently had a high opinion of her.

"It's all so confusing, Sister." Corinne stared at her intently. "Gloria Steinem is a feminist and she believes…" She paused and made an exasperated gesture. "Never mind, you'd never agree with her anyway, so there's no use arguing."

"I'm willing to listen," Angie assured her, although she privately felt that Corinne might have chosen a better time and place for this discussion.

Corinne slumped her shoulders in a gesture of defeat. "I'd rather talk to you about the Church. I have a lot of questions. Jimmy's parents are Baptists and he says Mary wasn't a virgin her entire life and he even showed me what the Bible says."

Angie stiffened, prepared to defend the truth of the

Gospel. "We know it's true. Scripture tells us that our Savior was born to a virgin and—"

"But *after* Jesus was born, Sister," Corinne inserted. "Mary was married to Joseph, remember? According to what Jimmy showed me in the Bible, Jesus had brothers and sisters, the children of Mary and Joseph. They were married and they had sex, and if…if the birth control pill had been around then, they probably would've used it."

"I'm sure Jimmy has misinterpreted the Bible," Angie said in what she hoped was a calm and collected voice.

"The entire book of James was written by Jesus's brother—that's what Jimmy says."

"Corinne, please, I think you're getting all upset over nothing."

"Sister, think about it! What kind of man—and Joseph was a man—would live with a woman he loved and behave like her brother? It doesn't make sense to me. If the Church is wrong about something this important, then I have to question everything else it teaches."

"I don't believe the Church is wrong, Corinne," Angie told her. She couldn't imagine why Jimmy would put such ideas into Corinne's head—unless he wanted to undermine the girl's faith. Of course, Mary had remained a virgin! Angie's whole life was modeled on the Virgin Mother. She'd taken the vow of chastity, accepted virginity for life, based on the ideal of the Lord's earthly mother.

"Don't you *see,* Sister?" Corinne pleaded, wide eyes staring up at her. "If the Church is wrong about this, it could be wrong about other things, too."

Angie was speechless.

"Jimmy says—"

"Corinne," she said, snapping out of her stupor.

"Jimmy isn't a religion expert. He isn't even Catholic. It's obvious that he's been raised with a number of misconceptions."

"Maybe it's us who have the misconceptions, Sister. Did you ever think of that?"

Frankly, Angie hadn't. "I'll tell you what I'll do. I'll ask for a meeting with Father Sanders and have him answer your questions. Then I'll report back to you what he says."

"While you have his attention, you might ask him about purgatory, too." Corinne's tone was skeptical.

"Purgatory?" Was nothing sacred anymore? It was a mistake to date a boy outside the faith, but Angie hesitated to mention that for fear of driving Corinne away completely. She had to wonder what Corinne's parents were thinking to let her get involved with a Protestant boy, but then she remembered that they weren't fond of Jimmy and had discouraged the relationship.

"There's not one single word in the entire Bible about purgatory, Sister. I asked Jimmy's mother after he told me that, and she said the same thing. Not a single mention in all those pages. The Church just made it up so people will think they're going to suffer when they die."

Angie raised both hands, ending this discussion before it went any further. It was best saved for another time. Once she'd talked to Father Sanders, Angie would be able to reassure Corinne; as it was now, the girl was too emotional and in no mood to listen to reason.

"The thing is, Sister, I *want* to be a good Catholic."

"I know you do," Angie said, not doubting her sincerity.

"My parents are both strong Catholics and so are my grandparents. It would hurt them if I turned my back on the Church, but I have to honestly believe in its teachings.

I have to know deep in my heart that the Church wants what's best for me, that it won't force me to have more children than my husband and I can support."

"Corinne, you're worried about things that shouldn't be troubling a girl of your age."

"Sister, oh, Sister." Corinne closed her eyes and then she shook her head in a small, knowing way.

"I have to go," Angie said. She had mixed feelings about ending the conversation—regret at not helping Corinne find a way to resolve her doubts, and relief at escaping, for the moment, these uncertain waters.

"When I was in grade school," Corinne said, her voice low, "I used to dream about being a nun one day."

"Did you?" Angie said, touched by her words.

"I can't do it. I realize that now. I just can't."

"Not everyone has a vocation," Angie said, thinking a girl like Corinne would certainly add a bit of energy to convent life.

"Not everyone has the ability to accept what's told to them without ever asking a question," the girl added. "I couldn't deal with that. I'd never be able to do it, Sister, no matter how much I love God."

{22}

Sister Joanna

Joanna sat across from the shocked, grieving husband, wishing there was something she could say or do to ease his pain. She'd come to comfort Richard Dougal after Dr. Tripton had informed him that his wife, Maryanne, had died. This father would have to raise three young children by himself. He'd have to remain strong for their sake and—somehow—survive her loss.

"I'm so very sorry," she whispered, her heart aching at the unmasked grief she read on the man's face.

Richard Dougal glanced up. "I don't understand. She's only thirty-one. How could this happen? I should've been here. I thought everything was all right after the surgery. Then the hospital called and said there was a…complication." His voice caught and he paused to compose himself before continuing. "I had to get a babysitter. I hurried, but by the time I got here, it was too late."

Joanna was well aware of the details. The physician had already explained the medical reason for the young woman's death. It was a rare heart condition no one had known about and no one could have anticipated. As a result, she'd gone into cardiac arrest following the hysterectomy.

"Is there someone I can phone for you?" Joanna asked.

As if in a stupor, he shook his head. "My neighbor's watching the kids. My mother-in-law was going to fly out to help once Maryanne got home from the hospital. We don't have any family in the area." His voice cracked and his shoulders shook with the effort not to break down.

"Would you like me to pray with you?" she asked softly.

He nodded.

Joanna knelt and briefly raised her eyes to heaven, pleading with God to give her the words to comfort this man. As soon as she bowed her head, Mr. Dougal broke into deep, mournful sobs.

Joanna spent an hour with him, until he'd calmed down and the neighbor's husband arrived to drive him home. Richard Dougal thanked her, his voice a monotone, and let his neighbor lead him away. He was numb with grief; Joanna knew that numbness would get him through the next few days, but afterward... All she could do was pray for him and his family.

Returning to the nurses' station, Joanna felt emotionally depleted. She barely noticed when Dr. Murray approached. He took one look at her and said, "You need a cup of coffee."

She needed something, but she didn't think caffeine would help her any more than it would that poor, grieving husband. To her surprise, Dr. Murray took her into the doctors' lounge on the second floor and then poured coffee for her. She noticed that he'd added a liberal amount of sugar.

"I'm not in shock," she protested.

"No, but you just might be when I tell you who's here."

"Someone's here?" she asked in confusion. "But…"

Dr. Murray pulled out a chair and sat across from her. He met her eyes and placed his hand on hers. He waited a moment as they both stared down at their linked hands, then asked, "Do you know a Greg Markham?"

"Greg?" Joanna nearly swallowed her tongue. Was Dr. Murray telling her that Greg, her one-time fiancé, was at the hospital? That seemed completely improbable. "What's he doing here?" she demanded.

"You'll have to ask him that yourself."

"But…" Joanna was too flustered to think clearly.

"He's in the staff lounge and he insists on talking to you personally. He won't take no for an answer."

She stared at Tim Murray, silently begging him for advice.

"This is the man you once mentioned, isn't it? The one who went overseas?"

She nodded. "We were engaged. He met a woman while he was stationed in Vietnam." She lowered her head, surprised by the flood of memories. They came and went with incredible swiftness, leaving her shaken in their aftermath. He'd been an important part of her life at one time—but now he didn't belong in her life at all.

"Do you still have feelings for him?" Dr. Murray asked. His gentleness rocked her as much as knowing that Greg was down the hall waiting to see her.

"No." Her response came automatically.

"He wants to talk to you. Are you up to it?"

Joanna wasn't sure that meeting Greg would be right for either of them. With some embarrassment she recalled the hours of torrid passion in the backseat of his car. They hadn't been able to keep their hands off each other. They'd lost their virginity together, shared a time in their lives that would be impossible to recapture.

"Sister?"

Joanna raised her eyes and blinked, not knowing what to say.

"As I said, he insisted that he speak to you personally." Dr. Murray frowned. "Do you want to do this? Because if you don't, I'll get rid of him."

Joanna knew that Greg wouldn't leave until he got what he wanted. She also knew he hadn't found her without help. She was fairly certain that assistance had come from her mother.

"I'll talk to him," she said, her voice gaining confidence.

Dr. Murray escorted her to the lounge, where Joanna found Greg pacing the room with his hands clenched at his sides. He stopped abruptly when she entered the room.

"Joanna." He breathed her name as though he were praying.

She felt his look in a physical way. His gaze wandered up and down her body, lingering on her face and then her short veil.

"You're as beautiful as I remember," he said, his voice filled with awe. "I wondered…" He closed his eyes, perhaps to chase the image of a younger Joanna from his mind. When he opened them again, he seemed to be comparing his memory with reality.

"I'll leave you two alone for a few minutes," Dr. Murray said, sounding gruff and none too cordial.

"That was one unpleasant fellow," Greg said, scowling after him. The scowl quickly turned to a smile as he looked back at Joanna. Striding toward her, he reached for her hands. "I don't care, though. He brought you to me and I'm grateful for that."

Joanna pulled her hands free of Greg's clasp.

"It takes some getting used to seeing you in a habit," he said.

A habit that had only been modified a short while ago, she wanted to tell him, but didn't. He wasn't here to discuss the changes in convent life. "How are you, Greg?" she asked instead.

"We need to talk." He gestured for her to sit on the sofa. The coffee table beside it was littered with used cups and old newspapers.

Joanna sat sideways on the very edge, while Greg sat next to her, a little too close for comfort.

He didn't speak for a few minutes, apparently trying to gather his thoughts. "I assumed that once I saw you, I'd know what to say," he muttered. "Now that I'm here, it's damn hard not to hold you."

Joanna stiffened. "You can't do that."

"I know…" He dragged in a deep breath. "Xuan and I are getting a divorce."

Although her mother hadn't told her, Joanna had read between the lines. There'd been a letter recently in which her mother had mentioned that she'd seen Greg and his wife having an argument in the grocery store. According to rumors—which Sandra was happy to pass along—the marriage was a troubled one.

"Is Lily with her mother?"

Greg nodded. "She's a beautiful child." He pulled out his wallet, opened it and removed a picture of his daughter for Joanna to examine.

The child had dark, almond-shaped eyes and a lovely smile as she stared into the camera. Joanna saw nothing of Greg in the little girl. In the blending of two backgrounds, the mother's heritage had clearly been favored. Joanna handed back the photograph. "You're right, she *is* a beautiful child."

"I miss her a lot," Greg said, tucking the photo inside his wallet. "Lily's the only good thing to come out of the relationship."

"I'm sorry to hear about you and Xuan."

Greg smiled weakly, and when he spoke, his bitterness was obvious. "So am I, but our marriage was doomed from the first. Xuan was looking for a way out of Vietnam and I was a convenient fall guy."

"I'm sorry, Greg," she said, noticing that he accepted none of the responsibility for his own actions. She *was* sorry about the divorce; the failure of any marriage was a tragic thing. And although Greg had badly hurt her, Joanna no longer held any ill will toward him— and hadn't in years.

"I'm afraid I'm the one to blame for the divorce," he said next, surprising her.

"In what way?"

"Xuan knew." At her questioning gaze, Greg continued. "She realized almost right away that I never stopped loving you."

"That's all water under the bridge now."

"Is it, Joanna?"

"It is for me."

"But not for me. I love you. I've always loved you."

At one time Joanna would have given anything to hear those words. Now they just seemed too little, too late—an avowal that had nothing to do with her.

"You're going through a divorce, Greg," she said calmly, her hands neatly folded in her lap. "It's wiped you out emotionally and you're hoping to return to the past. But that's impossible."

"It isn't, Joanna," Greg said, moving even closer to her. "We *can* have it all, the way we once did. I screwed up, but I swear to you it'll never happen again."

"Greg… You don't know what you're asking."

"I do know," he said firmly. "I want you to marry me."

"Marry you?" She bolted upright before sitting back down. "That's out of the question!"

He ignored her protest. "Leave the convent." He seemed to have everything worked out. To him, it was obviously a simple matter—once she was free, he'd be there to sweep her away. "You shouldn't be here. We both know you're a passionate, loving woman. Closing yourself off from life, from love—it just isn't you."

Joanna tried hard to hold back her irritation. "You're completely discounting the last six years of my life as if they mean nothing."

"They mean everything."

"Not if I listen to what you're suggesting," she said tartly.

"You kept yourself pure for me."

"What?" The man was living in a fantasy. "I kept myself pure for God. I think it's time you left." She stood, giving him little option but to stand, too.

"Joanna, please listen…"

She'd already heard more than enough. "I can't help you, Greg. I'm sorry, sincerely sorry that your marriage has fallen apart, but it's too late to recapture what we once had." Six years too late.

His eyes held a look of loss, of loneliness, and she understood why he'd tried to regain something that no longer existed.

Although she'd never said anything to her family, as the years progressed, Joanna realized she'd made a lucky escape by not marrying Greg. If he'd betrayed her once, he would again. She'd been young and naive and ruled by adolescent dreams and raging hormones. Those days were over. She was a woman now, a woman who'd made choices that had taken her life in a completely different direction.

Greg reluctantly left after two more attempts to change her mind. After the door closed, she needed a minute to calm her pounding heart.

She assumed that Dr. Murray had hung around to discover how her conversation with Greg had gone. As suspected, she found him leaning against the nurses' station, chatting with Mrs. Larson.

When Tim saw her, he slowly straightened. He searched her face for signs of what might have happened.

"Are you okay?" he asked.

Joanna smiled and nodded.

"He wanted to lure you away, didn't he?"

She neither confirmed nor denied his statement. "He was a good friend at one time."

"Is he sticking around for a while?"

Joanna laughed. "I certainly hope not."

"Yeah, me too. You've got enough on your mind without him following you around like a lost puppy."

The lead nurse's interest was piqued. She glanced at Joanna, her eyebrows raised in question. "What's this all about?"

"I had an old friend stop by to say hello," she explained.

"An old *boy*friend," Dr. Murray elaborated.

"The relationship died a painful death a long time ago."

"It's over?" he asked. "You're sure of that?"

Joanna nodded again.

Their eyes met and a flash of awareness darted through her. Greg, the boy/man she'd once loved, had asked her to leave the convent for him, and she'd turned him down flat. She hadn't needed to think about it, hadn't so much as considered his request.

Joanna wondered what her reaction would be if Dr. Murray were to ask her the same thing.

{ 23 }

Sister Kathleen

It came as no surprise to Sister Kathleen that there were discrepancies in the bank deposits for the first two Sunday collections in October. The first week it was only twenty dollars, but by the second week it had grown to a hundred and forty, an amount that shocked Kathleen. Father Doyle had made up the difference out of his own pocket, but this couldn't continue and they both knew it.

"Is Father Sanders upstairs?" Father Doyle asked, coming into the rectory late Wednesday afternoon. Kathleen was just getting ready to leave. His eyes met hers and she understood the real question he was asking. He wanted to know if Father Sanders was drinking again.

The truth was, Kathleen hadn't been able to tell. After the drunk-driving incident, the older priest seemed to be making a genuine effort at sobriety. Or perhaps he'd gotten better at hiding his addiction. Kathleen wasn't sure which. However, with money missing from the bank deposit, she realized he was spending that cash on *something*.

"You talked to Mrs. O'Malley?" she asked.

Father Doyle nodded. "She swears she's no longer buying him booze."

"Then he must be getting it himself," she said.

"Or he's found someone else to pick it up for him."

Kathleen was certain of one thing: Father Sanders hadn't taken that money to feed the poor.

"He didn't say much," she told him, meaning she hadn't been able to detect if the other priest was drunk or not. Father Sanders had become very good at avoiding her. It was only in conversation that she was able to hear the slur in his words. And only when she had the opportunity to see him walk for more than a few feet could she observe any flaws in his gait. These days, if he saw her at all, it was briefly and only when absolutely necessary.

"Allow me to walk you back to the convent, Sister," Father Doyle said. Without giving her an option, he handed Kathleen her jacket, then waited by the front door.

As they left the rectory, Kathleen carefully weighed her words, fearing she might be overstepping her boundaries. "I think perhaps it would be a good idea for us to speak openly, Father."

"Perhaps we should," he agreed. It seemed to her that he was relieved to have someone to talk to, someone who shared his concern for the older priest.

Kathleen chewed on her lower lip, a habit she'd had as a child and only reverted to in times of stress. "With you replacing the missing cash, I'm afraid we've created a protective environment for Father Sanders."

"In other words, I'm giving him permission to

drink," the priest murmured, and it sounded as though this was something he'd battled with more than once.

"It isn't fair to you *or* Father Sanders if you add money to the collection every week," she blurted out. "Father Sanders doesn't know what you're doing and he obviously assumes I'm so stupid I don't understand what's going on." She hadn't meant to be so blunt, but it all made sense to her now. This talk about Mrs. Stafford being away on vacation was wearing thin, too. Thin enough for Kathleen to see through it. No wonder Father Sanders had asked her to deal with the books. And no wonder things had been left in such a mess. He knew she had no practical experience and had figured she wouldn't pick up on what he was doing.

"I phoned Mrs. Stafford's house this afternoon," Father Doyle announced, his hands clasped behind his back as he matched his pace to hers.

Kathleen knew what was coming. "She isn't on vacation, is she?"

"No," Father admitted reluctantly.

"She quit," Kathleen supplied for him.

"I'm sorry to say you're right."

"Why do you feel you have to protect him?" she asked after an uncomfortable moment.

Father was silent for a long time. "The bishop has placed his trust in me to handle the situation with Father Sanders. He expects me to bring Father back to God and to a serious understanding of his responsibilities within the parish." He sighed. "I don't want to fail His Excellency—or Father Sanders."

"Bishop Schmidt told you all this?"

"No," he said. "But once I got to St. Peter's, I understood the situation and why I'd been transferred here." Then, as if he'd said more than he wanted, he murmured, "This is my problem, Sister. You shouldn't worry about it."

But she did worry; she couldn't help it. Kathleen was involved now, and she refused to abandon the younger priest. Her admiration and respect for Father Doyle and her anxiety about the burdens he carried grew stronger every day.

"You're right, of course," he said thoughtfully. "I have no option but to take the matter to Bishop Schmidt. I've let my pride stand in the way of doing what's right." His voice fell, and it was clear to Kathleen that he'd agonized over this dilemma for far too long. The bishop obviously knew that Father Sanders had a problem but exactly how much he knew remained unclear.

"Would you like me to go with you?" she offered.

Father Doyle shook his head. "That isn't necessary."

Instinctively she recognized that he was protecting her, although she wasn't entirely sure why.

"What about Sister Superior? Perhaps I should mention it to her?" Kathleen felt honor bound to do something, to help in some way. She was convinced that the head of the convent suspected something, but Sister Eloise hadn't pressured her for information.

"I'd prefer if you kept this to yourself, at least for now."

Feeling the heat of his gaze but not daring to look him in the eye, Kathleen nodded.

"Is that a problem?" he asked at her silence.

"No," she said quietly. She hadn't decided what she'd do or say if Sister Eloise did ask about Father Sanders; Kathleen didn't want to lie, but at the same time she'd given Father Doyle her word.

"I appreciate that, Sister," he said.

The distress in his voice gripped her heart. Kathleen knew she'd do anything she could to take this burden from him. Father Sanders's problem was a constant source of anxiety. For her own part, she hadn't slept a full night since discovering Father Sanders drunk behind the wheel of a car. Twice now she'd woken with nightmares about the priest causing an accident. She worried that he might hurt himself or some innocent bystander and she worried about the scandal such an incident would cause. Father Sanders's actions might do irreparable damage to the Church in Minneapolis.

"I'll call and ask for an appointment with the bishop first thing in the morning," Father Doyle told her as they approached the convent.

"I'll be praying for you," Kathleen assured him.

"Thank you, Sister. I value those prayers."

"What will happen to Father Sanders?" She hadn't wanted to ask, but she needed to know.

The priest sighed heavily. "I'm hoping the bishop will send him to a facility that will give Father Sanders the professional help he needs."

That was Kathleen's hope, too. "Have you known of other such…cases?" she asked.

Father Doyle shook his head. "No. Based on my own admittedly limited experience, I don't believe this is a common problem with priests."

"Father's drinking has gotten worse in the last six months, hasn't it?"

"I'm afraid so. He's worse than when I first arrived, although he's much cleverer about hiding it. The thing is…" Father Doyle paused and his face twisted with a look of torment as they reached the convent steps. "He tries so hard not to drink."

"What about Alcoholics Anonymous?" Kathleen couldn't believe she hadn't thought of that sooner.

The priest dismissed the idea with a shake of his head. "I suggested it once and Father wasn't open to attending the meetings." His shoulders slumped noticeably. "His greatest fear is that someone in the community might recognize him."

They paused outside the convent door, almost like teenagers saying good-night at the end of a date—lingering, not wanting to end the conversation.

"My prayers go with you, Father," Kathleen said when she realized she couldn't delay another moment.

"I can't thank you enough, Sister, for all your help and for your friendship."

Kathleen felt she had done so little, but she was warmed by his gratitude.

"It's such a relief to be able to discuss the problem honestly. I don't know what I would've done if I'd carried this burden alone for even one more day." He turned to leave, then turned back to say, "Thank you, Sister."

"God go with you," she whispered, watching him walk away. Her own heart was oppressed by the weight of their secret.

Kathleen entered the convent and was prepared to hurry into chapel when Sister Eloise stopped her.

"Sister," the older nun called sharply, "could I have a moment of your time?"

"Of course, Sister." Kathleen's heart sank as if she'd been caught doing something wrong. She stood motionless with an impassive expression on her face.

"You're still working on the church books, is that correct?"

"Yes, Sister."

"It was my understanding that the church treasurer was on vacation and would be back within a month. It's been more than that, hasn't it?"

"Yes, Sister." Kathleen kept her eyes lowered.

"Do you have any idea how much longer this *temporary* situation will last?"

Kathleen swallowed hard and shook her head. "Unfortunately, I don't."

Sister Eloise narrowed her eyes. "How is Father Sanders?" she asked.

"Father Sanders?" Kathleen repeated. "He…he seems to be doing well."

Again a lengthy pause, in which the older nun assessed Kathleen's response. "You're sure about that, Sister?"

"Oh, yes," she said quickly—perhaps too quickly, she thought, as soon as the words had left her lips.

The head of the convent considered her answer for minutes that seemed to stretch into hours. "There have been…rumors about Father Sanders. I wonder if you've seen any evidence proving these rumors?"

"I'm sure I haven't," Sister Kathleen said in what she hoped was a reassuring voice.

"No evidence of Father Sanders having a…certain weakness?"

"None." Father Doyle's request that she keep the news of Father Sanders's problems a secret from Sister Eloise rang in her mind. The echo of his words blocked out any other thought, any other consideration.

"You have never seen Father Sanders with a drink in his hand, is that what you're telling me, Sister Kathleen?"

"No, I've never seen that."

The tightness in her throat almost prevented Kathleen from talking as she forced out the lie. In fact, she'd never actually seen Father Sanders with a drink in his hand. Technically she *wasn't* lying, she told herself, although it was certainly a lie of omission because she'd seen the effects of his drinking.

"Never, Sister," Kathleen said again, uncomfortable with her superior's long silence.

Sister Eloise's lips thinned. "Very well."

{24}

Sister Angelina

Her tenth-grade Health class dragged all week and Angie couldn't put her finger on the reason until Thursday afternoon. Corinne. The girl had been quiet and introspective for days. She was usually so inquisitive, asking questions, disputing assumptions, challenging Angie at every turn. Often, the entire class revolved around something Corinne had brought up. This week, however, she had remained oddly silent.

"Can I see you after class?" Angie asked as she strolled past Corinne's desk. She'd given the class ten minutes to start their homework assignment.

Corinne reluctantly looked up from the textbook and stared at her with unseeing eyes. It was as though the girl looked straight through her.

"This should only take a few minutes," Angie assured her in case Corinne planned to meet Jimmy in the parking lot after school, as she often did.

"I can stay," the girl mumbled.

Angie moved down the aisle between the desks and

frowned as she glanced over her shoulder. She noticed Morgan Gentry studying Corinne, and she, too, wore a troubled expression. Angie decided then and there that she'd try to find out what the problem was.

The bell rang and the class disappeared from the room with a swiftness that never ceased to amaze her. Only Corinne remained. She slouched against the back of her desk chair and waited with her head lowered.

"You wanted to talk to me, Sister?" she said in the same lackluster tone she'd used all week.

"Yes." Angie slid into the desk across from Corinne. "Is everything all right?" she began.

"Sure, why shouldn't it be?" A defensive edge marked her words.

"You don't seem yourself."

Corinne shrugged.

Angie hesitated, wondering if she should pursue the issue. She didn't know whether it would be worth risking their fragile friendship. If Corinne had something on her mind, perhaps it was better to let her bring it up.

"Is that why you wanted to talk to me?" Corinne asked defiantly. "I can't stay if you're going to interrogate me like this."

"Actually I have another reason," Angie said, refusing to be hurt by the girl's remark. "I wanted you to know that I took your questions seriously."

"Questions?" Corinne repeated. "Oh, you mean my little tirade a couple of weeks back. It's no big deal, Sister. I was on one of my soapboxes. I get like that sometimes. Don't worry, I've forgotten all about it."

"Perhaps you've forgotten it, but I haven't," Angie said. She didn't believe for a moment that Corinne had put the issue out of her mind. "I took your questions to Father Sanders."

The girl's eyes lit up with interest and she straightened. "You did? What did you ask him?"

"My first question concerned what you said about James being the biological brother of Christ."

"Mary and Joseph's son. It's right there in the Bible," Corinne insisted, showing more life than she had all week. She leaned toward Angie, eager to learn what the priest had said.

"It's exactly as I assumed," Angie said, almost sorry to burst the girl's righteous bubble. "Mary and—"

"The Church is asking us to believe that Mary and Joseph lived like brother and sister all those years," Corinne said loudly. "You've got to know it didn't happen. They were in love! I told you before, Sister—Jimmy showed me right in his Bible where it says James was Jesus's brother."

"Corinne," Angie said stopping her before she could leap onto another soapbox.

"But Sister, anyone who's ever been in love will tell you that's impossible. I know Mary was the Virgin Mother and all that, and Joseph was a saint, but he was a man too, and Mary was human. They were in love and they were married. You can't make me believe they weren't intimate. Just think about it."

"Father said you were obviously reading a Protestant Bible and that their Bible is full of inaccuracies."

"Sister!" As if consumed by frustration, Corinne closed her eyes and shook her head.

"I'm sorry you're having a hard time accepting Father's explanation, but it's the truth."

Corinne continued to shake her head in disbelief. Sighing audibly, she crossed her arms and said, "I'd be curious to hear what Father Sanders had to say about purgatory."

His answer had come as a surprise to Angie. "You're right about that. There isn't a single word in the Bible about purgatory."

"See!" she cried.

"Purgatory and limbo might not be spelled out in Scripture, but the Church, under the divine direction of the Holy Spirit, has made these truths clear through the Holy Father."

"The Pope?"

"The Holy Father is our earthly guide."

"He's the same one who says it's wrong for Catholics to practice birth control, isn't he?"

Angie was sure she saw Corinne roll her eyes. "Why do you have such difficulty with Church doctrine?"

"Because it doesn't add up," the girl said. "I want to be a good Catholic, Sister. I make Jimmy attend Mass with me every Sunday and we try to do the right thing." Her gaze skirted away from Angie's, as if she was too embarrassed to meet her look. "It isn't easy because—" She stopped and drew a deep breath. "It just isn't easy, and now..."

"Now?" Angie pressed when the girl let her words fade.

Corinne's closed expression indicated she didn't have anything more to say. "You know what, Sister? I don't believe Father Sanders."

"I'm sorry you're disappointed," Angie said, hoping her soft tone would soothe the girl.

"He's a man, and it's time women in the Church began to think for themselves. These priests and bishops and the Pope aren't married. They don't have families to support. Even you, Sister—your vow of poverty and whatever else you vowed are no real sacrifice."

Before Angie could reply, Corinne started talking

again, and the anger seemed to rush out of her. "You have everything given to you. You're provided with a home and all your meals and everything you need. The priests are the same. You don't know what it's like in the real world, where people have to make life-and-death decisions."

"Corinne—"

"I think I've already heard more than I want," the girl muttered as she grabbed her books and stood up from her desk.

"I can't allow you to use that tone of voice with me," Angie said. She'd been patient long enough.

Corinne's eyes narrowed. "I used to think you were someone special, Sister. I used to enjoy your classes and do you know why?"

Angie wasn't sure she was up to having her pride shredded. "I believe you've said too much already, Corinne. School's out. Perhaps it would be best if you left now."

Eyes glittering, Corinne stared her down. "Okay, but I want you to remember this conversation, Sister. Think about it, think about all the brainwashing that's been going on for the last two thousand years by men like Father Sanders." With that she whirled around and marched out of the room, filled with righteous indignation.

Oh, teenage girls and all their angst, Angie mused. She recalled that period in her own life and how everything had gone smoothly until the one time she'd stood up to her father and announced she wanted to enter the convent.

As Angie cleaned the blackboard, she heard someone behind her and turned to find Morgan standing in the doorway.

"Oh hi, Sister. I thought Corinne might still be here."

Angie lowered the eraser to the ledge in front of the blackboard. "She left a few minutes ago. I'm sure you can catch her if you want."

Morgan shrugged. "She's been a real pill lately."

Angie murmured something noncommittal.

"She's on restriction," Morgan said. "Did she tell you?"

Angie shook her head.

"She hasn't seen Jimmy all week and it's driving her crazy."

"I see."

Morgan nodded. "I think this is the first time Corinne's parents ever put her on restriction."

"Really?" Angie's curiosity was piqued now. "What happened?"

Morgan lifted one shoulder, but Angie could tell the other girl was delighted to tell tales on her friend. "Corinne has a midnight curfew just like me, and her father caught her sneaking into the house at four in the morning last Saturday. He was furious, too."

"I can imagine," Angie muttered.

"She's grounded for a week, so she's only gotta go three more days before she can see Jimmy again."

"No big deal, right?" Angie said casually.

"Right," Morgan agreed. "It isn't like the end of the world, and anyway, that's what Corinne gets for stepping over the line."

It wasn't only with her parents that Corinne was pushing the boundaries, however. She had serious problems with the Church, too.

{ 25 }

Sister Joanna

Dr. Murray pulled up to the bus stop in front of St. Elizabeth's Hospital in his shiny red Corvette. He was directly in front of Joanna, who stood waiting for the bus. Leaning across the passenger seat, he rolled down the window, despite the crisp October afternoon.

"Hi," he said, giving her the full effect of his smile.

Joanna's heart skipped with excitement at the sight of him. "Hi, yourself."

"So, have you decided to run away and marry your high school sweetheart?"

"I wouldn't be taking the bus if I had," she said with a laugh. Despite everything, Joanna couldn't disguise how pleased she was to see him, even if Tim Murray teased her at every opportunity. She hadn't seen much of him in a while. They'd both been busy—or pretended to be. It was the oddest thing, this…non-relationship of theirs. Joanna couldn't deny her growing attraction to Tim, and yet, she had to. For the first time since entering the convent, she'd begun to question her vocation. But that brought an avalanche of unpleasant questions, questions she preferred to ignore. As a result, she hadn't spoken to him, other than to exchange information about patients, for almost two weeks.

"Can I give you a ride, or is that forbidden, too?" His voice rang with challenge.

Joanna bit the inside of her cheek and glanced down the street. The bus wasn't due for ten minutes, but she really shouldn't go with Dr. Murray. It went against all the convent's rules of propriety. If anyone found out, Joanna would have to answer for her actions. Still, even knowing the risk she was about to take, she found she couldn't refuse.

"Is it really such a difficult decision?" he asked.

"All right, I'll go, but you have to drive me directly to the convent," she said. She didn't wait for him to agree, but walked eagerly toward the car. All her life, she'd longed for a ride in a red Corvette, but the sports car was only a small part of the temptation.

Dr. Murray leaned across the bucket seats again and opened the passenger door. The vehicle was impossibly low to the ground. Joanna slid into the soft leather seat and automatically reached for the safety harness.

"So, heard from Mr. Markham lately?" he asked, keeping his eyes on the road.

"Would you kindly stop?"

"No. I find it interesting that lover-boy would show up wanting to steal you away from the convent."

"You find it interesting, do you?" Joanna was enjoying herself too much to let him provoke her. The Corvette drove oh-so-smoothly, rounding the corners with the ease of a race car.

"You mean to say you weren't tempted?" he pressed.

"I'd think any woman would be flattered to have an old boyfriend seek her out."

Joanna *had* been flattered—and dismayed. Five or six years ago, she'd dreamed of this happening, and now that it had, all she felt was pity for Greg.

But she hadn't been tempted. At least not by Greg Markham. She sighed and could see that she was in for a lot of teasing until she explained herself. Although Tim Murray appeared to be joking, there was an undercurrent of seriousness in his remarks.

"His coming here wasn't a joke and it wasn't for old times' sake," Dr. Murray continued. "He wants you back. I'm having a hard time believing you didn't at least consider his proposal."

"Greg is part of my old life," she said simply.

Tim's gaze briefly met hers before he returned his attention to the road. "You mean to say you're a nun now and the religious life is all you care about?"

She nodded and intuitively realized it was a lie. She'd found serenity and peace in the convent, and there was comfort in the rituals of her daily life, but it was her work as a nurse that fulfilled her. Lately, at the end of the day when she returned to the convent, she'd become aware of a new longing—a deep, unspoken, barely recognizable part of herself that hungered for something more. The stark life, the repetitive prayer regimen, the lack of human touch was beginning to lose its meaning for her. In part, she suspected it was her growing attraction to Tim that was responsible for these feelings; she hoped that eventually it would pass. She didn't *want* to feel the things she did, and yet she couldn't help herself.

"Greg sought me out for his own reasons," she said. "He was trying to recapture his youth. What he didn't understand is that there's no going back, not for either of us."

"You sound very wise."

Joanna smiled, pleased by the compliment. "Do I?"

He nodded. "And sincere."

"Greg's hurting just now, feeling the pain of his divorce. He's looking for what used to be comfortable and easy. In his view, I entered the convent because of him. He actually believes I've been waiting for him all these years. He's free now, so of course he assumed I'd want him back."

"It must've been a shock when you turned him down."

"Yes," she agreed, "I imagine it was."

"In other words," he said, inhaling sharply, "you never have any doubts about being a nun?"

She hadn't said that, and she wasn't willing to make such a confession now. "There are days," she said, feigning a lightness of tone, "that I'd give it all up for a gooey hot fudge sundae."

"Really?" He glanced away from the road and his grin broadened to a full-blown smile. To Joanna's surprise, Tim roared past the convent and down the street.

"We just passed the convent," she said, looking over her shoulder and watching the building disappear in the background.

"I know," he murmured as though it didn't matter.

"Where are you taking me?"

"You'll find out."

She wasn't sure she liked the sound of this.

"You don't trust me, Joanna?"

She noticed the *Sister* was suspiciously absent. "Should I?" she asked.

"That depends," he said and pulled up to the drive-in

window of a Dairy Queen. "I have a weakness for hot fudge now and then myself."

"Oh…" was all Joanna could manage to say. It'd been years and years since she'd indulged in anything so decadent, but that didn't concern her nearly as much as the implication behind Tim Murray's words.

"So, what would you like?" he asked, studying her before placing his order. The teasing light was gone from his eyes.

Joanna hesitated—and then asked for the largest hot fudge sundae they had. With whipped cream.

By the time she returned to the convent, she was sure there was chocolate fudge smeared across her face. They'd sat in the parking lot and must have talked for an hour. As if she needed to convince him—and herself—she'd told him about her experiences as a nun and the peace she'd discovered in the religious life. He asked her a lot of questions and his interest seemed genuine. In the process, she'd succeeded in reassuring herself of her vocation, of her calling to work for God.

When Joanna finally glanced at her watch, she felt immediate alarm. Arriving back at the convent this late was certainly going to raise eyebrows.

Because of her tardiness, she had to rush to the chapel. If Sister Superior noticed when Joanna slipped into the pew with her fellow nuns, she didn't indicate it in any way. Following chapel, they went in to dinner.

Another space at the table was empty that night. Sister Julia was gone as if she'd vanished by some magician's hand. No one needed an explanation. Sister Julia, like five others that year, had decided to leave the religious life. Joanna felt her absence profoundly. Had she pursued the possibilities she sensed with Tim, she might have found reasons to leave herself.

That night she removed her simple habit, and tired though she was, knelt on the hard floor and reached for her rosary. Her mind drifted as she slid the beads through her fingers and recited the Our Father followed by ten Hail Marys. It took a determined effort to finish without falling asleep right there on the floor, with her head resting against the side of the mattress.

When Joanna finally climbed between the cool, coarse sheets, she closed her eyes and almost instantly fell asleep.

The first thing Joanna felt when Tim came to her in her dreams was that he shouldn't be with her. But he refused to leave. He said he'd given careful thought to all her talk about being a nun and her reasons for staying in the convent, but frankly he wasn't buying it.

He told her she was just as attracted to him as he was to her. He sat next to her in his red Corvette, looking so intense and so handsome she couldn't force herself to glance away.

Then, because she knew he was right, she nodded. Yes, she was attracted to him, but— She wasn't allowed to finish. With a small shout of triumph, Tim kissed her. Really kissed her.

At first Joanna resisted, telling him such contact was strictly against the rules. But he wouldn't listen, because they both knew how desperately she longed for his kisses.

He tasted so good, just as she'd feared. It was everything she remembered and had missed so much. Again and again his mouth sought hers. Again and again she gave him all that she was, all the woman she longed to be.

At some point he took off her clothes. Joanna was embarrassed that he'd see her nude. But when she saw the look of admiration and wonder in his eyes, she lowered her arms and stopped trying to conceal her body from him. How they'd ended up in bed together she couldn't figure out. Everything seemed to be happening so fast; first they were in the Corvette and then they were in bed. Tim's eyes had filled with love as he stared down at her.

She smiled up at him and wove her fingers into his hair. She didn't need to urge his mouth to hers; he released a small, soft moan as his lips met Joanna's.

He made slow, thoughtful love to her, revealing tenderness and care. It was so beautiful that she struggled to hold back the tears. Then he gently placed his arms around her and held her close.

An alarm rang, so loud and piercing that Joanna panicked. Throwing him off her, she leapt out of bed and glanced wildly around, certain they were about to be discovered.

It was then that Joanna realized she stood in the middle of her darkened cell in the convent of St. Bridget's Sisters of the Assumption in Minneapolis, Minnesota.

She wasn't in Dr. Tim Murray's arms, but in the convent. The alarm that had so terrified her—announcing her sin to the entire world—was merely the bell calling her to pray.

Joanna fell to her knees beside the bed, her eyes misting with guilt and regret. She was a nun and such dreams, such longings, were forbidden to her.

And yet her body felt warm and she ached with the deep need to be loved, to be touched. To be treasured.

{ 26 }

Sister Kathleen

"Oh, Sister," Mrs. O'Malley said the moment Kathleen entered the rectory on Monday afternoon. "I'm glad I caught you. Father Doyle needs to speak to you right away."

The housekeeper's face was drawn, her voice low and hoarse. Something must be very wrong.

"What is it?" Kathleen asked.

The older woman reached for a wadded handkerchief in her apron pocket and dabbed at her eyes. "It would be best if Father Doyle told you himself. He went to the church to pray a few moments ago. He's waiting for you there."

Her heart thundering with alarm, Kathleen hurried out the door and swiftly walked down the hill toward the large Catholic church. The sky was dark and leaden, and it felt cold enough for snow. It was early yet, mid-October, but in Minnesota winter sometimes arrived before Halloween.

She hurried into the church, but her eyes didn't adjust

to the dim light for a moment or two. Gradually a lone figure took shape, kneeling at the railing in front of the altar, bent over, his head in his hands.

It was Father Doyle and he appeared to be in some spiritual distress. Kathleen's imagination went wild. Father Sanders was nowhere to be seen and she couldn't help wondering if this problem involved the other priest.

Tentatively Kathleen stepped toward Father Doyle, unsure if she should interrupt his prayers.

He must have sensed her presence, because he raised his head and slowly turned to look her way. Kathleen saw such anguish in his eyes that she automatically stretched out her hands to him, in an overwhelming urge to comfort.

"What happened?" she whispered.

Father Doyle took her fingers in his and together they moved to the front pew. They sat angled toward each other, so close their knees touched. The priest squeezed her hands and then released them. Kathleen placed them in her lap, missing the warmth and reassurance of his touch.

"I've been transferred."

"Transferred?" Sister Kathleen couldn't take it in. There had to be a mistake. "But why? Where?" She knew Father Doyle had gone to the bishop about Father Sanders and his drinking problem, but surely Bishop Schmidt wouldn't send him away because of that. None of this made sense.

Father Doyle nodded. "I'm afraid I've been ordered to leave."

The questions crowded her mind and she couldn't get them out fast enough. "You went to Bishop Schmidt? You told him about Father Sanders? What did he say? How could he do this?" The lump in her throat thickened.

Father Doyle seemed resigned to this news, whereas she had yet to deal with it. "I'll try to answer your questions," he said, and his eyes held a distant look. "I did speak privately to the bishop regarding Father Sanders."

"What did he say?"

He hesitated, then shook his head "Perhaps it would be best if I kept that to myself, but suffice it to say that I have failed Bishop Schmidt just as I'd feared."

"But *how?*" Surely the bishop understood that Father Doyle could do only so much on his own.

"It doesn't matter now," he whispered. "The last thing I want you to do is worry."

How could she not? Kathleen was deep in this mess. She was certain Sister Eloise knew of Father Sanders's weakness for the bottle, but if her superior discovered that she and Father Doyle had covered for the priest, there was no telling what would happen.

"I know what you're thinking, Sister," Father Doyle said, "but I want to assure you I didn't mention your name."

At this point Kathleen no longer cared. "How could the bishop do this?" she demanded, her raised voice echoing in the church.

"There's an emergency," he said flatly, revealing no emotion. "Father Wood from Holy Family in Osseo has died suddenly and the parish is desperately in need of a priest."

"What about right here at St. Peter's?" she asked. Surely the bishop wouldn't leave the parish in the hands of an alcoholic priest, a priest who was more often drunk than sober?

This all seemed so unfair. Father Doyle hadn't gone running to the bishop to report on Father Sanders; in fact, he'd waited until the situation had reached crisis proportions, and prior to that, he'd done everything humanly possible to help the older priest. Father Doyle was well aware of his mission at St. Peter's, but what did the bishop expect him to do? No one could protect Father Sanders forever.

"A new priest has been assigned to St. Peter's," he told her.

"Why didn't Bishop Schmidt send the new priest to Holy Family? You belong here. I don't want you to go." She recognized that she was being selfish, but she didn't know what she'd do without Father Doyle.

From the anguish she read in the priest's eyes, Kathleen knew he didn't want to leave the parish, either.

"Sister," he said and he gripped her hands once again. "I want you to tell Father Sanders that you can no longer manage the books. Make up whatever excuse you want, but you must promise me you'll disentangle yourself from this matter as quickly as possible."

She nodded. "What…what about Father Sanders?" she asked, her eyes pleading with him for answers she knew he didn't have.

He shook his head as though he had nothing more to tell her.

This was so wrong! "He could injure or kill someone if he gets behind the wheel of a car," she said urgently. "Not to mention the harm he might do himself."

The priest's jaw tightened. "I have my orders and this parish is not my concern anymore." He said those words as though he was repeating what he'd been told. "I've been given a new assignment."

"You *can't* leave us," she protested.

"Sister Kathleen," he cried. "I have no choice! Do you understand what I'm saying? I can't do anything, and neither can you. It's in the hands of Almighty God now."

"Oh, Father." Kathleen blinked back tears. "I can't believe this." Mortified that the priest would see her weep, she covered her face.

"I'm so sorry," he said and gently laid his hand on her shoulder. "So very sorry."

Kathleen was, too. After a moment she composed herself and raised her head. "When do you have to leave?" Surely the bishop would give Father Doyle a few days to put his affairs in order before forcing him to move to another town and another church.

"Tonight."

"So soon?" She was aghast.

"Holy Family…" He let the sentence dwindle into nothingness. He was obviously as aware as she that this new assignment was just an excuse to get him out of the picture and the sooner the better.

"Who'll be replacing you?" she asked.

"Father Yates. Donald Yates."

Sister Kathleen had never heard of him. "Do you know Father Yates?"

The priest nodded. He offered no assurances about the man, no words of advice.

"What's he like?" she asked, needing all the information she could get.

"He taught me in the seminary," Father Doyle said guardedly. Then he added, "I didn't know he was serving as a parish priest. I…wouldn't think it was his calling."

This was worse than she'd imagined. In all the time she'd worked with and known Father Doyle, she'd never heard him utter a disparaging word about anyone. His intimation that Father Yates wasn't a suitable parish priest was the strongest warning he could have given her.

She realized Father Yates was the reason he'd told her

to find a way out of the bookkeeping task as quickly as possible. He was worried about what would happen to her. A chill raced up her back.

"Why is Bishop Schmidt sending you away and not Father Sanders? Does he honestly believe this new priest will do any better than you did? I don't—"

He stopped her with a raised hand. "Father Yates is more…exacting." He sighed. "I can't delay leaving any longer," he said and started to rise.

"No, not yet!" She astonished herself with the demand. "Please," she added softly. "Stay for just a few more minutes."

He nodded and sat back down.

But now she didn't know what to say and fought down the urge to weep. "Will I ever see you again?" she whispered. Father Doyle had become a friend. He was everything that was good about priests and the Church. His genuine love for God and his parishioners exemplified what the religious life should be.

"I don't know," he told her. "Perhaps our paths will cross again."

Kathleen had said farewell to those she cared about before this, but she'd never experienced such a profound sense of loss as she did in that moment. "Is there anything I can do for you, Father?" she asked.

After a few seconds, he said, "Pray for me, Sister."

"I will," she promised. "Every day."

"I'll pray for you, too."

"Thank you," she whispered.

He stood to leave and this time she didn't stop him. As he walked away, she bowed her head in sorrow. The lump in her throat made it difficult to choke back tears.

"Sister," he said, his voice calm now and reassuring, as though he'd found peace within himself. "If there's an audit or if Father Yates decides to check the books and you need me, then all you have to do is pick up the phone. Call me at Holy Family. Call me anytime you need my help. Understand?"

"Yes."

He smiled softly. "God be with you."

"And with you," she returned. But it seemed that God had abandoned them both.

{27}

Sister Joanna

Joanna didn't see Dr. Murray again until Friday of the following week. Halloween skeletons decorated the nurses' station, along with giant orange pumpkins. All the talk was of the upcoming presidential elections.

Joanna passed Dr. Murray in the hall and kept her gaze averted. It was an obvious attempt to pretend she hadn't seen him, which appeared to suit his purposes, too. Irrational though it might be, Joanna felt slighted. The least he could do was acknowledge her even if *she* chose to ignore him.

It was all too apparent that Dr. Murray had taken her words to heart. God had called her into His service, she'd told him over and over. She knew now that she'd worked so hard to convince him because she feared what would happen if she admitted otherwise. It was chilling to realize how strongly she was attracted to him. The dream had made that completely clear—her subconscious at work, although her conscious mind tried to suppress the attraction. This flirtation had gone on long enough. For both their sakes it had to end. And yet...

They'd walked past each other when Joanna heard him call her name. "Sister Joanna?"

Despite her resolution to the contrary, relief rushed through her as she turned to face him. She was unable to hold back her smile. "Hello, Dr. Murray," she said, and wanted to kick herself for sounding as perky as a Dallas Cowboys cheerleader. That wasn't how she'd *meant* to sound. She'd hoped to appear sober and professional.

If he noticed anything was amiss, he didn't comment. "When was the last time you checked Mrs. Wilson's blood pressure?"

"I just did. I made my notations on the chart." Her tone was perfect this time.

"Good." He nodded once, and without another word, continued down the corridor.

So much for that, Joanna mused as she entered her next patient's room. As far as the doctor was concerned, their outing had been time shared between friends. That was the way it should be. She was the one obsessing about it, the one who'd built it into this wildly romantic fiasco.

"Did you hear the latest?" Lois Jenson asked Joanna at the end of her shift. Joanna was preparing to go off duty and head to the bus stop.

"Hear what?" she asked. Lois took delight in passing on rumors, usually adding a comment or two of her own.

"About Dr. Murray and Jenny Parkland. Jenny's that sweet maternity nurse."

"They're dating," Joanna said casually. She hadn't heard, but it wasn't a guess. Somehow she knew—and understood. She was off-limits to Tim. He was right, of course. She was a nun; this was the life she'd chosen, the life she wanted.

Lois seemed unaware of Joanna's drifting thoughts. "Three nights this week."

Joanna returned her attention to the other woman.

"Dr. Murray and Jenny," Lois repeated. "They had three dates last week alone. They're seeing each other every day now."

"That's great," Joanna said, forcing a smile. "It's about time he made the rounds."

Lois laughed. "Cute, Sister, very cute. A little play on words there."

The joke was a pitiful attempt to disguise how the news had made her feel. But Joanna had no right to feel anything whatsoever regarding Dr. Murray. He was a handsome, eligible bachelor and she was as good as married. Her vows had been spoken and she was wedded to the Church, a bride of Christ.

"I'm pretty sure Jenny's had her eye on Dr. Murray, too."

Frankly Joanna didn't blame the other nurse. He was everything a woman could want in a man.

That night Joanna knelt before Sister Superior for the weekly Chapter of Faults. Her heart was heavy, the load of guilt weighing upon her shoulders.

Although Joanna knew she couldn't be held responsible for her dreams, she suffered from repeated pangs of guilt. She'd invited Dr. Murray—she refused to call him Tim again—into her thought life. In the process, she was risking serious trouble, jeopardizing her vows and her emotional health. Furthermore, she was setting herself up for major disappointment.

"Sister Superior, I confess before you and Almighty God a weakness in my thought life." She paused, debating how much to elaborate. She heard herself say something vague about "inappropriate reactions" and then all at once, on her knees with the entire convent looking on, she broke into huge sobs. She didn't know why she was weeping or how to stop.

An hour later, Joanna was called before Sister Eloise. "Tell me what has upset you so much," the older nun said gently.

Joanna reached for her handkerchief and blew her nose. Her eyes were puffy and her nose felt raw. Still, the tears came and she couldn't seem to make herself quit.

"Sister." Once more Sister Superior urged her to speak.

"Oh, Sister Eloise, I'm afraid I've done something foolish."

The other nun waited patiently as Joanna struggled for words. "There's a physician at St. Elizabeth's— and…and I've let my attraction for him build in my mind." She hid her face, fearing the revulsion the other nun might feel toward her.

"Sister, you are still a woman. It's only natural for you to be attracted to a man. We took a vow of chastity, but that doesn't mean we have no heart or no feelings."

Joanna hadn't expected Sister Superior to be sympathetic to her predicament.

"Does this physician return your feelings?"

A week earlier she might have answered yes, but now she knew better. "No…he's involved with another nurse."

"I see," Sister Eloise said after a long pause. "And that upsets you, doesn't it?"

Joanna felt torn. She wanted Dr. Murray to be happy and to have a good life. He was a talented surgeon, but more than that he genuinely cared for his patients. She knew, too, that one day he'd be a wonderful husband and father. He'd marry someone else, someone free to return his love, and that awareness brought an ache to her heart she dared not examine.

"I want him to be happy," Joanna whispered, her voice ravaged with emotion.

The other nun nodded approvingly. "How can I help you?"

Joanna didn't think anyone could help her through this. She felt sick to her stomach now, as though she was coming down with a bout of the flu.

"You see this physician routinely, do you?"

Joanna inclined her head.

"If you worked in a different part of the hospital, would that help?"

So her superior was going to have her transferred to another floor. Perhaps that would be for the best; perhaps then Joanna might get her life back into perspective. "I think...that would be a good thing, Sister."

The other nun promised to see to it.

Although Joanna knew that a transfer was in motion, she didn't expect it to happen quite so quickly. On Monday she learned she was being sent to work in the Emergency Room, assigned to the swing shift. Her entire schedule had been altered. She wasn't given the opportunity to tell the other nurses she'd worked with about the change or to say goodbye. More importantly, she didn't see Dr. Murray again.

Two days later he sought her out. "You might have said something about a transfer," he said, interrupting her as she dressed a young woman's wound. He completely ignored her patient. The woman, a housewife who'd cut herself with a bread knife, stared up at him.

"I apologize," Joanna said to the woman. "Dr. Fuller

will be in to give you the stitches in a moment." She turned to glare at Dr. Murray.

He followed her out of the room.

"What are you doing here?" she demanded.

"Why'd you ask to be transferred?"

"The answer to that should be obvious."

"Unfortunately it isn't that easy, so spell it out for me."

She wasn't sure he could handle the truth any more than she could admit it. "I don't believe it's a good idea for us to see each other again."

"Fine, you want to skip the occasional stop at the Dairy Queen, that's perfectly all right with me. But there's no reason to drop out of sight for three days."

"I didn't drop out of sight."

"No, you disappeared."

Joanna couldn't remember ever seeing him this angry. His face was red and he obviously had to make an effort to keep his voice controlled.

"You don't understand," Joanna whispered.

"Explain it to me."

"I can't see you again. Not at the Dairy Queen, not here, not anywhere."

"What the hell are you talking about?"

She knew he'd ask but she didn't have an answer for him. Not one she could live with for the rest of her life. "Please don't ask me that—just accept that I wanted this transfer."

"Are you *sure* this is what you want, Joanna?"

"Sister Joanna," she corrected.

He didn't say anything for a while. "Sister Joanna," he repeated, frowning darkly. "That's all the answer I need." Then he was gone. The way he left told her he would abide by her wishes.

She'd never see him again.

{28}

Sister Kathleen

On All Saints' Day, a week after Kathleen gave notice that she could no longer work on the church books, she stopped at the rectory to find out if a replacement had been hired. There was information she needed to convey to the new person—if there *was* a new person. Father Sanders had had plenty of time to hire a bookkeeper, but thus far she'd seen no evidence of anyone stepping into her role.

She refused to let him talk her into continuing in the position; a few words of praise and encouragement weren't going to persuade her to stay on.

She carefully rehearsed her speech in case she needed it. Father Doyle had insisted she get out before she became so entangled in the mess that escape would be impossible. She'd taken his advice and spoken to Father Sanders right away. The older priest had pleaded with her to reconsider, but Kathleen had held her ground. She wanted out—and the instant she met Father Yates she was even more sure of it.

Unfortunately Father Sanders was gone when she arrived and, despite his promise the week before, there was no replacement for Kathleen to train. Now she'd have to talk to Father Yates, a prospect that sent shivers of apprehension down her backbone.

As Father Doyle had implied, the new priest was an unpleasant man who seemed to find little in life with which to be happy. He was often harsh and unfriendly toward parishioners. His manner bordered on rude.

He'd been at St. Peter's a little more than a week, and already Kathleen had heard a number of complaints. She didn't think he was a bad priest, just an angry one, and that anger seemed to come in the form of a sharp tongue and judgmental attitude.

"Father Sanders is out?" Kathleen asked the housekeeper in a tentative voice.

Mrs. O'Malley nodded. "I'd disappear myself if I could," she said. She glanced toward the ceiling and shuddered. In a conspiratorial whisper, she added, "He doesn't like my cooking."

The housekeeper didn't need to identify whom she meant. "My meat loaf is too salty, my mashed potatoes taste like library glue, and he complained about my pumpkin pie. At lunch today he said he'd tasted better black bean soup out of a can." Her voice quavered with indignation as she repeated the criticism.

"You're a wonderful cook," Kathleen told her. The housekeeper made melt-in-your-mouth biscuits and cooked delectable meals for the priests. Her Irish stew rivaled the best Kathleen had ever tasted. Feeding the priests well was Mrs. O'Malley's mission in life, so Father Yates's complaints had deeply wounded her pride.

"Thank you for saying that," Mrs. O'Malley said,

sniffling. "It's a shame, you know, about losing Father Doyle. It won't be the same around here."

"How's Father Sanders?" Kathleen asked.

The cook met her eyes. "Poorly, I'm afraid," she said with a sigh.

The message was clear. Father was drinking again, more than ever. Losing Father Doyle and having to deal with Father Yates had tipped the scales for the priest.

Footsteps could be heard coming from the priests' living quarters. Mrs. O'Malley leapt as if someone had pinched her from behind and hurried back to the kitchen.

Kathleen returned to her small office and sat at the desk, thinking she'd better speak with Father Yates today. She waited for him to acknowledge her. However, he continued down the hallway without as much as a nod in her direction.

After another moment, Kathleen approached him, knocking politely on his office door.

The priest glared up at her from his desk. "Can't this wait?" he asked, frowning.

Kathleen stiffened at his lack of welcome but forged ahead. "I need to speak to you this afternoon. At your convenience, Father."

Scowl lines marked his otherwise attractive face. "What is it?" he demanded.

"Today's my last day doing the church books," she said. "I told Father Sanders a week ago that I could no longer continue to teach full-time and do the book-keeping, too."

"Overburdened, are you, Sister?"

She detected more than a hint of sarcasm, but chose to ignore it. "When Father Sanders asked me to take on this task, I was told it would be temporary. But apparently the previous bookkeeper has decided...not to return." The woman had resigned in August, but Kathleen didn't want to expose Father Sanders entirely.

"Now you're walking away as well."

"I did tell Father Sanders of my intentions two weeks ago. He's had that period of time to hire a replacement."

The other priest refused to look at her. "Which he hasn't done, now has he?"

"I... I wouldn't know."

"Fine, you can be on your way."

"Thank you." Relief rushed through her. But when Kathleen turned to leave, he stopped her.

"To be honest, Sister, it doesn't surprise me that you've quit."

She made no comment but clasped her hands in front of her as he continued to write.

"As it happens, I had a chance to go over the books this morning," he said. "I don't suppose you know of my own bookkeeping background?"

Kathleen froze. He must have noticed the discrepancies between the donations and the deposits. She'd hoped that with Father Doyle making up the difference, the matter would settle itself.

"There appear to be a number of small...*deliberate* errors."

Kathleen didn't agree or disagree.

He glanced up and met her eyes before she had a chance to lower her own. In those brief seconds, Kathleen read his contempt. He was about to say more when the rectory door opened and in strolled Father Sanders.

The priest staggered a couple of steps, then paused in the office doorway. She could smell the liquor on him and immediately noticed his unfocused gaze.

"I'm happy to see you, Father," the other priest said

with open disgust. "You're just in time for this rather unfortunate discussion with Sister Kathleen. As you know, she's chosen to give up the bookkeeping."

"Fine job she's done, too," Father Sanders said approvingly.

"I disagree, Father."

"There's a problem?" Father Sanders sounded shocked. As though he found it difficult to remain standing, he leaned against the doorjamb. The stench of liquor seemed to permeate the office; she was sure Father Yates smelled it, too.

The new priest sat back in his chair. "Your silence doesn't do you credit, Sister Kathleen." He waited, obviously expecting her to speak. She didn't defend herself and wouldn't.

"I believe you owe this parish an explanation."

Her head lowered, Kathleen bit her tongue to keep from defending her actions. She had done nothing wrong. If there *was* a crime, it was in not reporting the shortfalls to the bishop. Little good *that* would have done her, she reasoned sadly. Father Doyle had tried, and look where it had gotten him.

"I don't know what possessed Father Sanders to ask you to work here in the first place," he said, turning his scowl on the older priest. "It was a bad idea from the first."

How nice to know her efforts were appreciated, Kathleen thought to herself, struggling to hide her irritation. For two months, three and often four times a week, she'd spent hours balancing the church's books, and this tongue-lashing was all the thanks she received.

"Seeing that you have nothing to say, you leave me no option," Father Yates said in a way that told her this would bring him pleasure rather than regret. "I'm going to have a talk with Sister Eloise regarding the questionable methods you've employed."

She nodded, hoping, praying, that Sister Superior would realize she was in an impossible situation. Perhaps it had been wrong to protect the older priest, but she'd followed Father Doyle's lead. His name, however, would not pass her lips. He'd already paid dearly for his efforts to fulfill the bishop's expectations of him and to help Father Sanders.

"May I go now, Father?" she asked her voice small despite her attempt to conceal her reaction.

"By all means," he said, standing. "You're a disgrace to the good name of St. Bridget's Sisters of the Assumption."

Kathleen nearly ran out of the rectory, so desperate was she to leave. The afternoon was cold and she was chilled to the bone by the time she arrived at the convent. She'd barely stepped in the door when Sister Eloise asked to see her.

"Is what Father Yates told me true?" she demanded the moment Kathleen entered her office. Before Kathleen had a chance to reply, she was hit with a second question. "Did you alter the books?"

The answer wasn't easy. Kathleen *had* altered the books, but only slightly and only to correct the discrepancies once Father Doyle had replaced the missing cash. "I...it isn't as bad as it looks, Sister."

The older nun was clearly angry. "Is it true you took money for your own purposes and then repaid it at a later date?"

"Absolutely not!" Kathleen cried, aghast that anyone would believe such an outrageous lie.

"That's what Father Yates says happened. He has proof."

"I'm not the one who took the money," Kathleen said reluctantly. "I wasn't the one who made the deposits." The fact that Father Yates had blamed her when he *knew* Father Sanders had done it was shocking to Kathleen. She hadn't expected behavior so…so calculated, so unconscionable, from a priest.

Her defense didn't appear to placate her superior. "Are you telling me you know who did and you said nothing?"

Kathleen nodded.

"This is even worse than I imagined. Father Yates is right. Disciplinary action is necessary. I'm going to sleep on this, Sister, but I think it would be best if you returned to the motherhouse for a period of contemplation to acknowledge your sins."

Kathleen couldn't take in what she was hearing. "You're sending me away?"

"You've disgraced us, Sister."

"But…but you haven't heard my side of it." Tears clogged her throat as she struggled to get the words out.

"Nothing you say will change the fact that you were dishonest in dealing with the church's books. You have ridiculed us all."

Kathleen opened her mouth to explain, but Sister Eloise was too angry to listen. Dragging Father Doyle's name into this mess would do more harm than good. He was her friend, her confidant and he'd done what he could to protect her. Now she had to return the favor.

Still, the unfairness of the situation was more than Kathleen could endure. "I don't deserve this, Sister."

The older nun frowned at her. "As I recall, you were certainly eager to accept the job. 'Practical experience' would benefit you, or so I remember you saying. This is what you wanted. I let you do it against my better judgment. I was not in favor of the idea, but in the spirit of cooperation between the rectory and the convent, I gave in.

"I knew it would end like this, and I blame you, Sister, for your refusal to tame your ego and for surrendering to foolish pride."

The silence that followed seemed deafening.

"Very well, Sister," Kathleen whispered.

"You will do without dinner and be ready to leave tomorrow."

"Yes, Sister."

Kathleen left the office and had to find a chair so she could sit down, she was trembling so badly. The shaking didn't seem to abate as she burned with anger and humiliation.

For almost ten years Kathleen had given her life to the church and to God, and *this* was the thanks she'd received. The priests were paid decent salaries but because she'd taken a vow of poverty, as all nuns did, she worked for a pittance. Kathleen taught school, sewed her own clothes, cooked, cleaned and lived a Spartan life. Her reward was loneliness and a variety of thankless tasks. For the first time since she'd entered the convent, Kathleen began to question the rightness of staying.

That night, unable to sleep, her stomach growling, Kathleen packed a small bag. She could only imagine what the other nuns would say or what they'd be told once she was gone. It would soon be apparent that she was leaving in disgrace.

The doorbell chimed in the distance. Then again, more insistently. Two long peals followed by a burst of short ones.

She didn't know who was on duty, but obviously

whoever it was had gone to bed. Since she had yet to disrobe, Kathleen took the task upon herself.

To her surprise, an agitated young man was pacing on the other side of the door.

"How can I help you?" Kathleen asked, opening the door a crack.

"I need to talk to Sister Angelina."

"I'm sorry, but the sisters have all gone to bed."

"It's important!"

"I'm sorry," Kathleen said again. She was sympathetic, but there were strict rules about admitting visitors, and she didn't have any choice. "Come back tomorrow and Sister will speak to you then."

"No—I have to talk to Sister Angelina now."

"I'm truly sorry," she said and without waiting for him to argue further, she closed the door.

{ 29 }

Sister Joanna

At ten, Joanna had another hour to go until the end of her shift and already she was exhausted. Normally she didn't drink coffee this late at night, but she needed a jolt of caffeine to help her adjust to her new schedule. Working in the Emergency Room was exhausting—periods of boredom alternating with bursts of frantic, high-adrenaline activity.

With only a couple of days until the national election, all the talk around the hospital was of Nixon and McGovern.

"McGovern hasn't got a chance," one of the nurses, Gloria Thompson, said as she added sugar to her coffee.

"Have you checked the price of bread lately?" another complained. "You can thank Nixon for that. He sold our wheat to Russia, and fifty cents for a loaf of bread is the result." She rolled her eyes and nodded when Joanna strolled past. "Good to have you with us, Sister."

"Thank you," she said. It would take time to adjust,

not only to this schedule but to the staff. She missed Sylvia Larson, Lois Jenson, Julie and the others.

And she missed Dr. Murray with an ache that refused to leave her. Countless times each day, her mind drifted to him, despite her efforts to discipline her thoughts.

When she'd finished her coffee, she returned to the Emergency Room. It'd been a slow night, with several minor injuries and one serious situation—a teenage girl who'd been brought in by her boyfriend. The girl had apparently been to a backstreet abortionist and was hemorrhaging badly. Dr. Barlow, the attending physician, was working on her while Gloria and two other staff members rushed to meet his demands.

"Sister Joanna," Dr. Barlow called out when he saw her. "Would you find out what you can from her boyfriend?"

"Right away," she said. She'd just started toward the waiting room when a tall, solidly built teenage boy came barreling through the swinging doors.

"I want to be with her," the boy said belligerently. "Let me see her!"

Two orderlies restrained him from advancing farther.

"Will someone shut him up?" Gloria yelled.

"Where are the parents?" one orderly asked.

"Corinne. Corinne! It's going to be all right, baby." The youth strained against the two men holding him back. "Hang on, Corinne. Hang on." His young face was twisted with torment as he struggled. When he caught sight of Joanna, he went slack. "Sister! Sister."

"Can I help?" Joanna asked.

"Get me Sister Angelina," he pleaded. "Corinne begged me to get her. She needs to talk to her."

The young man didn't know what he was asking. "That's impossible."

"That's what the nun at the door said, but Corinne wants to talk to her. Please, Sister. They'll listen to you."

"You went to the convent?"

The boy nodded, tears brightening his eyes. "Corinne says she has to talk to Sister." The tears came in earnest now, washing down his pale face. "She was bleeding so much and she was afraid… I didn't know she was pregnant. I didn't even know."

The orderlies released him and Joanna took him into a vacant cubicle. The young man collapsed onto a stool and sobbed openly. Joanna laid her hand on his shoulder, trying to comfort him.

"She never wanted me to use any protection—she said it was against the Church and Corinne wanted to be a good Catholic."

Joanna sat with him for several minutes and let him talk. She couldn't imagine how a teenager could rationalize not using birth control and then decide on abortion. How desperate this girl must have been.

"Sister, find out what's happening. I need to know. Please, Sister, please."

Joanna left him for a moment and learned that Corinne Sullivan had been rushed into surgery in an effort to stop the bleeding.

"It doesn't look good," Dr. Barlow said as he peeled off his blood-smeared plastic gloves. "She waited too long to get here. Are the parents on their way?"

A knot in her stomach, Joanna nodded. "Admissions called them."

"Make sure they have privacy when they arrive," he said, and with sadness in his eyes, he turned away.

Joanna recognized that forlorn, hopeless look. It was too late. Nothing more could be done. She wanted to shout at the injustice of it all, to scream how terrible it was that a girl so young would waste her life. Didn't she realize how precious life was? Hers and that of her unborn child.

About ten minutes later, as Joanna passed the Emergency Admissions desk, a middle-aged couple hurried in, looking shaken and unsure. "I'm Bob Sullivan. Where's our daughter?" the man asked.

"Mr. and Mrs. Sullivan." The teenage boy went over to Corinne's parents.

"We've been so worried," Corinne's mother cried. "She didn't come home after school. We've been phoning everyone, and no one knew where she was."

"None of that matters now, Sharon," the father said. "For the love of God, tell us what happened!"

"Yes, Jimmy, tell us what happened," Sharon echoed. "The hospital phoned but they wouldn't give us any details."

"She was—she was pregnant," Jimmy said in a faltering voice.

"Pregnant?" Bob Sullivan grabbed the teenage boy by the shirtfront and rammed him against the wall. The boy's feet were suspended two inches from the floor before Joanna could get the older man to release him.

"Shall we discuss this privately?" she said, steering them to an area the hospital had set aside for families. Once inside the room, the parents huddled together on the sofa and Jimmy stood by the door, as though ready to flee. Joanna sat in the remaining chair.

"Is Corinne suffering a miscarriage?" The question was directed to Joanna by the girl's mother.

Joanna shook her head. It was hard to even say the words. "Apparently Corinne decided to…abort the baby."

The blood drained from the mother's face. "An abortion? Corinne decided to get rid of the baby?"

Joanna nodded reluctantly.

"You arranged this?" the father asked Jimmy, his eyes narrowed and his face reddening.

"No! I swear I didn't know anything about it! Corinne told me she was going to see a friend and had me drop her off at a street corner downtown."

"You didn't know what she was doing?"

"I didn't have a clue. How could I, when she didn't even tell me she was pregnant." He hung his head and his tears dripped onto the tile floor.

"Why would she go to a backstreet abortionist?" Sharon Sullivan asked her husband, wringing her hands in shock. "Why wouldn't she talk to me about this?"

"How did she pay for it?" Bob asked Jimmy.

"I don't know," he told them. "I don't know anything."

"She was saving her money for Europe this summer," Corinne's mother whispered, gripping her husband's hand. "Where is she now?" she asked. "I want to be with her."

"Corinne's in surgery," Joanna explained.

"Surgery?" the mother repeated. "She'll be able to have other children, won't she?"

"I don't know," Joanna told them.

They sat in silence after that. Perhaps fifteen minutes later, the surgeon entered the room. He was dressed in surgical greens, a protective mask hanging around his neck. From the look in his eyes, Joanna knew. The girl was gone. She'd bled to death.

"I'm sorry," he said, and exhaled sharply.

Corinne's parents and Jimmy stared at him in confusion.

"Sorry?" Sharon Sullivan repeated. "Corinne can't have babies?"

The physician's gaze sought out Joanna's and she

saw his regret and his sadness at relaying such horrific news to these parents. "Your daughter died on the operating table," he said. "We did everything we could."

A few seconds passed and then came an unearthly wail of anguish and disbelief. Corinne's mother buried her face in her hands and sobbed loudly.

"There's been a mistake. I'm sure this is all a mistake." Bob Sullivan stood and looked first to the physician and then to Joanna. He clenched his fists at his sides. "Corinne sat at the breakfast table with us this morning. She had a test in her Health class this afternoon. It was the only thing she talked about—this test was important. Now you're telling me my little girl is *dead?* No. There's been a mistake. Something isn't right. Corinne can't be dead."

"I'm sorry," the doctor said again. "She'd lost too much blood. It was too late."

Jimmy seemed close to shock. "She said I had to take her to Sister Angelina first," he whispered, his voice barely audible. "She should've told me, she should've talked to me about the baby." Turning away from them, he slammed his fist into the wall. He howled in grief and pain, then collapsed in sobs, huddled in agony on the floor.

Joanna felt tears pricking her eyes, unable to bear witnessing their pain.

"She can't be gone—this can't be happening," Sharon burst out. "Corinne and I are going to Europe this summer. We've been planning the trip for months."

"She's only sixteen," her father said to no one in particular.

"Is there someone I can phone?" the physician asked.

Bob Sullivan looked up as if he hadn't heard. "My baby girl can't be dead. She sat at the breakfast table with us this morning."

"Sister," Dr. Johnson whispered. "Perhaps you should call the rectory and ask that one of the priests come down to be with the parents."

Joanna nodded and wiped the tears from her own cheeks.

"I'll phone Father Sanders," she murmured, wrapping her arms around Sharon Sullivan. If there was any way she could take this pain away from them she would, but that was impossible. Death had struck again like a thief in the night, stealing what was most dear.

{ 30 }

Sister Angelina

The November morning was clear and crisp, and Angie's spirits were high. The day before, she had received a letter from her father. His letters were so rare that she cherished each one and read them countless times. He seemed to be doing well and his news, as always, was about the restaurant. Angie had written back immediately. Knowing it would please him, she suggested she fly home to Buffalo that summer if it could be arranged. Her summers were often full of college classes and other commitments, but it had been far too long since she'd seen him.

That night she'd dreamed she was cooking in the restaurant kitchen, adding spices to a large pot of red sauce. When she woke that morning, she could almost smell the garlic cooking.

Humming to herself, Angie walked to the high school. She wasn't inside the building ten minutes before she heard the terrible news.

"Corinne? Dead?" she repeated, shocked, as Morgan

Gentry came to her weeping hysterically. Surely there was some mistake. Corinne *couldn't* be dead.

"It's true, Sister, I swear it's true. My mother woke me up to tell me. She's with Corinne's mother now. They're at the funeral home picking out the casket."

Instant tears sprang to Angie's eyes.

As students filed into her first-period class, Angie noticed that a number of them were crying. Several came to her looking for consolation, but Angie had none to give. She assigned pages to be read and then sat at her desk numb with disbelief and pain. By noon she realized she could no longer teach that day.

With Sister Alberta's permission, she returned to the convent and sought out Sister Joanna.

"She was in your class?" Joanna asked, sitting in the chapel with Angie after they'd prayed together.

Angie nodded, still numbed by the pure shock of the news. "She was…just a child, with an inquisitive mind. I…can't accept this." She listened with horror as Joanna relayed the events of the night before. "Jimmy was there?"

"Yes," Sister Joanna said. "He took it hard. It would help if you talked to him," she told Angie. "He blames himself, but he didn't know. He would never have let her go through with the abortion if he had, I'm convinced of that."

"The abortion…" Even now, Angie couldn't absorb the fact that Corinne had done this. In class, they'd talked about the physical hazards of such actions, as well as the legal and moral questions. Corinne had voiced her opinions loud and clear, repeating the popular secular cry of a woman's right to control her own body. Angie had been dismayed by her attitude. The child she'd carried was a precious life. No less than her own...

"Talk to Jimmy," Sister Joanna advised again. "He badly wanted to speak to you. He came here looking for you. Apparently Corinne was desperate to find you before going to the hospital."

Angie jerked her head up. "He was here? Last night?" she whispered. "*Jimmy* was the one who came to the door. Sister Kathleen told me there was a young man asking to see me, but I couldn't imagine who it might be." She wanted to kick herself now because the answer should have been obvious.

"I'm sure it was him," Sister Joanna said, confirming her suspicions. "He mentioned your name and said Corinne had insisted on talking to you."

Angie's heart ached, and this news did nothing to ease that pain. The girl had looked for her, and Angie had been unavailable. The agony of knowing this settled on her with an almost unbearable weight.

That same afternoon, Angie was able to speak to Jimmy when he showed up at the convent a second time. The boy's right hand was in a cast, but when Angie questioned him about it, he shook off her concern.

"Corinne wanted you, Sister. Instead of letting me take her directly to the hospital, she begged me to drive to the convent and get you first. I should never have agreed but I didn't have any idea she was bleeding so much. She didn't want me to know."

"Oh, Jimmy." Tears streaked Angie's face as she tried to understand the reasons Corinne might have wanted to see her.

Jimmy wept too as he sat with her in the convent's visitor area. Looking away, he drew in a shaky breath. "I didn't know she was pregnant. I swear it, Sister!"

"I believe you." It seemed important to tell him that.

"Corinne insisted we couldn't use any protection," he muttered. "She wanted to live up to the Church's rules, even when she didn't agree with them."

"Why would she get an abortion then?" Angie cried.

Jimmy hung his head and the tears slipped from his eyes. "I don't know, Sister. I honestly don't know, but I think it was because of her parents. I… I don't think she could face her mother or her father. She didn't want to disappoint them or…you."

"Oh, Jimmy." This was not something Angie wanted to hear.

"We did try to be careful, Sister.…" He lifted his uninjured hand to his face and rubbed his eyes.

The young man left soon afterward, and Angie sat in shock and grief as she tried to make sense of what she'd learned. Sister Joanna had been so sure that talking to Jimmy would help the boy deal with his sorrow, but it had the opposite effect on her.

If anything, her own feeling of loss had grown worse. This young girl was dead. Corinne had challenged Angie constantly, forcing her to defend the Church and her own beliefs. But in the end, Angie had let the girl down. Without ever meaning to, Angie had hurt Jimmy, too.

Angie's tears began in earnest then. Not knowing where else to go, she went into the chapel, knelt at the altar and buried her face in her hands. It felt as if her world was askew, as if nothing was right and never would be again.

She didn't know how long she stayed there, but when she raised her head, afternoon shadows loomed against the chapel walls. Angie had grown emotionally numb, unable to feel, unable to react.

She returned to her cell and collapsed onto her bed. In all her years of serving Christ she had never experienced anything like this sense of emptiness. Corinne had asked Angie if she'd ever questioned authority. The girl had challenged Angie to reconsider Church decrees against birth control. She'd bombarded her with questions and when she didn't like the answers, she'd scoffed at what she saw as outdated views.

To Corinne it was ridiculous that priests couldn't marry and have families. She'd startled Angie once by suggesting that nuns should be able to celebrate Mass. Such thinking was sacrilegious. Angie couldn't imagine a nun being allowed to administer the Holy Sacrament.

Lying on her side on the bed, Angie saw a shadow outside her room. She'd assumed she was alone in the convent's sleeping quarters. She sat up. Perhaps someone had come looking for her.

Standing, Angie went to the doorway and glanced in both directions. "Sister Kathleen," she called when she saw the other nun who wore her coat and carried a small bag. Her veil was missing. Alarm bells rang in Angie's head.

Kathleen turned to face her, dropping her suitcase at her feet. "Sister Angelina," she said in a rush of sympathy. "I'm so sorry."

Angie bit her lower lip in order to keep fresh tears at bay. "Thank you," she whispered. "You're…leaving?"

Sister Kathleen nodded. "Yes, Sister. I'm going away."

"But where?"

Sister Kathleen leaned against the wall and searched her pocket, pulling out a tissue. It took Angie a moment to realize the other nun was weeping.

"What happened?" Angie asked. "What's wrong?"

Kathleen straightened. "It doesn't matter now… I'm

going to Seattle. My brother lives there, and he told me years ago that he'd help me if ever I decided I had to walk away from this life. I phoned him."

"You're leaving the order?" They'd lost so many sisters already this year.

"I don't know… I need to think all of this out." Sister Kathleen dissolved into sobs. "I've been ordered to return to the motherhouse, but I can't go back to Boston and disgrace my family. I'd never be able to look my parents in the eye if they believed I'd…" She let the rest of her words fade.

It was clear to Angie that her friend was in agony over leaving. "Is there anything I can do to help?" she asked, although she doubted she was in any state to lend assistance.

Sister Kathleen shook her head. "Nothing. No one can… Sister Angelina, I'm sorry about not waking you last night. Had I known…"

"You did what was required." Had the situation been reversed, Angie would've done the same thing.

The other nun's relief was unmistakable.

"God be with you, Sister Kathleen," Angie whispered.

"Thank you," she whispered as she started down the corridor, carrying her small suitcase.

"Will you write and let us know what's happening with you?" Angie asked.

Sister Kathleen shrugged. "I will if I can. Goodbye, Sister."

"Goodbye," Angie returned. It seemed to be a day for farewells. First Corinne, and now her friend.

{ 31 }

Sister Joanna

Joanna was concerned about Sister Angelina, who'd taken Corinne Sullivan's death hard. When she first heard the news, Sister Angelina, like so many others, had reacted with shock and disbelief. Joanna had suggested Sister Angelina speak with Corinne's boyfriend; he needed emotional support and counseling to help him deal with his role in this tragedy. In retrospect, Joanna realized that while Sister might have consoled the young man, the conversation had only made her feel worse.

For reasons she couldn't fathom, Sister Angelina blamed herself for what had happened to Corinne. She wasn't sleeping, wasn't eating and hadn't been able to return to school for a week following the funeral.

All Sister Angelina seemed capable of doing was staring at the wall and weeping. Everyone was worried, including Sister Superior, who'd called in a physician.

Joanna didn't know what was said, but she suspected the doctor had prescribed tranquilizers. Now, as she sat in the hospital chapel, Joanna prayed for her friend, prayed for Corinne's parents who'd suffered such a grievous loss. She prayed for Jimmy whose life was forever altered by the death of his girlfriend and his unborn child.

While she was whispering her prayers, Joanna prayed for herself. More and more she'd grown dissatisfied with her life. For six years she'd constantly reassured her mother that she hadn't entered the convent on the rebound. Yes, if Greg had come home from Vietnam without a wife they would've been married and by now she would have produced the requisite two point five children and lived in a house with a white picket fence. But Greg hadn't come home to marry her, and Joanna's future had taken a detour.

In her pain and humiliation, she'd turned to God for comfort. She'd believed with all her heart that He was calling her to the religious life. She had trusted to the very depths of her soul that becoming a Sister of St. Bridget's was the right decision for her.

Then she'd met Dr. Murray and everything changed. For six years she'd ignored every part of her femininity. Yet God was the one who'd created her as a woman. He'd been the one who'd given her breasts and a womb, who'd given her sexuality. Being a nun meant rejecting all sexual feeling, and she was no longer sure she could do that.

Shortly after Corinne Sullivan's death, Joanna had gone to the maternity floor. The nurse Dr. Murray was seeing worked in the delivery room and Joanna wanted to catch a glimpse of her. She had no intention of introducing herself or making any effort to speak to the other woman. Curiosity had nagged her into taking this action, but in the end Joanna hadn't seen Jenny.

Instead she'd gotten waylaid at the nursery. For reasons

she didn't want to examine, she'd stopped in front of the nursery window and stared at the babies. These perfect, beautiful children had caught her attention as soon as she stepped off the elevator.

It had been years since Joanna had held an infant, years since she'd smelled that special scent. Years since her maternal instincts had struck this hard.

Seeing that she was enraptured by the newborns, the head nurse had invited her inside and urged her into a rocking chair. Then, as if knowing exactly what Joanna wanted, the grandmotherly nurse had placed a newborn in her empty embrace.

The little boy fit perfectly in the cradle of her arms. For a terrifying moment, Joanna had been afraid to breathe, afraid to move. But gradually instinct took over, and she began to rock the baby. Softly, gently. Peace, unlike anything she'd experienced in years, came to her then. A sense of wonderment settled over her, and in that moment she felt completely happy.

Tears had pooled in Joanna's eyes, embarrassing her. Yet no one spoke. Thirty minutes later, when she walked toward the elevator, her original mission forgotten, she was a changed woman.

It was as if she'd seen into her own heart. She was like women all through the ages. She wanted what women had always wanted: to be loved and cherished by a man, and to have that love bring forth children. She wanted a husband and family, and the ache of having neither left a void inside her that couldn't be ignored.

The chapel door opened and Joanna realized she wasn't alone anymore. She made the sign of the cross, sat on the wooden pew and folded back the kneeler. But as she was ready to stand and leave, Dr. Murray moved into the pew beside her.

The shock of seeing him stole her breath. For the longest moment they stared at each other, saying nothing.

Tim spoke first. "I've been worried about you."

Who had told him? How could he possibly have known her doubts and her thoughts when she'd shared them with no one but God?

"Why?"

"I heard about Corinne Sullivan. Did you know her?"

Joanna shook her head. "She was a student at St. Peter's High School but I didn't know her."

"I heard you were with her family when they received the news."

"Yes." It was one of the saddest nights of her life. To the day she died, Joanna would remember the haunting grief of Corinne's parents. To lose a child, especially under such conditions, was a tragedy beyond words. And Jimmy Durango—the poor boy felt guilt as well as grief. None of their lives would ever be the same.

"How are they doing?" Tim asked. He sat only a few inches away, but after their initial greeting he hadn't looked at her again.

How was any family able to cope after the loss of a child? "About as well as can be expected," Joanna said.

He nodded and then, his voice the merest of whispers, he added, "I've missed you. The entire third floor misses you."

"I miss everyone there, too." And she did. Working E.R. wasn't the same. The staff had welcomed her, but Joanna felt like a stranger, trying to find her place and fit in with the others. The suddenness of her transfer had created a certain amount of suspicion and plenty of speculation.

"I know why you asked to be transferred," Tim went

on, "and I agree it was for the best, but that doesn't mean you aren't missed."

She bowed her head, not wanting him to read what she could no longer hide. Almost from the beginning Joanna had been physically and emotionally attracted to this man. That attraction had blossomed and taken root in her dreams, those disruptive sexual dreams that continued to obsess her. It was as though the womanly part of her, once repressed, had broken free. Refusing to be ignored, the fantasies had lingered in her mind, in her waking moments, invading even her prayer life.

"But even though I understand why you asked for the transfer, I don't know if it was the right thing for either of us." His words were low and intense. He reached for her hand and held it firmly in his own.

Joanna was astonished by how much his touch affected her. A lump formed in her throat as she splayed her hand and let their fingers intertwine.

"I know I shouldn't touch you, shouldn't even be this close, but Joanna…" He bent his head near hers and his lips brushed her cheek.

Eyes closed, she swayed toward him and their foreheads touched. "So much is happening all at once," she murmured.

"I'm falling in love with you…."

"Don't say it, please." She placed a finger against his lips.

"Just let me know where I stand with you. That's all I ask."

"I can't…" Before she could finish, the chapel door opened and Sister Nadine walked inside. She paused when she found Joanna sitting with Dr. Murray and frowned darkly.

Joanna eased her head away from Tim's, but the other

nun's gaze lowered to their locked hands. Almost immediately, she turned and walked out of the chapel.

"Does that mean trouble?" Tim asked, exhaling forcefully at the other nun's rapid departure.

Joanna didn't know what it would mean; nevertheless, she tried to reassure him. "It's probably nothing to worry about." He seemed to accept that and she was grateful.

But Joanna was wrong. Sister Superior asked to see her the following afternoon; Joanna didn't need to be told why. It was as if this confrontation was meant to be.

By now, Sister Eloise's office should be a familiar place to her. Joanna recalled the troubles she'd had in the beginning, while she was a postulant and then a novice at the motherhouse in Boston. Battling her stubbornness and her lack of submissiveness had never become any easier.

"Sister Joanna," the head of the convent said, looking up from her desk. She hesitated and seemed to search for the right words. "The last time we spoke, you mentioned your attraction to one of the physicians at St. Elizabeth's."

Joanna merely nodded.

"At that time we both felt it would be best to have you transferred to another area of the hospital."

"Yes, Sister."

"That hasn't helped, has it? You haven't been able to subdue your rebellious nature, have you?"

"No," she admitted, struggling to hold back the guilt. "But Sister, you reminded me that while we're nuns, we're still women, too. I love this man with all my heart." Never before had Joanna dared to acknowledge her feelings out loud.

"And he returns your love?" she asked.

"Yes… Maybe… I don't know." She prayed he did, but yesterday was the first time they'd spoken honestly, however briefly, about their feelings.

"What do you want to do, Sister?"

Joanna bowed her head, unable to meet her superior's eyes. "I don't know… I just don't know."

"Would you like to transfer to another convent?"

Joanna looked up and shook her head. The ache inside her intensified. "I want to go home," she whispered.

"You are home, Sister," the other nun said.

"Home to my family," Joanna elaborated. "I need to think about all this. I need time. I'm sorry, Sister Eloise, I'm so sorry. I feel like I've failed you and failed God."

Sister Eloise was quiet for so long that Joanna wondered if she was about to refuse her. "You're sure this is what you want?" she finally asked.

"Yes… I'm not saying I'm leaving the order. What I need is time to sort through these feelings and know my own heart, to consider the future."

"A leave of absence then?"

"Yes," Joanna whispered as the tears burned her eyes. Suddenly the life that had seemed so calm and predictable had become confused. Chaotic. Sister Kathleen was gone. Joanna wasn't quite sure what had happened, but she'd left the day after Corinne Sullivan died. Then there was Sister Angelina, who was devastated by Corinne's death and had been in a state of depression ever since. Now, Joanna, too, was experiencing a crisis of faith.

"Very well," Sister Eloise said reluctantly. "Return to your family."

{ 32 }

Sister Angelina

Something was wrong with her, Angie decided. She couldn't seem to get enough sleep. That morning, she'd embarrassed herself by falling asleep during lauds. Right in the chapel, she'd nearly keeled over onto Sister Martha. Fortunately the other nun had managed to catch her.

Angie's appetite was nonexistent and the skirt she'd shortened only a couple of months earlier was so loose it hung on her hips.

Only recently she'd tried to talk to her father on the phone and all she'd been able to do was weep. He'd been upset and tried to discover what was wrong, but she couldn't tell him, couldn't bring herself to admit how bad she was. Instead she'd made light of her tears and ended the conversation as quickly as she could.

Sister Superior was worried about her, too. Worried enough to call for a Catholic physician to come and talk to her. Angie didn't need a doctor to tell her she was depressed—or to give her medication.

She knew why she felt the way she did. What she didn't know was how to deal with this never-ceasing mental anguish, this constant sense of guilt and doubt.

Everyone had been so kind and gentle with her. She tried, she really did, to shake off the mantle of grief, but it clung to her. The world seemed dark and ugly, and it seemed that nothing good would ever happen again. All gaiety and laughter had evaporated into the darkness.

As the Christmas holidays approached, there was an air of celebration at the convent, an anticipation of joy. Angie experienced none of this. It was difficult to function, to pretend she was preparing the next day's lessons when she rarely put any thought or effort into her classes anymore. Luckily, with Thanksgiving, there was a four-day break coming this very week.

Staring down at the textbook as the nuns around her worked at the long tables, silence filling the room, Angie tried to force her thoughts onto the next day's lessons, but to no avail.

Instead, her mind continually returned to Corinne's parents. Again and again she was tormented by the question of how Bob and Sharon Sullivan were going to face this holiday season without their beautiful Corinne. How would it be possible for them to put up a Christmas tree and decorate their home when their only daughter had recently been buried? Where was their joy? Where was—

"Sister?"

Angie looked up from her book and realized Sister Martha had been speaking to her.

"I'm sorry," she said. "I didn't hear you."

"There's a man here to see you."

"A man?"

"Yes, Sister. He's quite insistent. He says he's your father."

"My father?" Angie was sure she'd misunderstood. "My father is in Buffalo, New York." The Thanksgiving week was one of the busiest of the year for the restaurant. He would never leave Angelina's to travel at such an important time.

"He would like to see you," Sister Martha said.

Angie got up from the table. Although she knew there must be a mistake, her heart raced. Could her father really be here in Minneapolis?

As she entered the foyer, her steps slowed. It was indeed her father. He stood in the entry, still in his thick overcoat, hat in hand as he waited.

"Daddy," she whispered.

Tony Marcello looked up, his face dark with concern. When he saw her, a smile came to his lips and he held out his arms.

As if she were a little girl again, Angie ran into his embrace. By the time she felt his arms around her, the tears had come, ravaging her with huge, breath-choking sobs.

He cradled her like a child, his hand on her head as he hugged her close. He murmured to her in Italian, in words she hadn't heard for so many years that she barely remembered their meaning. Then they were sitting on the sofa, where he continued to hold her protectively. "Angelina, my poor, sweet Angelina, what has happened to you?" He brushed the hair from her forehead, and in the process dislodged her veil. His eyes searched hers.

Through her tears, his features swam before her. She felt his love, and God help her for being weak and emotional, but Angie needed his strength—just as much as the motherless child she'd once been.

"What has happened to you?" he repeated in a broken whisper as though he too was close to tears.

"She's dead, Daddy. Corinne is dead. I told her it was wrong—I'm the one to blame. I'm the one who urged her to be a good Catholic girl. Then she got pregnant."

"This high school girl?"

Angie nodded. "She panicked—she was so afraid. I knew things weren't right. I sensed it and I did nothing. *Nothing.*" She wailed in grief and guilt and hid her face in his shoulder. "She came to find me instead of going to the hospital…and she bled to death."

"Oh, Angie, sweet, sweet Angie."

"She's dead…gone, and it's my fault."

"No, Angie, no."

Others had attempted to tell her the same thing, but Angie discounted their words and refused to accept her innocence in Corinne's death.

Because Angie believed she *was* responsible. Corinne had come to her time and again and argued against the Church's stand on these important issues. Angie realized now that the girl had come to her seeking answers, searching for a way to rationalize what she and Jimmy were experiencing. Corinne had been seeking a tacit blessing to use birth control.

Angie hadn't given it to her, hadn't agreed with her arguments and as a result, Corinne had chosen to engage in unprotected sex. Then she'd discovered she was pregnant and her world had come crashing down. Angie's world had toppled, too.

As she'd mulled over her conversations with Corinne, Angie reached a conclusion. The girl *was* right. Such intimate decisions as whether or not to use birth control were between a man and a woman, between husband and wife. The Church had no business interfering, no Biblical ground on which to stand. The consequences of this decree were more and more apparent every week at Sunday Mass. Catholics were revolting and walking away from the Church, or at the very least choosing to follow their own consciences in the matter of birth control.

Corinne's words haunted her. If the Church was wrong about birth control, then what else might be a mistake? Angie was afraid to examine that question.

"Angelina, Angelina," her father crooned. "I'm taking you home with me."

She looked up at him, frowning. "I don't think I can leave."

"You aren't in jail. You need to come home."

She didn't argue. She didn't have the strength.

"Go, collect what you need and send Sister Superior to speak to me."

With one exception—her insistence on becoming a nun—Angie had always followed orders. First from her father and then from the sisters who ran the order and the convents in which she'd lived. She never questioned authority, but accepted whatever she was told, did whatever she was asked. Her thoughts were subordinate to those of others—older, wiser people, whom she'd entrusted with her life.

She stepped away from her father.

"Go," he ordered. "It's time you left, time you realized this place is not for you. It never was, but I couldn't refuse you."

Angie found Sister Eloise in the room where the other nuns sat and quietly worked or studied. "Sister," she said, "my father is here."

"So I understand." Her disapproval was evident.

"He would like to speak to you."

Sister Eloise nodded. "He couldn't have come during the day? It is highly unusual for family members to stop by unannounced this late in the evening."

"No," she said without emotion. "He's here now."

While Sister Superior met with her father, Angie went to her cell, pulled out her overnight case and packed her things. She placed her clothes neatly inside the case; it didn't take long to pack. With her coat over one arm and her suitcase in the other, she returned to the foyer.

Her father stood as she approached.

"I can't allow you to leave," Sister Superior said, her expression severe.

"You can't stop us," her father said, his jaw set. "I've come to take my Angelina home."

"Sister Angelina, I implore you to reconsider."

Without speaking, Angie moved closer to her father's side.

He took the suitcase from her hand and held open the door. The cold night air stung Angie's face as she stepped into the darkness.

"We're going home, Angelina."

"Yes, Daddy. We're going home."

{ 33 }

Sister Kathleen

Kathleen added cream to the large pot of mashed potatoes and turned on the hand mixer. Sean's wife, Loren, was busy preparing the platter of turkey and stuffing for the dining room table.

"Aunt Kathleen, Aunt Kathleen, help me," four-year-old Emma cried as she chased the calico cat around and around Kathleen's legs while two-year-old Paul sat in the middle of the room pounding on an overturned pot with a wooden spoon. The television blared in the background.

"Emma, go see your daddy," Loren said.

"Daddy sent me in here."

The phone rang in the distance. "I'll get it," Sean shouted from the living room, where he was watching a football game. This was like no Thanksgiving Kathleen could remember. In Boston it was a huge family affair, with as many as twenty people, and her mother supervising in the kitchen. At the convent it had been another matter entirely, a formal and subdued celebration but with the same roasted turkey and pumpkin pie. With Sean and his family, it was three adults and the two children in a cramped two-bedroom house.

Her brother, God love him, had taken Kathleen in on a moment's notice. He'd even given her money for the flight to Seattle. She was well aware that she couldn't continue to impose on Sean and his wife. She had to make a decision and move forward.

"Kathleen," her brother called, standing by the telephone.

She turned off the mixer and peered around the corner. "Yes?"

"Do you know a Father Brian Doyle?"

She was so stunned all she could do was nod.

"He'd like to speak to you." Sean held out the receiver, and when she'd accepted it, he returned to his football game, but lowered the volume.

"Father Doyle?" Kathleen asked, pressing the receiver to her ear.

"Sister Kathleen, how are you?"

"I'm well, and you?"

"Good," he said. "Good. It's taken me this long to find you."

"I'm sorry, I should have contacted you."

"No one seemed to want to tell me where I could reach you," he said. "I was finally able to locate your parents in Boston and they gave me this number."

"I'm in Seattle."

"So I understand." He sounded out of breath. "What happened?"

It all seemed too complicated to explain. In the two weeks since she'd left, Kathleen had made an effort to forget.

"Tell me," he urged.

"I told Father Sanders I could no longer keep the books for him," she said, going back to their conversation shortly before his move to Osseo. "Just like you suggested."

"Yes, that's good, but apparently there was some kind of trouble afterward."

"There was," she whispered. All at once she felt too weak to stand and sank down onto the sofa arm. "Father Yates decided to audit the books and almost immediately discovered the discrepancies."

She heard the slow release of Father Doyle's breath. "I was afraid of something like that," he muttered.

"Then Father Yates contacted Sister Eloise."

His silence said everything. He knew without her elaborating how uncomfortable the situation had been.

"I assume you didn't explain that I was the one making up the shortfalls?" he said heavily.

"No."

"Why not?" His voice was incredulous. "I would've stepped forward and told the truth. There was no need for you to go through this alone." She heard him sigh. "In my eagerness to serve the bishop and help Father Sanders, I was more of a hindrance than anything else. Now I see I'm responsible for your troubles, as well."

Kathleen disagreed. "I was ultimately the one in charge of the books. Not you. It was only right that I accept responsibility for my role in all this."

"But at what cost?" His words were angry—and regretful.

She had no answer to give him.

"Why did you leave the convent?" he asked next. "Or did Sister Eloise send you away?"

"Sister Superior instructed me to return to Boston,"

Kathleen said reluctantly. "But I chose to come to Seattle instead."

"But isn't Boston your hometown?"

"Yes, but I was going back in disgrace, an embarrassment to the order and I… I couldn't. I just couldn't look my parents in the eyes and tell them I'd done wrong."

"You didn't," Father Doyle insisted. "I was the one who—"

"We both did," Kathleen whispered.

"Sister Kathleen, I can't tell you how sorry I am."

He had nothing to apologize for. Worse, he blamed himself for not being there to protect her.

"It's my fault," he said. "I'm the one who should've been reprimanded. If I hadn't tried to protect Father Sanders, none of this would have happened."

"I don't think it's necessary to assign blame, Father. What's done is done." Kathleen felt better just hearing his voice. She'd missed him terribly. Other than a few of the nuns she taught with, Father Doyle was her only friend; they'd shared this burden and helped each other and in the process had developed a certain closeness, careful though it was.

"What can I do?" he asked, obviously distressed.

"Do?" she repeated. "Nothing."

"I don't believe that. First thing tomorrow morning, I'm contacting the motherhouse and explaining the circumstances," he said. "I refuse to allow you to be punished."

"Please don't," Kathleen pleaded. "Father, I'm sincere about that. This business with Father Sanders and Father Yates has helped me."

"How?" He didn't sound as though he believed her.

"It's clarified some issues I…hadn't realized I needed to deal with."

"What issues?"

"We don't need to discuss those now." Kathleen preferred not to delve into the whole complicated mess. She felt resentful and angry and misjudged. With Father Doyle gone, she'd been left vulnerable, facing a difficult situation on her own. She'd hoped, had *believed* that her own order would come to her defense; instead her superiors had condemned her without even hearing her version of events.

"If that's what you want." Father Doyle didn't seem happy with her reticence.

"I do." She felt strong, stronger than she had in a long while.

"What about the future?"

"I don't know what to tell you."

"You're leaving the convent, aren't you?"

No one else had asked her that question. Not her brother or her sister-in-law, not her parents. Had they voiced it, Kathleen wasn't sure how she would've responded, but the minute Father Doyle asked, the answer was clear.

"Yes," she whispered, "I've decided to leave."

She heard the priest's harsh intake of breath. "I was afraid you were going to say that."

"I'm positive it's the right decision," she assured him. She stood, easing herself off the sofa arm. She had given nearly ten years of her life to the Church without ever truly questioning her vocation. But in that time, the world had changed—and so had she.

"I called for another reason," Father Doyle said. "I got word this morning that Father Sanders was in a car accident."

"No," she gasped. "Was he drunk?"

"Yes."

"How bad is it?" Her greatest fear was that Father Sanders had injured an innocent party or killed himself in a drunken crash.

"He walked away from the accident and thank God no one else was hurt."

Kathleen murmured her fervent relief.

"God used the accident to get Father the help I couldn't," the priest continued. "He was arrested for drunk driving and the judge placed him in a facility that specializes in the treatment of alcoholics."

She said a silent prayer of thanksgiving.

"Unfortunately—" he sighed "—the press got hold of the story and it's front-page news."

As far as Kathleen was concerned, it was Bishop Schmidt who'd brought the bad publicity down upon the diocese. If he'd listened to Father Doyle and taken steps to help Father Sanders earlier, the outcome might have been very different.

"What about Father Yates?"

The priest laughed softly. "He's been promoted and will be assuming Father Sanders's position as head of St. Peter's."

Kathleen laughed, too.

The line went quiet for a moment, and Kathleen supposed it was the end of their friendship. They had no reason to maintain contact. "Thank you, Father, for calling, and for telling me about Father Sanders."

"I'm the one who should be thanking you."

"Would you mind… I mean, if it would be all right, I'd like to talk to you every now and then." Where she got the courage to ask, she didn't know. But he was a link with her past and she faced so many transitions as she moved toward the future. It would be good to have a special friend she could call when she needed to.

"I'd like that, Sister Kathleen."

"Just Kathleen," she corrected.

"Kathleen," he repeated softly. "Write down my number and phone me anytime you wish."

"Thank you."

After a few words of farewell, she replaced the receiver and looked up to see her brother and Loren and the two youngest O'Shaughnessys waiting by the table. She joined them, their Thanksgiving feast about to begin.

"Are you ready?" Sean asked.

Kathleen nodded. She was ready now for whatever the future held.

Part Four

OUT OF THE HABIT

But small is the gate and narrow the road that leads to life, and only a few find it.

—**Matthew 7:14**

{34}

Kathleen O'Shaughnessy

Sean and Loren insisted Kathleen stay with the family until after the Christmas holidays. By the first week of January, she realized she had to stop relying on her brother. It was time to make her own decisions and to begin relying on herself. Walking away from the convent the way she had, without a word to her superiors, had been an act of defiance and anger. Only recently had she been in touch with the motherhouse. The conversation had been brief; by mutual agreement it was determined that Kathleen would take a one-year leave of absence. She would continue to receive her small salary and she'd start attending classes at Seattle University. St. Bridget's Sisters of the Assumption would pay her tuition fees.

"Are you sure about this?" her brother asked as he loaded her suitcase into the trunk of his car. Retired from the Army, Sean worked at Boeing building airplanes and his wife stayed home with their children.

"Of course, I'm sure," Kathleen told him, although

she was frightened out of her wits. She would be living in a group home called House of Peace, a facility set up by a group of former nuns who had dedicated themselves to helping other women like themselves move from the convent back into the world.

Mother Superior had agreed to give Kathleen this year, with the stipulation that she would accept counseling. It was Sister Agnes's fear that Kathleen's desire to leave was primarily a reaction to the unfortunate circumstances with Father Sanders. Mother was afraid Kathleen would regret her decision later.

"I'll do whatever I can to help you," Sean said, opening the car door.

"You already have," Kathleen said and impulsively hugged him. Nervous as she was, she found it difficult to release him. "I don't know what I would've done without you and Loren these last two months." It was disconcerting to have no home. She'd been under her parents' roof until she'd entered the convent and now, when she was nearing age thirty, she had no place to call her own.

"You'll come see us soon, won't you?" Loren asked, standing on the damp lawn with the two children leaning against her.

"Of course I will," Kathleen promised. "As often as you want." Crouching, she held her arms open to her niece and nephew. Emma threw small arms around her neck, while two-year-old Paul hugged her upper arm. After a few moments, Loren pulled her protesting children free.

Tears filled Kathleen's eyes as her brother backed out of the driveway. "I can't thank you enough," she whispered, not wanting him to hear the emotion in her voice.

"Mom and Dad think you should come home."

"I can't. I don't want to be a burden to them—or to you."

"You're not a burden to me. And Mom and Dad would never think of you as a burden, either."

Perhaps not, but she was a disappointment to her family and she knew it. Kathleen didn't have the emotional strength to answer her parents' questions. Dealing with her new life was complicated enough.

As for seeing a counselor, she welcomed the opportunity to talk about her feelings. Her one wish was that if she had to sort through all the emotions associated with leaving the convent, it be with a counselor she knew and trusted—preferably Father Doyle. The priest, however, was in Osseo, Minnesota, and she was in Seattle.

"You're going to be all right," Sean assured her.

"I know." But she didn't entirely believe it. The world outside the convent was a frightening place. Kathleen didn't know what to expect or how to cope with all the changes that were hurtling toward her.

"You can call Loren or me anytime."

"Thank you." She swallowed hard.

"It can be a cruel, lonely world when you're alone," her brother warned, "but you *aren't* alone. Remember that."

"I will." It was as though Kathleen was in high school all over again and her big brother was giving her advice.

She knew Sean was worried about her, but her brother had his own life and his own problems. Sooner or later, Kathleen needed to start taking care of herself, and there was no better time to learn than right now, at the beginning of a brand-new year. The world of 1973 was a different place than it had been ten years ago.

When Sean pulled up in front of the House of Peace,

Kathleen saw that it was a large, two-story white home with one large dormer above a screened-in porch. There was a trimmed laurel hedge on each side of the narrow walkway that led to the front steps. A Christmas wreath still hung on the door inside the porch, and she saw the welcoming glow of lamplight, dispersing a little of the day's gloom.

After a moment, with her brother at her side, Kathleen walked up the steps. She held her breath and rang the doorbell. Someone must've been waiting on the other side, because it opened immediately.

"You must be Kathleen." A woman of about sixty with short white hair and a pleasantly round figure greeted her. "I'm Kay Dickson. We spoke on the phone."

Kathleen felt warmed by Kay's smile.

"Come in, come in." The other woman held open the door for them.

Sean hesitated as he set down Kathleen's suitcase. "I should be getting back home." His eyes questioned her, as if he felt uncertain about leaving her at this stranger's house.

"I'll be fine," she told him, and in that instant she knew it was true.

This was a new beginning for her. She could walk away from her life as Sister Kathleen with her head held high. Yes, there was some bitterness, some anger and hurt feelings, but she would learn to deal with that. Overall she had no regrets. She was ready for this second stage of her adulthood.

"There are five others living here," Kay explained as she led Kathleen up the stairs and showed her the bedroom reserved for her. It had a double bed, a dresser with a mirror and a nightstand that held a small lamp. This would be the first time in her life that she'd slept in a double bed. That room was luxury beyond anything she'd ever known.

"Breakfast is served at six. When's your first class?"

"Eight."

"That's perfect then."

"Am I the only one going to school?" Kathleen hated to ask, but the thought of navigating a college campus on her own felt overwhelming. It wasn't as though she'd been completely sheltered in the convent. For that matter, she'd traveled from one end of Boston to the other on city buses in her teens. But being friendless in a strange town, attending a strange school, was suddenly terrifying.

"Sandy and Pauline are both taking classes at Seattle University. They'll be happy to have you join them."

Kathleen set her bag on the end of the bed. "Thank you." Everyone was being so kind.

"We're having lunch in a few minutes. Please join us. There's a work schedule in the kitchen. We'll ask you to sign up for chores, but it isn't necessary to do anything for the first couple of days. We recognize that this is a major adjustment."

"I want to help," Kathleen said. She needed the comfort of routine and a sense of giving back instead of merely receiving. Although she deeply appreciated everything Sean and Loren had done for her, they'd treated her as though she was recovering from a long debilitating illness. It was only at her insistence that they let her help with even the most mundane household tasks.

After a lunch of pea soup and warm bread—just right for such a cold, gloomy day—Kathleen sat down and wrote her parents a letter, in which she reassured them that she was happy and well. When she'd finished, she tore a second sheet of paper from her notepad and wrote

Father Doyle. Her purpose was the same; he'd sounded concerned when they'd spoken on Thanksgiving Day and she wanted to let him know she was fine. She'd mailed him a short letter with a card at Christmas but hadn't heard back.

The phone rang and Kay came into the kitchen, holding open the swinging door. "It's for you, Kathleen," she said.

Surprised, Kathleen walked into the hallway, where the phone rested on a small table by the stairs. "Hello," she said, assuming it was her brother. No one else knew she was at the House of Peace.

"Sister Kathleen—Kathleen—it's Father Doyle. I hope you don't mind that I tracked you down. Your brother told me where I could reach you."

"I was just writing you!"

"I apologize for not answering your Christmas card. How are you?"

She opened her mouth to tell him what she told everyone else—but he was the one person she could trust with her real feelings. "A little shaky, actually."

"I thought so. How can I help?"

He could move to Seattle, become her counselor, hold her hand for the next twelve months and reassure her that she was doing the right thing.

"You could be my friend, Father."

"I already am." He chuckled softly. "We're friends, Kathleen. Good friends."

{ 35 }

Joanna Baird

"Can I get you anything, honey?" Sandra Baird asked, checking on Joanna one evening early in the new year. Joanna sat in front of the television watching the eleven o'clock news. Five Watergate defendants had pled guilty that day to burglary. The news was dominated by the break-in at the Watergate complex and the possible link to President Nixon.

"I'm fine, Mom," she said, reaching for the remote control. This device was new since she'd entered the convent and she found it both amazing and ridiculous. What was the world coming to when people couldn't be bothered to walk across their living rooms to change channels or turn off the TV?

Dressed in her robe, her mother came into the darkened room and sat on the edge of the sofa. Her father was already asleep. Sandra took Joanna's hand and held it loosely. "It's good to have you home."

It didn't feel good to Joanna. Her mother was suffocating her with attention. And her father, her dear sweet father, was as confused as she was. Half the time he called her Sister and then with a look of pain and regret apologized profusely. He'd loved the fact that she was a nun and had taken such pride in her vocation. Now that she was home, he didn't know how to react to her. All her life, Joanna had been close to her parents. This uneasiness and concern grated until she wanted to scream.

Her father didn't understand why she'd asked for a leave of absence, and she couldn't explain it to him. He wanted her to be happy, but he also wanted her to be a nun.

Her mother, on the other hand, was thrilled to have her home and came up with a hundred reasons each day to entice her back into the world. Since Joanna's return, Sandra had made hair appointments for them both, plus she'd arranged for a manicure and pedicure. She'd taken Joanna clothes-shopping and bought her several new outfits.

As a result, Joanna felt as though she was living with a foot in each world. Part nun, part not—and all of her very confused.

It had seemed so simple when she'd first decided to ask for a leave of absence. All she needed was time away—a few weeks, a couple of months at most. Just enough time to review her options.

However, the longer she was away from the convent, the more complex her emotions became. She missed the order and ritual of her life. There was a certain comfort she hadn't appreciated in rising and going to bed at the same time each day, in praying and eating according to schedule. It was a life of symmetry. Of harmony. The unfamiliar freedom she experienced living with her parents was awkward and confusing.

"You seem so quiet since you've been home," her mother complained.

"Mother, I observed Grand Silence for years. I'm not as talkative as I was when I was a teenager."

Her mother glanced uncomfortably toward the blank television screen. "Remind me what Grand Silence is again."

"Every night after seven-thirty, we didn't speak."

"Ever?"

"On rare occasions. It was the time we set aside to pray and meditate."

"You were always praying. I never did understand what you had to pray about at all hours of the night and day."

"Mother, I was a nun."

"I know, dear, but…" She gave a wry smile. "Well, that's all behind you now."

"Is it, Mom?" Joanna asked because she wasn't sure.

Her mother patted her hand as though to convince her that soon everything would be as it always had. "By the way, Greg phoned and asked to see you."

Joanna shook her head. "I don't want anything to do with Greg."

"I know. I told him that, but he seems to think—"

"That I left the convent because of him."

"Yes," her mother confirmed.

"I didn't. His visit to Minneapolis had nothing to do with my coming home."

Her mother's fingers tightened around hers. "All your father and I want is for you to be happy."

Joanna gave her mother a reassuring smile and stood. "I'm going to bed now."

"Good idea. You have a big day ahead of you."

Joanna nodded. She was applying for a job at the

local hospital. Although her parents wanted her to live with them indefinitely, Joanna couldn't do that. The walls felt like they were closing in on her; she wanted her own place. Thankfully, because of her nursing degree, she could support herself. Joanna was also convinced that through her nursing skills she could find a sense of balance in life.

"Good night, honey," her mother called as Joanna entered her bedroom.

"Good night." Sitting in the dark at the end of her bed, Joanna thought about her interview the next morning. Then, out of habit, she slipped to her knees and reached for her rosary.

When she'd finished the five decades—ten Hail Marys each—of the Joyful Mysteries, she kissed the crucifix and set the rosary back on her nightstand. As soon as she'd nestled her head on the pillow, Tim Murray's image appeared in her mind. She allowed herself this one extravagance: while in bed, alone, she talked to him. She told him about her day and how confused she felt and she mentioned her regrets. He was involved in several of those. Her feelings for him were tangled up with her dissatisfactions, and she knew she needed a clear head before she spoke to him again.

One regret was that she'd left the convent without telling him goodbye. There hadn't been time. Perhaps he'd assume she'd returned to Providence because of Greg. She hadn't, of course, and she hoped Tim wouldn't think that.

Sometimes, usually at night, she wondered if he still thought about her at all. Did he ask about her? Did he know where she was? Did he care? Or was he relieved that their paths would no longer cross? Joanna could only speculate about the answers. Whenever she did, a sinking sensation settled in the pit of her stomach.

The house was quiet when Joanna woke the following morning. Her father had gone to work, and her mother had a volunteer committee meeting first thing. As though Joanna were a child, her mother had left a note that told her what to eat for breakfast.

Reading the list propped against the sugar canister, she smiled and helped herself to a banana, which wasn't on the suggested menu.

Standing under the hot spray of the shower a few minutes later, Joanna luxuriated in the perfumed soap and creamy shampoo. This was decadence unlike anything she'd known in six years.

While combing her hair, Joanna stared at the fog-covered mirror. As the steam from the shower slowly dissipated, her facial features began to take shape. For a long time she studied her own reflection. It was like watching herself emerge from behind a veil. As good a metaphor as any, she thought wryly. She was becoming reacquainted with Joanna Baird—but this Joanna was a different person from the one who'd entered the convent six years before.

After dressing for her hospital interview, Joanna poured a cup of coffee and on impulse, picked up the phone. It had been wrong to leave Minneapolis without talking to Tim. He deserved to know what had happened and why she'd left the way she did.

She got his office number from directory assistance and then promptly changed her mind. Wadding up the paper, she threw it in the garbage. Halfway out the door, Joanna changed her mind again and retrieved the phone number. If she called him now, she'd have a legitimate excuse—asking him for a reference.

Her skin went cold and clammy as she dialed the number. The phone rang, jolting her. She closed her eyes, waiting for his receptionist to answer.

"Dr. Murray's office."

"Ah…"

"Would you like to make an appointment?"

Not knowing what else to say, Joanna answered, "Yes."

"Are you already a patient?"

"No, actually—"

"I'm sorry. Dr. Murray isn't taking any new patients without a referral."

"I see." It didn't surprise her to learn that he was a popular surgeon. "In that case, would it be possible to leave a message?"

"Of course."

"Would you please tell him Joanna Baird phoned?"

"B-a-i-r-d?"

"That's correct."

"And your message?"

"Tell him…tell him Sister Joanna phoned to say goodbye."

"Oh. Goodbye," the receptionist said, sounding confused.

"Also, could you please tell him I'd like to use him as a job reference?"

A moment of silence followed and Joanna could hear a pencil scratching. "I'll let him know."

"Thank you," she whispered feeling more foolish than ever. She hung up the phone.

{ 36 }

Sister Angelina

The shades were down and shadows flickered across the bare walls in Angie's childhood bedroom. Her father had left it exactly as it was in 1958, when she'd entered the convent. Judging by outward appearances, not a month had passed. Everything looked exactly the same. Only it wasn't. Angie was vastly different from the eighteen-year-old who'd left home to become a nun.

Her father had stormed into the convent and wrapped her in his protective arms and brought her home. But now that she was back in Buffalo, he didn't know what to do with her. Angie was lost and confused and in such emotional anguish that it took more effort than she could muster to get out of bed in the mornings.

Her father knocked on her bedroom door. "Angelina, are you awake?"

She didn't answer and prayed he'd go away. It wouldn't do any good, but she already knew that.

After a second knock, he opened the door and flipped on the light switch. "It's morning."

She was sitting up in bed, staring at the wall. She squinted at the bright light and wanted to shout at him to turn it off, but that would demand energy and she had none.

"It's a beautiful morning. Look." As if turning on the lights wasn't bad enough, he raised her window blind and sunshine invaded the room.

Angie closed her eyes. She didn't *want* to look at the sunshine. She didn't *want* to speak to her father.

"Angelina!" His voice rose with exasperation. "What's wrong with you?"

Angie said nothing.

"All day you sit here and stare at the wall. You don't talk, you barely eat. Even my zabaglione doesn't tempt you. I heard of a man ready for death who sat up in bed when his wife brought him my zabaglione. Yet my own daughter barely takes a bite."

Angie wanted to reassure her father that it wasn't his cooking. He had surrounded her with his love, spoiled her with gift after gift and tempted her with his desserts, all to no avail. She wanted none of the things he tried to give her. What she wanted, what she *needed,* was forgiveness. But no one could give her that—least of all her father, who couldn't understand her grief.

Angie had failed Corinne and in the process she'd failed herself. The pain of knowing that refused to leave her.

"How can I help you?" he asked, sitting on the corner of her bed.

"You can't, Daddy."

"Talk to me," he pleaded. "Tell me what happened."

Tears moistened her eyelids and she shook her head, unable to get any words past the constriction in her throat.

"A girl in your class died, and you think you killed her?"

Angie nodded. "Yes…in a way, I think I did."

"How?" he asked. "Did you hold a gun to her head? She got pregnant and she tried to get rid of the baby. It's not your fault, Angie. God knows why a beautiful young girl would try to kill her baby, but these things happen." He lowered his voice, frowned and then added a few other comments in Italian, none of which Angie could translate.

"She trusted me."

"She didn't have a mother to talk to?"

"Yes…but I was the one she turned to."

"And you knew this teenager was pregnant and advised her to make an appointment with this abortionist?"

Of course she hadn't! Why did her father insist on asking her these ridiculous questions?

"You won't answer me because you're hauling around this load of guilt you have no business carrying." Impatience sharpened his voice.

"I knew something was wrong," Angie argued, her own voice emotionless. "I knew it but I didn't ask."

"And that's the reason you're nailing yourself on that crucifix up there next to Jesus?" He pointed at the large crucifix on the wall across from her. A palm frond from the Palm Sunday service fifteen years earlier was tucked behind it.

Angie lowered her head and refused to answer.

"What can I do for you?" Her father was shouting now. "Please tell me!"

She shook her head.

Exasperated, he turned and walked out of the room, leaving the door open and the irritating lights on. Angie groaned in frustration. All she wanted was to be left alone and to sleep. She was so tired. But despite her exhaustion, she either tossed and turned the night away or wandered the hall, pacing back and forth. Her eyes burned, and she cursed her inability to escape into sleep. Then just before dawn she'd drift into a fitful slumber, which inevitably ended when her father got up.

She could hear him now, thumping down the stairs. In a few minutes she'd smell the scent of freshly brewed coffee. A little while after that, she'd hear him climbing upstairs again. He would return to her room, carrying a breakfast tray in an effort to persuade her to eat. To satisfy him, she'd nibble one or two bites and leave the rest. She had his routine all worked out.

Sure enough, right on schedule, he trudged up the stairs and brought the tray of breakfast into her bedroom. "I made you coffee," he said as he did every morning. Then he set the tray on her lap. Coffee and a croissant, jelly, butter and a small pitcher of cream.

"Thank you," she whispered, although she wished with all her being that he'd take it away. She wasn't hungry. Sometimes she was afraid she'd be violently ill if she so much as lifted a fork.

Usually her father left then, but he didn't this morning. He walked back and forth at the foot of her bed. Angie watched him, wondering at this sudden break in their routine.

"Angelina," he said, facing her. She suddenly saw how much the years had changed him. Her father was in his early sixties, but he was still robust and she'd never thought of him as growing old. It was a shock to see how lined his face was and how his once-gray hair had gone completely white.

"Yes?" she asked. Trying to please him, she stirred cream into her coffee.

His eyes were sad and empty; his shoulders drooped in defeat. "Do you want to go back to the convent?"

If she had an answer, Angie would have given it to him, but she simply didn't know. For fifteen years she'd dedicated herself to the Church. She'd loved her life, enjoyed teaching and her students, but in her soul Angie knew she'd never stand in front of a classroom again. It just wasn't in her to teach anymore. That wasn't completely Corinne's doing; Angie had burned out. At a loss, she hung her head and didn't answer.

"You can't speak to your own father?" he cried. "If you can't tell me, then who can you tell?"

His pain unsettled her. Angie loved her father more than anyone or anything other than God, and it grieved her to cause him anguish. "I...don't know."

"If you want to go back to Minneapolis, I'll take you." The fact that he'd made such an offer revealed how truly desperate he was.

"I don't want to go back," she wept, breaking into sobs. "I can't..." If she couldn't teach, she'd be given some other assignment and Angie could think of nothing else that would suit her.

Her father moved closer and set the breakfast tray aside. Then he gently gathered her in his arms. "You cry. Go ahead and cry it out, and then it's over with, okay?"

"I...don't know."

He sighed. "Angelina, I can't stay home any longer."

"Stay home?" She realized it'd been weeks since he'd spent more than an hour or two at the restaurant. In her pain and self-absorption she hadn't recognized the sacrifice he'd made for her.

As if struck by a brilliant notion, he said, "Come to the restaurant with me."

She stared up at him through her tears. He hadn't left her alone in weeks. Weeks! Even when he was away, he made sure someone was in the house with her. All at once it dawned on her why. Her father was afraid she'd commit suicide if he gave her the opportunity.

Angie would never take her own life. That hadn't even entered her mind. Yes, she was depressed and angry with the Church, but taking her own life would condemn her for eternity. And it would destroy her father. She couldn't bear the thought of putting him through such an ordeal. Surely he knew that!

"Angie, come with me," he said, his eyes shining with hope. "It'll be just like when you were a little girl." His large hands gripped her shoulders. "Get dressed now and I'll meet you downstairs."

For the first time since she'd come home, Angie felt the beginnings of a smile. "Okay, Daddy. I'll go to the restaurant with you."

{ 37 }

Joanna Baird
April 1, 1973

Joanna had forgotten how lovely Providence could be in the springtime. The air was clear and fresh, and she marveled at the newly green trees and budding flowers. She had her own apartment now and was discovering that life as a single woman wasn't nearly as frightening as it had first appeared.

Twice now, Joanna had been asked out on a date. Both invitations had caught her by surprise. She wasn't looking for a relationship, but she'd felt flattered and more than a little flustered. She'd been a teenager the last time she'd gone out with a man—she didn't include that ice cream sundae with Dr. Murray. She'd declined both invitations because technically she was still a nun.

Her job on the surgical floor was fast-paced and interesting, and she loved her work. She was learning to manage her money and remained in close contact with her family. Every Sunday she attended Mass with her parents, keeping her ties to the Church strong. Her parents and the Church were her anchors during this time of adjustment. She'd found that her high school friends were mostly married and their lives were completely unlike her own. She felt uncomfortable with them and she was sure they did with her, too.

Once she had her own apartment and a job, Greg had called her, hoping for a chance to prove himself. Joanna had been kind but firm in her rejection and she hadn't heard from him again, which was a relief.

The phone rang on a beautiful Monday morning as Joanna stepped out of the shower. Her hair was longer now and permed. She liked this new carefree style that was so popular among her peers, although it reminded her a little of a dandelion gone to seed. Wrapping the towel around her, she answered on the third ring.

"Hello," she said breathlessly. Since this was her day off, it was either the hospital calling her in as a substitute or her mother about to suggest they meet for lunch.

"Good morning," her mother said cheerfully. "There's a surprise at the house for you."

"A surprise?"

"A man actually." A male voice could be heard in the background. "Hold on a minute," her mother said.

Joanna strained to identify the voice but it was too faint.

Then her mother was back on the line. "Here, you can talk to him yourself."

"Joanna?"

It was Tim. Dr. Murray! She sank onto the edge of the bed in shock. "Tim?" All these months and she hadn't heard a single word. Not one. Then, out of the blue, he showed up at her parents' home? Her breath went shallow.

"Are you there?" he asked.

"What are you doing at my parents' house?" she demanded.

"I came to see you. Why else do you think I'm here? Would it be all right if I came over?" He sounded impatient and excited at once.

"Yes, please…" Her anger melted away. "It would be very nice to see you. Do you know where I am?"

Her mother had already given him the address, he said, and he was leaving now.

In a record fifteen minutes, Joanna dressed, put on her makeup and dried her hair. Still, her nerves were frayed by the time Tim knocked on the door.

Joanna opened it and stepped back, hands clasped together in front of her, heart pounding hard.

"This, um, is a surprise," she said. She wasn't sure how to act or what to say. He looked wonderful, better than she remembered. It'd been almost six months since she'd seen him, but she hadn't forgotten a thing about him. Not a day had passed in which he hadn't been part of her thoughts.

"May I come in?" he asked.

Joanna wanted to die of mortification when she realized he was still standing in the doorway while she unabashedly stared at him. "Of course! Please." She hurriedly stepped aside.

He walked into the one-bedroom apartment, which was only beginning to reflect her personality. Her mother had helped her add dashes of individuality here and there. For six years Joanna had lived with the barest of necessities. It took her mother's eye to point out small things she could use—a photograph, ivy in a ceramic pot, some colorful tea towels—to turn this apartment into her home.

"You look—" He hesitated. "Different."

Her hand went instinctively to her hair. "Yes, I imagine I do."

He lowered his voice, as if in awe. "You're beautiful—but then you always were."

His compliments embarrassed her and she immediately looked around for a distraction. "Would you like a cup of coffee?" she asked brightly.

"No, thanks."

She poured herself one just to keep her hands occupied and then joined him in the compact living room, where he sat at one end of the sofa and she sat at the other.

"So," she said, holding her mug with both hands. "What brings you to the East Coast?"

"I was in Boston for a symposium. I heard you were in Providence and decided to take an extra day to look you up." He made it sound so matter-of-fact.

"How did you know I was here?"

He relaxed against the arm of the sofa and crossed his long legs, balancing his ankle on the opposite knee. "The hospital called. You gave them my name as a reference. There were six Bairds in the phone book, I hit Mark on the third try and your mother answered."

He'd gone to a lot of trouble, she mused.

"I didn't know what to think when you left without a word," he said. "I thought, I hoped—hell, I don't know, but it came as a shock."

"I'm sorry. I know I should've called."

"Why didn't you?"

"There wasn't time, and I wasn't sure it would be wise...."

"Why not? You had to know how I felt about you. That last day I saw you, I admitted I was falling in love."

Yes, and his admission had terrified her. "As I recall, you were dating someone else…and I was, am—" she corrected "—a nun." She sipped from the mug and noticed her hands were trembling.

Tim's eyes softened. "You don't look like any nun I've ever seen," he murmured, and his words reminded her of a similar statement he'd made last fall.

"I've taken a leave of absence."

"For how long?"

"A year," she told him.

"Then what?"

"If I feel the way I do now, and I know I will, I'll write a letter to Rome and ask to be released from my vows."

"Are you sure you're going to follow through with this?" He certainly had a lot of questions.

She nodded, set her coffee mug aside and sat up straighter. She had a few questions of her own. "I phoned and left a message for you," she said, "but you never acknowledged my call."

"Message? What message? You said goodbye. What did you want me to do? Track you down so I could say goodbye, too?"

"I don't know. It probably wasn't correct protocol to contact you, but… I didn't want it to end the way it did."

"I assumed the only reason for your call was to line me up as a reference."

"No," she said sharply, "that was the excuse I used. I wanted you to know…"

"Know what?"

She shrugged and called herself every kind of coward for being unwilling to confess the truth.

"More importantly, Joanna, tell me why you left."

She raised her eyes to his. "You mean you don't know?"

He reached out and gently grazed her cheek with his knuckles. "Tell me." His eyes pleaded with hers.

Joanna wasn't sure she could.

"I need to know," he continued in a low, seductive voice.

The tenderness in his eyes mesmerized her, and she was unable to look away. "I was falling in love with you, too. I tried so hard not to—but I couldn't discipline myself enough to prevent it."

"That was why you transferred to the Emergency Room?"

She nodded. "I had a talk with Sister Superior, and she advised the move. Later, when we were found together in the hospital chapel, she suggested I needed time away to review my feelings."

"Have those feelings changed?" he asked.

She swallowed tightly. While she was embarrassed about discussing her attraction to him, she was grateful for the freedom to speak honestly. "No."

"After all these months, you're saying you feel the same way about me?"

"Yes," she whispered.

"I'm glad, Joanna."

He lifted her chin until her gaze met his.

"Have I made a complete fool of myself?" she asked.

He shook his head. "I came back from Nam a different man. As far as I was concerned, God was dead. Either that, or he'd never existed. Just when it felt like my life was getting back to normal and I was starting a promising practice, I ran headlong into a beautiful hospital nun. You wouldn't let me forget about God. I remember you once told me that God hadn't given up on me, even if I'd given up on Him."

"I said that?"

"And more. Half the time, I came away from the hospital thinking about you, about arguments I wanted to make and hadn't. You had me muttering to myself. I don't know how you talked me into attending Mass again, but I'm grateful you did. I started sleeping better and my mother noticed a change in my attitude. I told her you were responsible and she assumed you were much older—a nice, friendly nun in her sixties or seventies. I didn't correct that impression."

She'd prayed so hard for Tim Murray and it felt as if God had smiled upon her when she saw him in church that first Sunday.

"I didn't know what to think when I realized I was in love with you," he said.

Joanna's hand went to her heart.

"It troubled me, Joanna. You'd dedicated your life to Christ and I didn't want to feel the things I did. I dated several women and was actually grateful when you got that transfer, but it didn't help. I think you were already a part of me. I've missed you. Not a day goes by when you aren't in my thoughts."

"I miss you, too," Joanna confessed.

"Then you were gone." He shrugged ever so slightly. "I'll admit that at first I was glad. You know what they say—out of sight, out of mind. But it didn't take me long to discover I wasn't going to forget you. Then I was annoyed because you left without a word of farewell. That one phone message only served to infuriate me more."

She smiled.

"I was invited to speak at the symposium and I accepted because it was the perfect excuse to find you. I had to know, Joanna."

"Know what?"

"If you feel about me the same way I feel about you." He stretched out his hand and caressed the side of her face.

"I love you, Timothy Murray. I loved you when I left the convent and I love you even more now." She turned her face into his hand and kissed his open palm.

He pulled her into his arms and brought his lips to hers with a tenderness that made her feel weak. "I just kissed a nun," he whispered.

"And a nun is about to kiss you back." Her lips found his.

Tim held her close, and his breathing was heavy when he lifted his mouth from hers. "Okay, where do we go from here?"

"I still have six months of my leave of absence."

"That long?"

"That long," she repeated. "But the time will fly by. Let's get to know each other as just two people, all right?"

He nuzzled the side of her neck. "That should be interesting with you living in Rhode Island and me in Minneapolis."

"We've both faced challenges before."

"You're going to make me wait, aren't you?"

She sighed as she wrapped her arms more securely around his neck. "You know what they say about good things coming to those who wait. The very best is yet to be, I promise you that." Closing her eyes, she pressed her head to his shoulder. In the depths of her heart she knew Tim Murray would be worth every moment of that wait.

{ 38 }

Angelina Marcello

The first day Angie visited the restaurant, she sat on a stool and watched her father move between his chefs, tasting the sauces and correcting the herbs and spices. For weeks she simply sat and watched. Then one day, she suddenly realized how much she'd missed the pungent scent of simmering garlic. She closed her eyes and breathed it in the way someone who stands on a beach inhales the scent of salt and sea. At that moment Angie truly felt she'd come home.

Shortly afterward, for reasons she didn't understand, her appetite returned. Every day her father had tried to entice her with his favorite dishes. She refused each one until he offered her spaghetti alla puttanesca, which had been her childhood favorite.

The sauce, made with anchovies, tomatoes and olives, was hot and spicy. Long ago she'd heard that the recipe originated in the red-light district of Rome. Women of the night would cook the sauce and set it on their windowsills, hoping to lure patrons to their establishments.

The spaghetti tasted as wonderful as she remembered. *Better* than she remembered. That night she had two huge plates of spaghetti, heaped high with the spicy sauce.

It was as though she'd been awarded an Olympic medal for her appetite. The entire kitchen crew applauded when she finished her second helping. Her father beamed, his eyes brimming with unshed tears. He hurriedly brought her his signature zabaglione, and stood by watching as she ate every last bite.

That was the beginning. The next day it was fettuccine Alfredo. Angie hadn't noticed how thin she'd become—and she'd forgotten how wonderful food tasted—until she started visiting the restaurant. *Everything* smelled so good, and once she'd sampled the familiar dishes, it seemed as if her father's food offered her the comfort she hadn't found anywhere else.

Then one afternoon six months after she'd left the convent, Tony Marcello insisted he had paperwork that needed his attention and asked Angie to do the daily tasting. Reluctantly she'd agreed, seeing through his ploy. He wanted her to assume his role; it had been his plan for her from the time she was a child and she didn't have the heart to refuse him.

Mario Deccio and the other cooks had been with the restaurant for years and knew the recipes as well as—or better than—Angie. Still, they respectfully stepped aside and waited for her approval, the same way they did with her father. The gift she'd once shared with him had never left her, she discovered. Her instincts for the nuances of a dish were as reliable as ever.

In the summer of 1973, Angie began working the restaurant floor, greeting their dinner guests and making recommendations when called upon. It was her job to see that the patrons were satisfied and that their dining experience was everything they had anticipated. People liked her unobtrusive manner and asked after her if she wasn't there. By the end of the season, profits were up twenty percent.

Her father had never been happier, Mario said. That wasn't all he told her. "Your papa was not the same after you went to the convent," the chef confided. "For a long time we worried. He seemed to lose all interest in life. But you're home now."

It was good to be back. Angie felt guilty for enjoying her role in the restaurant so much. It was almost as though the last fifteen years had somehow disappeared from her memory. From her life…

She might've been able to continue pretending indefinitely if Mario's granddaughter hadn't stopped by early one afternoon. Angie saw the teenager enter the kitchen and nearly collapsed. Gina Deccio was sixteen years old and wore her hair in the same teenage style as Corinne Sullivan. They both had dark, inquisitive eyes. Gina smiled at Angie and it was as if Corinne had stepped into the room.

"Angelina, come and meet my granddaughter," Mario said. His expression revealed his pride as he placed his arm around the girl's shoulders.

"Hello," Angie said, barely able to contain her panic. "If you'll forgive me, I have an errand to run." No one questioned her as she pulled off the apron and hung it on the peg and nearly dashed from the building. It was muggy and warm, late in the summer; Jim Croce's "Bad, Bad Leroy Brown" was playing on a nearby radio as Angie began her walk. She walked and walked for blocks on end.

Her feet hurt but she kept up the punishing pace, her mind racing, driving her further and further from everything that was familiar, everything that had given her solace.

She didn't stop until she found a church. It wasn't a Catholic church, but Angie didn't care. She hurried inside and made her way to the front, then fell onto her knees at the railing. Burying her face in her hands, she silently wept.

She cried until there were no tears left and when she was finished, she sat in a pew and realized those tears hadn't been for Corinne. They'd been for her.

In the months since Angie had set aside the habit of St. Bridget's Sisters of the Assumption, she'd found her place outside the convent. She wasn't going back. This time away wasn't a leave of absence. She wouldn't be returning to the convent in a few weeks or months. She was *never* going back.

Glancing up, she closed her eyes and prayed fervently, begging forgiveness. When she'd joined the convent she had devastated her father. Now she was afraid she'd be disappointing her heavenly Father by leaving it.

She waited for the guilt to come over her like a dark storm. Inwardly she cringed and feared another depression; instead she experienced a new sense of peace. She wondered if it was just wishful thinking; she wasn't convinced God would so easily forgive her for abandoning her vows. There'd be a price to pay. Surely penance would be required before God Almighty would set her free from debilitating guilt and remorse. She'd failed Him, and that couldn't be without consequences. She didn't know how long she sat and waited for some act of penance to reveal itself. It never did.

When she left the church, Angie felt almost giddy. She was free. The emotional shackles were gone. Without guilt, without remorse, she could walk away from her life as a nun.

Her father was white with panic by the time a taxi returned her to the restaurant. "Where did you go?" he demanded, following her inside.

"For a walk."

"You were gone *four* hours!" he shouted.

"It was a long walk."

He put his hands on his hips just as he used to when she was a child who'd disobeyed. "Is that all you have to say for yourself?"

"Yes," she said, and kissed his cheek before reaching for her apron. "On second thought, no."

"No?" His eyebrows shot upward.

"No," she repeated, feeling jubilant. "I've decided to write Rome."

He scowled ferociously. "What are you going to write?"

"I'm going to ask that the Holy Father release me from my vows."

Angie waited, expecting her father to express relief and delight, but he showed no outward sign of happiness.

"Did you hear me, Dad?"

"I heard you." He turned abruptly and went back into his office.

Bewildered, Angie went after him. "Don't you have anything to say?" she asked, standing in the doorway of the small, meticulously organized office.

He looked up, his weathered face lined with worry. "Where are you going next?"

"I'm not going anywhere, Daddy. I'm home to stay."

"You mean it?"

Angie nodded.

Her father took out his handkerchief and dabbed at his eyes. "It was my zabaglione, wasn't it?"

Angie stared at him in disbelief and then realized he was teasing. "Without a doubt," she said.

Her father burst out laughing. He leapt up from his chair, threw his arms around Angie and hugged her. She laughed, too, until the tears ran down her cheeks and the kitchen staff came to investigate.

{ 39 }

Kathleen O'Shaughnessy

In August of 1973, shortly after Nixon refused to hand over the secret Watergate tapes as ordered by Judge John Sirica, Kathleen moved out of the House of Peace and into her own apartment. She'd been hired as a lay teacher at St. Joseph's Parochial School, teaching fifth grade, and was jubilant to be self-supporting.

It was the first time in her life that she'd lived on her own. Her parents had visited earlier in the summer; they'd accepted Kathleen's decision and encouraged her to move back East while she reflected on her choices for the future. But Kathleen liked Seattle and this was where she wanted to make a fresh start. Sean was close by and she could visit her parents during the summers. Her mother and father had reluctantly agreed with her plan to live on the West Coast. They parted on warm terms, and Kathleen felt absolved from the lingering worry that she'd disappointed those who loved her most.

More and more, she recognized that she had no desire to return to the convent. Her counselor, a former nun herself, had helped Kathleen immeasurably. They discussed the complex issues of her role in the Church, past and future, as well as coping with life on the outside. They talked about everything—finding jobs, feeling guilt, the possibility of meeting men...

For part of the summer, Kathleen taught a catechism program. She also led the children's choir, and for pure fun, she was teaching herself how to play the guitar again. That last summer at home, before entering the convent, she'd managed to learn a repertoire of easily played songs.

One afternoon toward the middle of August, Kathleen strolled through Elliott Bay Park after one of her counseling sessions. The blue sky and the warm breeze off Puget Sound enticed her to linger. Someone was playing the guitar and it sounded so much better than her own simple strumming that she paused to listen.

Kathleen found the musician sitting under a tree, dressed in jeans with his long dark hair tied in a ponytail and a kerchief headband. He played a folk song and she sat down on a nearby bench.

"Want to sing along?" he called out.

She shook her head, embarrassed that he'd noticed her.

"I'm Pete," he said.

"Kathleen."

"Good to meet you, Kathleen." He began to play an old song she remembered, "House of the Rising Sun."

"I've been teaching myself the guitar," she said when he'd finished. "I've discovered it isn't as easy as it looks."

"All you have to do is practice."

"I know." She supposed that was something she could be doing right then, but it was such a glorious day, Kathleen didn't want to go home to an empty apartment. So she stayed. Never mind that she owed both

Father Doyle and her sister Maureen a letter. Or that she could be getting a head start on her classes for September. This was where she wanted to be.

After another half hour, she finally stood to leave.

"Goodbye, Lady Kathleen. Hope to see you again."

"You too, Pete." He'd begun to play a melody she didn't recognize. So many of the more recent songs were unknown to her.

She waved as she passed him, her mood free, swinging her bag at her side. Another thing she'd had to get used to—carrying a purse.

It soon became a habit to pick up something for dinner from the Pike Place Market and then stop at Elliott Bay Park to listen to Pete. That first time, she hadn't noticed he was a street player, or more accurately a park player. He collected coins in his guitar carrying case; because she considered him a friend, she didn't give him money. However, she often brought him fruit or a drink.

One afternoon she'd bought him a sandwich, and the two of them sat on the lawn and talked. Summer was winding down and Pete was heading south. To school, she assumed, although he'd never actually said.

"You're a teacher," he said, opening a soda can and handing it to her. "You'll be going back to school next week." He sat with one knee raised as he ate his turkey sandwich. She envied the way he seemed to fully enjoy each moment, each sensation.

"I'm starting right after Labor Day." This wasn't a date, she reminded herself. They were just friends, but it felt good to sit with a man and simply talk. This was new to her, this easy camaraderie with the opposite sex. Even as a girl, her exposure to boys had been limited. Sean was almost ten years older and her youngest brother was barely more than a baby while she was living at home. She'd attended an all-girl high school.

Pete lowered his sandwich and studied her with undisguised admiration. "I certainly never had any teacher as beautiful as you."

She must have blushed because he leaned forward and traced the bridge of her freckled nose. Those freckles had been a curse when she was a teenager, but Pete seemed to find them intriguing.

"Don't men say pretty things to you, my lady Kathleen?"

She lowered her eyes, afraid that if she mentioned the fact that she was still technically a nun, he would leap up and race away. That was what the boys in her high school class had done even *before* she'd entered the convent.

Her dates had been few and far between. The minute a boy learned she was interested in the religious life, the relationship, such as it was, would immediately end. Kathleen didn't want that to happen with Pete.

"I'll miss you when you leave," she confessed.

"I won't be gone more than a few months," he said. Then with a small laugh, he leaned forward and kissed her cheek. "Maybe I won't go at all."

Kathleen's spirits lifted. "Really?"

"It's hard to walk away from a red-haired lady."

His compliments flustered her and to distract them both, she asked a practical question. "How will you support yourself?"

He shrugged. "I'm not into material things. My life is simple. Anyway, I could always get a job in a tavern or maybe a coffeehouse. Summer's too beautiful to waste on a real job. That's why I enjoy playing in the park."

Kathleen smiled, loving his free and easy life. She wasn't materialistic herself. When you weren't allowed to own goods of any kind, the hunger for material possessions quickly disappeared. *Things* didn't satisfy. Love was what mattered.

Pete straightened and reached for his guitar, playing a lovely song, one she'd never heard before. People stopped to listen as he strummed.

"That was beautiful," Kathleen said.

"It's a love song. I wrote it for you."

"Me?"

Pete chuckled. "Don't you know how I feel about you, Kathleen O'Shaughnessy?"

Her heart pounded furiously at his words, as though she were running straight into a flaming building.

"You like my music, don't you?"

"Oh, yes—very much."

"Want to listen to a tape of it? We can get a bottle of wine and go to your place."

Kathleen wasn't completely naive. She could listen to Pete and his guitar in person; she didn't need a tape to do so. She suspected the tape was an excuse to come to her apartment so he could kiss her. The silent debate inside her didn't last more than a couple of seconds. "That would be fun."

Pete purchased a bottle of red wine and held her hand in his as she led him into her apartment. She didn't have any wineglasses, so they sipped the merlot out of tumblers. It was mellow, easy to drink, and quickly went to her head.

"This is very good," she said, sitting on the sofa next to him.

His smile was incredible. Pete was incredible. He moved closer and settled his arm around her shoulders. Kathleen rested her head against his neck and when he turned to kiss her, she closed her eyes.

Almost right away, her head started to swim. She'd rarely drunk wine, and it seemed impossible that a single glass could make her tipsy, but it had. Pete kissed her, gently at first and then with deepening passion. His tongue invaded her mouth; Kathleen let it happen. This was foreign to her, but exciting, and she enjoyed their mutual exploration.

"How does that feel, my lady Kathleen?" he whispered.

"Good."

"For me, too. How about this?" He rained kisses along the side of her neck and then opened the top two buttons of her blouse. His mouth left a fiery trail down to the edge of her bra, where he let his tongue delve into the valley between her breasts. When he paused, Kathleen held her breath, hardly able to believe what he was doing.

His hands cupped her breasts, taking in their fullness, while he continued to kiss her. She was hardly aware that he'd unfastened her bra, and she groaned aloud as he slipped her blouse over her arms. The bra fell from her shoulders, leaving her breasts exposed.

Kathleen freed her mouth from his. "I don't think—"

"No—don't think, because we're here to feel." Taking her hand he pressed it against the bulge in his pants. She reacted as if he'd burned her and pulled loose.

Pete laughed and stripped off his shirt. "There," he said, "how's that?" Then he kissed her again with long, slow seductive kisses that dissolved her objections.

Kathleen started to relax and Pete leaned her back until she was flat against the sofa. Then he lay on top of her, pushing her into the cushions. She felt his erection, which seemed to have grown even harder. Pinning her hands above her head, he kissed her lips and worked a line of moist kisses toward her breasts. When his lips took in her nipple and sucked on it, sensation shot through her like an electrical shock. Involuntarily, Kathleen arched upward.

Pete chuckled softly. "That's only the beginning."

"No…"

"Yes, honey." He drugged her with kisses once more, but a moment later, slid off her.

With her eyes closed, Kathleen relaxed again, grateful this had come to an end. They were moving too fast. Then she heard him release his zipper. She tried to sit up, but Pete wouldn't let her. He shoved her against the cushions, and before she had a chance to protest, he was on top of her again. When she attempted to squirm free, he forcefully held her down.

"You don't lead a man this far and then tell him no," he said.

He tried to kiss her, but Kathleen twisted her mouth away from him. The gentle musician she'd met in the park underwent a personality change as he jerked up her skirt and tore off her cotton panties.

"We can make this easy, baby," he murmured.

"No…no! Don't do this. I don't want this."

"Yes, you do," he countered in the same seductive voice he'd used earlier. Even while she tried to push him away, he pried open her legs and rammed his rigid penis deep inside her.

Kathleen gasped at the pain, but if Pete was aware of her discomfort, he gave no indication. Eyes squeezed shut and teeth gritted, he continued to pound her, his body repeatedly slamming against hers. Again and again. Faster and more furious. The pain was dreadful and it didn't ease even when he cried out and then slumped, his deadweight holding her down as he heaved and panted.

"That was fantastic," he whispered.

Kathleen was too shocked to move. Her mouth had gone completely dry and her tongue felt glued to her teeth.

"Oh, honey, you're so tight. So good."

It took her a moment to free her arms enough to push him off her. This horrible man had stolen her virginity. He'd taken advantage of her inexperience. He'd ignored her protests. Standing on wobbly legs, her skirt torn, she grabbed her blouse and held it against her bare breasts. Pointing a shaking finger at him, she cried, "Get out of here!"

Pete sat up, looking stunned. "What's wrong?"

"Get out," she cried, near hysteria now. "Get out." She picked up one of his sandals and threw it at the door.

Pete raised both hands as if to ward off an attack. "I'm going, I'm going. I don't know what you're so upset about. You wanted this as much as I did."

"No! No, I didn't." To be fair, she *had* wanted him to kiss her and had enjoyed their foreplay, but she'd never wanted him to go any further. What he'd done felt like abuse, like an assault. It felt as if he'd crushed her soul. "Now leave." She refused to let him see the tears in her eyes.

"All right, all right." He dressed quickly, then slipped into one sandal and grabbed the second on his way out the door. As soon as it closed, Kathleen picked up his tumbler, still half-full of wine and hurled it at the door. The glass broke and red wine splattered across the carpet and the wall.

Falling onto her knees, she covered her face with her hands and wept. When she rose, the room was completely dark.

Emotionless, she stumbled into the bathroom and turned on the shower. She scrubbed every inch of her skin as she stood under the high-pressure spray, wielding the washcloth with such force she threatened to leave abrasions. The water ran cold before she'd finished.

Dressed in her nightgown, Kathleen sat in the darkened room and wept again. She needed a friend, someone she could talk to, someone she trusted. Sean would be furious and God only knew what he'd do to Pete if he found him. She didn't want her brother to end up in jail on her account. Her counselor came to mind, but she was afraid of what the woman would say if she admitted her stupidity.

In the end, at two in the morning, when she was sure she'd go crazy unless she heard another human voice, Kathleen phoned Father Doyle in Minneapolis.

He answered the phone himself, sounding groggy. "Father Doyle," he murmured.

"You said I could call you anytime of the day or night," she whispered, uncertain he'd recognize her.

"Kathleen?" He seemed instantly alert.

She checked her watch and realized that with the time difference it was 3:00 a.m. "I shouldn't have called."

"What happened?"

Now that she had him on the line, she found it impossible to admit what she'd done. Struggling to keep the panic and the pain out of her voice, she whispered, "I met a man in the park."

"Tell me what happened."

She started to sob. "I can't…"

"All right," he said calmly. "Tell me this. Are you hurt?"

"I… I don't think so."

"Are you in pain?"

"Yes!" she nearly shouted.

"Do you need a doctor?"

"I need a priest," she cried.

There was a short pause and then he said, "I'm here."

They talked nonstop for an hour, and when they'd finished Kathleen felt she had her soul back. The guilt was gone, but her heart ached and so did her body. Father Doyle suggested she swallow a couple of aspirin and try to sleep.

Kathleen took his advice and, to her amazement, fell quickly into a deep, undisturbed slumber. The phone woke her in the morning, and before she had time to consider that it might be Pete, she answered.

"How are you feeling?" It was Father Doyle.

She sat on one end of the sofa and brought her feet up while she tried to find an answer. "I don't know yet. I was in bed… I haven't had a chance to think."

"Ah, so I woke you." Apparently he found that amusing. "Turnabout is fair play."

Kathleen smiled. "Thank you so much for talking to me last night. I didn't know where else to turn."

"I'm glad I'm the one you called."

She swept the long, tangled hair away from her face and sighed. "I did something very foolish. I learned a painful lesson because of it."

"Yes, you did, but I don't want you berating yourself over this. What happened wasn't entirely your fault. In fact, it was more his than yours."

"It doesn't matter whose fault it was." To her, it didn't. What mattered was that she'd lost her virginity to a man who neither valued her nor appreciated what he'd stolen.

"There's something we didn't discuss last night that you need to do," he said.

"What?"

"I want you to see a physician. This is important, Kathleen, so don't ignore me."

He wanted her to tell a doctor what had happened. She *couldn't* do that. "I can't," she whispered, half-tempted to weep. "I can't tell anyone else...."

"Don't worry—I've already made arrangements for you to see a physician friend of a friend. I talked to him and explained the situation. You won't need to say a word. I've taken care of everything."

Kathleen was so grateful she didn't know how to thank him. "What would I do without you?" she asked.

"What are friends for?"

{ 40 }

Joanna Baird

"Nixon's done it now," Joanna said, sitting on the carpet, her back against the sofa and the phone to her ear. It was early November 1973 and she spoke to Tim every night. She could only guess what he was spending on long-distance charges as their conversations sometimes went on for two and three hours. Because of this, he'd had a second phone line installed in his home so they could talk for long periods of time without worrying that he might miss emergency calls.

"Do you seriously think Leon Jaworski is going to grant Nixon any political favors?"

"I don't know," Joanna said, "but as far as I'm concerned that's what you get for voting Republican." She didn't know his political allegiance for a fact, but she had her suspicions.

"You mean to say you voted for McGovern?"

"Darn right I did."

"I don't believe it," Tim cried. "The woman I want to marry is a Democrat."

Joanna's hand tightened around the receiver. "What did you just say?"

"I can't believe you're a Democrat."

"Not that, earlier."

"Are your parents Democrats, too?"

Joanna sighed in frustration. "I don't know how my parents voted in the last election. I want to know what you meant when you said the woman you want to marry."

"*Did* want to marry," he said archly.

"Tim!"

He chuckled. "Okay, okay. You must've guessed by now that I haven't been calling you every night for the last five months because I like the sound of your voice."

"I like the sound of *your* voice." Every night she looked forward to hearing from him. In August, he'd flown out to spend a week with her, but that was all the time he could spare away from his practice. Those seven glorious days had gone by far too quickly.

"Well, okay, I do like the sound of your voice," Tim said in low fervent tones. "But I like a lot more than that." He paused and she held her breath. "You know I love you."

"I love you, too." So much that sometimes she could barely stand being apart from him.

"I've been waiting, Joanna, but I have to tell you I'm getting kind of impatient."

"Waiting for what?"

"That letter from Rome," he said, as if it should be obvious.

"I'm sure it'll be here soon."

He muttered something under his breath.

"You can ask me, though." She didn't need any letter; she knew her heart and had mentally separated herself from the religious life over a year ago. More than anything in the world, she longed to be married to Tim.

"Once you're free, I'll propose."

"Yes."

"Yes, what?"

"That'll be my answer once you get around to proposing. Listen, perhaps you could talk to my father. He's…a little old-fashioned and it would mean a lot to him if you'd discuss marrying his daughter with him first."

"Are you always this bossy?" he asked.

She was annoyed that he'd called her bossy, because Joanna didn't see herself that way at all. "It was only a suggestion."

"I've already talked to your father and your mother, too."

"You have? When?"

"This summer when I was out there."

"You didn't tell me! What did they say?"

"Oh, they seemed pretty pleased," he said smugly. "But I may have to rethink my plans, since that was before I found out you voted for McGovern."

"A Democrat didn't break into the Republican party headquarters, you know? A Democrat would never do anything as underhanded as that."

His laugh echoed over the line. Joanna was smiling, too. She'd always enjoyed bantering with Tim, and as they'd grown more familiar with each other, their friendship had deepened.

"It's a good thing you live as far away as you do."

"Why?" she teased. "Do you want to throttle me?"

"No, I'm dying to make love to you. I don't know how I'm going to keep my hands off you next week."

Joanna was flying to Minneapolis for Thanksgiving

and staying with his mother. "Your mom will make a wonderful chaperone."

He grumbled some remark she couldn't quite catch— and probably wasn't intended to hear. "It's three months since I saw you. I know you were a nun, Joanna, but I was never a priest, and I'm telling you right now, it's damned difficult not to touch you...."

"Good." She loved knowing she tempted him. What Tim probably didn't realize was how tempted she was, too. He knew she wasn't a virgin, but he'd accepted her decision that they should wait until they were married before they made love. With Tim, she didn't want any regrets. When they said their vows, it would be because they were committed to each other for life. With that commitment came the God-given privilege of intimacy. Joanna had cheated herself once and refused to repeat that mistake.

"Good?" he repeated. "Do you *enjoy* torturing a man?"

"Only you." She smiled at the way he grumbled, but she also knew that he respected and loved her enough to honor her wishes. "Before I forget, Mom told me this morning that Greg Markham's remarried."

"So lover-boy is out of the picture."

"He married a woman from the Philippines."

Joanna had been somewhat taken aback. Greg had repeatedly complained about the problems in his marriage due to the differences between Xuan's culture and American attitudes. She'd never learned English properly and seemed to hate Greg for what she perceived as his lack of attention. Naturally, Joanna had only heard Greg's side, although she'd been reluctant to discuss the matter at all.

"I don't care if he married a space alien as long as he accepts that you don't want him in your life."

"He's been out of my life for years. Are you going to be a jealous husband, Timothy Murray?"

"Very."

"Well, I intend to be an extremely jealous wife. I only want you working with male nurses."

"I'd like to work with you," he said. "The hospital still hasn't found a nurse who's even come close to replacing you."

"You certainly know how to flatter a girl."

"I try," he said with mock shyness.

That was the way most of their conversations went.

On Tuesday afternoon the following week, two days before Thanksgiving, Joanna's flight arrived in Minneapolis. It was the first time she'd been back since she'd left the convent.

Tim was waiting for her inside the terminal. She was so eager for the sight of him that she felt she might break into tears when she finally saw him. Wearing a dark overcoat and clutching a bouquet of roses, he made his way through the crowd.

They walked toward each other and when she was close, Tim took her in his arms, crushing the roses against her. And if she hadn't known it before, she knew it now: he needed her in his life with the same intensity that she needed him.

She'd never approved of public displays of affection but she couldn't wait a second longer for him to kiss her. He half lifted her and the flowers fell to the floor as his mouth descended on hers.

"Timothy. Timothy."

His name seemed to come from far away. So far that Joanna almost didn't hear it.

"In a moment, Mother," he said.

Tim had brought his mother to the airport? Oh, great!

They'd never met, and Joanna was nervous about this first encounter. Tim knew that.

Slowly he released her. With his arm still around her, he turned to the woman in the long wool coat and 1960s-style pillbox hat with matching purse. "Mother, this is Joanna Baird. Joanna, my mother, Alice Murray."

Joanna felt the other woman's perusal of her. "You're the nun."

"Former nun," she said.

Tim's arm tightened around her waist. "The letter arrived?"

She smiled up at him and nodded.

"We're getting married!"

Joanna gave him a puzzled glance. "Yes, I know."

"I mean now. Tomorrow, if it can be arranged."

"Timothy," his mother protested.

"Tim." Joanna had a few objections of her own. "I intend to marry only once and I want a real wedding."

His scowl was fierce. "I hope you can pull it together in a month because that's all the time I'm giving you."

Joanna met his mother's gaze and she noticed her smile. "Can we do it?" she asked Mrs. Murray.

His mother laughed. "I don't think we have any choice. My son took a long time to choose his bride and it wouldn't be a good idea to keep him waiting."

Joanna was in full agreement.

{ 41 }

Kathleen O'Shaughnessy

Luckily St. Joseph's Parochial School was within walking distance of Kathleen's tiny apartment. With the gasoline shortage and the long lines at service stations all across America—not to mention the discrepancy between her salary and the cost of living—it would be a lifetime before she could even dream of purchasing her own car.

Walking into the apartment complex, Kathleen stopped to bring Mrs. Mastel her newspaper and mail. "Is there anything else I can do for you?" she asked the eighty-year-old widow.

"Not a thing," the woman told her. "Be sure and pet Seymour on your way out."

"I always do," Kathleen told her. Seymour was the ghost cat who'd died five years earlier and, according to Mrs. Mastel, had joyfully returned to her in spirit form. Kathleen had managed to convince her elderly friend that it wasn't necessary to feed the cat or keep his water dish filled, since he didn't exist as a corporeal entity.

Spirits didn't eat or drink, she'd explained gently. The woman's married son had phoned to thank Kathleen. Apparently she was the only person who'd been able to convince his mother that she didn't need to buy cat food anymore—and the smell of rancid tuna no longer pervaded her apartment.

"Oh, dear, it looks like I have one of your letters," Mrs. Mastel said just as Kathleen was heading out the door.

The woman studied the envelope. "It looks important, too." She handed the letter to Kathleen, who thanked her and quietly left.

As she walked upstairs, Kathleen glanced at the return address, and her heart started to pound. Entering her own apartment on the fifth floor, she set her purse and newspaper on the kitchen counter, then examined the envelope a second time. It was the one she'd been waiting for all these months. Her exemption from Rome. A deluge of emotions overwhelmed her and for a moment she could hardly breathe.

After the degrading episode with Pete, she'd felt serious doubts about her decision to leave. Life inside the convent was safe. Protected. It'd taken several long conversations—not with her counselor, but with Father Doyle—before she'd finally made up her mind. In the end, she'd followed through with her original intention and applied to Rome to be released from her vows.

As she sorted through the mail, Kathleen set the bills to one side and found a second, smaller envelope. This one contained a letter, too, and as soon as she saw who it was from, she tore it open. Father Doyle wrote only on rare occasions. Since the incident that summer, he'd made an effort to keep in touch with her as her spiritual advisor. Kathleen was grateful.

He wasn't much of a letter-writer, and she knew that maintaining contact with her must be a chore. Several times she'd been on the verge of telling him it wasn't necessary to write. She couldn't make herself do it; she enjoyed his letters too much. Perhaps it was selfish of her, but in the overall scheme of things, that seemed a comparatively small sin.

She read over the few paragraphs, savoring each word, and then smiling to herself, refolded the single sheet and returned it to the envelope. The letter from Rome remained unopened. Kathleen knew what it said. Her request had been granted.

The phone rang, startling her. Phone calls were infrequent, since she knew so few people and was only now beginning to make friends, outside of other former nuns. Like her, they tended not to use the phone very often. "Hello?"

"It's Sean," her brother said.

Loren was generally the one who phoned, and it was unusual to hear from him. "What can I do for you, big brother?"

He hesitated. "I'm calling to ask a favor. Loren and I are having a bit of a disagreement, so I'm phoning myself."

"What's the favor?"

"I have this friend. Now listen, it isn't like it sounds."

Kathleen didn't have any idea what it was supposed to sound like.

"I want you to meet him," Sean said. "His name's John. John Lopez. His wife died two years ago, and he's got a couple of kids. I think you'd make him a good wife."

"Wife," Kathleen repeated, laughing. She hadn't even *met* the man and already her brother had the two of them married. He certainly seemed to be leaping ahead. But then, Kathleen knew he was worried about her living alone, even though she'd never told him about Pete. She loved him for his care and concern.

"Well, why not? You want to get married, don't you?"

"Yes, one day. But I'd prefer to choose my own husband and in my own time."

"I'm not saying you have to marry him," Sean insisted, although he clearly had hopes in that direction. "John's a good man and he's had more than his share of bad breaks." He paused and Kathleen heard Loren's raised voice in the background. Obviously her brother and sister-in-law were continuing their argument.

"Will you meet him?" Sean asked. "I'm not asking you to do anything but meet him."

"Okay. I'm willing to do that."

"Just… Kathleen, listen. If you aren't interested in him, don't lead him on, all right?"

"You have my word."

A dinner date was set up for the following night. Kathleen was to walk down to a fish-and-chips place on the Seattle waterfront. John would meet her there. Sean had told her to tie her hair back with a pink ribbon, so John would know it was her. She figured he'd recognize her because she looked like Sean, but she didn't waste time arguing, since her brother already had everything worked out.

The next evening, Kathleen went to a well-known fish-and-chips stand and watched as a solidly built man with blunt features stepped away from the building. "Are you Kathleen?" he asked.

"You must be John."

"I am." As if he wasn't sure what to do, he thrust out his hand.

Kathleen shook it and noticed his handshake was pleasantly firm—neither crushing nor limp. That was a good indication of a man's character, her uncle had always said. "It's nice to meet you," she murmured.

"You, too." He gestured to the inside seating and a large menu posted there. "Would you like to order?"

"Yes, please."

Once they'd decided, John went up to the counter to place their order, then waited to carry it back to the table. While he stood there, Kathleen had an opportunity to study her brother's friend. He seemed nervous and a bit uncomfortable. She understood that; it was how she felt herself. After Pete, she'd socialized some but always in a group. This was the first time she'd been alone with a man since the musician. She trusted her brother, and if he'd set it up, she could be assured of John's decency—and her own safety.

John returned with two cardboard containers of deep-fried fish and salty French fries, plus a small container of coleslaw. They sat across from each other at a red picnic table.

"Sean tells me you're a teacher," he said.

Kathleen licked the salt off her fingers. "Fifth grade. He told me you're a widower."

He nodded. "My wife died in September a couple of years ago. She had breast cancer."

"I'm sorry."

He reached into his wallet and pulled out two pictures. "These are our kids," he said, turning the bent photographs to face her. He pointed at the petite blonde smiling into the camera, holding two small children in her lap. "That's Patty a month before she was diagnosed." Next he pointed at the boy. "That's Steve. He was four then, but he's seven now, and Chelsea. She was two in this photo, but she's just turned five." The second picture was a more recent photograph of the children.

"They're beautiful," Kathleen said.

He stared down at the photographs. "They miss their mother."

"You miss her, too, don't you?"

He looked up as if she'd surprised him with the question. "More than words can say." He replaced the photographs and she noticed that his hand shook slightly.

Kathleen sprinkled vinegar over her fish.

"Patty liked vinegar on her fish, too."

She wasn't sure his comment warranted a response.

"Is there anything you want to know about me?" he asked.

Picking up a French fry, Kathleen paused. "This isn't an interview, John. Why don't we just have dinner and talk?"

"All right," he agreed and seemed to relax. "That would be good, except I have to leave in forty minutes. I don't like to leave the kids at night. Anyway, the neighbor lady said she could only stay until seven-thirty."

"That's not a problem."

"Would you like to meet my kids?"

"Perhaps later," Kathleen said. "I think it would be best if you and I got to know each other first. I wouldn't want the children to get close to me too soon, in case the two of us decided...you know."

"That we aren't compatible."

"Right," she confirmed.

"Good idea. I hadn't thought of that."

"Have you dated often since losing Patty?"

He shook his head. "No. You're the first."

She could've guessed that.

"You like kids, don't you?" he asked.

"Very much."

"Good," he said, sounding relieved. "You're Catholic, right?"

"John, you're interviewing me. I'm not applying for any position here."

"Right, right. Sorry."

"Relax, okay? I'm about the least scary woman you're likely to meet."

He grinned. "I don't know about that." He reached for a piece of fish, took a bite and then glanced up at her. "I like you, Kathleen. Thanks for putting me at ease."

She helped herself to another French fry. "Thank you for inviting me to dinner."

They smiled at each other. John Lopez was a good, decent man, just as her brother had said. And even if it turned out that marriage wasn't a possibility, friendship was.

{ 42 }

Angelina Marcello

Working with her father at Angelina's, Angie discovered a sense of peace she'd thought was lost to her after Corinne's death. She woke each morning and, instead of being overwhelmed by the crushing weight of sadness, she felt purpose and fulfillment.

Until then, she'd never truly understood her father's devotion to his restaurant. It didn't take her long to catch his fervor. In serving good food, Antonio Marcello was opening his home and his culture to the country that had welcomed him and his wife. He was a natural host, and sharing his beloved family recipes was his way of expressing his thanks, as well as providing for his family.

In the mornings, Angie worked with the kitchen crew and the head chef, Mario Deccio. When the restaurant doors opened at five-thirty, she played the role of hostess, greeting each guest personally. She remembered people from previous visits and always asked about their health, their families, their businesses. Often she told the story of her parents' flight to America and recounted her earliest memories of the restaurant. With Angie and her father working side by side, the restaurant's reputation continued to soar.

In August of 1974, just days after Richard Nixon resigned from the Presidency and Gerald Ford was sworn in as the thirty-eighth president of the United States, Angie found her father sitting in his office intently watching the television news.

"Dad," she said, needing to discuss a pressing problem. The truckers were out on strike and the restaurant's daily deliveries hadn't been made. Unless they had fresh produce, they'd be unable to open their doors that night.

Without moving his eyes from the television screen, her father held up his hand to silence her. "In a moment."

"But Dad…"

"Gerald Ford is the new president."

"I know." Angie had never been interested in politics, but these days it was all her father talked about. Again and again he reminded her how crucial it was to be informed about current affairs. He feared that what had happened in Italy in the '30s and '40s could happen in his new country.

"He is the first president in all of America's history to become president without a national election," he said urgently.

"Yes, Dad, but this is important."

"Very important," he agreed, obviously assuming that she was referring to the political situation. "We must keep a close eye on Gerald Ford."

"I couldn't agree with you more." Knowing she wasn't going to get his full attention, she left the small office, smiling to herself.

"What did your father say we should do?" Mario

asked her, nervously fidgeting in the kitchen. "When I spoke to him, he didn't even seem to be aware that there's a truckers' strike going on. The fruit and vegetables are sitting at the warehouse rotting. We have to do something."

Angie didn't have the heart to tell their chef that her father was more concerned about politics than his own restaurant. "He said I should go after the order myself."

"He said that?"

He would have if she'd asked; Angie was convinced of it. "My father has a truck. That's the practical solution, don't you think? I'll drive over and pick up as much as I can haul on my own. If the strike continues, I'll make the run again." She didn't stop to think that she hadn't driven the old truck in years and while she had a driver's license, it wasn't a current one.

"It's a hundred-mile round trip!"

"Yes, I know. I'll be as quick as I can."

The tension eased from Mario's face, and the lines between his eyebrows relaxed. "I don't know what we'd do without you, Angelina."

"Nonsense." But she smiled, aglow at his praise.

Hurrying back into her father's office, Angie said, "Dad, I need the keys to your truck."

"You're driving the truck?" he asked, looking away from the television long enough to regard her with questioning eyes. "Why?"

"Because there's a truck drivers' strike and if we don't get our supplies, we won't be able to open for dinner tonight."

"You're going to drive it all that way by yourself?"

"Yes, I am."

"You can do this?"

She nodded impatiently.

Standing, he slipped his hand into his pocket for the keys. When he placed them in her open palm, his fingers folded around hers and the tears sprang to his eyes. "You came home just in time, Angelina. I always dreamed of this day." Then, as if he'd embarrassed himself, he reached inside his back hip pocket for his handkerchief and loudly blew his nose. Sitting down again, he returned his attention to the TV.

Angelina felt a little misty-eyed herself as she walked out the back door. After all these years, her father's dream of having her work by his side had become a reality. Someday soon—when she'd sufficiently proved her devotion to the restaurant—he would hand over Angelina's to her. In most ways he already had.

It took Angie the better part of three hours to pick up their supplies and drive back. The moment she pulled up to the rear entrance, the entire kitchen crew was there to unload the boxes of fresh produce. Getting everything finished before the doors opened that night would be difficult, but Angie knew that if any staff could manage such a feat it would be hers.

"Where's my father?" she asked.

"I don't know." Mario sounded surprised. "Last time I saw him, he was in his office."

For three hours? While the staff rushed about their duties, Angie searched for her father. He wasn't in the office, which was something of a relief. A lot of people were interested in what was happening politically, but his interest was becoming an obsession.

No one answered the phone at the house.

"Mario," she said, interrupting the chef. "Where could he be?"

"I don't know," Mario said again, growing a little

flustered. "Do you want me to cook or do you want me to look for Antonio?"

Angie left him to get on with his work and decided to drive around until she found her father. He sometimes went for a walk or played boccie with friends at a nearby park, but those occasions were increasingly rare. His life was the restaurant and his outside interests were few. She sometimes wondered if he had lady friends. He'd been a relatively young man when her mother died, but if there'd been some romantic interest, Angie had never been aware of it.

When she didn't find him at any of the usual places, she drove home. Although she was outwardly calm, her fears mounted. This wasn't like him. Never, ever, had he disappeared without a word.

Entering the house, she looked around. "Dad!" she called.

No answer.

"Dad, where are you?" *Oh, dear God, where is he?* It was a prayer, as fervent as any she'd ever uttered. She hadn't prayed much since leaving the convent. Some mornings when the alarm rang, she automatically threw back the covers, got out of bed and went to her knees. Reality would assert itself in a moment or two, and she'd remember that this ritual of prayer was no longer part of her life.

On Sundays she'd fallen out of the habit of attending Mass. Then a few weeks ago, she'd gone back to the Protestant church she'd visited during the deepest part of her depression. That was where Angie had found peace, so she'd returned there. Not every week, just once or twice so far, but she liked the sermons and the change from the formal rites she'd always known.

For some reason, Angie thought Corinne would approve of her seeking other answers.

Taking the stairs to the second floor, Angie checked in her father's bedroom. To her shock, she found him lying on the bed sound asleep.

"Dad, you've had me worried to death," she cried. Napping in the middle of the day was one thing, but refusing to answer the phone was another.

He didn't respond. Looking more closely, she saw that he was pressing the photo of her mother, which he usually kept on the nightstand, to his heart.

Then she knew. Her beloved father was gone.

Just that morning he'd said Angie had come home just in time.

She couldn't possibly have realized how true those words were.

{ 43 }

Kathleen O'Shaughnessy

"Here's your newspaper, Mrs. Mastel," Kathleen said, dropping by the widow's apartment on her way out. It was a bright, sunny August afternoon.

"Oh, thank you, dear." The old woman sat in her overstuffed chair in front of the television, petting her imaginary Seymour. Even after his death the cat gave her comfort. "Are you off to summer school?" she asked.

"Actually I'm meeting a friend for lunch."

"That widower?"

Mrs. Mastel might be eighty years old, but she had the memory of a woman half her age. The moment she'd learned Kathleen was dating John Lopez, she hadn't let up with the questions.

"Not this time. Just a friend."

"Male or female?"

Kathleen laughed. She didn't really mind her neighbor's interest, but she needed to leave if she was going to be on time. "Male. He's a priest, though."

"Oh, well, God bless you both."

"God already has," Kathleen said and hurried out before the widow could waylay her with more questions.

As she walked out of the apartment building, Kathleen hummed a recent hit "Please, Mr. Postman," which was an appropriate song for seeing Father Doyle. They'd exchanged letters—brief on his part—for the last two years, and talked intermittently over the phone. He was her spiritual advisor and just as importantly, her closest and dearest friend.

His trip to Seattle had come about unexpectedly, and she was delighted. She hadn't seen him face-to-face since before she'd left the convent, back in the days when they'd struggled over Father Sanders's drinking. When Father Doyle had phoned to say he'd be in Seattle for a conference, they made arrangements to meet at a popular coffeehouse near Seattle University.

Kathleen arrived ten minutes early, just to make sure they had a table. To her surprise, Father Doyle was already there. The minute he saw her, he stood. Kathleen maneuvered her way across the crowded space and held out both hands to him. He looked exactly the same—as though time had stood still. She noticed that he wasn't wearing his Roman collar, though, which surprised her; he was dressed casually in jeans and a dark sweater.

The priest's face broke into a wide smile when he recognized her, and while he looked no different, Kathleen knew she did.

"Hello, Father."

"Kathleen," he said, his eyes glowing with warmth as he smiled, studying her after a long hug. "You look wonderful!"

She flushed with his praise. Outwardly she'd changed, and inwardly too. The woman he'd known as a nun had been unsure of herself. But two years out of the convent, Kathleen had learned some valuable lessons. She now moved freely and confidently in the world she'd once feared.

"How are *you?*" she asked, wanting to hear about him for a change. It seemed so many of their conversations centered on what was happening to her.

"I'm doing well," he said. "And you?"

The waitress came just then, before Kathleen could question his answer. She sensed that his conventional response was far from accurate.

"What would you like?" Father Doyle asked.

Kathleen closed her eyes and breathed in the scent of freshly brewed coffee. It was little things like this that she loved about her life now—sitting with friends and spending time with them, eating in front of them and talking openly. "I'll have a cappuccino," she told the waitress.

"I will, too," Father Doyle said.

The woman left, and Kathleen leaned across the table, eager to return to their conversation. She wasn't about to let him sidetrack her, either, as he did all too often. "We've been friends too long for you to fool me, Brian Doyle. What's wrong?"

Her honesty appeared to surprise him. Before her eyes, he closed up, sitting back and crossing his arms. He might as well have raised a sign that said Keep Out. "Nothing. Can't we just have a pleasant conversation after I came all this way?"

"And here you are. So friend to friend, tell me what's wrong."

His refusal to confide in her was upsetting. Hurtful. Particularly because, over the last two years, she'd confided in *him* frequently. He was the only person who knew about Pete. He'd advised her, counseled her and supported her in making her own decisions dozens of times. She loved him for being her priest and her friend.

"You can't tell me?" she asked, frowning.

"No."

"Why not?"

"It's...personal," he murmured an uncomfortable moment later.

"Okay," she said, struggling to disguise her disappointment. "What do you want to talk about?"

"This widower you're dating..."

"Yes. John." They'd discussed the relationship countless times. This was old news.

"How's it going?"

"Fine, I guess." She couldn't understand why he'd asked her about this, of all things. "John's a very nice man."

"You haven't mentioned him in a while. I was just wondering."

Kathleen was doing some wondering of her own. Had she been wrong in her assumptions about Father Doyle? Apparently they *weren't* the kind of friends she'd thought they were. Not if he couldn't share his deepest concerns, yet expected Kathleen to confide hers.

"Are you going to marry him?" Father Doyle asked.

John hadn't asked Kathleen to be his wife but she realized he was thinking along those lines and frankly so was she. "I don't know. Probably." Their relationship seemed to be headed in that direction. It wasn't a passionate romance; mostly they were friends. They were emotionally compatible and the children loved Kathleen. It was more for their sake that John was interested in her, and in all honesty, Kathleen in him.

"Do I sense hesitation?" Father Doyle murmured.

She watched the waitress set their coffees down

before she glanced at Father Doyle. He seemed to be waiting for her answer. But for the first time, she didn't feel comfortable sharing her life with him.

"I don't know," she said again. She got along well with John. At almost thirty, she was eager to start a family. After her one unfortunate experience, dating terrified her, but John was comfortable and safe and he seemed genuinely fond of her. Women had married for less.

"How's Minneapolis?" she asked, thinking that would distract him. It was her way of letting him know that certain parts of her life were closed off to him, too.

"The same as always. Oh, before I forget, I brought you some wild rice," he said. Leaning down, he reached for a small bag on the floor by his chair.

"Thank you." She sipped her cappuccino. Father Doyle had always been thoughtful.

They talked for a little longer. The discussion revolved around her and her teaching position and her family, but there was nothing more about her future. Not once did Father Doyle mention his parish or anything other than the most mundane facts about his life. After twenty minutes, they'd run out of things to say.

"I guess I'd better go," she said. All these years she'd considered Father Doyle someone special in her life, but the relationship obviously hadn't been reciprocal. Disheartened, she stood, collecting her purse and the small bag of wild rice. "It was good to see you," she said formally. "Thank you for keeping in touch. Goodbye, Father Doyle."

He stood, too.

Making her way out of the coffeehouse, Kathleen felt weighed down by disappointment. She wasn't sure what she'd expected from this meeting, what she'd hoped for—but not this awkward, almost painful exchange. She'd made a mistake, assumed things about their relationship that weren't true.

Kathleen was about a block away when she heard Father Doyle call her name. She turned around, thinking she must have left something at the coffeehouse.

He was breathless when he caught up with her. He stood directly in front of her and blurted out, "Don't marry John."

She frowned. "I beg your pardon?"

"Please, Kathleen, don't marry this man."

Had he learned something about John Lopez she didn't know? "Why?"

His face was red but his eyes were clear as they met hers. "I'm leaving the priesthood."

He couldn't have shocked her more. She stared at him, too shaken to respond.

"I've already been released from my duties and have applied to Rome for a dispensation."

Kathleen still didn't know what to say.

"I realize this is a surprise. I wanted to tell you earlier, but I couldn't."

"You don't want to be a priest anymore?" That was hard to accept. Brian Doyle was a wonderful man, the best priest she'd ever known. It would break her heart to see him abandon the Church.

Brian's gaze held hers and she read his sorrow and regret. "I want to serve God. That desire has never left me, but I can no longer remain silent about certain things happening in the Church. The bishop and I cannot agree. This is the only way I have of voicing my dissatisfaction."

All this time he hadn't complained or let her know

any of his feelings. He'd helped her through *her* struggles but had never shared his own. She couldn't understand it.

"You never said a word," she whispered.

"I couldn't tell you what was happening. I couldn't tell anyone, not even my family. I decided to leave very recently." He looked around for someplace they could talk.

"There's another café with a patio a couple of blocks over," she suggested.

Within minutes they were seated at the sidewalk restaurant, sipping coffee neither of them wanted.

"I didn't have a conference in Seattle," Brian confessed. "I came because of you."

Kathleen shook her head, hardly able to take in what he was saying.

"When the moment came, when you walked into the coffeehouse, I decided I couldn't tell you. And that wasn't the only thing.... I've been in love with you for years, Kathleen."

Her hand flew to her heart. "I...never knew. Never suspected."

"I made sure you didn't. It wasn't my intention to tell you."

Stunned as she was, Kathleen could barely think. "Is it because of me that you're leaving?"

"No," he said and lowered his head. He reached for her hand and held it tightly in his own. "I released my love for you, Kathleen, when you left the convent. I prayed for you, prayed God would bring a good man into your life, a man worthy of your love. When you mentioned John, I felt He had answered my prayers."

"And now?"

"Now I know God has other plans for us both."

"What happened? Can you tell me that much?"

She could see that whatever it was had broken him in ways she hadn't thought possible. "A new priest joined the parish," he finally said. "He was young and dynamic—and a practicing homosexual."

Before she could stop herself, she gasped.

"He seemed to think I shared his sexual preference and… I went to the bishop."

He didn't need to say more; Kathleen knew what had happened. Bishop Schmidt had reacted in the same manner as he had when Father Doyle had taken Father Sanders's problem to him.

"He transferred you?"

"No, he sent Father Galen to another parish. But Father Galen isn't going to change. I'm not judging his… inclinations, Kathleen. What I object to is his behavior, which is flagrant to say the least—and in a man who took a vow of celibacy. But the bishop and I…" He paused and shook his head. "I love the Church. I have dedicated my life to serving God, but I cannot remain silent and obedient to what I know is wrong."

Her fingers tightened around his.

He raised his probing gaze to her. "Kathleen, if you sincerely love John, then please tell me. I don't want to do anything to hurt you." His voice fell. "I wasn't sure what would happen when we met today."

"I…didn't know what to think when you refused to talk about yourself."

"When you walked into the restaurant, so beautiful and so vibrant, it was all I could do not to blurt out my feelings right then and there. But I realized I'd be doing you a grave disservice. I have nothing to offer you. I'm unemployed and I don't know what the future holds."

"I do," she said, smiling up at him. Turning over his

palm, she rubbed it with the edge of her thumb. "Did I ever tell you about this gift I have for seeing the future?"

He smiled back. "I don't think you ever mentioned it before."

"An oversight, I assure you."

"What do you see?" he asked, staring down at his palm.

"I see your life surrounded by love."

"That's encouraging."

"You attract it to yourself by the love you give others." She glanced up and saw he was enjoying her little game.

"Anything about a wife?"

Until that moment, she didn't know how beautiful that word could sound. "Oh, yes, there's lots here about a wife. You'll marry a redhead."

He leaned down and kissed her hand. "I'm partial to redheads."

"My goodness," she said, rubbing her thumb across his palm. "Look at all these children."

"Children?" he repeated, leaning forward for a closer look. "How many?"

She sighed and closed his fingers over hers. "As many as God sees fit to give us."

Part Five

THE REUNION

But for me, I know that my Redeemer lives
And that He will stand upon the earth at last.
And I know that after this body has decayed
This body shall see God.

—Job 19:25–26

Open House for
St. Peter's Convent House
in Minneapolis
August 30th, 2002
From 1–3 PM

All St. Bridget's Sisters of the Assumption
And Former Sisters
Are Cordially Invited
The Convent House has been sold
And has been slated for destruction.

Reconnect with old friends
Let us gather
and
Praise God for our time together

Joanna Murray
1335 Lakeview
Minneapolis, MN 55410
June 12, 2002

Dearest Angelina,

I couldn't mail off this invitation without enclosing a short note. My goodness, where has all the time gone? It's hard to believe it's been thirty years since we were last together. I've thought of you so often and blame myself for not keeping in touch. I think it would've helped us both if we'd made the effort. I deeply regret that we didn't have an opportunity to talk before I made my decision to leave the convent. I tried to contact you shortly after I left, but I learned that you were no longer living there, either.

Those were turbulent times for all of us—personally, professionally and emotionally. I know you blamed yourself for what happened with Corinne, but you shouldn't. You weren't at fault. I sincerely hope the years have been good to you and you've been able to put the pain of those days behind you.

As you can tell from the letterhead, I married Dr. Tim Murray who worked at St. Elizabeth's—this happened in 1974. We have two sons, Michael and Andrew. That's the short version of my news. I hope we'll be able to catch up in August.

It would mean so much to me if you'd attend the Open House. It could be a time of healing for us both. A time for laughter, too, and many, many good memories.

Sincerely,
Joanna
(Formerly Sister Joanna)

June 30, 2002

Dear Joanna,

To say it was a surprise to hear from you after all these years is an understatement. Thank you for thinking of me. I appreciate the personal invitation to the Open House. How sad that the old convent's about to be demolished. But I understand it's been empty for almost ten years and if the order was able to sell it, then all the better. Still...

As for your invitation, I've thought about it constantly since it arrived. I hope I'm not disappointing you, but I've decided against attending. I could give you a list of excuses and all of them would be valid, but the truth of the matter is that I don't have any desire to return to Minneapolis or to the convent. There are too many ghosts I'd need to face, and I'm unwilling to do that.

Don't feel bad about not keeping in touch. I haven't talked or written to anyone since I left. I couldn't. Have you? What about Sister Kathleen? She was always one of my favorites.

You're right—we certainly did have a lot of laughs together. Do you remember those rubber brownies? I still giggle every time I think about the look on Sister Eloise's face.

I'd enjoy hearing from you again, Joanna. Please give me more details about your life, but don't expect me at the Open House.

Sincerely,
Angelina Marcello
(Formerly Sister Angelina)

July 1, 2002

Dear Joanna,

Thanks so much for sending the invitation, which came to me through my oldest brother. What a treat to hear from you after all these years! I had no idea the convent in Minneapolis had been sold. How sad. My life is so different than it was when I was a nun. I imagine yours is, too.

Frankly, I'm surprised you stayed in Minneapolis. I couldn't get away from there fast enough. But all's well that ends well, right?

Count me in for the Open House. I can't wait to see you and everyone again.

Yours in Christ,
Kathleen Doyle (formerly O'Shaughnessy)

August 1, 2002

Dear Angelina,

I heard from Joanna that you've decided not to attend the Open House at the end of this month. I'm so sorry you won't be there. Is there anything I can say that will change your mind? I'd love to see you.

Dealing with the past is a tricky business, isn't it? Forgive me for being so bold, but I think that unless you face what happened to Corinne—and to you as a result—this tragedy will forever haunt you.

I'm married now, happily so, and have a wonderful family. (I'll tell you more later!) What about

you? How have the years treated you? If you can't
find it in you to attend the reunion, I'll understand.
I'll be terribly disappointed, but I'll understand.

Your friend,
Kathleen

{ 44 }

Joanna Murray
August 30, 2002

The day of the reunion had finally arrived. An hour before the scheduled event, Joanna, Tim and their two sons opened the doors to what had once been the Minneapolis convent of St. Bridget's Sisters of the Assumption. The convent had closed ten years earlier, and now with the building sold and due to be destroyed, this was possibly the last time she and the others would step inside.

While her men carried in the necessary equipment and supplies, Joanna wandered down the long hallway to what had once been the chapel. Just by the door, she searched the wall for the light switch and flipped it on. Some of the bulbs had burned out, but the room was clearly illuminated.

Looking around the stark chapel with its hard stone floor and rows of wooden pews, Joanna held her breath. Slowly her gaze drifted toward the altar, now stripped bare.

Closing her eyes, she could almost hear the chants of her fellow sisters as their voices rose in worship all those years ago.

Thirty years had passed since she'd walked out of the Minneapolis convent. St. Bridget's Sisters of the Assumption had dwindled down to a few hundred members now. The average age was sixty-nine and there were fewer and fewer women entering the community— and many of them, she'd learned, were in their forties and fifties. Usually widows who'd raised their families and were hoping to serve God in a deeper capacity.

The conservative order had undergone a transformation in the years since Joanna had joined in February of 1967. St. Bridget's Sisters had held out against the changes brought about by the Second Vatican Council much longer than the smaller orders. For one thing, they were one of the last orders to modify the habit. These days, the habit had been discarded entirely. A few still chose to wear a simple black veil and crucifix, but those were mainly the older nuns who, early on, had so rigorously resisted the changes. The Grand Silence was another aspect of convent life that had disappeared.

Women who entered the novitiate were no longer subjected to the Year of Silence, either, the year that had been such a trial for her. How she'd struggled those twelve months, and what valuable lessons she'd learned about herself...

Gone, too, was the Chapter of Faults, public penance and the austere living quarters. While she was organizing the reunion, Joanna had visited a woman who was currently a St. Bridget's sister in Minneapolis. Joanna had a vague recollection of Sister Colleen, who'd been transferred to the convent here shortly before her own departure. This visit had made her aware of the many differences between then and now. In fact, a tour of the apartment the nuns rented had shown her exactly how far the order had come. Sister Colleen had proudly pointed out the cheerful decorations. Even the bedrooms revealed the personality and character of their inhabitants. Joanna recalled her own cell, a bleak room with no hint of either.

The one change that impressed and pleased her most was the openness and friendliness of Sister Colleen and the other two nuns she'd met. They had invited her to lunch and then before the meal, they'd all joined hands for a communal prayer. When she'd expressed her surprise, Joanna learned that the sisters now saw hospitality as akin to godliness. She'd been a nun in the days when eating with anyone other than fellow sisters—or occasionally family—was actively discouraged.

Joanna wondered if these changes, had they come sooner, would have influenced her decision. In retrospect she doubted it. Ritual or lack of it wasn't the issue. Remaining a nun would have deprived her of the children she longed to love.

She walked down the center aisle of the chapel and slipped into a pew. As she sat on the hard wooden bench, emotion swept through her. Her years serving Christ had been good ones. She had no regrets. Not about entering the convent and not about leaving. She'd fulfilled her mission, met Tim and—

"Mom," Michael, her oldest son, grunted as he came into the chapel, carrying a hefty floral basket. "Where do you want me to put this?"

"Over there," she said, pointing to the left of the altar.

"What about this one?" Andrew asked, following his brother.

"On the other side."

As her sons placed the floral displays by the altar, Joanna watched them with a deep sense of pride. They were strong, handsome young men and the joy of her life. She and Tim had decided to wait for two years after their marriage to start their family. She'd wanted to cement their relationship first and Tim had agreed.

"Dad's getting the table set up in the foyer. He'll be along in a minute."

Michael stood with his hands on his hips and glanced around. "You really lived here?"

"I really did."

"It's hard for me to think of my mother as a nun, you know." Like his father, Andrew was six feet tall, but he had the blond hair of the Baird family. Michael possessed his father's interest in medicine and was currently serving his residency in Abbott Northwestern Hospital. Also like his father, Michael wasn't in a hurry to marry and settle down.

Andrew, on the other hand, a recent graduate of the University of Minnesota at Duluth, had majored in chemistry and girls. Odds were her youngest son would be engaged by the end of the summer.

"Do you mind if we take a look around?" Michael asked. "It's not like I'll have the opportunity to explore a convent again anytime soon."

"Feel free," Joanna told them. "But it hasn't been a convent for quite a few years."

"Does that make you sad?" Andrew asked. He was the more sensitive of her sons.

Joanna shook her head. "Not really. It was no longer part of my life by the time it closed."

As soon as the boys had left, Tim walked into the chapel. "I thought I'd find you in here." He slid an arm around her waist and kissed her cheek.

Joanna leaned against her husband of almost thirty years and gave a long, slow sigh. "You wouldn't believe the hours I spent in this chapel." Every morning and evening, she was here for lauds and Compline. And if she wasn't at the hospital, working her shift, then she was here at noon for the Angelus, too.

"Praying?"

"Always. We worshiped here as a community. Oh, Tim, I remember how lovely our voices sounded. As a postulant I struggled with the singing, but I came to sincerely love it."

"I came to sincerely love you." He rested his jaw on the crown of her head.

"Most of my prayers here in those final days were for you," she confessed. "Or more accurately, for me and the way I felt about you. Again and again I begged God to keep my heart pure." She turned her head slightly to face him. "You can't imagine what it was like to be a nun and at the same time desperately in love with you."

"Yes, I can," he said, tightening his hold on her waist. "I was a man desperately in love with a nun. How do you think that made *me* feel?"

"Culpable and depraved."

"You know what they say about forbidden fruit," her husband teased, releasing her.

Smiling, Joanna walked to the front of the chapel and straightened the floral displays. After months of careful planning she was suddenly nervous about seeing the other nuns again. This was far different—far more significant—than the high school reunions she'd attended over the years.

"You're anxious," Tim said, sounding surprised.

"A little," she admitted. Naturally, every now and again she'd run into other women like herself who'd once been nuns. Most people, however, were unaware of her previous life, and she was reluctant to mention it. If anyone asked what she'd done before she married Tim, she simply said she was a nurse. She knew from experience that the minute people learned she'd been a nun, there would be an awkward silence or worse, a double take, and then the inevitable questions. Answering those was the hardest.

Only people who'd lived it themselves could appreciate how important that time had been to her. The woman she was now—the wife, the mother, the nurse, the Catholic—had been created by the years she'd spent as a sister.

It was for this reason that Joanna eagerly anticipated the reunion. Like her, almost all the nuns she'd known had left the order—the statistics were staggering. The last article she'd read reported that between 1969 and 1980, seventy percent of the order had either died or left.

Despite her own decision to leave, it saddened her that so many priests and nuns had forsaken the religious life, and that so many Catholics had abandoned the Church. The scandals that had recently become public were devastating spiritually and emotionally to those who'd remained faithful.

Slowly the Church would recover. Devout Catholics—like her, like Tim—were working hard to rebuild what had been lost.

"I don't regret the time I spent here," she told her husband.

"Neither do I," Tim replied. "We never would've met otherwise."

"Oh, you would've married someone else," she said, confident that one of the lovely nurses who'd pursued him would have captured his attention.

"I don't think so," he said, his eyes serious. "I needed you, Joanna. After Vietnam I came back emotionally empty. I'd turned away from God and anything that had to do with religion. You were the one who showed me the way back."

"And you showed me how to love. You taught me that loving a man, a family, didn't mean loving God any less."

"Thank you, Joanna," he said quietly.

"Mom." Andrew stuck his head in the door. "Someone's here."

"Already?" She glanced at her watch with a sense of panic. She wasn't nearly ready yet! She still had the front table to organize and the food trays to set up and coffee to brew. It would be impossible to do all that and still greet everyone as they arrived.

"I'll start the coffee," Tim said, giving her a chance to greet the first guest.

Kathleen O'Shaughnessy—Joanna recognized her instantly—walked into the chapel.

"Joanna?" she asked.

"Kathleen?"

With small cries of delight, they hurried toward each other and hugged fiercely.

"I thought I'd come a little early and help you get ready."

Joanna relaxed. "I'm so glad you're here."

Kathleen looked around the chapel, and Joanna could see that her friend was experiencing the same emotions she had when she'd first walked inside.

Oh yes, this reunion was going to be good for them all.

{ 45 }

Kathleen Doyle
2002

Kathleen felt such joy to be attending this reunion. "I can't believe we're finally here," she said excitedly.

"When did you arrive?" Joanna asked.

"Just this minute. We drove from Seattle. Brian's parking the car and then walking over to the rectory."

The two hugged again. "I'm just thrilled you could make it."

"I think that means Joanna welcomes the help," a tall man said, entering the chapel. Kathleen assumed he was Joanna's husband. "The coffee's going," he said, smiling at his wife.

"I was hoping I could lend you a hand. It's wonderful that you're doing this." Kathleen had enjoyed her brief correspondence with Joanna and was anxious to catch up with everything that had happened in her friend's life and the lives of the other sisters she'd lived with.

"Wait a minute. Doyle? Brian Doyle?" Joanna said

slowly. "Wasn't there a priest at St. Peter's with that name?"

Kathleen nodded.

"You married Brian Doyle, the *priest?*" Joanna asked, not disguising her shock. "I never made the connection."

"Technically Brian is still a priest."

"Whoa!" Joanna's husband held up his hand. "You'd better explain that."

"Tim?" Kathleen suddenly grinned. "I remember now—you're the doctor who came to Mass that one Sunday. Joanna nearly fell out of the choir loft trying to get a better look at you."

Joanna blushed.

"You never told me that," Tim said with a laugh.

Joanna playfully jabbed him in the ribs.

"Explain the comment about Brian still being a priest," Tim said curiously.

"He's a married priest," Kathleen said. "We never intended for this to happen. He made the decision to leave and applied to Rome, but Rome never responded."

"You mean to say it's more than just his letter getting lost in the mail?" Joanna asked, frowning.

Kathleen nodded. "Much more. It's become a political battle of wills. Rome was losing so many American priests that the ecclesiastical authorities decided to ignore requests for the dispensation of vows. Apparently they hoped the priests would ultimately change their minds. In our case, that strategy didn't work."

"I didn't know anything like that was happening."

"Few people do."

"Does he continue to celebrate Mass?" Joanna asked. It was a frequent question.

"Every Sunday. There are so many disenfranchised

Catholics in the Seattle area. Over the years we sort of found one another. Brian works a forty-hour week as a loan officer, but on Sunday mornings he's a priest."

"Do you have a meeting place?" Tim asked. "A church?"

Kathleen smiled. "In a manner of speaking. We have everyone over to the house and our living room becomes our place of worship." She marveled at how many people had heard about their Sunday-morning Masses. Former Catholics arrived, needing to talk; Brian offered a willing ear and a way to return to God and the Church, even if the road back was a bit unconventional.

"You actually celebrate Mass in your home?" Joanna repeated.

"We've had as many as fifty people show up, and afterward there's a potluck breakfast. That way, people get to know each other. It's really a wonderful time of fellowship."

"You must have a huge house."

"We have a large family. Once we decided we wouldn't wait for the dispensation from Rome any longer, Brian and I decided to have our family all at once." At Joanna's puzzled look, she explained. "We had a set of triplets and then twins."

"Oh, my."

"A year and a half apart."

Joanna burst out laughing, and Kathleen didn't blame her. There were no multiple births in her family, but Kathleen had broken that statistic—twice. Those early years hadn't been easy, but they'd managed and grown close because of it.

"I don't know whether to give you my condolences or to congratulate you."

"Congratulate us," Kathleen said. "They're all adults, all married and we're already grandparents."

"That's wonderful," Joanna said.

"Now." Kathleen rubbed her hands briskly together. "What can I do to help?"

"Let's get the food set up out front," Joanna suggested.

Kathleen followed her out of the chapel, but just as she was about to leave, she turned to face the altar, now bare and somehow desolate. It'd been years since Kathleen had stepped inside a Catholic church. Years since she'd even thought about this chapel. She smiled at the thought that these days her home was also her church.

Many of the people who came to their house on Sundays knew she was a former nun and Brian a priest. That seemed to comfort those who sought them out. People felt free to express their own differences with the Church, knowing Kathleen and Brian had experienced similar troubles themselves.

Turning resolutely away from her past, Kathleen hurried out to the front foyer, where a wooden table had been set up.

Joanna had everything neatly organized. Under Kathleen's admiring eye, she brought out a lace tablecloth and together they placed that on the table.

"Who all is coming?" Kathleen asked eagerly.

"Sister Martha was the first to respond."

"The choir director?" Kathleen could well remember the woman who'd led them in song, who'd insisted it was their duty to provide music for Sunday Masses.

"That's the one."

"What about Sister Eloise?" She'd had her share of differences with Sister Superior, but she'd always respected the nun who was the head of the Minneapolis convent.

Joanna set a small bouquet of flowers on the table. She straightened and her face became somber. "Unfortunately, Sister Eloise died in the mid-nineties."

"I'm sorry to hear that."

"Julia will be here," Joanna continued. "Judging by what she wrote, she went back to her hometown in Kansas and stayed there. She's still teaching."

"Still?" It had to be in a Catholic school, Kathleen guessed. After leaving, many of them had accepted teaching positions. This time, however, when they stepped into a classroom, they collected a paycheck. Unfortunately many of the parochial schools had closed after the exodus of nuns. It became impossible to keep tuition costs down and still pay teachers a living wage. Until her own children were born, Kathleen had taught first in a Catholic elementary school and when they were older, she'd been a teacher for the Seattle school district. She'd recently retired and now worked for the state in Children's Protective Services.

"What about Sister Angelina?" Kathleen asked.

Joanna shook her head. "I tried to convince her, but she wasn't interested."

"I was afraid of that. I wrote her after hearing from you and I tried to get her to come, too. She never answered my letter. It's a real disappointment not to see her."

"It is," Joanna agreed. "Remember those fabulous Italian dinners she threw together without so much as a recipe? The woman was a marvel in the kitchen," she murmured as she displayed a guest book. "Now I know why. Her father owned a restaurant, which Angelina runs."

"Doesn't surprise me. I never ate better Italian food in my life. Not before and not since."

The front door opened and Kathleen glanced up to see her husband. They'd been looking forward to this trip; it was a vacation and much more for them. A reconciliation with the past, a chance to visit places that had meant so much.

"Was there anyone at the rectory?" she asked.

He nodded. "A young priest from the Philippines."

"The Philippines?"

"Yes, Father Apia is the assistant. And our parish priest is from Nigeria," Joanna said. "He's wonderful. We feel fortunate to have them both."

"Nigeria," Brian said, looking to Kathleen. It didn't surprise her that many of America's parish priests now came from foreign countries. They'd seen this trend developing when priests started leaving the priesthood at a rate that was impossible for the seminary graduates to replace.

"Did you learn anything about Father Sanders?" Kathleen asked.

Regret showed in her husband's eyes. "He died several years back. Father Apia had heard of him, but didn't have a lot of information. Apparently he was killed in an automobile accident."

Kathleen met her husband's eyes. Her question was reflected in his. They both wondered if he'd been drunk at the time.

"It was a sad situation," Joanna said.

"He had a drinking problem," Kathleen ventured, wondering how much, if anything, she should say.

"Yes, that came out afterward."

"Was anyone else killed, do you know?"

"No," Joanna said, "and we're all grateful. Father

Sanders was driving the wrong way on the interstate. Apparently he realized what he'd done and was trying to cross over the embankment. He gathered speed and hit the median at ninety miles an hour."

"Dear God." Kathleen covered her mouth with her hand.

"He flipped the car and was killed instantly." Joanna's mouth trembled. "It was a tragic loss. Father was so well-liked. The entire Minneapolis church grieved for him."

"Do you know anything about Father Yates?" Brian asked, a moment later. "The priest who replaced me?"

"You don't know?" Joanna asked, sounding surprised. "He became Bishop Yates after Bishop Schmidt passed away."

Kathleen couldn't believe it, and from the look on Brian's face, he couldn't, either. On the other hand, Father Yates's ambitions weren't exactly a secret, she thought.

"He wasn't a popular bishop."

"I can imagine," Kathleen murmured.

"He died of cancer a couple of years later."

"I'm sorry to hear that," Brian said, and Kathleen knew her husband well enough to recognize that his sentiments were sincere. This generosity of spirit was one of the many qualities she loved about him. Not a day passed that she didn't thank God for bringing this man into her life.

Without Brian, she might eventually have married John Lopez. She wondered now if it would've been a good marriage. Especially when it was discovered that Kathleen had a reproductive "peculiarity," as her doctor described it. Not until after the twins were born did they learn that her body released more than one egg at a time. All her births were destined to be multiple.

For five years straight, Kathleen didn't sleep through a single night. Neither did Brian. Such demands might have destroyed some marriages, but her husband had been a helpmate in every sense of the word. After giving birth to five children in such a short time, they had no problem resorting to birth control, although Brian had preached against it only a few years earlier.

"Mom." A tall, blond young man came in the door. He stopped when he saw Kathleen and Brian. "Hi," he said, then turned to Joanna. "There's someone outside. I think she might be one of you guys."

"Us guys," Joanna said out of the corner of her mouth.

"She's sitting in her car and I think she's crying. Maybe you should check it out."

Kathleen and Joanna exchanged looks. "Do you think it might be Angelina?" Joanna asked.

"Oh, I hope it is. She *should* be here. This day might wipe out thirty years of pain."

Joanna started for the door and then came back for Kathleen. "Come with me," she urged. "She might be able to refuse me, but she can't say no to both of us."

{ 46 }

Sister Angelina
2002

Even now, Angie couldn't believe she was in Minneapolis. She knew Joanna was right, that unless she confronted the past, she'd never be able to deal with the future. At the last possible moment, with some encouragement from friends, she'd made plane reservations and arranged for a rental car.

There was a second reason she'd decided to attend the reunion: to visit the Sullivan family. It didn't seem possible that Corinne had been dead thirty years. Thirty years! Countless times Angie had thought about the girl and wished that things had been different—that Corinne had talked to her, that she'd been summoned to the door when Jimmy came looking for her...

Normally Angie would have arranged a meeting with the Sullivans well in advance. Years in the restaurant business had taught her the importance of handling situations in a businesslike manner. Had she thought this through adequately, she'd have phoned ahead.

She hadn't, because she wasn't sure she had the courage to face Corinne's parents. Then she'd awakened less than thirty hours ago and realized she'd been given an opportunity to settle the complex issues of her past. As Joanna had said, she'd regret it if she didn't attend this reunion.

What Angie should have considered was that the Sullivans might no longer live in the area. In fact, a short investigation had revealed that Bob and Sharon Sullivan had moved to Arizona after his retirement in the late eighties.

Almost in afterthought, Angie had sought out Jimmy Durango. She'd looked up his name in the phone book and was amazed to find it. He answered the call himself and the conversation had been one of the most cathartic of her life.

"Sister, I can't believe it's you!" he'd burst out.

She hadn't bothered to correct him about her status. "How are you, Jimmy? Have the years been good to you?"

"They've been very good. I'm married, and Sandy and I have two kids. Matt's twenty and Carol Anne's twenty-two. I ended up doing a stint in the Army a couple of years after Corinne died."

"Did you see the Sullivans often?" she'd asked.

He released a heavy sigh. "No, they didn't want much to do with me, and I can't say I blame them. Having a daughter of my own now, I can understand a lot better what they must've gone through."

Angie felt that was generous of him. She could only imagine the guilt he'd carried with him. He didn't say it, but she suspected that the Sullivans blamed Jimmy for their daughter's death. For most people, it was easier, somehow, to deal with tragedy if they could point a finger at someone else.

"Sister," Jimmy had said. "I don't want you to think I forgot Corinne." His voice wavered slightly. "For almost two years, I went to the cemetery nearly every day. My folks were worried about me. They were right because I felt—I don't know—that life wasn't worth living after she died."

Angie understood that feeling far better than he realized.

"Then one day, it came to me that Corinne had loved me. She died loving me. The last words I ever heard her speak were to tell me she was sorry and that she loved me. She wouldn't want me killing myself because of what happened to her. That would've made her death even worse.

"Shortly after that, I walked into the Army recruiter's office and enlisted. It was the best decision I could've made at the time."

"I suppose it gave you a new kind of life."

"Yes," Jimmy agreed, "it did. Over the years I kept in contact with Jerry, Corinne's older brother. Her parents went through a rough stretch for a couple of years, too, but like me, they eventually learned to cope with their loss in their own way. Her mother got real active in a pregnancy hotline. Her father retired about fifteen years ago, and they moved almost right after that. Jerry says they seem happy and that they've made a lot of friends in Arizona."

"I'm so glad to hear it."

"Me, too," Jimmy said.

They'd ended the conversation a short while later, and Angie had been fighting back tears ever since. Although it was early, she drove to the convent house and sat in her car, letting the memories wash over her.

A car was parked out front, but she wasn't sure whether it belonged to Joanna or to someone visiting the church. Outwardly, the convent house hadn't changed much. She'd been saddened to learn that it was sold and being torn down. There was no reason for the mother-house to hold on to the building, which had apparently sat empty for a number of years.

So many memories. Her gaze drifted toward what had once been the high school. That, too, had closed. Years and years of students had walked through those now-vacant halls. Girls like Corinne and Morgan, and boys like Jimmy Durango. Teenagers who were adults now, with grown families of their own.

Angie could only hope that the skills she'd taught there had served her students well throughout the years.

Looking back at the convent, Angie saw two figures step out of the building and walk across the street toward her. She squinted against the bright sun, but instantly recognized Sister Kathleen. How could she miss her with that mass of red hair? And—oh, my goodness— was that Sister Joanna?

Not waiting to find out, Angie climbed out of the car and with outstretched arms, approached the two women.

"Joanna? Kathleen?"

"Angelina?"

Soon she was enveloped in a three-way hug.

"Most people call me Angie now," she said, laughing as they stood apart to study each other and the changes thirty years had brought. She brushed at the fresh tears spilling down her cheeks.

"I'm so *happy* you decided to join us," Joanna said,

slipping her arm around Angie's ample waist. She was forty pounds heavier since leaving the convent.

"I'm happy to be here, too." She sincerely meant that.

As soon as she was inside the old convent, Angie was introduced to both their husbands.

"I never got married," Angie told them with a tinge of regret. "I always thought I would. Always wanted to, but it just never happened."

"You have a restaurant?"

She nodded. "The one my father started over fifty years ago." Given the choice, though, Angie would have preferred a husband and children. As she'd told her friends, it just hadn't happened, but not for lack of wishing. Or trying. Twice she'd met and seriously dated men she was interested in; both times the relationships had looked promising. But then, for reasons she'd never really understood, both men had ended the relationships.

As the years passed, she'd come to think the problem might be hers rather than theirs. One of her theories was that having entered the convent at eighteen, her social and emotional development had remained that of an adolescent. She cringed whenever she thought of it, and wondered if it could be true. There was no one she trusted to be honest enough to tell her the truth.

Both men had been married previously; Mark was a widower and Kenneth divorced. Each had been eager to marry again, but after a while, she'd found herself withdrawing. Despite her own desire for a family, she could never make a complete commitment to either man.

However, she'd remained good friends with Mark's two daughters. Angie kept in touch with them and they often turned to her for advice. Although Mark had eventually remarried, neither Janice nor Nikki was close to his second wife.

Their fondness for Angie had been a sweet balm through these last few years. Childless years. When Mark's daughters learned of the reunion, they'd urged Angie to attend. Janice had driven her to the airport and stayed with her until it was time to go to her gate.

Angie liked to think she would've remained friends with Corinne had the teenager lived.

The foyer, with its dark carpet and straight-backed chairs, looked exactly the way Angie remembered, except that the statue of Mary was missing from its alcove.

Joanna and Kathleen stood behind a long table, and while Joanna had Angie sign the guest book, Kathleen sorted through the name tags until she found the one that read Angelina Marcello.

"Sister Martha's coming and Julia, too," Kathleen announced cheerfully. "And Sister Joan, Sister Dorothy, Sister Anne—oh, it'll be so good to see everyone again."

"Would it be all right if I wandered around for a bit before the others arrive?" Angie asked.

"Oh, sure, but there's not much left to see."

"The chapel's still there, but the altar's been stripped," Kathleen told her.

Angie stopped at the chapel first. She stood in the entrance and closed her eyes, listening with her heart as the echoed prayers of the sisters seemed to reverberate around her. So much devotion and love had been sent to God from this room. It was as if Angie could hear those prayers now. She hadn't expected to feel such strong emotion. Perhaps a vague sense of loss and regret, but not these intense feelings that transported her to that most innocent time in her life.

She turned to leave and nearly walked into a young man.

"Oh, hi," he said, balancing a large deli tray. "You

wouldn't happen to know where the kitchen is, would you?"

"Right this way."

"Mom thought it'd be a good idea to keep these meat trays refrigerated until we need them."

"Mom is Joanna or Kathleen?"

"Joanna. You were a nun too?" He looked at her in a way that said he found it hard to believe.

"Many years ago," she said smiling to herself.

"Did you know my mom when she was a nun?"

"I did," Angie told him.

"What was she like? I mean, I only see her as my mother."

"I don't imagine she's any different." Angie didn't know the woman Joanna had become, but she could well remember the nun she'd once been. "What did she tell you?"

"Not much, but she's talked about this reunion for months. She's been filling us in—my dad, my brother and me—on where some of the other sisters ended up. I'm sure you'll hear all of that soon enough."

And she did. Angie stayed in the kitchen for much of the reunion. It was where she felt most comfortable. But nuns and former nuns frequently sought her out to exchange stories. It became obvious that the adjustment for her had been relatively easy compared to some of the others.

She carried out deli trays and brewed several pots of coffee. Between trips in and out of the kitchen, she caught snippets of conversation.

"I married the first man I ever kissed. Our marriage didn't last six months. I was devastated," one woman said sadly. "I failed as a nun and then my marriage ended in divorce. I went from being a highly exalted Catholic to an outcast in two fast lessons."

Angie understood. She, too, had fallen from grace.

"I used to drive down to the convent at nights," she heard Sister Martha—now plain Martha Shaw—confess to Joanna. "I missed my life here so much and yet I knew I could never go back. It was months before I stopped doing that. I'm so happy to have this opportunity to say goodbye to our old building."

Angie felt the same way herself. Attending the reunion had been the right decision; she was glad she'd come.

"For me it was a hurting and healing process at the same time," Angie heard Kathleen tell the former Sister Loretta. "I lived in Seattle in the House of Peace and talked about my feelings with a counselor. But just when I was sure everything was going to be all right, something would happen and I'd stumble into a depression. The convent was a safe haven. Here I had community, liturgy, theology and love. The world can be a cruel place when you're alone."

Angie had been saved from that by her father. He'd always been there for her, from the beginning until the end. She felt his love even now, years after his death from a massive stroke.

Once inside the kitchen again, she refilled the coffeepot with water and spooned the grounds in the container before turning it on.

"You should be mingling with the others," Joanna said, stepping into the room.

She smiled. "I will later."

"I never intended for you to take on this task."

"Why not? I saw a need and I filled it. Isn't that what we were taught in the convent?"

Joanna laughed. "You have me there. Kathleen and her husband are coming to my house afterward. Could you join us? I don't feel we've had near enough time to catch up."

"I'd enjoy that very much," Angie said.

{ 47 }

Joanna's House

Joanna sat on the large sofa in her spacious living room as Tim opened the wine. The reunion had been exhausting but well worth the months of effort that had gone into the planning. Gathering the community of nuns and former nuns one last time had been everything she'd prayed it would be. Now with Kathleen and Angie, Joanna could unwind after a hectic afternoon.

"I can't thank you enough for doing this," Kathleen said, sitting next to her husband. The sky was only beginning to darken, the last rays of the sun casting a warm glow over the lake that was visible from the large living room windows.

Brian Doyle placed his arm around his wife. "It was smart to do this while the convent was still intact. I only wish something like this could be arranged for priests and former priests—the guys I went to seminary with, for instance."

"I didn't know how I'd feel about this weekend," Angie said, accepting a glass of merlot from Tim Murray. She sat in the recliner and leaned back, her gaze focused on the setting sun. "Even after the plane landed, I wasn't sure coming here was the right thing." She raised her glass. "Now I know it was."

Joanna remembered how Angie had spent much of the reunion secluded in the kitchen. She'd worried about it at first but then realized this was where Angie felt most comfortable. Not only that, she was grateful for the extra help.

"Did you get to visit with everyone?" she asked, fearing Angie had been so busy with details she'd missed out on the most important aspect of the reunion.

"I had a wonderful time. I talked to Sister Julia and Martha and a number of others. Oh, and Sister Colleen."

"I don't remember Sister Colleen," Kathleen said, frowning. She glanced from Angie to Joanna.

"She taught ninth-grade French," Angie explained.

"Oh, yes," Kathleen said. "She must have left the community after we did."

"No," Joanna said. "Sister Colleen's still a member of the order, although she no longer wears a habit."

"Surely she's retired from teaching by now?" Kathleen murmured.

Angie crossed her legs. "I believe so—quite a while ago, I'd say. She didn't mention exactly when, but she did tell me she shares an apartment in the city with two other nuns. All three of them work with the homeless."

"Yes," Joanna said. "I've visited the sisters at their place. And I've seen Sister Colleen at parish events."

"Did she tell you why she stayed?" Kathleen asked Angie. "There must've been tremendous pressure to leave when so many other women did."

Angie shook her head. "We didn't get around to discussing that, but I have the feeling Colleen's been completely content with her life. As I remember it, she always was. She felt then as she does now, that she was doing God's work." Angie paused and sipped her wine. "It did come as a shock to her that I'm no longer a Catholic."

"You mean you don't attend Mass?" Tim asked, moving to the edge of the cushion, openly curious.

Joanna smiled to herself. Her husband was a strong Catholic, and a Eucharistic minister in their church. No one who knew him would believe that at one time he'd rejected God and Church.

"I attend a Protestant church in Buffalo now," Angie explained.

"In our day, that was like joining ranks with the enemy," Joanna said with a laugh. "We didn't dare so much as walk on the same side of the street as one of those *other* churches."

"I talked to two or three women today who've left the Church," Kathleen said. "In fact, not one of them wants anything to do with the Catholic Church. Remember Sister Janet? She's dropped out, and so has Sister Ruth."

Joanna had been so busy acting as hostess that she hadn't had the opportunity for more than brief conversations with any of the visitors. She was hoping her friends would enlighten her.

"I had the most wonderful afternoon," Kathleen murmured. "It was such a validation of the decisions I made, and it was so great to talk to women who understand everything I went through when I first left the convent."

Everyone looked to Kathleen, nodding in sympathy. "That time wasn't easy for me," she said softly. "But I was fortunate in that I had a supportive older brother and a place to go."

"I've heard of nuns who were given little or no support by their communities," Angie added.

"Can you imagine," Kathleen said, "coming out of the convent after twenty or more years with no retirement funds, no savings and sometimes no skills?"

Tim frowned and shook his head. "That didn't happen to any of you, though, did it?"

"No," Kathleen was quick to respond, "but we were relatively young when we left." She gave a slight shrug. "We all went our own ways for different reasons—but there were similarities in each case, too."

Joanna agreed. "I left because I'd grown into a completely different woman from the nineteen-year-old girl who'd entered the convent with a broken heart. I was so certain I had a vocation. I wasn't prepared six years later to find myself feeling restless and uncertain."

Tim loudly cleared his throat. "You mean to say *I* didn't have anything to do with your decision?"

Everyone laughed, including Joanna. "Yes, dear," she said, playing along. "I was in love and longing for a family, too." But it was more than that. In her pain over the broken engagement, Joanna had turned to God for comfort, convincing herself that He was calling her into His service. Her vocation hadn't been genuine, although no one could have convinced her of that in 1967. If it had been, she'd still be a nun to this day, the same as Sister Colleen.

"I was one of the lucky ones," Angie said. "I had a home and a career waiting for me. Never once did I feel displaced or a burden to my father. According to his friends, the minute I was back, my dad was happier than he'd been since I left."

"A lot of the women I talked to mentioned feeling guilty," Kathleen said.

To Joanna, that made sense. For a time, soon after she'd come home, she too had experienced the burden of guilt.

"I think a lot of us felt lost and displaced," Kathleen said. "For myself, I went from Grand Silence to my brother's house with two preschool children. Emma and Paul had no appreciation for silence."

That comment produced smiles all around.

"I talked with one former nun—I don't think she was part of the community when we were—who spoke of that feeling of displacement," Kathleen continued. "She couldn't go back to live with her parents, nor could she afford to rent a place of her own."

"What about friends?"

Kathleen shook her head. "She didn't say, but I sort of had the feeling that she's been drifting for years, no roots, no real home or family."

"That's sad," Angie murmured.

"I was surprised how many of us have married and divorced," Joanna said. She'd talked to four former nuns who'd married quickly after leaving the convent; after a child or two, their marriages had fallen apart. It made her feel all the more blessed to have Tim in her life.

"A lot of the women I spoke to had problems with relationships," Kathleen added. "Especially relationships with men."

One of the most telling conversations of the afternoon had been with a woman who'd come out of the novitiate at the same time as Joanna. "Sister Joan's been married three times in the last twenty-five years. She said she'd failed God as a nun and then was divorced within a year of her first marriage."

"Talk about going from respected to rejected in two

short steps," Tim said, and sipped his wine. He reached for Joanna's hand and they entwined their fingers.

"I want to go back to this issue of relationships with men," Brian said. "Was it a recurring theme?"

"It was," his wife confirmed.

"It must have something to do with how submissive we were taught to be," Angie said thoughtfully. "Remember custody of the eyes?" She rolled her own eyes now, mocking the custom of always lowering one's gaze while in the presence of a man.

"I think that submissiveness set many of us up for exploitation by men," Kathleen muttered.

Joanna noted the way Brian's arm tightened around his wife's shoulders, as if offering her love and reassurance. "My biggest problem was money," she said.

"Not enough?" Angie asked.

"No—managing it. Before I entered the convent, as well as when I left, I lived with my parents. As soon as I could, I got my own apartment but I had no idea how to budget my paycheck."

"She still has problems with budgeting." Tim winked, then went around with the wine bottle and refreshed everyone's glass.

"If you had it to do over again, Angie, would you have joined the convent?" Kathleen asked, nodding her thanks at Tim.

Angie hesitated. "Given everything I know now?"

"Yes, everything."

Gnawing on her lower lip, Angie nodded. "I would. I loved being a nun and part of a community. You two," she said, gesturing toward Joanna and Kathleen, "and the others… You were the sisters I never had—the big family I always wanted. It was good for a lot of years, but finally I had to move on. There was the whole mess with Corinne, which was a real catalyst for me. And as it turned out, my father needed me. Just hours before he died, he told me I came back just in time."

A silence fell over them. "I'd do it again, too," Kathleen admitted. "To this day I can't say for sure whether I had a vocation or if I was just living up to my family's expectations. All I know is that I was raised with the knowledge that one day I'd be a nun. That life was everything I'd anticipated and more. After a while, though, I started to wonder about my role in the Church."

Joanna knew that Kathleen might have continued with the community for years if not for Father Sanders, God rest his soul.

"What about you, Joanna?" Kathleen asked. "Would you join the convent if you had a chance to do it all over again?"

Like her friends, Joanna nodded. "I wouldn't be the woman I am today if I hadn't spent those years in the convent. Nor would I have met Tim." She smiled at her husband, this man whom she'd loved for thirty years, and their eyes held for a long moment.

Joining the convent *had* been right for Joanna at that time in her life. She'd found warmth and healing in those years with St. Bridget's Sisters of the Assumption.

"No regrets?" Angie asked, looking around at her friends.

"None," Kathleen said.

"None," Joanna said.

The three raised their wineglasses in a silent toast to the years they'd lived in love and trust and faith. Their lives might have changed in every conceivable way, but those feelings had not—and never would.

* * * * *

GLOSSARY

Convent: The residence of a religious community, especially nuns.

Mother Superior: The nun who is the head of a religious community.

Motherhouse: The residence of the head of a religious community. Central home for the Order. Nuns are sent from the motherhouse on assignments or missions. Postulants and Novices are trained at the motherhouse. Nuns take their vows there.

Sister Superior: The head of a convent or house away from the motherhouse.

Divine Office: Compilation of prayers based on scripture, prayed at different hours of the day. The Divine Office consists of Prime, Lauds, Matins, Compline and Vespers, each prayed at different times of the day, also known as Hours.

Custody of the Eyes: The habit of keeping the eyes lowered in order to meditate and pray, and away from things that would distract from God.

Postulant: The first-year candidate for admission into a religious order.

Novice: A second- and third-year candidate for the second stage of becoming a nun. A woman is admitted into a religious order for a period of probation before taking vows.

Diocese: The area under the jurisdiction of a bishop. There are 184 dioceses in the United States.

Chapter of Faults: A humbling, cleansing way to deeper prayer. A nun kneels before her fellow sisters and her superior once a week to confess the faults of the week and receive a penance from the superior.

Grand Silence: The practice of keeping silent from 7:30 p.m. until 7:30 a.m.

The Year of Silence: Novitiate candidates are asked to maintain a year of silence while contemplating their vocation in their first year.

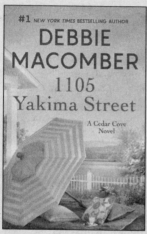

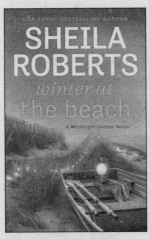

Get 4 FREE REWARDS!

We'll send you 2 FREE Books plus 2 FREE Mystery Gifts.

FREE Value Over **$20**

Both the **Romance** and **Suspense** collections feature compelling novels written by many of today's best-selling authors.

YES! Please send me 2 FREE novels from the Essential Romance or Essential Suspense Collection and my 2 FREE gifts (gifts are worth about $10 retail). After receiving them, if I don't wish to receive any more books, I can return the shipping statement marked "cancel." If I don't cancel, I will receive 4 brand-new novels every month and be billed just $6.74 each in the U.S. or $7.24 each in Canada. That's a savings of at least 16% off the cover price. It's quite a bargain! Shipping and handling is just 50¢ per book in the U.S. and 75¢ per book in Canada.* I understand that accepting the 2 free books and gifts places me under no obligation to buy anything. I can always return a shipment and cancel at any time. The free books and gifts are mine to keep no matter what I decide.

Choose one: ☐ **Essential Romance**   ☐ **Essential Suspense**
               (194/394 MDN GMY7)   (191/391 MDN GMY7)

Name (please print)

Address   Apt. #

City   State/Province   Zip/Postal Code

Mail to the **Reader Service:**
IN U.S.A.: P.O. Box 1341, Buffalo, NY 14240-8531
IN CANADA: P.O. Box 603, Fort Erie, Ontario L2A 5X3

Want to try 2 free books from another series? Call 1-800-873-8635 or visit www.ReaderService.com.

---

*Terms and prices subject to change without notice. Prices do not include sales taxes, which will be charged (if applicable) based on your state or country of residence. Canadian residents will be charged applicable taxes. Offer not valid in Quebec. This offer is limited to one order per household. Books received may not be as shown. Not valid for current subscribers to the Essential Romance or Essential Suspense Collection. All orders subject to approval. Credit or debit balances in a customer's account(s) may be offset by any other outstanding balance owed by or to the customer. Please allow 4 to 6 weeks for delivery. Offer available while quantities last.

Your Privacy—The Reader Service is committed to protecting your privacy. Our Privacy Policy is available online at www.ReaderService.com or upon request from the Reader Service. We make a portion of our mailing list available to reputable third parties that offer products we believe may interest you. If you prefer that we not exchange your name with third parties, or if you wish to clarify or modify your communication preferences, please visit us at www.ReaderService.com/consumerschoice or write to us at Reader Service Preference Service, P.O. Box 9062, Buffalo, NY 14240-9062. Include your complete name and address.

STRS19R

DEBBIE MACOMBER

36869	CHOIR OF ANGELS	___	$7.99 U.S.	___	$9.99 CAN.
36000	1022 EVERGREEN PLACE	___	$7.99 U.S.	___	$9.99 CAN.
33125	NAVY FAMILIES	___	$7.99 U.S.	___	$9.99 CAN.
33121	NAVY BRIDES	___	$7.99 U.S.	___	$9.99 CAN.
33032	HANNAH'S LIST	___	$7.99 U.S.	___	$9.99 CAN.
33019	ALASKA HOME	___	$7.99 U.S.	___	$9.99 CAN.
33018	ALASKA NIGHTS	___	$7.99 U.S.	___	$9.99 CAN.
33017	ALASKA SKIES	___	$7.99 U.S.	___	$9.99 CAN.
32918	AN ENGAGEMENT IN SEATTLE	___	$7.99 U.S.	___	$9.99 CAN.
31926	THE SOONER THE BETTER	___	$7.99 U.S.	___	$9.99 CAN.
31917	BECAUSE IT'S CHRISTMAS	___	$7.99 U.S.	___	$9.99 CAN.
31913	CHRISTMAS IN ALASKA	___	$7.99 U.S.	___	$9.99 CAN.
31903	WEDDING DREAMS	___	$7.99 U.S.	___	$9.99 CAN.
31894	ALWAYS DAKOTA	___	$7.99 U.S.	___	$9.99 CAN.
31888	DAKOTA HOME	___	$7.99 U.S.	___	$9.99 CAN.
31883	DAKOTA BORN	___	$7.99 U.S.	___	$9.99 CAN.
31860	THE MANNING BRIDES	___	$7.99 U.S.	___	$9.99 CAN.
31624	ON A CLEAR DAY	___	$7.99 U.S.	___	$8.99 CAN.
31580	MARRIAGE BETWEEN FRIENDS	___	$7.99 U.S.	___	$8.99 CAN.
31551	A REAL PRINCE	___	$7.99 U.S.	___	$8.99 CAN.
31535	PROMISE TEXAS	___	$7.99 U.S.	___	$8.99 CAN.
31441	HEART OF TEXAS VOLUME 2	___	$7.99 U.S.	___	$8.99 CAN.
31413	LOVE IN PLAIN SIGHT	___	$7.99 U.S.	___	$9.99 CAN.

(limited quantities available)

TOTAL AMOUNT $ _____
POSTAGE & HANDLING $ _____
($1.00 for 1 book, 50¢ for each additional)
APPLICABLE TAXES* $ _____
TOTAL PAYABLE $ _____
(check or money order—please do not send cash)

To order, complete this form and send it, along with a check or money order for the total above, payable to MIRA Books, to: **In the U.S.:** 3010 Walden Avenue, P.O. Box 9077, Buffalo, NY 14269-9077; **In Canada:** P.O. Box 636, Fort Erie, Ontario, L2A 5X3.

Name: _____

Address: _____ City: _____

State/Prov.: _____ Zip/Postal Code: _____

Account Number (if applicable): _____

075 CSAS

★ mira

Harlequin.com

MDM0319BL

*New York residents remit applicable sales taxes.
*Canadian residents remit applicable GST and provincial taxes.